CORRUPTION

ALSO BY MITCHELL HOGAN

THE NECROMANCER'S KEY

Incursion

THE SORCERY ASCENDANT SEQUENCE

A Crucible of Souls

Blood of Innocents

A Shattered Empire

At the Sign of the Crow and Moon—novella

THE INFERNAL GUARDIAN

Shadow of the Exile

Dawn of the Exile

THE TAINTED CABAL

Revenant Winds

Tower of the Forgotten—novella

A Goddess Scorned—novella

SCIENCE FICTION

Inquisitor

CORRUPTION

THE NECROMANCER'S KEY: BOOK TWO

MITCHELL HOGAN

This book is a work of fiction. The characters, incidents and dialogues are products of the author's imagination and are not to be construed as real. Any resemblance to any persons, living or dead, events, or locales is entirely coincidental.

CORRUPTION

Published by Mitchell Hogan

First Printing, 2020

WIRAYA
Scale in Miles
0
500
1000
THE WASTES
Ruruc
SIMORGA SEA
Atya
PLAINS OF KHISIG-UGTALL
NIYAS
Ivrian
Kroe
Sohrab
JARGALAN
PLASSE
2017

YMALTIAN MOUNTAINS
THOUSAND LAKES
Caronath
Nantin
Crital River
STATES
Kyuth
KAILEN
Sansor
Nagorn City
Valborg
GREAT SOUTHERN MOUNTAINS OF EALYSIA
ISTART
OMBINE
Mazin
AK-SETTUR
Gessa
Manela
SEA OF MINGOL
JARGALAN MOUNTAINS
TRACKLESS OCEAN

WHAT'S GONE BEFORE

NECROMANCY BEGAN ON THE island of Niyas, when humans were little more than savages roaming the wilderness. The dawn- and dusk-tides were already known, but Niyandrian sorcerers discovered the corrupted tidal forces absorbed into the earth. They grew obsessed with the earth-tide's promise of immortality, and with the secrets of the dead.

When Queen Talia of Niyas sought to raise her people to eternal life, the powerful countries of the mainland conspired to put an end to her rule. Allied armies invaded Niyas. Battles were fought with steel and sorcery. Thousands died. Cities fell. And, at last, the mainland allies, led by the Order of Eternal Vigilance, prevailed. Queen Talia died when her capital, Naphor, fell, and Niyas was placed under mainland occupation.

But there were rumors of a child: the heir to Niyas; the daughter of Talia, the Necromancer Queen. In secret, a guardian was appointed to protect her.

The Order of Eternal Vigilance stole Niyandrian girls from their homes in their search for the heir, but they never found her. They re-educated those they had taken within the walls of their strongholds. Many of the girls were trained as knights of the Order.

BOOK ONE: INCURSION

Carred Selenas, Captain of the Last Cohort and Queen Talia's former lover, leads the resistance against the foreign invaders as they await the return of the Necromancer Queen and the reemergence of the Niyandrian people and culture. But it has been years since Talia died, and her people are losing heart. With one failure after another, Carred's resolve crumbles, but duty keeps her searching for the lost heir—the symbol all Niyandrians could rally behind, and the key to Queen Talia's return from the dead.

Anskar DeVantte has been raised in the sacred disciplines of the Order of Eternal Vigilance his entire life. Born with the mark of sorcery and the ability to manipulate the dawn-tide, Anskar must endure the Order's brutal initiation trials if he is to become a consecrated knight.

In the first trial, a sword-fighting tournament, Anskar emerges triumphant, but is injured in his final fight.

During the second trial, that of forging one of the ensorcelled blades the Order is famous for, Anskar is obsessed with perfection and works late into the night at the smithing hall. Against the rules of the trials, he assists his friend Orix, and one night agrees to help Sareya, a Niyandrian trainee who has previously tormented him. In the heat of the forges, Anskar and Sareya become lovers, but he is immediately beset with guilt: intimate relations among trainees are forbidden by the Order. Conflicted in his faith to Menselas, the God of Five Aspects, Anskar shuts Sareya out.

Before the end of the second trial, the blind sorcerer Luzius Landav arrives with his assistant, a dwarf woman named Malady. Landav has brought the trainees crystal catalysts, which will enable them to draw upon the dawn-tide for their protective sorceries. Landav senses Anskar also has a dusk-tide repository, and more disturbingly can also store the dark-tide. As Anskar experiments with his catalyst, it grows discolored, and black threads weave through its strata.

Using their catalysts, the trainee knights finish forging their swords and imbue the blades with strengthening cants using the dawn-tide. Anskar and Sareya are reconciled, and he names his sword *Amalantril*, after her Niyandrian name—meaning "moontouched".

Their swords are tested against the battle hammer of Beof, a priest of the Warrior aspect of Menselas. Orix's and Sareya's blades hold up under Beof's assault, but when it is Anskar's turn, *Amalantril* cleaves straight through the haft of Beof's hammer. The Warrior's priest stalks away in a fury.

After they pass the second trial, Anskar and Sareya become lovers again, and each find out the other also has a dusk-tide repository.

The third trial forces the trainees to confront their fears and to use dawn-tide sorcery in the creation of a protective "ward sphere." When Anskar's turn comes, he is attacked by the vengeful Beof. An uncontrolled burst of shadow blasts from Anskar, knocking Beof unconscious.

Anskar, Orix, and Sareya are among the seven trainees to pass the trials and are raised to the interim rank of knight-liminal. The Seneschal, Vihtor Ulnar, declares he will take Anskar DeVantte under his wing. Beof is sent to the mainland to be disciplined by his bishop.

Anskar questions Vihtor about his past and his parents. The Seneschal is guarded and forbids Anskar from asking again.

Landav and Malady implant the catalysts beneath the skin of the trainees. Anskar's body rejects the dark-threaded crystal and he grows critically ill.

As Anskar recovers under the care of the priests of the Healer, a golden-eyed crow disturbs him in the middle of the night. Anskar enters a fugue-like state as he follows the crow where it leads him. They enter a Niyandrian crypt, where the crow reveals a passage concealed in the back of a sarcophagus. They exit the citadel and, for days, the crow leads Anskar through the wilderness.

Anskar is hunted by a dead-eye, a defiler of corpses and one of the constant menaces in the wilderness, but with the crow's help manages to kill it.

The crow brings him to Hallow Hill, atop which sits a Niyandrian ruin. A wraithe meets Anskar there—one of the ancient beings that haunt Wiraya. The wraithe urges Anskar to enter the ruin, where he finds a statue of a woman carved from bone, upon her forearm a vambrace crafted from a peculiar silver alloy.

Anskar snatches the vambrace and flees from the tomb's spectral guardian. The wraithe tells him to wear the vambrace, which grows invisible against his skin.

Vihtor and a search party find Anskar and return him to the citadel. Anskar keeps the vambrace's existence to himself.

Carred Selenas receives word from her spies that one of the Order's newest knights, a woman named Sareya, could be the Niyandrian heir, and also that Hyle Pausus, the Grand Master of the Order of Eternal Vigilance, is on his way to Niyas from the mainland city of Sansor. She comes up with a plan to bloody the Order's nose and snatch Sareya away from them.

Carred and her rebels are attacked by Luzius Landav and Malady, who have been charged by their mainland employees with putting down the resistance. In the ensuing fight, Landav transports himself and Carred to a shadowy realm, where she meets a secret consortium who put pressure on Carred to disband her rebellion. She refuses and uses a ring Queen Talia gave her to break Landav's power and return to Wiraya. The rebels capture Landav, but Malady escapes. Carred cuts off the sorcerer's head.

Once Anskar has recovered, he resumes training with the knights-liminal, and they congregate to welcome the dawn-tide every morning. As they continue honing their sorcerous wards and making mail, they learn that the sale of enhanced weapons and armor is a lucrative business for the Order.

Anskar approaches his namesake, the knight Eldrid DeVantte, to ask about his mother and father. Eldrid claims to know nothing except that he gave Anskar his surname at the request of Vihtor.

Vihtor summons Anskar to quiz him about his journey to Hallow Hill. The Seneschal orders Anskar not to speak to anyone of his ordeal, and to cease greeting the dawn-tide with his friends, as he is putting himself in temptation's way with Sareya.

The trainees undertake their first mission, each mentored by a fully consecrated knight. They are led by Noreina Lanwitch, and to everyone's surprise Vihtor announces he will join them.

The expedition journeys to the site of Quolith, a new city the Order is building atop the ruins of Naphor, the Niyandrian capital. As they survey the work from afar, Niyandrian rebels spring an ambush. Anskar punches a hole through the Niyandrian line, breaking their charge. When he is knocked from his horse, Sareya comes to his aid, dusk-tide sorcery spilling from her hands, turning Anskar's attacker into a charred and smoking corpse. The surviving Niyandrians flee.

The expedition has lost almost half its number, including the trainee Petor. Vihtor chastises Anskar for disobeying orders, and Sareya for using forbidden sorcery.

As dusk approaches, they find a farm with a cottage to shelter in. Outside, dozens of cattle have been slaughtered by dead-eyes. Vihtor orders defenses prepared against the coming night and the inevitability of the dead-eyes' return.

Anskar hears a woman screaming inside the cottage. He and Vihtor investigate, only to find the cottage empty apart from the corpse of a woman recently killed.

After nightfall, dozens of sickly, spindle-limbed dead-eyes attack, clambering over the farmhouse's makeshift defenses. The knights and trainees defend the horses in the front yard, using their arcane wards to protect themselves, but the dead-eyes are seemingly endless and two more appear for every one slain.

Vihtor is isolated and overwhelmed, and somehow Anskar steps through shadows to appear at the Seneschal's side and save him. The dead-eyes keep coming, and Vihtor orders a retreat to the cottage.

Anskar uses dusk-tide sorcery to create a strong ward sphere. He surges into the fight to save Orix and others, but as he does so, he is surrounded by dead-eyes. Anskar's dusk-tide repository fails and his ward sphere vanishes. He reaches for his dark-tide repository to create a new ward sphere, which flings the dead-eyes from him.

The remaining knights and trainees barricade themselves inside the cottage. The knight Abizar makes a last stand to enable everyone to get to safety, and is eventually ripped to shreds.

The knights and trainees fight desperately as dead-eyes break through the roof and windows. Anskar uses dark-tide to hold up the ceiling, which bows under the weight of dead-eyes. He explodes his ward outwards and kills the dead-eyes on the roof. Sareya uses sorcery to incinerate the rest of the dead-eyes with violet flames, and then, exhausted, she collapses.

Carred Selenas discovers that Niyandrians are being rounded up a few at a time and sold by the Order of Eternal Vigilance as slaves. After years of failures and self-doubt, she cannot stand by. She frees Niyandrian slaves from a warehouse and burns down the building.

Carred receives word that her rebels attacked a group of knights from Branil's Burg and their trainees, but had been driven back by a young knight who bristled with sorcerous energy, aided by a young Niyandrian woman, Sareya. Carred speculates that Sareya is Queen Talia's daughter and that the young knight may be the heir's guardian. Both must have been conditioned by the Order, unaware of who they really are.

After the expedition returns to Branil's Burg with Petor's body, Anskar examines his vambrace using dark-tide power. He has a vision of a full suit of intricately forged plate armor and is inexplicably overcome with a burning need to possess the armor.

Vihtor commands Anskar to cease using the dusk- and dark-tides forever.

The trainees are given a day's break, and Anskar, Sareya, and Orix enjoy good food and too much beer. Late that night, disinhibited by alcohol, Anskar and Sareya renew their relationship.

Grand Master Hyle Pausus gathers the Order in the chapel of the Hooded One, which has been converted into a bankers' vault. Anskar is not impressed with Hyle Pausus, who has offended the priests of the Hooded One by desacralizing the chapel, believing him to be a fraud who places the needs and wishes of the noble elite of the mainland above those who represent Menselas. The Grand Master announces that the Niyandrians who built the vault begged to be received into the family of Menselas. Sareya tells Anskar that Hyle must be lying, as no Niyandrian would willingly forsake the old gods, but they both watch in fascinated horror as the Niyandrians are branded with the five-pointed star of Menselas.

That same day, Luzius Landav's servant, Malady, turns up at the Burg, carrying Luzius's severed head in a sack. The decomposing head seems to speak to Anskar, who is horrified. Malady is revealed to be a demon, and tells the Grand Master that he has been deceived. Malady escapes, and fearful of betrayal, Hyle Pausus orders the recently branded Niyandrians killed. Four of the Niyandrians, however, can't be found.

The atmosphere within Branil's Burg deteriorates. Lessons become somber affairs, Forge Master Sned drinks more, Vihtor becomes aloof and unapproachable, and Sareya withdraws into herself, seldom speaking and barely eating.

The trainees are raised to the rank of knight-inferior. In another year, they will be expected to take solemn vows or leave the Order and never return. Afterwards, Vihtor again questions Anskar about the crow and Sareya. Anskar lies and says he has remained distant from Sareya.

To clear his head, Anskar leaves the Burg, intending to find some space. When he stops to rest, he sees the golden-eyed crow sitting on a branch, staring at him. Anskar rides away, and as he eats and drinks at an inn, he wonders why the strange bird has returned and what it wants.

Anskar heads back to the Burg and finds Naul's dead body, which speaks to him, telling him to help Sareya. Anskar wakes Orix and sends him to get help, then heads to Sareya's room. He breaks through the locked door and finds Sareya bound and gagged, kneeling at the center of a circle formed from a golden chain. Within the circle stand four Niyandrians: the four escaped converts.

As Anskar fights two of the men, the dark-tide within him bursts its bindings. One Niyandrian's hand withers, and the second's face putrefies. The Niyandrian woman, a sorcerer, confronts Anskar, her dagger dazzling with silver fire. But she holds back and gasps with reverent awe: "*Melesh-Eloni!*"

The two remaining Niyandrians knock Sareya unconscious, drag Anskar to the center of the circle, and use a sorcerous portal to escape.

They manhandle Anskar into a waiting carriage and speed away. The woman sorcerer claims Anskar is *Melesh-Eloni*, though Anskar doesn't know what the words mean. Anskar attacks his kidnappers and causes the carriage to crash. He escapes, only to find the wraithe from Hallow Hill in the middle of the road. The wraithe clutches the golden-eyed crow in one hand, then crushes the bird, leaving it twitching on the road, before disappearing.

The Niyandrian sorcerer begs Anskar to come with her, but knights of the Order arrive. Vihtor kills the sorcerer and is shocked to see Anskar's eyes are now somehow cat's eyes, like those of a Niyandrian.

Back inside the Burg, Anskar is sure Vihtor knows more than he is revealing, but Hyle Pausus decides Anskar is a gifted knight-inferior and will take him to Sansor with his retinue. Vihtor doesn't voice an objection, and agrees that it could be dangerous for Anskar to remain in Niyas.

Anskar visits Sareya in the infirmary, where she tells him that *Melesh-Eloni* means "godling."

Anskar departs Branil's Burg by ship the next morning, consumed by questions that he feels he may never get answers to.

Carred and a small group of her followers watch the passage of the lone galleon as it heads out to sea.

Noni is possessed by the spirit of Queen Talia and tells Carred that there is no daughter: the heir to Niyas is Talia's son, the knight-sorcerer Anskar DeVantte. Talia reveals that Carred is Anskar's guardian, and now is the time for her to step into that role.

Carred vows to bring Anskar back to Niyas so that the entire country will rally to her cause. Under Anskar's lead, the faithful will take back Niyas for Niyandrians. Queen Talia will return. And the dead will live forever.

ONE

THE TREES LEANED DOWN.

Pressed in all around.

Reached out to touch her.

"Mama," Carred whispered—afraid the trees would hear. "Mama, where are you?"

She could feel the rag doll trembling in her hands. Little Nally's big blue eyes seemed wider than ever.

The sun's gone, Little Nally said in her squeaky voice. *It's nearly dark.*

"Don't worry, I'll keep you safe." Carred was proud she kept her tears at bay. *Four-year-olds don't cry,* Mama always told her.

Lightning shivered across the gray sky, edging the clouds with silver. Carred's heart skipped then pounded: one, two, three.

Thunder boomed and she remembered to breathe.

"Mama …" Louder this time, a quaver in her voice. "Mama, I'm scared."

The wind gusted. Clouds roiled overhead, bathing the forest floor in shadow. Rain began to fall, faster and faster, till it pelted the treetops and drenched her hair.

And then there were shapes moving between the trees. They shifted the second she saw them, pretending not to be there. She held Little Nally out before her—*she'd* be able to see better, what with her big eyes. But Nally just shook and said nothing. If she'd spotted anything, she was too frightened to say. The rag doll's trembling spread to Carred's hands. Maybe it had started there. Another flash set the sky ablaze, then flickered away and died. This time the thunder rolled after just two heartbeats.

And the rain poured down, forming puddles all around.

"Mama?" Now she spoke in whimpers. "Mam—"

"Shut it!" Father's voice in her head. "Or I'll give you something to cry about."

And there were other voices. She couldn't tell if they came through her ears or not. Maybe they were thoughts turned loud.

Carred, they seemed to say. *Carred Selenas.*

Wingbeats.

Something fluttered down to an overhanging branch. A bird, black all over till it opened its eyes—gold, like twin shining suns.

And still figures moved through the gloom, whipping and snapping like clothes drying in the wind. They made her think of fangs and claws and eyes of blood. Fingers, not quite solid, brushed her skin. She gasped and held tight to Nally. The crow peered down from its tree, golden eyes flashing with reflected lightning.

One heartbeat, and thunder crashed.

Riding its echo, a shape sped through the gloom toward her. She covered her face with the rag doll. Risked a peek. Frowned in confusion.

It was a helm like the kind soldiers wore, only different. Theirs were open-faced, but this helm covered the whole head without even a slit for the eyes. A hairline crack split it down the center, widening as the front of the helm started to open.

And Carred screamed as she turned and ran.

She mustn't look.

Mustn't see.

Howls echoed behind her. Claws strained to reach her. Icy breath blasted her back.

And someone was cackling.

"Theltek, save me!" she shrieked.

The woods were home to the moontouched—what the grownups called witches.

The cackling rose ever louder till it swamped her.

Hands grabbed her and she wailed.

Mama stepped out from behind a tree.

"That'll teach you! Wander off, would you? Well, now you've learned your lesson." Mama wrinkled her nose and fanned a hand in front of her face. "You messed yourself?"

Shame drove the fear out of Carred.

"You hear that, Sanjor? Your daughter's shit herself."

Carred's father stumbled into view. Took a swig from a bottle.

"Clean her up," Mama said.

"Don't you go giving me jobs, woman. Clean her yourself." And with that, he walked away.

Carred could see it now: the path through the forest that led back to town.

Mama grabbed her by the collar. "You did it to spite me!" Slapped her. Snatched Little Nally from her hands. "And you don't need this, not if you're going to grow up."

"No! Nally!" Carred cried as Mama slung the rag doll into the trees. She dared not look in case the helm was there. In case she should see.

"And you're not coming indoors in those clothes," Mama said as she led her away. "You'll strip outside and let the rain wash them clean."

Carred stole a look over her shoulder. No crow looking down at her. No helm.

Was that Nally? She could hardly see through the downpour.

"Come on!" Mama said, pulling her along.

One last look as they reached the path.

The trees stooped down, branches reaching for the ground.

For Nally.

And then they snatched the rag doll away.

Carred knew things were different when she woke. She was bigger for one thing. Older. Scarred. It took a few moments to realize she was in her tent at the new camp in Rynmuntithe—a good hundred miles from the part of the forest that so often formed the backdrop of her dreams. Dream singular—for it was always the same dream of being left alone. Except this time it had been different. There had been voices, clearer than the usual vague whisperings. A voice calling her name. There had been the golden-eyed crow. And there had been the helm. Even now, the thought of what might have been inside throttled the breath in her throat.

Sounds came from outside her tent. A commotion. A man's voice—not a woman's as in her dream—calling her name, coming nearer.

"Carred!"

Taloc pushed his way through the entrance flap. "They've

found us."

"Shit." Carred flung aside her covers and rolled her eyes as Taloc turned his face from her nakedness. Still so lacking in confidence despite being a good-looking man, tall and broad; and his red skin had a healthy glow, now he was eating properly. He had Carred to thank for that. She'd saved him from a life of slavery. But it was warriors she needed, not more lovers. By Theltek of the Hundred Eyes, she'd already lost enough of them.

"There's more than two hundred knights a few miles out."

"They found us so soon?" she said as she quickly dressed.

"They had help."

"You can look now," Carred said as she fastened her shirt. What would Taloc have made of her battle scars? Marith loved them, but Marith was an odd woman. It hurt like a sword to the guts that they'd been parted when the assassins had come for Carred. She could use Marith's gentle touch. Then, at least, she might be able to sleep without the past creeping into her dreams—and bringing with it something new. "Help from who? No, let me guess … Olana." Another of the Niyandrian slaves she'd freed at Lowanin.

"Riding with them. You said she was trouble."

"I should've left her in that cage I found you all in," Carred said.

"You should have killed her."

"You could have done it."

Taloc licked his lips. He was new to this.

"You get used to it," Carred said as she pushed past him and stepped outside into the creeping light of dawn.

Tents were already coming down, no need for her to give the order. Canvases were rolled, poles bundled with twine to be carried on backs. Children with ferns for brushes set about erasing tracks in the sun-dried mud. The night's ashes were scattered amid the trees. A few men stood about arguing, then turned disapproving looks on Carred.

"Everyone knows what to do!" she shouted above the ruckus. "Scatter. We'll regroup in the highlands the day after tomorrow."

Her voice drew Noni nearer, as detached and unheeded as a ghost. The young woman's hair was neatly brushed and plaited—Vilintia Yoenth had always wanted someone to mother, having sacrificed her best years to military service. It was no surprise to see the veteran rushing to keep up with Noni. No surprise either when she met Carred's gaze with a "whatever you need" look. Her hair might have matched the color of her mail, but Vilintia was still, first and foremost, a soldier.

Carred caught the weaselly Fult Wreave shaking his head. The sole survivor of the Ickthal dynasty—if that's what he really was—no doubt thought this was a lost opportunity for a famous last stand. But that had been Naphor, and Carred, unlike Wreave, had actually been there when the ancient capital fell.

"You want to fight, Fult," Carred said, "then by all means stay. The rest of you, let's go. Taloc, Noni, Vilintia, with me."

"Welcome to Ahz!" the fat man said as he raked the last of Taloc's coins across the table. "Enjoy your stay."

"You already said that," Carred grumbled from behind her cards. She slapped them face-down on the table. Another shit hand. She was starting to see why the game was called Five-card Malice. She slid two more talents toward the fat man, leaving her with one.

"Twice," Taloc grumbled as he stood. His chair tipped over

with a loud clatter. He was drunk. Very.

So was Carred.

Not the fat man, though. Sober as a bloody shark.

One of the onlookers—all of them were Niyandrian, which should have made her feel safe—whispered something to the woman beside him, then tried to pretend he'd been looking at something over Carred's shoulder. Perhaps he thought he recognized her ...

She'd come to Ahz to lie low and lick yet another wound. Olana's betrayal hadn't surprised her, but the timing had been bloody inconvenient. And it had diminished her newfound resolve. Crushed it underfoot.

"What kind of name's that for a town, anyway?" Vilintia said. She was seated at another table with Noni, just watching—too sensible to gamble, too responsible to drink, and making sure everyone knew. Reminded Carred of her mother.

"Appropriate's what it is," Taloc said.

"Ahz," the fat man said, picking up one of Taloc's coins and biting it, "is Old Niyandrian for—"

"Haven," Carred said. Taloc was right, though for the wrong reason. The town was one of the few not under direct Order control, a haven of Niyandrian culture. Probably because it was too much of a shithole for the Knights of Eternal Vigilance to set foot in without staining their white cloaks and their pure thoughts.

"You surprise me." The fat man pursed his lips and set the coin amid the ever-growing stack before him. Evidently he'd decided it wasn't a fake. "Most people in the occupied towns are forgetting how to speak regular Niyandrian, let alone the old tongue."

"Who said we're from an occupied town?" Carred said.

"And, in case you've not noticed, we've done nothing but speak Niyandrian all night."

As had the fat man and the crowd of local drinkers who'd gathered around the table to watch the game. So many crimson faces and not a single mainlander to ruin things. For one drunken moment Carred could almost imagine the invasion had never happened.

"True, true," the fat man said. "Which leads me to wonder—"

"Drink!" Carred said as she caught the eye of a server, who gave her a disapproving look. "And no, I've not had enough, before you ask." The fat man looked annoyed at her interruption. Let him be annoyed. The less any of the locals knew, the better. "By the way," she said somewhat smugly, "I know a smattering of Old Niyandrian."

"Again, I'm surprised. You don't look the type."

The type he implied was a descendent of one of the ancient noble families, like that weasel Fult Wreave. Perhaps like the fat man himself: his severe widow's peak, his arched eyebrows, gave the impression of nobility, though he'd clearly fallen on hard times, or been displaced by the invaders.

"I picked up the odd word and phrase here and there."

"Oh? Where, exactly?"

"Here and there." Old Niyandrian had been the official language of Queen Talia's court. Not that a mere captain of the Last Cohort should have spent much time at court, but Talia had insisted, on the pretext of threats to the queen's person—though in reality to stave off the unnatural chill in her bones once the hangers-on had gone home.

"Well, now that you've established my coins are good," Taloc said with an impressive edge of manly belligerence while neglecting to mention that Carred had loaned him the coins, "I'll call it a night. Unlike Carred, I've drunk more than enough."

"Carred Selenas?" the fat man said. Murmurs passed among the onlookers. "You should have said."

"He wishes." Carred gave Taloc a withering look. "You've got a thing about that loser and her failed rebellion, haven't you, Taloc?"

He almost grimaced at his mistake. Would have done if they were alone. "Not any longer," he said. "Ran out of patience with that bitch some time ago. Too many failures."

Carred felt a twist in the pit of her stomach. Was he playing along, or did he really mean that?

"Good night," Taloc said. He glanced Vilintia's way before he headed upstairs. Was there something between ...? Surely not. Vilintia was old enough to be his mother.

"Night," Carred grumbled. She became acutely aware of eyes on her, and the murmuring continued. Still, some of the punters looked impressed, as if they might sign up to her cause if she'd only admit who she was. But doing so would just increase the chances of being given away. Almost twenty years of occupation, and Niyas was teeming with Olanas.

"You do have a surname, I take it?" the fat man said.

Carred thought on her feet. "Pelhur." Marith's surname. For some reason that made her feel guilty. It was the booze, she figured as the server returned with her mistberry wine, mixing up her emotions like it always did. She shouldn't drink, and certainly not so much. "Thanks," she said, accepting the glass and taking a healthy sip. "And now you have me at a disadvantage. Or should I go on thinking of you as—?" She stopped herself just in time.

"Thinking of me as what?"

"The refined gentleman," she said, and he seemed to like that.

Ass, she added to herself, or was that the town?

"If you must know," the fat man said, "I am Count Vasseyli ap Murbian."

Carred was right: just like Wreave.

"My friends call me Vaz," he added with a diffident wave.

"You have friends?"

"Oh ho, a wit as well as an appalling gambler." He leaned across the table to her and whispered, "And a worse liar." With an expansive gesture, he raised his voice so everyone could hear. "But don't worry. As a leader, a symbol of resistance, you are admired here."

A dozen pairs of eyes watched for her response. She was too drunk to maintain the facade, just as she was too drunk to bluff at cards. Of its own volition, her mouth curled into a smile.

People gasped, shook their heads, then started to cheer.

"I said it was her from the scars," the man who'd whispered about her told the woman next to him. "Didn't I say it was her?"

Niyandrians pressed in around Carred, wanting to shake her hand, telling her she was a hero.

"You realize we'll have to leave now," she said. She wiped a tear from her eye—why was she crying? Because they looked up to her, that's why. Valued what she stood for. She gave them hope, but that hope was a lie.

Through the press of bodies she glimpsed Vilintia rise from her chair and head upstairs, leaving Noni sitting at their table alone.

"It's all right. I'll look after her," Carred called.

Vilintia stiffened at the sarcasm. Turned on the stairs. "I was . . . I was just . . ."

"You were cold, I know. Go easy on Taloc."

"What? Taloc?" Vilintia wrinkled her nose.

"Go on. You're convincing no one," Carred said.

Vilintia gave a sheepish smile and hurried upstairs.

Carred glanced at Noni—hands folded in her lap, chuckling at something only she could hear. Following Carred's gaze, a few of the locals muttered and rubbed their eyes in the sign of Theltek. They probably thought Noni was moontouched, or more likely that she was mad.

"Another hand?" Vaz said. "Just you and me?" He fixed Carred with a penetrating stare—his idea of flirting? She washed the bile back down with a swig of wine.

"I've only a few coins left ..."

"Ah, but you have that ring. I'd wager all I have for such a beauty."

Carred hadn't realized the void-steel ring on its chain was hanging outside her shirt. She tucked it back out of sight.

"No?" Vaz said, unashamedly staring at her chest. "Surely you have something else to gamble?"

"Just the clothes I'm wearing."

He smiled. "I'm more interested in what's beneath."

Someone in the crowd groaned. Others shook their heads and started to move away. They'd seen this sort of thing from Vaz before, no doubt. Either they didn't approve, or they knew when to give him space.

"Are you in?" Vaz asked with a raised eyebrow.

Don't be an idiot, Carred told herself. She could hear Marith's voice in her head: *You're better than that.*

"Fuck it," she said, draining the rest of her mistberry wine and waving the glass for a refill. The bastard server pretended not to see her. "What do I have to lose?"

"A woman of your reputed experience?" Vaz said. "Nothing, I'm sure. And yet so much to gain."

"Yes, you do have a large pile of coins."

"I wasn't referring to that."

The vile prick really fancied himself. Well, he wasn't her type ... although, appearances weren't everything. Despite his general air of sleaziness, she felt an old familiar stirring. *Don't go there,* the shrinking voice of sobriety said.

The sound of a chair grating on the floor snapped Carred out of herself. Noni stood, staring at her with wide, warning eyes and shaking her head.

"Sit down, girl," Carred said. "It's all right. I don't intend to lose."

"Such confidence," Vaz said as he dealt her five cards, then five for himself.

Carred arranged hers swiftly into a fan and studied her hand.

"Everything still all right?" Vaz asked from behind his cards.

"Of course," Carred said, biting her lip.

She was fucked.

Carred tripped on the stairs as she went up to her room. "Shit," she said, catching herself on the banister, "I left Noni by herself."

"I'm sure she'll be fine," Vaz said from behind. He gave her ass a rough squeeze. But for the booze, it would have hurt, but Carred barely felt it. "Firm," he said appreciatively. "Firm is good."

She fumbled with the doorknob, then they fell into the room together, though Carred had the impression Vaz was pretending, even if she wasn't. Already he was undoing her shirt, rather too deftly for insobriety. She bit back the urge to shove him away from her, or to be sick. A bet had to be honored.

Vaz tugged her shirt open and his eyes widened. "You've seen better days," he said as he traced the outline of the scar between her breasts. She winced at the memory: the knight's sword had pierced her mail and almost killed her, cut right down to the sternum. "And not just the scars. You must be—what?—fifty?"

"Thirty-six," she said, "which is half whatever you are."

"Not even close." A hard edge had crept into his voice. He gripped her arms and forced her down to the bed.

"Easy," Carred said. "I'm willing, you know." Or rather, indebted.

He growled and set to work yanking her pants off. He cursed when they got caught on her ankles, gave up and forced her onto her belly. The way he gripped her hips from behind was painful, even through the alcoholic haze. Carred felt a stab of panic and rolled to her back, scooting away up the bed. He followed, got on top, pinned her down with his weight. She really panicked then, pounding at his ears with her palms. He responded by ripping into the flesh of her breast with his teeth.

"Ouch!" Carred cried. "That bloody hurt, you bastard!"

"It was meant to." He commenced sucking at the wound he'd made.

"Get off!" And now she was too angry to be drunk. She pounded the back of his head with hammer fists. He roared and reared up to hit her, but she raised her hips, wrapped a leg around the back of his neck and locked it down with the other leg. Vaz gasped as she squeezed, occluding the blood flow to his brain. He thrashed and slapped at her, but still she squeezed. Vaz let out a pathetic wheeze and his body went limp.

The door burst open. Taloc barged in. Sword in hand. Naked. Not quite flaccid—Carred couldn't help noticing. Good for Vilintia.

"Interesting position," Taloc said, taking in the situation with raised eyebrows, going to sheathe his sword, then realizing he hadn't brought the scabbard.

"Piss off, Taloc." Carred unhooked her legs from around Vaz's neck and let him slump to the bed unconscious.

"You wouldn't catch m—"

"Didn't I tell you to piss off?" Carred said, shoving Vaz off the bed. He hit the floor with a thud and remained unmoving. Maybe she'd held the choke too long? No, his shirt shivered with the faintest of breaths. Pity, that.

"Go check Noni's all right," she said. "You might want to put some clothes on first."

Taloc turned, then hesitated at whatever he'd seen down the corridor.

"She's all right," he said, though he sounded uncertain as he stood aside and Noni stepped into the doorway, arms clutched over her chest as she shivered.

Carred sprang off the bed and pulled Noni into the room, then slammed the door in Taloc's face.

Noni's teeth chattered. It wasn't even all that cold, and besides, she was fully dressed. Carred's heart was thumping from her scuffle with Vaz. Theltek, what had he done to her? Her breast stung like crazy, and when she touched it, her hand came away sticky with blood. He'd bitten her and drunk her blood! Pervert.

Her eyes burned, and she dashed away tears. *Pull yourself together,* she told herself. *You're supposed to be a leader, the guardian of Queen Talia's heir.*

Noni pressed herself to Carred, still shivering, icy, even through her clothes.

"Remember how you used to warm me, Carred?" she said, the voice not her own. "There's no one to warm me in the realm of the dead."

Carred stepped back and held her at arm's length. Noni's eyes glowed golden. "Talia?"

"Hold me, Carred. No, let's get under the covers. I'm so cold."

From the floor by the side of the bed, Vaz grunted and stirred awake.

Noni swept toward him, flung out her arm in a grand gesture—Theltek's eyes, she even moved like Queen Talia. Vaz grabbed the bedclothes and tried to pull himself up, but Noni barked at him in Old Niyandrian, the words not ones Carred knew. The air tingled with sorcery.

Vaz stiffened, fell back to the floor, shook violently.

"What did you just say?"

"Reveal yourself," Noni said in Talia's voice.

With a shriek of rage, Vaz thrashed about, fists hammering the hardwood floor. He writhed and twisted, bucked and flailed. His exposed skin mottled, then darkened, limbs stretched and thinned, face contorted and lengthened. His nose receded until it was just slits. His eyes turned to yellow sickle blades. The thing Vaz had become ripped its clothes from its gangly body as hairs erupted from every inch of skin. No, not hairs: spines, like those of a porcupine, until the only things not covered by them were the sickly eyes. The creature rose into the air, feet a couple of inches above the floor. It turned its hungry glare on Carred and hissed.

Noni spoke another command in Old Niyandrian, and the thing that had been Vaz backed away toward the window. Apparently unafraid, Noni approached and opened the window wide. Another command, this time scarcely more than a whisper, and the creature floated outside. It hung there in the air for a moment, then drifted slowly away, eyes still fixed on Carred until they receded into the night.

"What in Theltek's name was that thing?" Carred breathed. "I almost let it fuck me!"

Noni—or was it Talia?—chuckled as she closed and latched the window. "What it was doesn't matter. It won't be back, not while I'm with you."

"That's a relief," Carred said as Noni turned to face her, eyes still golden. "So why don't I feel reassured?"

She couldn't move, could barely breathe, as Noni slid toward her and took her hand, her grasp clammy.

"Let's get warm," Noni said.

Carred lay on the bed, and Noni lay beside her, pulling up the sheet and blanket to cover them. As Noni snuggled into her, Carred turned her head away. She couldn't look at those eyes.

"You're trembling, Carred. You never used to feel the cold."

"I'm not cold."

"No," Noni said, "you're still my little furnace." She pressed up close to Carred's back, leeching the warmth away, giving contented gasps, just the way Talia used to.

"I'm not disappointed by your failure to take my son and heir from the Knights of Eternal Vigilance, Carred. Well, perhaps I am a little. You are, after all, his guardian."

"It might have helped if you'd told me," Carred said. "But it's out of my hands. Anskar's been taken from Niyas."

"I know. And I know how much you have struggled on my behalf. No one else would have done as much as you. Given so much."

"But it wasn't enough," Carred said.

"No." Noni reached over and made Carred look her in the eye. "No, it wasn't."

"What else am I supposed to do? Your son's beyond my reach

now. Or should that be your daughter?" For years the Knights of Eternal Vigilance had hunted for the Queen's daughter, and Carred, the supposed guardian, had too.

"Don't be bitter, Carred. The deception was necessary."

"Because you didn't trust me?"

"The less anyone knew, the better."

Carred tried to roll out of bed, but Noni prevented her with a grip of ice and iron.

"I need you to find him."

"Do it yourself, if you're so all-bloody-powerful!"

Noni released her. Turned over. Let out a shuddering sigh. "I can't. He is obscured from me. Every effort at contact drains me."

"Try looking in Sansor. Isn't that where the Grand Master's based?"

"I think ..." And here the dead Queen's voice reverted to Noni's, quavering and close to sobs. "I think he hides himself."

"He doesn't want you?" Nothing. No reaction, not even the slightest movement. Noni's stillness told Carred she'd hit a nerve. Told her she had to be careful.

"Anskar is my son, Carred. He is my heir."

"He's more than that to you, Talia. I've worked that much out for myself."

"Find him, Carred! Keep him safe."

Or what? Carred didn't dare ask. "How? The Order has blockades!"

"Malady, the dwarf woman who served the sorcerer Luzius Landav. It sickens me, but you must enlist the help of the abyssal realms. The old man, Maggow, knows what to do."

"You've spoken with him?"

Noni's hips bucked on the bed. Her golden eyes rolled up

into her head, came down white. Her fingers made clutching motions as she started to spasm, her face a mask of anguish. When the seizure passed, she lay still, drool glistening from the corner of her mouth.

Already, she was snoring lightly.

Carred leaped out of bed and started putting her clothes on. "Vilintia!" she yelled. "Stop rutting and get your ass in here!"

Curses came from down the corridor. A door opened and shut. Footsteps, and then Vilintia entered, buttoning her shirt, nothing covering her long legs.

"We're leaving," Carred said, buckling her sword belt.

"At this time of night?"

"Now."

As Vilintia started to turn away, Carred asked, "Well? How was it with Taloc?"

Vilintia's face went from crimson to pink. "We'd barely started before all that commotion."

"Same here," Carred said, glancing at the window, flinching as she recalled the thing that had been Vaz.

Taloc appeared in the doorway, tucking his shirt in. He shared a look with Vilintia.

"Ah, good," Carred said, cocking her thumb at the still-sleeping Noni. "You can carry her."

"Where're we going?" Taloc asked.

"The highlands, a little earlier than planned. To see a man about a demon."

TWO

A SOUTHERLY WIND BELLIED THE sails of the *Exultant* as she glided across the calm waters of the Simorga Sea. The rills and ripples left in the ship's wake reflected starlight, and Anskar DeVantte watched them from the aftcastle as if they were forerunners of the sorcerous currents he would welcome with the dawn-tide.

It was a relief to reach the end of the first day at sea. Captain Hadlor had insisted Anskar and his fellow knight-inferior, Orix, scrub the decks. He'd worked them till their hands were raw and their knees were swollen, and only then did he let them eat. The Captain, on the other hand, had done nothing but eat since they left the harbor at Dorinah. Well, eat and criticize the two of them if they missed the slightest patch of a plank or strake.

Orix had been too tired and too green with seasickness to eat the proffered food—some kind of gray-looking gruel that smelled of fish. He'd gone below decks to their dorm.

A droplet of water struck Anskar's face. He turned a palm up to see if it had started to rain. Nothing. Probably just the spray coming off the sea.

And then he felt it: the crawl of tiny insects over his skin, the steady drip of intangible water on his clothes and hair, the persistent caress of the darkness all around him, trying to get in.

He'd wondered when it would come.

It wasn't a rushing wind like the dawn- or the dusk-tides. The dark-tide was more subtle, more insidious. The fact that he'd only now noticed its touch told him that the barriers he'd erected were working. He sent slivers of awareness inside himself, to probe at the forbidden sorcery he'd woven around each of his three repositories. He'd observed Sareya doing the same, controlling the ebb and flow of her repositories, and he had simply copied her.

Sareya …

What they had done together still inflamed him.

Shamed him.

What was he doing, emulating her, a Niyandrian, when he'd resolved to make good on his vocation this time round? The Church of Menselas forbade all sorcery save for the knights' use of the dawn-tide for their ward spheres and the forging of weapons and armor, yet here he was sinning again. It was an act of supreme arrogance to think he could use his own power to resist the dark-tide.

Only the God of Five Aspects had the right.

"Menselas," he muttered through gritted teeth, "come to my aid."

Anskar felt self-conscious. They were the words of someone else, a petition that his old mentor, Brother Tion, might have made.

Not the Melesh-Eloni.

The thought sliced through the center of his mind. Was it his own?

Melesh-Eloni: what his Niyandrian kidnapper had called him before the knights had come to his rescue.

Sareya had translated the word: *Godling.*

"Ignore it," Anskar told himself—exactly what Tion would have said. Errant thoughts were the rotten fruit of an undisciplined mind, or they came from the abyssal realms. Never from Menselas.

Queen Talia was supposed to have had a daughter, not a son ...

"Ignore it!" he said again, this time so loud he had to look around to check he hadn't been heard. But there was no one else on deck. He was alone, though he didn't feel *quite* alone.

The dark-tide seeped into his pores, slowly filling him to the brim.

Tightening his jaw with new resolve, he began again. "Menselas, come to my aid. Elder, cleanse my mind. Warrior, protect me. Healer, restore me. Mother, wrap me in your arms. Hooded One ..."

And again he stalled. Invoke the darkness to drive away the dark? The Hooded One had once been known as Death. But still, he had to pray.

"Hooded One, take my will and place my reliance upon the Five."

He began the prayer again, reciting it like a cant. Over and over, the words spilled from his lips almost of their own volition. All the while he shivered at the violations of the dark, fought the urge to resist them, begged for the strength to leave it all to Menselas. A test of faith, Tion would have said.

When, after what felt like an hour, nothing changed, Anskar

had to assume he had failed the test. Either that, or Menselas had abandoned him due to the sins he and Sareya had committed at Branil's Burg, and the times he had succumbed to the tides of the dusk and dark.

The sway of the deck beneath his feet, the lap of the waves against the keel, the tang of the brine drew him out of himself, and before he knew it, they had lulled him into an unfamiliar sense of calm.

The newfound peace remained with Anskar hour after hour, save for the knot of worry he had about voyaging into the unknown.

He watched the clouds racing across the faces of the two moons—the red Jagonath and white Chandra—then studied the patterns of the stars strewn across the black background of night. He tried to make out the shapes of the saints in the constellations, men and women who had given their lives in the service of Menselas. Of course, Sareya used to mock him, insisting the constellations depicted gods, not saints—the demons worshiped by her people.

Were they really his people too, at least in part?

He became aware of a cold weight on his forearm, pulled back his shirtsleeve, and the moonlight revealed the vambrace he'd taken from the Niyandrian tomb on Hallow Hill. It was glowing, aswirl with scintillant colors. He swiftly covered it. In the daytime it would be invisible once more. He shivered as he recalled his vision of a suit of armor made from the same eldritch metal as the vambrace.

"Thought you'd be tired after all that deck scrubbing," Captain Hadlor said, startling Anskar. He'd not heard the Captain approach. "Have to work you harder tomorrow." Hadlor bit into a pastry, then took a slug from an earthenware bottle to wash it down. "Before we reach the mainland, I'll have you lads tying all sixteen knots a sailor should know and climbing the rigging like a pair of Ealysian gibbons."

The Captain came to lean against the gunwale, staring out into the night. He crammed the rest of the pastry into his mouth and chewed vigorously. Hadlor was half a head shorter than Anskar, but he was as wide as he was tall, a blubbery man with thick arms and thicker legs. His coarse-weave pants were hoicked up beneath his barrel chest but did nothing to disguise the bulge of his stomach. He wore an open-necked white shirt, which contrasted sharply with his dusky skin. His head was completely bald, huge ears sticking out, the lobes stretched by looping rings of gold. Around his neck, the Captain wore a chain with a pendant in the form of an axe. Anskar had seen him discreetly kiss it on and off throughout the day.

"Ah," Hadlor said, breathing in the chill sea air, "I love the smell of a well-scrubbed deck. You lads did well, for your first day at sea. Where's the pudgy Traguh-raj boy?"

Orix wasn't really pudgy, just thickset, though he enjoyed his food almost as much as the Captain did. "He's down below, Captain. Fast asleep."

Hadlor laughed at that. "I got him good, eh? He'll be sore in the morning, and then I'll get him even better. No slackers on the *Exultant*. That way, when the crisis strikes, we'll all know what to do." He jiggled his belly, then took a long pull on his drink.

"Crisis?" Anskar asked. "You're expecting trouble?"

"At sea, boy, you plan for the worst and hope for the best. If the behemoth rises from the deep and cracks open our hull, or if the devil-beak wraps us in its tentacled embrace, who knows how many sailors we could lose? Then it's the passengers who need to crew the ship. Either that, or we'll all go under together, and I don't plan on going under. I'm too young to die a cold death at sea." He must have been close to sixty. "And there are too many ladies who'd miss me," the Captain added with a mischievous grin.

Anskar peered warily into the dark waters slurping and sucking at the keel. "There are beasts down there?"

Hadlor slapped him on the shoulder. "Even if there aren't, there's the threat of storms. The Simorga's a capricious sea, young Anskar. Best be prepared, I always say, which is why you'll be working twice as hard come sunrise."

"And the knights?" Anskar asked. "The priests?" He'd seen none of them helping on deck throughout the day.

"They think they're as far above a sailor's work as Menselas is above their sordid desires," Hadlor said. "But they'll only have themselves to blame when their bloated corpses go bobbing into shore, assuming the sharp-tooths don't get to them first. But not you two lads, eh? Too young to think yourselves above hard work, which is what will save you in the end. Keep doing what I tell you, and the crew will respect you. Who knows, maybe the Simorga Sea will respect you too. What I want to know, though, is why a couple of green-gilled lubbers like you and the pudgy one are traveling with the Grand Master."

Anskar didn't know the Captain well enough to disclose the real reason: that there was concern for his safety after the kidnap attempt. He shrugged. "Maybe there's something they can teach me in Sansor that they couldn't at the Burg."

"Maybe," Hadlor said, then hawked up phlegm and spat it over the side. "Just you be careful, is my advice." He rubbed his axe pendant between thumb and forefinger, lips working in what looked like a silent prayer.

"What is that?" Anskar asked.

"The Axe of Juagott. The storm god worshiped by the island folk of Ak-Settur, and a good patron for men of the sea."

"You worship the heathen gods?"

Hadlor turned back to him, eyes widening as he saw something over Anskar's shoulder. "Praise be to Menselas," he said. "All five aspects. And may he bless this ship and bring us safely to Sansor."

Anskar frowned, then followed the Captain's gaze to where a man in a white robe was ascending the steps to the aftcastle.

Again, Hadlor clapped Anskar on the shoulder, and again he uttered, "Just you be careful," then he stoppered his earthenware bottle, nodding at the man coming onto the aftcastle as he passed by on his way back down to the deck.

Some obscure sense made Anskar shudder, and his fingers tightened about the hilt of *Amalantril* sheathed at his hip. He'd worn the sword all day despite it getting in the way as he scrubbed the deck. He wasn't used to being away from the Burg, and he needed the reassurance of ensorcelled steel. The mail he'd made for the final test of initiation before taking simple vows, however, had been scoured with sand and vinegar and well oiled, and was stowed in a hemp-weave sack beneath his bed.

As the white-robed man came closer, Anskar started to make out his features: dark eyes that glittered in the starlight, a mouth like a gash, and thin strands of greasy hair plastered to his scalp. The first time Anskar had seen him, the acolyte had worn a half-mask, but that had been when he'd branded the flesh of the Niyandrian builders who'd converted the Hooded One's chapel into a vault for the storage of mainland wealth. When the builders had been revealed as spies of Carred Selenas, the acolyte had presided over their executions.

"I see your eyes have not yet recovered," the acolyte said. "I pray to Menselas that the alteration is not permanent."

The leader of the kidnappers, a Niyandrian woman named Aelanthe, had done something to Anskar using sorcery. He'd not known what at the time, but later the healers had given him a mirror. His eyes, once as normal as any self-respecting mainlander's, were now slitted like a cat's and tawny. They were the eyes of a Niyandrian.

"Does it affect your vision?" the acolyte asked, cocking his head to one side.

"Not now." At first his sight had grown blurry, but then it had adjusted. If anything, he saw things more clearly now, especially at night.

"Feral," the acolyte said. "Tell me, Anskar DeVantte, do you have Niyandrian blood?"

Sareya had asked him the same question repeatedly, on account of the reddish tint to his skin. Anskar had always rejected the idea vehemently. Sareya's implication had been that his father must have been a knight who had defiled a Niyandrian woman during the war against Queen Talia.

The acolyte was frowning at him, and Anskar looked away, heat flushing his cheeks.

"Forgive my impertinence," the man said. "I ask too many questions, yet I have neglected to tell you anything of myself." He offered Anskar his hand. "Gadius Menashin, acolyte to the priests of the Elder at the Mother House."

"What does that even mean?" Anskar asked. "Acolyte?"

"It means I assist."

"With sorcery?" Anskar had sensed Gadius's mark of sorcery when he and Orix had first come aboard—a strong mark, smooth and well cultivated. The acolyte had two repositories that Anskar could detect: dawn and dusk.

Gadius raised an eyebrow. "I carry the thurible for the incense, light the candles, find the right page in the holy scriptures for the priest to read from."

"Back at Branil's Burg …" Anskar started, hesitating when Gadius narrowed his eyes. He didn't need to finish his sentence about what he'd seen the acolyte do to the Niyandrian spies.

"My function is to serve," Gadius said. "Without question. Well, Anskar, I am glad to have finally had the chance to speak with you, but I'm dallying. A group of us are meeting for Nethers on the forecastle. You're welcome to join us."

"Nethers?"

"Oh, the priests at Branil's Burg didn't pray so early? Nethers is a Skanuric word. It means 'last dark.' Nethers is the first prayer of the day. Most important, don't you think, for those who must use sorcery—even you knights—to place Menselas first, before the dawn-tide blows through you?"

Anskar had never thought of it that way, but it made a kind of sense.

"Join us," Gadius said, not waiting for an answer as he turned and set off down the steps.

Anskar didn't feel he had much of a choice.

When he reached the main deck, white-robed priests carrying lanterns were processing toward the forecastle, a lone knight at their rear. Anskar followed them, and as they reached the top of the steps, the knight offered him a hand in greeting. He was a tall man, slim yet broad-shouldered, with black hair tied at the nape of his neck.

"You must be Anskar DeVantte," the knight said in a low voice, as if he didn't want to be overheard. "Seneschal Vihtor Ulnar's an old friend of mine. He asked me to look out for you. Lanuc of Gessa."

"Gessa?" Anskar said, taking Lanuc's proffered hand.

"A coastal city to the east of the Great Southern Mountains of Ealysia. I'm not surprised you haven't heard of it. Gessa's about as far from civilization as you can get, and its people are somewhat insular. Not me, though. I found it oppressive and couldn't wait to get out."

"So Vihtor asked you to look out for me ..."

"Don't take it the wrong way," Lanuc said. "You're a grown man and already a knight-inferior. But Sansor's a complicated city. It's an easy place to lose your faith, or to make enemies with no idea how you did. It's also a long way off, even by sea, and our stopover has hazards of its own."

"We're stopping somewhere else?"

"They didn't tell you? No, I don't suppose they did. Don't trouble yourself about it, Anskar. And remember, if you need anything, come to me."

The priests had by now formed themselves into a circle, their lanterns held aloft. Gadius was watching Anskar and Lanuc with forced patience, waiting for them to stop talking and take their places. Lanuc squeezed in between two disgruntled priests, then politely asked one of them to make room for Anskar.

Once everyone was in place, Gadius announced the opening of the time of prayer with an invocation in Skanuric; then the priests began to chant a Skanuric litany Anskar had heard Brother Tion use on several occasions. He could make out the odd word but not enough to understand the meaning. The chant was sonorous and rhythmic, and he was soon caught up in its currents. When the priests began to sway in time with their singing, Anskar swayed too, and beside him so did Lanuc.

As soon as he realized what he was doing, Anskar was overcome with feelings of guilt and unworthiness. The forecastle at that moment was holy ground, and the collective chant was a direct channel to the ears of Menselas.

After the prayers, the priests embraced each other, then one at a time shook hands with Anskar and Lanuc before filing back down the steps. As Anskar followed Lanuc onto the main deck, knights were coming up from below and finding themselves positions around the gunwale.

At Anskar's querying look, Lanuc explained, "Time to greet the dawn-tide."

Anskar felt foolish. He should have known. He found himself a spot near the prow, gazing out across the dark waters, focusing on the sliver of gray on the horizon.

He turned back at the sound of voices and saw the Grand Master emerge from his cabin, immediately surrounded by a gaggle of priests. Hyle Pausus was dressed in a white cloak, the hood pulled up against the breeze. By the ship's wheel, Captain Hadlor fiddled with his axe pendant as he looked on with a handful of crewmen.

They didn't have long to wait for the dawn-tide to come. Anskar felt it first as an icy tingle over his skin. He braced himself against the gunwale as it hit him in waves and gusts, crisp and fresh, a quickening wind that blasted through him, scouring him inside and out, swelling his dawn-tide repository to bursting. He gripped the gunwale, breathing in the dawn's potency with deep, shuddering gasps. Never before had it felt so cleansing, so overawing, so blissful. And when the tide passed, skirling out over the sea, he staggered back from the gunwale, exalted and refreshed, as if he'd had a good night's sleep.

He caught a glimpse of the Grand Master amid his huddle of priests, standing with his arms outstretched, mouth agape in a soundless howl. Hyle Pausus shuddered violently in the throes of some private ecstasy.

All around the deck, knights and priests started to head below. Anskar became aware of the smells of bacon and toasted bread, the bitter aroma of coffee. He spotted Orix coming up onto deck, a steaming mug in hand, still chewing whatever he'd just grabbed for breakfast. Anskar waved, and together they made their way back to the aftcastle to watch the sun rise.

"Not eating?" Orix said.

"Once the line's gone down. I take it you missed the dawn-tide?"

"I caught a little of it in the mess, through the gaps in the planks. Anyhow, it's not like we're going to need to cast ward spheres any time soon."

Anskar gazed out at the crimson-splashed sea, Orix beside him, slurping noisily at his coffee.

"That's odd," Orix said, frowning at the red orb of the sun.

"What is?"

"Sun's rising off the stern."

"So?"

"Rises in the east, don't it?"

"Your point?"

Orix took another slurp of coffee. "Sansor's north."

And then Anskar understood. He turned so he could look across the deck toward the prow.

The *Exultant* was heading west.

THREE

"YOU TWO," A KNIGHT SAID, striding along the deck toward Anskar and Orix. He was a big man with a forked beard. "Come here and earn your keep."

"Earn our—!" Anskar started, but Orix stopped him with a hand on the shoulder.

"For Menselas, remember?"

An act of humility. Orix was right. But it still grated that a do-nothing knight had the nerve to boss them around. Following Orix's lead, Anskar set down the length of rope he'd been practicing tying knots with. "What do you want us to do?" he asked.

"There's rats in the bilge, in case you ain't heard. I want you to feed them."

"Feed rats?"

The knight took them to the mess and gave Anskar a bucket containing scraps of food left over from breakfast. "You, carry this," he told Orix, indicating a keg of rainwater.

He led them down a flight of steps to the belly of the ship, stopped at a door with a barred window, opened it for them and gestured for them to carry the food and water inside. "Shut the door when you're done," he said as he headed back up top.

The stench inside was appalling: sweat and human waste. In the gloom, chained by their ankles to the planks up and down the belly of the hold, were upwards of fifty red-skinned Niyandrians, men and women, naked and covered in their own filth.

Anskar set down the food bucket.

Orix, clutching the water keg to his chest, cursed.

"You are ..." a woman said in broken Nan-Rhouric. She was painfully thin, and her skin bore the marks of a whip. "You are Niyandrian?" She might just as well have added: "And you would do this to us!"

Anskar became aware of dozens of cat's eyes watching him. They had seen his own. Dipping his head in shame, he moved back to the steps that led up to the deck. Behind him, he heard the thud of the door.

"So that explains the detour," Orix said. "The Plains of Khisig-Ugtall are west of here. The port of Atya's famous for its slave markets."

"But the Order would never ..." Anskar didn't bother to finish the thought. What other explanation could there be? "And the Grand Master knows about this?"

"What do you think?"

Of course he did.

"And Vihtor?"

Orix didn't answer that. He didn't need to.

It was hard for Anskar not to think about the slaves in the hold as he worked alongside seasoned sailors, learning to repair nets and continuing the endless scrubbing of the deck. He tried to reassure himself that the Niyandrians would have done the same to mainlanders if Queen Talia had won the war, but doubts had started to enter his mind.

Since learning the rebels thought he was the Queen's son and heir, he had begun to take things Sareya had told him more seriously. What if Talia's hadn't been a war of conquest, but of self-defense? And what if the Necromancer Queen had been forced to delve into dark and hidden sorceries in a desperate bid to survive the aggressive expansionism of the mainland allies?

He and Orix worked until the sun was at its zenith. Anskar's skin itched from the heat, his mouth was dry, and he stumbled as he fetched the next bundle of netting he was supposed to repair.

"Take a break, lads," Captain Hadlor said from the quarter deck. He was watching them work, earthenware bottle in one hand, some kind of fish in the other, which he appeared to be eating raw.

Anskar moved to one of the water butts that stood in the shade of the sails and splashed his face and hair before using a ladle to take a long drink. He passed the ladle to Orix, then seated himself on the deck in a patch of shade.

Almost at once, half a dozen knights began to congregate around the water butt. Several wore broad-brimmed hats against the sun, and a couple were bare chested and already showing the angry signs of sunburn. They were all drinking beer, and judging by the exaggerated way they swayed with the ship's movement, they had been for some time.

The sole woman among them stood half a head taller than Anskar. The sleeves of her shirt had been cut away to reveal colorful tattoos of snakes and skulls and axes. She was lean and muscular, and her face, while square jawed, was not unattractive, on account of her icy blue eyes. Her hair was bound closely to her scalp in tight braids. Despite the beer she was pouring down her throat, she seemed the least drunk of them all as she approached Anskar, walking lithely on the balls of her feet. He shrank back from her, and she grinned at that—a knowing grin. Predatory.

"Anskar DeVantte. They said you were a boy. I see that you're a man. Ryala Mitredd. You've heard of me? No? Eldrid is an old … acquaintance of mine." Some of the men chuckled at that. "What's he to you, Anskar, a big brother? Uncle? Long-lost cousin? Because I refuse to believe Eldrid is a father. Parenthood would do nothing for his reputation."

"We're not related," Anskar said.

"Really? Such a rare surname. So noble. I'm surprised. And those eyes: like a Niyandrian's. You a half-blood?"

Anskar's jaw tightened, but he said nothing. Ryala intimidated him. There was a confidence about her he wasn't used to.

"Don't worry," she said. "I like half-bloods. Full-blood Niyandrians too. For a bunch of death-worshiping necromancers, they sure know how to have a good time."

Anskar almost retorted that there were Niyandrian slaves in the hold, but Ryala presumably already knew that. Probably she'd helped to put them there.

"I think I should like to kiss you," Ryala said, leaning in so close Anskar could smell the beer on her breath. He recoiled, much to the amusement of the men.

"We should be getting back to work," Orix said.

"The heathen speaks!" a knight said, a stocky man with red hair and freckles. "Say something else, fat boy? Let's hear that accent."

"Boy?" the fork-bearded knight who'd sent them to feed the slaves said. "I thought it was a girl." He stepped forward and pinched Orix's chest through his shirt. "See? Tits! Sure you ain't no woman?"

Orix's face flushed. Before he could do anything stupid, Anskar stepped between him and the fork-bearded knight.

"Please … in Menselas's name."

The others laughed loudly at that, Ryala loudest of all. But the fork-bearded man glowered and raised his fist.

"Colvin, enough!"

Lanuc hurried across the deck toward them. The knights all tried to stand to attention without spilling their beer. Ryala muttered something under her breath.

"We all know you're a bunch of uncouth, beer-swilling peasants," Lanuc said in a cheery voice as he drew near, "but at least try to act like knights."

"Sir," said the fork-bearded knight Lanuc had called Colvin.

Captain Hadlor appeared around the mast. "I don't care who you are or who's in command of you lubbers," he said, "but you either get busy helping around my ship, or I'll have you thrown overboard for the sharp-tooths."

"What sharp-tooths?" Ryala said with a sneer.

"Those sharp-tooths," the Captain said, pointing out to sea, where three dorsal fins were circling off the starboard side. "Consider yourselves warned."

Exhausted from the day's work, Anskar and Orix made their way below deck. The dorm was in darkness save for a hooded lantern that swayed gently with the movement of the ship. The dorm was essentially a large cabin that slept six knights, as well as Anskar and Orix. Men and women sleeping in the same quarters struck Anskar as odd. Presumably the higher ranked knights had achieved a level of discipline and self-regulation that as yet eluded him. But he would need to acquire it quickly. He and Orix had taken simple vows only days ago, yet in another year they could be up for solemn vows, and then they would be expected to function and behave as any other fully consecrated knight. *By drinking beer and loafing around!*

He told himself not to be so cynical, that the knights aboard ship were just a bad bunch, but he wasn't convinced. Surely the Grand Master would have surrounded himself with the best of the best?

The air was ripe with sweat, and the background of rhythmic breathing was interspersed with the occasional loud snore.

Orix didn't even bother taking off his shirt and pants, both sweat stained and crusted with salt from the day's work on deck. He even kept on his boots and his sword belt as he fell on his bed, and he was asleep within minutes.

Not Anskar, though. He just sat on the edge of his bed, irritated by the snores and the stench. He was used to a room of his own—at least when he'd not been with Sareya. He smiled at the memory of her touch, then winced with shame. He shouldn't entertain such thoughts, same as he shouldn't succumb to the insistence of the dark-tide once more pitter-pattering over his skin. He had to shut it out. Keep it out. For good.

At some point he must have lain down and fallen asleep. But then he rose to the surface of the blackness that had engulfed him. Gray mist surrounded him, tinged with flickering red light.

He started at the flutter of wings and turned, expecting to see the golden-eyed crow that had led him to the summit of

Hallow Hill. But the crow was dead. Instead, he glimpsed a shadow within the mist, lissome yet at the same time formless. His nostrils were assaulted by the stench of rot, and he recoiled. He turned to flee, but the shadow was still there in front of him, though its scent was now sweet, with hints of musk and rose, and its writhing formlessness now conveyed a presence striving to take shape.

It coalesced into the semblance of a woman, though woven of pure darkness and devoid of any features save snaking arms, a wisp of a tail, a crude and misshapen head. A slit appeared where the mouth should have been, and a sibilant voice spoke, the sounds at once familiar and yet incomprehensible to him—Niyandrian.

"Queen Talia?" he breathed, and the shadow form flickered in and out of reality. "Mother?"

The shadow spoke again, and this time its voice was shrill and full of urgency, echoing around inside his skull.

And then he heard a different voice, a man whispering, "Go on, boy, be my woman. Give us a feel of them tits."

With a gasp, Anskar opened his eyes. There was a man stooping over Orix's bed, naked from the waist down. All Anskar could see was the knight's sizable buttocks, but he instantly knew who it was: Colvin, the fork-bearded man who had ridiculed Orix on deck.

"Come on, fat boy," Colvin growled as he loomed over the bed, "roll over."

Orix grunted, then started awake. Colvin started to climb onto the bed, but Orix elbowed him in the face. Colvin swore and grabbed him by the throat.

"Get off!" Orix squealed.

And then the whole dorm was in an uproar as knights woke

up, demanding to know what the noise was about.

Anskar rolled out of bed and sprang for Colvin's back, got an arm around his neck. Colvin dipped and threw him over his head, slamming him into the floor.

Orix flew from the bed, thumping Colvin on the jaw. Knights were throwing off their blankets, calling for the fight to stop. Colvin punched Orix in the stomach, doubling him up, caught him with an uppercut that dropped him. Colvin followed Orix down to the deck, pounding away with hammer fists.

Anskar tried to get up, but his head swam. Ice coursed through his veins, answered by the frantic pulse of the catalyst buried beneath the skin of his chest. A spasm passed through his dark-tide repository; then he heard an almost audible snap as the barrier he'd placed around it failed. Vitriol gushed from the repository, streamed through his veins and into his fingertips. With a burst of rage, he launched himself at Colvin, grabbing his arm.

Colvin screamed; then he dropped to his knees, whimpering as the flesh of his arm blackened and sloughed away. Colvin's eyes were wide with terror, his mouth agape as pus and bloody slime dripped to the deck, leaving his hand and arm no more than bone.

And then he jerked, and blood spewed from his mouth. Steel burst through his chest, and Colvin dipped his eyes to stare at the tip of the blade before he slumped forward and hit the floor.

Orix stood there, red-faced and trembling, bloodstained sword in hand.

A woman moved quickly behind Orix and disarmed him without any resistance—Ryala. Ignoring the blood pooling on the floor, she stared instead at the slimy remains of Colvin's arm, then narrowed her eyes at Anskar.

Hands took hold of Anskar from behind, and like Orix he

didn't resist.

"What have you done?" Ryala said.

"It was him!" Orix kicked Colvin's corpse. "He tried ... He tried ..."

But Ryala was still looking at Anskar.

"What have you done?" she asked again.

Footsteps came from up top. The door swung open, and Captain Hadlor was there with three hard-looking sailors behind him.

"What's going on?" the Captain demanded.

"This is Order business," one of the knights said.

Hadlor glared at the man. "On this ship, everything is *my* business."

"Come," Ryala said, shoving Orix toward the steps. "Bring him," she told the two men holding Anskar. "The Grand Master will want to hear about this. If that's all right with you, Captain?"

Hadlor nodded, and then Anskar and Orix were dragged up the stairs to the deck.

FOUR

AN ARMORED KNIGHT STOOD guard outside the Grand Master's cabin, which was set a way back from the ship's wheel. It was the only cabin not below deck, and Anskar suspected it had been Captain Hadlor's cabin until the Grand Master had required it. The guard looked as though he'd stood sentry all night. His white cloak was drenched from the sea's spray and in places crusted with salt.

Ryala went in first, no doubt to give her version of events. The men holding Anskar relaxed their grip, allowing him to stand with Orix, surrounded by the rest of the knights from the dorm and the three sailors who had come with Captain Hadlor. The Captain stood in the center with Orix and Anskar, arms folded across his ample belly, eyes glinting with barely suppressed anger.

Eventually, Ryala came out and gestured for Anskar and Orix to go in. "You too, Captain," she said, and Hadlor nodded.

When a couple of knights moved to follow them inside, Ryala

stopped them with a raised hand. "No one else," she said, and didn't sound too happy about it.

"Ah," the Grand Master said, looking up from some papers atop his desk. "A moment, if you don't mind."

The cabin door shut behind them, cutting off the sea breeze. It was stifling inside, the air thick with tobacco smoke. A solitary lantern was suspended from a chain beside the door, and three candles burned down to stubs guttered upon the table. Empty wine casks hung from the low ceiling beams—too many to count at a glance. There was a wine rack against one wall, half full. An open bottle of red stood atop a torn and creased map spread out on the table, a glass filled almost to the brim beside it. A pipe with a wooden bowl carved into the shape of a boyish head lay in a copper tray, gently smoldering and sending up wisps of dirty smoke to join the haze beneath the ceiling. On the table there were also neat stacks of silver talents set into a foot-square wooden rack for the purpose, as if they had recently been counted. Behind the table, an intricately woven curtain divided the room. Presumably the Grand Master's bed lay on the other side.

Hyle Pausus continued to scan the parchment he'd been reading when they entered. He looked older in the dim light of the cabin, crow's feet rimming his eyes, yellow-stained beard straggly and unkempt. His bulbous nose was covered with purplish veins that worked their way to his plump cheeks. He was dressed in a red silk robe cinched beneath his gut with braided silver rope. The robe was open to the navel, exposing a flabby chest covered with gray hair.

With a sigh, the Grand Master snatched up a quill, dipped it in ink, and scratched his signature on the parchment. "Contracts, contracts, contracts." He sighed, grabbing his wineglass and taking a sip. "You young men don't know how good you have it right now, do they, Captain?"

Someone coughed from behind the curtain that partitioned the room. It sounded like a woman, but Anskar couldn't be sure. The Grand Master's eyes flashed with irritation.

"I am not a man to beat about the bush," Hyle Pausus said, "and I am sure the Captain here has better things to do, so let's get straight to it. Ryala has told me all that she saw. Now tell me your version. You first," he said to Orix.

He took a sip of wine, then shut his eyes as he listened to Orix's account of what had happened.

"So you were asleep when Colvin came to your bed?" the Grand Master said, eyes still shut tight, the faintest of smiles curling his wine-stained lips.

"I woke up," Orix said, "and he was … he was …"

"Yes," the Grand Master said, opening his eyes. "Terrible. Depraved. How Menselas tests us."

Orix glanced at Anskar.

"And you, Anskar DeVantte? What did you witness?"

Anskar told him, though he left out the dream that had awoken him to Orix's plight. All the while he spoke, the Grand Master's bloodshot eyes watched him, unblinking.

"And then you killed Colvin?"

"I accept full responsibility," Anskar said.

"For what? I am reliably informed that yours was not the hand that held the sword."

"It was me," Orix said. "I stabbed the bastard."

"Indeed." The Grand Master's lips quivered, and he took another sip of wine. "It sounds like he deserved it. Sometimes an evil spirit enters a man. Less often a woman. Either Menselas permits it, to test us, or one of the other gods seeks to undermine the sanctity of our Order."

Captain Hadlor discreetly touched his axe symbol.

"Sylva Kalisia, perhaps," the Grand Master said. "A dark and necrotic vixen. Jubal the One-Eyed. Coruth the Cripple. One of the old gods of the Niyandrians, even. Who can say, eh, Captain?"

Hadlor's fingers dropped from his pendant. He gave a theatrical shudder and muttered, "Terrible, Grand Master. Terrible how many false gods there are."

"You have lived a sheltered life at Branil's Burg, Anskar." The Grand Master raised an eyebrow. "Some might say too sheltered. On the mainland you will be exposed to the hundred and one churches that rival ours. They breed like rats. Once people stray from the one true path of Menselas, they will believe anything."

"But are these rival gods real?" Anskar asked.

"Some," the Grand Master said, setting his glass down on the desk. "When they are not demons. But before we deviate too far from the purpose of our little chat, tell me, if you can, what happened to Colvin's arm. Ryala said it was rather unpleasant."

"Aye, Grand Master," Captain Hadlor said. "It was that."

Orix looked at Anskar, but neither of them said a word. Anskar met the Grand Master's gaze and clenched his jaw, awaiting the condemnation to come, the punishment.

A glint of amusement shone in the Grand Master's eyes, and then he stuck out his bottom lip and shrugged. "Must have had a particularly aggressive case of the rot. I've heard of people spontaneously decomposing because of it. More fool him for not seeing a physician as soon as it started. Captain, have your men dispose of the body before anyone else gets infected. Those sharp-tooths you're always on about will think it's their lucky day."

As the Captain left the cabin, the Grand Master leaned back

in his chair, cradling his wineglass, and gave Anskar and Orix an appraising look. His lip curled as he took in the state of Orix's filthy clothes, his mussed-up hair.

"Run along now." He waggled his fingers toward the door. "Off you go."

Orix was first to the door, but as Anskar followed him, the Grand Master said, "Not you, Anskar. A word alone, if you please. *Alone*," he said to Orix, who was lingering in the doorway. "You do know what that means?"

Orix glanced at Anskar, then stepped outside and shut the door.

The Grand Master's eyes rested on Anskar for an uncomfortable moment, and then he took another mouthful of wine. "Your skin has a slight tint …"

"My parents were mainlanders," Anskar quickly put in. He'd believed that for the longest time. Maybe it was true of his father, for he lacked the crimson appearance of a full-blood Niyandrian.

"Of course, of course," Hyle Pausus said, leaning forward, elbows on the tabletop. "Inkan-Andil descent? They're dusky skinned. And maybe a dash of something … exotic? Striking. Quite striking. Though you do yourself no justice with your clothes crumpled and sweat stained."

"I'll change, Grand Master," Anskar said, turning toward the door.

"No, no, no. It can wait. The other one …"

"Orix, Grand Master."

"Traguh-raj?"

"From the Plains of Khisig-Ugtall."

The Grand Master cocked his head to glance at the map on the desk, and stuck out his bottom lip. "Shows," he said. "Such unforgiving features. But it's you that interests me, Anskar.

Seneschal Ulnar tells me you don't know who your parents are. Kailean nobility, I'd wager. It's in the bearing, and that little hint of exotic blood … not unusual among the noble houses. Glass of wine?"

Anskar hesitated, glanced behind at the door.

"No? Suit yourself. I'm a night owl, Anskar, working through the dark hours. Without a drop or two of red I'd despair. Menselas is a hard taskmaster, eh? But it's all worth it in the end." He topped up his glass, keeping the bottle upturned until it was empty of the last drop. Then, in a pensive tone, he repeated, "It's all worth it. So tell me, Anskar, have you recovered from your little brush with the Niyandrian rebels? Carred Selenas seems to have a thing for you. I wonder why."

"They were after Sareya," Anskar said.

"Yes, the Niyandrian girl. No doubt thought she was Queen Talia's daughter. It's not the first time something like this has happened. I'm always getting reports from our strongholds in Niyas. I had hoped Vihtor would have suppressed these blasted rebels by now. Not good for business, you know. Not good at all."

"Business, Grand Master?"

"The business of governing a province. The Niyandrians we can just about tolerate, but only if they fall into line."

"And if they don't?" Anskar was thinking of the slaves in the hold.

"Ours is a god of five aspects, Anskar. Mostly in balance, but from time to time it is necessary to give one or two aspects their head until order and harmony can be restored."

"The Warrior?"

The Grand Master shrugged. "If need be. Or the Hooded One. But let's not get pessimistic. Vihtor tells me things are improving across the isle. Balance may yet reign." He raised his eyebrows. "Niyandrians and mainlanders living together in harmony, praise be to Menselas. Now, are you sure you don't want me to open another bottle? Of course you don't! A good student, Vihtor said. An exemplary knight-inferior. Splendid, Anskar. Excellent. Play your cards right"—again, that appraising stare—"and you should fit in well at the Mother House. Thank you, Anskar. That will be all."

FIVE

"MY, THAT'S A BIG one," Carred told Maggow as he returned to the hideout in the high country to the northwest of Branil's Burg.

The old man scowled in response, tightening his throttle hold on the cockerel's neck despite it already being dead. "We need a lot of blood."

Taloc sniffed with distaste. He'd already made his case to Carred that he didn't think it right or wise to be playing about with demons. Vilintia stood at his side, no longer pretending there was nothing between them. Earlier, Carred had caught them holding hands. It was clear from the haughty tilt of her chin and the disapproving look she gave Maggow and his dead cockerel that Vilintia agreed with Taloc on the matter of demons. Ordinarily, they would have been right. Niyandrians had an innate gift for sorcery, though it needed to be coaxed out of them, nurtured and honed; but the sorcery of the abyssal realms was another thing altogether. It involved pacts that ran both ways. It involved facing the threat of rending and ripping, the ever-shifting chaos of demonic whims. And it always involved a good degree of risk.

But Maggow was a law unto himself. He came from the dwellers of the swamp who lived on eels, crawfish and boiled tubers. He had been raised in the ways of the old ones, and the old ones had known a thing or two about demons. Or so Maggow claimed.

And Queen Talia had said he would know what to do.

Noni had reverted to being a haunted, withdrawn child now that she no longer spoke for Talia. Or the wraithe, for that matter. Was that the poor girl's role in life, to be the mouthpiece of others, whether living or dead? More grist to Carred's growing doubts about Talia's cause, yet what would become of her if she left the Queen's service after all these years? A down-and-out drunk and gambler—she'd already seen how low that could lead her. And in any case, what if Talia didn't let her leave? It scared Carred, the things a queen who had survived death might be capable of.

"You still carry the stench of the earth-tide," Maggow told Carred as he walked past her on his bandy legs.

"I washed, like you told me."

"Then wash again."

The earth-tide—whatever that was—permeated her flesh, Maggow had informed her when she'd arrived from Ahz. In response to his questions, she told him about Vaz and the thing he'd turned into. According to Maggow, beings like Vaz had once been Niyandrians, but they had transgressed natural laws with their use of the earth-tide, a debased form of the energies of the dawn, dusk and dark that pooled in the bowels of the earth.

"The sap of the necromancers," Maggow called it. "The essence that grants them long life and more."

At a cost, though: such creatures had a burning need for blood, and their bodies were warped beyond recognition—just like Vaz and the porcupine quills that covered him when he wasn't disguised by a further abuse of the earth-tide. Carred shuddered and vowed to wash again, with scalding water and coarse soap if necessary. Anything that might remove the taint of Vaz's touch. Thank Theltek things hadn't progressed any further.

"I'll prepare some scouring powder from dried herbs and fungi," Kalij said.

"You can do that?" Another of the Niyandrian slaves she'd rescued back in Lowanin, Kalij had proven his worth tenfold, catching, skinning, and cooking squirrels and birds, foraging for edible plants and tubers, then miraculously making them taste good. He'd lost his entire family to the Order's slavers, but rather than curl up and die of grief, he'd adopted the rebels as his new family, and he'd do anything to meet their needs.

"My powder will cleanse and deodorize, and I'll cook you wild algath sprouts to boost your body's defenses in case this creature has infected you."

"Algath sprouts?" Even Kalij had failed to improve their dung-like taste. "Maybe I'll just drink more alcohol. That'll kill any infection I might have."

With dusk closing in on them, Carred, Taloc and Noni followed Maggow as he carried the cockerel he'd snatched from a nearby homestead. The tenants were mainlanders, so Carred felt no qualms about stealing.

The rest of the rebels—those who had returned—were seated around the fires Maggow had ordered them to set in a loose circle. Eight fires. The old man had insisted on eight. Something about the number was important to the demon lords. Or perhaps it was an old superstition.

Maggow produced a rusty knife and slit open the cockerel's belly. Blood and innards sloshed over his feet, and for a long while he rummaged through the offal, his crimson skin gaining a new coating of slick and viscous red from fingers to elbows. He separated heart from lungs, kidneys from liver, and then he proceeded to dice each organ up into eight roughly equal portions. He scooped up the slivers of the cockerel's tiny heart and stalked around the perimeter of the eight fires, flinging the meat into the flames, where it sizzled and smoked. Men and women looked on, eyes wide and glittering. He did the same with each lung, with each kidney, with the liver. Then he grabbed the hollowed-out carcass of the cockerel by the throat once more and began to cavort around the circle of fires, shaking the bird, turning its beady eyes to keep them always aimed at one fire or another. Spittle flew from the old man's mouth as he howled cants in some barbarous tongue that may have been a precursor to Niyandrian, or may have been the language of demons. Blood streamed down Maggow's arms from the slaughtered bird. It ran in rivulets down his naked chest and soaked into his stained and filthy loincloth.

Carred glanced at Noni, who watched impassively. Taloc and Vilintia held hands again, disapproval given way to fear. The rebels seated around the fires all now stood, cat's eyes aghast at the spectacle of the old man dancing around the flames, streaked with blood, a stream of garbled cries spilling from his lips to the accompaniment of the rhythmic pound of his bare feet.

Noni's masklike expression cracked for an instant, broke into the semblance of a crooked smile, but it vanished just as quickly. Carred looked from her back to Maggow and saw just what

Noni had seen. Beneath his rancid loincloth, the old man was erect. Then the old man's body jerked violently and he dropped to his knees, at the same time ripping the cockerel's head from its long neck, then throwing his own head back and unleashing a terrible, screeching cry. It was a jumble of strained and gargled syllables, which seemed to roll on forever, till they reached their strangled climax and the air within the circle of fires rippled.

Maggow stilled at once, staring at the spot with wide eyes that reflected the dancing flames, the cockerel's head in one bloodstained hand, its gutted body in the other. Carred smelled sulfur, and the air turned suddenly frigid.

The ripple became a shudder of the leaden dusk air. Then rime coated the ground and a rent of utter darkness appeared, untouched by the light of the flames. It gaped like a split wound, and something stepped through.

Or rather, it fell through the rift onto its ass.

And it was a small ass, relatively speaking. For it was a dwarfish woman who had tumbled through the veil between worlds.

The demon, Malady, was dressed in a motley coat and tricorn hat, which even now she twisted back into place as she stood and spun in a quick circle to locate whoever had brought her through the veil.

And she wasn't happy about it, Carred could tell from the snarl of rage on the dwarf-demon's face. She wouldn't have been Maggow for all the gold in Sansor. Carred only hoped the old man knew what he was doing, and that the bindings that were meant to enslave a summoned demon to a sorcerer's will were well and truly in place.

"How is it you could summon me, old man?" the demon spat. "Who gave you my true name?" Her face contorted under the immense strain of some internal struggle; then she gasped and let out a sigh of exasperation. "How can this be? Who told you my ranking in the order of demons? Was it a demon lord? You must tell me who has betrayed me, so that I can murder the bastard. No, murder is too good for them."

There was a flurry of activity in the sky above, and then birds began to alight on the ground around Maggow—wood pigeons, sparrows, thrushes, a broad-winged seagull with the red smear of blood staining its beak.

The old man grinned. "You would murder the birds of the air? Then it is a good thing I will not permit it, slave."

"Birds?" Malady said. "Birds betrayed me?"

Maggow held out his hand and a sparrow hopped onto his palm. With one finger, he stroked it beneath the beak and it emitted a contented chirp. "They are no fools, the birds. They know things, and they whisper such things to those with the ears to hear."

"Pah!" Malady said. "You're lying. A demon told you."

Maggow lowered his hand to the ground and the sparrow hopped off. The small flock that had gathered around him watched him attentively with beady eyes, as if they were waiting for him to tell them what to do. The demon noticed too, and she frowned.

"Not a demon," Maggow said. "The birds. You should be more careful. You and your former master."

"Well, he can't," Carred said, "if you're referring to Luzius Landav. He's dead."

Malady chuckled at that, and spittle sprayed from her lips. "Lost his head, poor dear. I carried it back to Branil's Burg. I hadn't felt such freedom to act of my own accord for a very long time. But now I'm bound once more. You have trapped me, old man, and I will eat your rancid liver for that."

Maggow made quick clawing motions, and the demon shrieked, throwing up her hands to protect her face. When she lowered them, there were three lines gouged beneath her eye, and they glistened with purplish blood.

"Next time I will blind you," the old man said. Malady pouted and grew sullen, but Carred didn't miss the calculating look in her eyes. "You are bound, demon," Maggow said, this time making a fist and yanking it toward himself. Malady stumbled and pitched to her knees. "Do not forget that. You can prod and pry at the bindings that compel your obedience, but you will find no flaws to exploit, no breaches to widen. You will do as I command, and you will not twist and manipulate my words. You will adhere to my intended meaning, and where you are in doubt, you will ask for clarification until you are certain of what it is I am commanding you to do. Is that understood?"

Malady gave a stiff nod.

"I can't hear you," Maggow said.

"Yes, I understand."

"Master," Maggow prompted.

Malady's lips worked as if she chewed gristle. Finally, she said, "I understand, Master."

"And understand this, too," Maggow went on, this time glancing briefly at Carred. "Should anything happen to me, should I die, for whatever reason—"

"Then I would be unbound," Malady interrupted. "Free to return to the abyssal realms."

"Then your bindings will pass to Carred Selenas, and you will obey her the same as you now obey me."

"No!" Malady said. "It doesn't work that way. You can't pass on a demon's bindings to another. That breaks every known law."

"What laws?" Maggow asked. "Whose laws? The laws of the abyssal realms? The laws of the demon lords?" The old man shook his head, amused. "It is not the demon lords who have bound you, Yashash-na-Agarot, demon of the Thirty-Third Order."

Malady winced at his voicing of her name and hopped from foot to foot, as if the ground had turned to lava. "Not so loud! Not so loud! Others will hear."

"Hear and have power over you?" Maggow said. "Others like the birds, perhaps?"

"Bastard," Malady spat. "You putrid, shit-sucking dehydrated afterbirth of a three-horned ass-burrowing rat."

"The insults and curses I will allow," Maggow said with a chuckle. "Because they amuse me. But for now, shut up."

Malady's lips drew into a tight line, and her eyes narrowed to dark slits.

"Now," Maggow said, "you will answer the questions of Carred Selenas. You will tell her everything she wants to know if it is within your knowledge and power."

Carefully, Carred asked the demon, "Do you know who Anskar DeVantte is?"

"Of course. I helped with the fitting of his catalyst."

"I mean really know. His lineage. What his destiny is?"

"Tell me," Malady said with a shrug.

"So you don't know?"

"I certainly don't know what his destiny is," Malady said. "Nor do I care. You Niyandrians heap too much importance on these ideas of destiny, and it makes no sense to us denizens of the abyssal realms."

"You have no overarching law to your lives?"

"No superior demon pulling the strings, if that's what you mean. Save for the council of demon lords, but they are in the thrall of the same forces of chance and necessity as the rest of us. So, no, we have no belief in anything as inexorable as destiny. But you go on believing in it if you wish. It makes your kind that much more predictable. But to answer your question about Anskar DeVantte a little more fully, before this bastard … my master … scratches my face again with his nasty little claw trick, I am aware—or rather, I have worked out for myself—what you believe he is. Or rather, who. It must be hard seeing the locus of all your hopes for your pathetic, dying culture spirited away across the sea, heading for the heartland of the Church of Menselas and the chief stronghold of the Order of Eternal Vigilance."

"So this is no temporary trip to Sansor for Anskar," Carred concluded. It was what she had started to fear. And she had to wonder how much she was to blame. Without her botched attempt to have Anskar kidnapped, the Order might not have sent him away. "So what do we do?"

Noni met her gaze briefly, then looked away again, shaking her head. If Talia was still in contact with her, she gave no sign.

"Personally, I'd stop worrying about it," Malady said. "It's out of your hands now, and if you believe in destiny, as you claim to, everything will work out as it's supposed to. Or have I misunderstood something? In any case, I doubt you'll have to worry about Anskar returning as an avenging sorcerer-knight. Probably the Order will use him for their own purposes, as they have done with most of the others who showed such potential. Either way, he is lost to you, so your rebellion will fail, and your civilization, if that's what you choose to call it, will fade away to nothing."

Carred clenched her fist, fought to hold her tongue. The demon was baiting her, that's all. But its words were tinged with truth. Half-truths, she told herself. No, they were lies! At least, she could make them lies if only she chose to act. But how should she act? What could she do?

She knew where to find a ship to take her in pursuit of the Grand Master's galleon, but she'd left it too late. The galleon under full sail was not only a huge ship, it was fast, and it had a long head start on her. And even if she caught up with it at sea, what then? In any clash of ships, the galleon was sure to win. Follow it all the way to Sansor and try to snatch Anskar when the Order considered him out of harm's way? That would be suicide. Any red-skinned Niyandrian would stand out like a sore thumb in Sansor, where the City Watch were said to be imbued with the eagle eyes and near-omniscience of some ancient goddess.

"It's no good," she muttered.

The seagull with the gore-stained beak emitted a screeching cry, and at first Carred thought it was echoing her despair, but then Maggow clicked his tongue and made a succession of grating, wheezing noises that the bird apparently understood.

"The Grand Master's ship has deviated from its course," the old man said as he petted the seagull. "It heads west, not north and east. It is not returning directly to Sansor."

"Not returning ..."

That made Carred wonder.

It gave her hope.

The Bilge Rat was heaving when Carred slipped through the door, and she supposed that was a good thing, as least as far as the owner was concerned—a thin Niyandrian turncoat by the name of Yasik. Like most of the successful business owners in the occupied town of Lensk, Yasik had quickly realized it was better for his livelihood if he welcomed the invaders and made a show of adopting their language and culture.

The tavern had been on its last legs not all that long ago, but the problem now was that it was heaving not so much from red-skinned Niyandrians as it was from dusky mainlanders, some of them in the white cloaks of the Order of Eternal Vigilance, most in the velvet robes of merchants. There were a few Niyandrian locals too, and a scatter of salty dogs taking a break from trawling for fish in the Simorga Sea that lapped against the town's stone wharves, but they were seated in the shadows of once-cozy nooks or at tables in the corners, about as far from the blazing hearth fire as you could get. And they spoke in low voices, as if they were afraid of being heard using their own language, rather than the Nan-Rhouric the invaders had brought with them from overseas more than sixteen years ago.

Carred ran her eyes over the babbling merchants closing out deals while they ate sumptuous meals of breaded eel and golden, crisp potatoes smothered in a mountain of cheese. They raised brimming glasses of blood-red mainland wine to seal their agreements, most of them feigning drunkenness and good humor, their cunning eyes glinting, appraising every last opportunity.

Carred was starting to think she should give up and return to the hills that enclosed the town's western flank. It had been hard for her coming here. She'd already lost too many people she loved, and she had no right putting any more of her lovers at risk. But what was the alternative?

She'd left Vilintia in charge of the hideout in the highlands. Taloc had been put out by that, but Vilintia said not to worry; she knew how to make it up to him. Carred had considered bringing Noni, but since Queen Talia had spoken through her lips, the girl had grown sullen and silent. She barely retained the volition to piss and shit without soiling her frayed and tattered dress; she never washed and seldom ate. She was too much of a liability to lug around and take care of.

But she'd brought Maggow and the demon he'd bound, and made them wait on the edge of town.

"What'll it be, Haijin?" Yasik the proprietor asked in fluent Nan-Rhouric, which sixteen years and necessity had taught Carred to understand. She hated the language with a vengeance and rarely used it, but in her line of work you neglected your enemy's tongue at your peril. She almost laughed in the cocky bastard's face. He was so smug, thought he was so superior because all the mainlanders loved him, yet he still believed Haijin was her real name.

She forced a grin for his benefit and approached the bar.

"Mead," Carred said. "Niyandrian mead."

Yasik frowned. For not only had she ordered in Niyandrian, but as Yasik reached for the earthenware cask, a few of the wealthy merchants glanced up and exchanged hushed words. Some of the Order knights did too.

Yasik had barely slammed the glass of mead down on the bar top in front of her when Carred heard a woman hollering her name, or rather the false name she had given Yasik.

"Haijin, you tart!" Captain Jada Hellequis called, and then Carred spotted her seated by herself beneath an open window overlooking the wharves. Jada was keeping an eye on her ship like she always did, and drinking enough mead to fell a herd of cattle, like she always did too.

Carred slapped a coin down on the bar to pay for her drink, and then made her way to Jada's table. It had been many months since they'd last seen each other, possibly even more than a year. Jada was as big as ever—broad, muscled like a man, and tall. Not attractive in the classical sense, mostly on account of her pox-scarred cheeks, but there was something Carred had always found striking about Jada. Something exciting, dangerous, and at the same time homey.

"Come here, you beautiful woman," Jada said as she stood, looming over Carred. She spoke Niyandrian fearlessly, and though her booming voice drew looks from the tables, no one, it seemed, had the will or the courage to challenge her. She wore a huge cutlass at her hip, and its pommel jabbed into Carred's side as Jada smothered her in a crushing bear hug. "Gods, you have a woman's ass," Jada said, squeezing Carred's rump to illustrate.

"That's because I'm a woman," Carred answered. It was a ritual they went through every time they met up.

"And you have a woman's—"

"Not here, Jada," Carred said, grabbing the big woman's wrist and guiding her hand anywhere but where it had been heading. "People will see."

"Then let them see!" Jada said, slurring her words from too much mead. "Bunch of goat-shagging hypocrites. They only obey their own rules when their superiors are watching. Out here, they do whatever they like. You know their Grand Master was only just in Niyas? I heard some of the knights in here talking about his love of young boys. So let them watch as I stick my tongue down your pretty little throat. I don't care."

"But I do, love," Carred said, stroking Jada's cheek with affection.

"Later?" Jada asked in a small voice.

"Later."

They sat and exchanged news, none of it good. The mainland

merchants had pretty much bought up the whole town. Niyandrians who remained had to pay rent to live in their own homes. The schoolhouse was only permitted to teach Nan-Rhouric, and any children who dared break that rule were rapped on the knuckles with a heavy stick and made to stand in the corner for the rest of the day's lessons.

"I tell you," Jada said with a shake of her massive head, "I'm getting out."

"Where will you go? It's the same all over Niyas."

Jada leaned across the table, as if she had a secret to tell. "The sea," she said, touching a finger to her nose. "I have a ship."

"I know," Carred said. "That's why I came to see you. That, and other things."

"What things?"

Carred reached beneath the table and Jada almost squealed at her touch.

"Ah, those things."

"It's been a long time, Jada," Carred said.

"Too long, Haijin. Theltek's eyes, I've missed you."

Through the open window, Carred caught the smell of brine and rank seaweed, and she could hear the heartbeat of the Simorga Sea, the relentless crash and spray of surf on the shore, and beneath it the creak of yards from the ships berthed in the harbor.

"Do you have a crew at the moment?" Carred asked almost whimsically.

"Why?" Jada sounded sober all of a sudden. "Where'd you want to go?"

Carred told her about Anskar then, about how he was one of "theirs." Jada had long known that "Haijin" was involved in some way with the rebels, but she would have been shocked to know she was their leader.

"And they're taking him to Sansor, you say?" Jada shook her head, and Carred could read the doubts setting in. Sansor wasn't the kind of place a Niyandrian wanted to go, especially a struggling trader like Jada. The sharp-tooths among the Sansor merchants there would eat her alive, and while she pretended to be at times, Jada was no fool.

"Not directly. I have information they've detoured west to Atya in the Plains of Khisig-Ugtall."

"They're not slavers, are they?"

"It wouldn't surprise me."

"Which brings me to the question of how you'll pay," Jada said.

"I could share your cabin," Carred suggested.

"That's a given," Jada said with a smirk. "But times are tough, Haijin. I'm going to need coin as well."

"Will this do?" Carred deposited a heavy purse in her lap. It was everything she'd been able to collect at such short notice from the unoccupied towns and villages on the way to Lensk. It wasn't a lot—most of the coins were copper, the rest silver. The people of Niyas had grown tired of the constant demands of coins for the rebellion, and Carred hadn't exactly brought them results.

Jada grinned, then assumed a look of mock seriousness. "And you'll still share my cabin?"

"I hope you're up to it."

SIX

THE BREEZE ROSE STEADILY till it became a gale. Waves that had lapped at the keel now surged and roiled, crashing over the prow and flooding the decks. Under gray skies, Anskar and Orix joined a team of sailors constantly bailing water overboard, while others took shifts of four to work under the pump. "Work hard; work tirelessly," Captain Hadlor frequently reminded them. "Else we'll all go under together." The Captain grinned as he said it, but even so, Anskar redoubled his efforts. All his life he'd been behind Branil's Burg's walls and there had been no chance to learn how to swim. But even if he could, he reckoned, he wouldn't have fancied his chances in the angry sea, and especially not with the behemoth, the devil-beak, and the sharptooths that lurked beneath the waves.

The knights stayed mostly below deck in their dorms, and the Grand Master never left his cabin. "Their funeral," the Captain cheerfully commented the one time Orix asked why they weren't helping.

The teams bailing water were rotated every few hours, and during those breaks Anskar and Orix retreated to the galley, where the cook—a kindly old man called Swen—rewarded their efforts with salted fish broth and hunks of black bread.

When night fell and the storm still hadn't abated, the Captain insisted that Anskar and Orix get some rest. "Don't worry," Hadlor said. "I always hold crew back for the night shift, and then you'll be fresh again in the morning, though I doubt there'll be much pumping and bailing to do by then. I can smell it in the air, you see. Weather's turning."

Lightning forked across the black sky in marked disagreement with the Captain's words. Hadlor shrugged, then frowned as thunder boomed, shaking the deck.

"I've prepared new quarters for the two of you," he said. "In a section with some of my sailors. They're filthy, foul-mouthed dogs, but they're all right. You should sleep more soundly from now on."

The Captain had arranged for Anskar's and Orix's armor and spare clothes to be stowed beneath their new beds, and when they entered the long cabin, they were greeted with sullen nods from the dozen or so sailors within, lying or sitting on their beds, drinking, talking, sharing jokes as the ship rocked and lurched and thunder cracked overhead.

Anskar got out of his wet clothes and hung them from pegs set into the wall to dry. He took a clean shirt and pants from his pack and put them on before climbing into bed, exhausted.

Anskar awakened to the squawks of seabirds, the smells of bacon and toasted bread wafting in from the galley. He could hear the hubbub of sailors talking, the chink of knives and forks, the sounds of good cheer and laughter. The long cabin was empty save for Anskar and Orix, who still snored on the adjacent bed. And save for the man peering in through the open doorway, silhouetted in the bright sunlight streaming in from outside.

Lanuc, in his white cloak, beneath which Anskar caught the gleam of a mail hauberk. His steel helm was tucked under one arm.

"I've been calling you for ages," Lanuc said, a big grin on his face. "You must have been tired."

"Not as exhausted as Orix," Anskar said, rolling out of bed and shoving his friend until he snorted himself awake. "See, it's easy to wake us when you know how."

Lanuc frowned. "I didn't want to. Not after …"

Anskar sighed, then nodded. "Thank you. That was thoughtful."

"It's a glorious day," Lanuc said, "and we're coming into port."

"Atya?" Orix said, rubbing sleep from his eyes.

"Yes, Atya."

Orix glanced at Anskar, but neither of them said a word about the *Exultant*'s cargo of Niyandrian slaves.

Captain Hadlor hadn't been wrong about the weather turning. The skies above the *Exultant* were cloudless, their pristine blue reflected in the calm waters of Atya's harbor. Anskar stood with Lanuc and Orix on the main deck as sailors swarmed around them. Knights congregated all along the gunwale in mail that glinted in the sunlight from where it had been scoured with sand

and coated with oil. All had on their white cloaks and helms, swords scabbarded at their waists.

"Are they expecting a fight?" Orix asked.

Lanuc shook his head. "Appearances are important to the Grand Master. The Order's presence is not strong in the Plains of Khisig-Ugtall, so we must be at our best."

The Grand Master emerged on deck in his winged helm and polished breastplate, every inch a heroic figure, save for his paunch.

There were dozens of other ships moored at jetties inside the harbor's massive stone walls. Most were fishing vessels, but Lanuc pointed out a few mainland traders and even a warship from the Pristart Combine, a galleon larger than the *Exultant*. Atya was a popular city for shore leave, Lanuc explained.

Orix was staring out toward the sprawling city that lay beyond the harbor: squat, flat-roofed buildings without end, most made from some kind of pale, sun-baked mud. There were several districts of taller sandstone buildings, and the occasional structure of dark gray stone, all with red or brown roof tiles. Along the harbor wall and the extremes of the city stood tall watchtowers, and nearby was a stone bell tower.

"One of ours," Lanuc said. "Built with the Order's coins."

Probably the wealth amassed from the selling of Niyandrian slaves, Anskar thought.

"Not much of a foothold in the Plains of Khisig-Ugtall," Lanuc said, "but it's a start."

One building a fair distance away caught Anskar's eye. An imposing granite building, cube-shaped, with sharp edges. His skin prickled and his arm hairs stood on end. His dark-tide repository stirred, as if sensing kindred sorcery.

"What's that place?" Anskar asked, pointing.

Lanuc touched the four fingers and thumb of his right hand to his chest—the sign of the Five's protection. "That, Anskar, is one of the infamous depots of the Ethereal Sorceress."

"That wasn't here when I was a child," Orix said.

"Her business interests expand all the time," Lanuc said.

Anskar looked away from the strange building and caught Ryala Mitredd studying him from her position against the starboard rail. Like the other knights, she was dressed in her full finery, her arm tattoos covered by her mail and cloak.

"Anskar," Gadius Menashin said, causing Anskar to turn, "you missed our predawn prayer. I trust you greeted the tide?"

"I overslept."

"Oh," Gadius said with a slight wrinkling of his nose. "Never mind. Menselas is merciful. I'm sure he'll understand. And you," Gadius said to Orix, "are you recovered from your ordeal?"

The acolyte didn't wait for an answer and instead set off across the deck to stand with the Grand Master.

"Be wary around Gadius Menashin," Lanuc whispered. When Anskar shot him an enquiring look, Lanuc shook his head. "That's all I'm prepared to say."

As soon as they made their way down the gangplank and across the wharves to reach the shore, Lanuc took Anskar and Orix with him deeper into the city.

"I volunteered us to find a suitable establishment for the Grand Master and his entourage," the knight explained. "He dislikes staying aboard ship, and we may be in Atya for a day or two."

Anskar glanced back at the ship, where the Niyandrians from

the hold were being herded down the gangplank by armored knights. The Grand Master oversaw the disembarkation from the forecastle, Captain Hadlor at his side, arms folded across his chest.

"Now that we're away from the ship," Anskar said, "there's something I wanted to ask you."

"Oh?" Lanuc said.

Orix nodded. He knew what was coming. He and Anskar had discussed it whenever they were alone.

"Colvin," Anskar said, and Lanuc immediately stiffened. "Why weren't we punished for his death? I thought the Grand Master would—"

"Enough," Lanuc snapped. "I will not speak on behalf of the Grand Master, or anyone else for that matter. Just be thankful he is lenient." His mouth twisted in disgust. "But it's whatever you did to Colvin's arm you should be more concerned about. Forbidden sorcery is an offense to Menselas."

Heat flushed Anskar's cheeks. Lanuc turned away and gestured for them to follow.

Atya was only the second major city Anskar had seen, and it was very different to Dorinah. The air was thick with complex aromas—animal musk, ordure, incense from the charcoal braziers that burned on virtually every street corner, which Orix said was to ward away evil spirits; the rich scent of spiced lamb, spit-roasted by street vendors; bitter coffee, sun-baked mud, pungent herbs smoked in long-stemmed pipes. The stench of seaweed and brine wafted in with the breeze, and there was even an underlying metallic scent, which Anskar suspected was the blood of butchered animals. He guessed there must be a slaughterhouse nearby.

The streets were packed with ruddy-skinned Traguh-raj, and in among them were dark mainlanders and even the odd crimson-skinned Niyandrian, which made Anskar uncomfortable. What if Carred Selenas's reach extended this far? Many of the mainlanders wore armor—not the pristine mail of the Order, but crude splinted mail or the heavy molded bronze favored by the City States. Everybody seemed to be haggling for something with the robed and eagle-eyed street traders who called out to passersby in brash and broken Nan-Rhouric.

There was a constant hubbub of voices, sonorous and rhythmic. Orix pointed out several wattle-and-daub buildings with thatched roofs that looked out of place. "They're house temples to the god Olan."

"Your god as a child?" Lanuc asked, but Orix shook his head.

"Olan's a thief in the night, they say. My father called him an infiltrator god. His worshipers slipped in among the Traguh-raj generations ago, leaving hundreds of these temples in their wake. They taught my people their ways, then left."

"So the Plains people worship only this Olan?" Anskar asked.

"We have our own gods," Orix said, then quickly added, "Not me, though. I belong to Menselas."

As they passed through narrow streets, the sound of drumming and pipes drowned out the prayer chants, a pounding rhythm with skirling melodies that repeated over and over. There were wild dogs and cats all over the place, and rats gamboling amid the sludge that ran through channels down the middle of the roads.

Lanuc seemed familiar with the city and swiftly led them to a large building fronted with acacia boards and surrounded on all four sides by a verandah with a pitched roof of rushes. The ground-floor windows were shuttered, but the upper-story windows were open to the morning sun, though a thin mesh curtain hung over each, which Lanuc explained was to keep the insects out.

While Anskar and Orix waited on the verandah, beneath a painted sign depicting a bucking horse, Lanuc went inside to arrange rooms for the Grand Master and his entourage. Two Traguh-raj women reclined on cushioned benches in the shade of the verandah's roof. Both were dressed in strips of diaphanous cloth, slender chains of silver adorning their hips, and they wore anklets with tiny bells. One had glistening black hair piled up atop her head with fine-toothed combs. The other's hair was dyed shades of purple and red and braided into long ropes.

Anskar felt the ladies watching him but couldn't meet their eyes. His face prickled with embarrassment as sordid thoughts muscled their way into his head. Orix, though, merely looked bored, tapping his foot impatiently and swiping at flies as they buzzed too close to his face.

After several minutes, Lanuc emerged, nodded to the ladies, then took Anskar and Orix through a network of narrow alleyways until they came to a tavern bustling with drinkers and diners, even this early in the day. Strange music drifted out from inside—pipes and bells and drums playing together in a jaunty, yet haunting, melody.

They entered through a curtain of beads. Inside, the air was heavy with smoke, both pungent and sweet. The entire first floor was a single large room dotted with tables and chairs and dominated by a large circular bar at its center.

A trio of musicians performed in one corner, all Traguh-raj, dressed in motley. One sat on a wooden crate, which he banged rhythmically with his hands and heels. Another clutched a skin sack bristling with bone pipes beneath her armpit. She blew on one of the pipes while squeezing the sack with her elbow, and the resultant sound was brash and grating, but not altogether unpleasant. The third musician—an old man—cavorted around with bells strapped to his wrists and ankles, a flat drum in his hand.

Most of the patrons were Traguh-raj locals, but in among them Anskar spotted several people of Inkan-Andil descent, probably from the City States and Kaile. Some were lightly armored and might have come in with the warship docked in the harbor. And there were two massively muscled, obsidian-skinned women sitting at the bar, apparently engaged in a drinking contest—barley wine, by the looks of it.

"Don't stare," Lanuc said. "Those are part-blood Orgols from the far south—the Jargalan Desert. Strong as oxen and fierce as lions. They live to fight, and see even the slightest glance as a provocation. They'll snap you in half like a twig."

"Really?" Orix said. "You're joking, aren't you?"

Lanuc looked deadly serious, but then he grinned.

"Come on," he said, leading them to a vacant table. "Are you lads drinking yet, or would you prefer milk?"

"Beer," Anskar said. He hadn't realized how parched he was. The heat in Atya was dry and scratchy, and it had sapped his strength.

Orix hesitated. Last time he'd drunk, Anskar and Sareya had needed to drag him out of the tavern and drape him over the saddle of his horse to get him home. "Perhaps a small beer," he said eventually.

"I'll ask about rooms here," Lanuc said. "It has to be better than the *Exultant*'s cabins."

"For the crew and the knights, too?" Orix asked.

Lanuc shook his head. "Most of them will stay on board. They'll be allowed ashore in rotation, but it's never a good idea to leave a ship unattended, especially in hostile territory."

"Atya is hostile?" Anskar asked.

"It's not under mainland rule," Lanuc said. "Customs are something other than we're used to here. To our way of thinking, Atya's virtually lawless."

Lanuc approached the bar and spoke to an elderly Traguh-raj woman in a stained leather apron—presumably the landlady. He returned with two mugs of beer.

"You're not drinking?" Orix asked.

"Later. First, I must return to the wharves and inform the Grand Master that I've found him accommodation, and then I'll board the ship and arrange for your gear to be brought here."

"How long are we staying?" Anskar asked.

"A day or two. Maybe longer if the Grand Master hears of anything interesting."

"Hears of?" Anskar said.

"I'll be as quick as I can." Lanuc hurried out through the beaded curtain.

"You look nervous," Orix said.

"I do?" It was a shrewd observation, and Anskar became aware he was asking too many senseless questions. He felt exposed, seated in a tavern in a foreign city. He still hadn't gotten used to being outside Branil's Burg's walls. The music was unsettling him, too. It was tuneful enough, but the sounds were unfamiliar, inviting him at once to dance, to sing, and to flee in panic. Once or twice he caught locals staring at him, and wondered if it was on account of his eyes.

Orix took up his mug of beer. "My folks used to bring me to places like this all the time. They had no choice. They were musicians, like this lot. Earned their coin playing the taverns."

"I never knew you were musical."

"I'm not. Can't even whistle in tune," Orix said, taking a long pull on his beer.

"Careful," Anskar said. "Remember what happened last time?"

"Can't be helped," Orix said. "Water's undrinkable in the Plains. They say it was polluted centuries ago, when the Niyandrians used to inhabit this part of the world. Dark sorcery, they say, which seeped into the water table."

"Your people blame the Niyandrians for that?"

"They ruled here for centuries," Orix said. "Till some calamity wiped most of them out and sent the rest scurrying back to Niyas."

"What calamity?"

Orix shrugged. "Their sorcery, I guess. My mother used to sing a song about them consorting with demons and summoning up the dead. They had a huge empire once."

"I know," Anskar said. "It's what Queen Talia was trying to emulate."

Queen Talia. He winced at his use of her name. His mother. Could it really be true? He offered up a silent prayer to Menselas that it wasn't, but deep down … how could he deny it, after the things he'd seen—the crow, the wraithe, the vambrace on his forearm?

"What is that they're smoking?" Anskar asked, glancing around at the locals, many of whom were puffing on long-stemmed pipes.

Orix shrugged. "Henlap, maybe laced with demondew. They're types of fungi. They say it's relaxing and helps you to see spirits if you smoke enough."

"You've not tried it?"

"I left the Plains of Khisig-Ugtall before I was old enough. Still, now I'm back …" he said with a chuckle that abruptly ended.

"What is it?" Anskar said, starting to turn in his chair.

"Don't look," Orix said, "but there's a woman seated at the bar, watching us."

"A local?"

Orix sipped his beer, talking into the mug. "Definitely not. Dark hair, tied back. Rings in her lips and nose, and a dozen of them in her ears. Olive skin. Dressed like a freebooter—black pants, tall leather boots, open-necked shirt." He coughed to clear his throat. "Weird eyes, though. Slanted. And violet."

Now Anskar wanted to look, but Orix gave a barely discernible shake of his head. "Uh-oh," he said, "she's coming over."

"Always good to see new blood in the Cockatrice," the woman said in fluent Nan-Rhouric, pulling out the chair they had intended for Lanuc and seating herself next to Anskar. She sat so close he could smell something sweet on her breath and the faint scent of sandalwood coming from her black hair.

"That's what this place is called?" Orix said, glancing around the tavern.

"Clever boy," the woman said. "And I had wondered if you even spoke the common tongue. Of course, if you prefer, I could use Plains speak?"

"*Yinail arga slaftwaec*," Orix said. It didn't sound polite.

"Perhaps not, then," the woman replied wryly. If she'd been offended by whatever Orix had said, she kept it to herself. "Bariya is such an unforgiving language, don't you think? And I lack the provincial accent for it."

Anskar glanced at her face, then swiftly away again. Lean and hard, age not easy to determine—early thirties, at a guess. Her lips were full and pierced with three silver rings, her teeth impossibly white. And her eyes ... Orix had been right: they were almond-shaped and violet. Her earlobes were heavy with silver loops, and a brightly colored tattoo—the head of a serpent—covered much of her throat, its sinuous body threading between her breasts and disappearing beneath her open-necked shirt.

"What brings you to Atya?" she asked. "Rumors of riches? Don't believe a word of it."

"We're on our way to Sansor in Kaile," Anskar said, still unable to meet her gaze.

"From Niyas," Orix put in.

"Then you must be terribly lost," the woman said. "Atya's hardly on the way to Sansor. It's actually considerably out of the way. So you came in with the Order ship. I guess that explains the white cloaks. You seem awfully young for knights. What are you, new recruits?"

"Knights-inferior," Orix said, as if it were a badge of honor.

"Inferior to what?"

"We've recently taken simple vows," Anskar explained.

"Presumably before you go on to take complicated ones. A word of advice: don't swear too many oaths. In time you'll forget what you've agreed to, and an oath broken … like eggs, if you know what I mean."

"What oaths have you broken?" Anskar asked, and this time he looked her in the eye.

She smiled at that and leaned back in her chair, clasping her hands behind her head. "That's a personal question to ask a lady, and we've only just met. So tell me, what's the Order of Eternal Vigilance doing in Atya this time? Come to build another church, or to sell more slaves?" The smirk on her face told Anskar she already knew, and that she was baiting him with the Order's apparent hypocrisy.

"We're waiting for someone," Orix said. "And you're in his

chair."

"Lanuc of Gessa," the woman said. "I know."

"You know him?" Anskar asked.

"You two certainly have your wits about you. Wasted on the Order. Utterly wasted. You think he'll worry about my firm backside keeping his chair warm? Perhaps I've misjudged his character."

"How well do you know him?" Orix asked.

"Another personal question." She shook her head at Anskar. "These Traguh-raj boys … no manners."

She lowered her hands to the tabletop and interlaced her fingers, at the same time sitting up straight and pulling her shoulders back. Anskar found his eyes drawn to the skin of her breasts above the open neck of her shirt; one of them had been tattooed with swirling script in a language he didn't recognize. In the furrow between her breasts, the tattooed serpent's scaled body seemed to writhe each time she breathed in.

The woman dipped her eyes, following his gaze, then translated the script on her breast for him: "*Shlyan na eleis*: 'The best there is.' It's a Soreshi dialect, and I admit it's pretentious, but I rather liked the sound of it. You approve?"

Anskar licked his lips as he looked away to the beer in his mug.

The woman looked round as the bead curtain parted and Lanuc came in with a couple of sailors who'd helped him bring Anskar's and Orix's packs from the *Exultant*. Lanuc hesitated on the threshold, looking over at their table, then said something to the sailors, who carried the packs toward the stairs leading up to the second floor. Lanuc made a show of straightening his cloak, then approached the table.

"Blaice Rancey," he said with a curt nod.

"Lanuc of Gessa," she said, rising and dusting off the chair she'd been sitting on. "Just keeping it warm, the way you like it."

"Kind of you," Lanuc said. "Good to see you." It was more of a dismissal than a greeting.

"I know." With a quick smirk, Blaice Rancey returned to her stool at the bar.

SEVEN

THE ROOMS LANUC ARRANGED for them were small but clean, and fragrant with the sweet scent of oil burning in ceramic bowls. At Lanuc's suggestion, rather than more comfortable clothes, Anskar and Orix donned their mail, strapped on their swords, and wore their white cloaks. The Grand Master wanted the Order's presence in Atya to stand out, and he wanted the knights to convey the impression of discipline and strength. Anskar left his spare clothes in his pack, which he stowed beneath the bed. Then, with a swift prayer to Menselas for protection in this strange city, he met Orix and Lanuc as they came from their own rooms, and together the three went outside.

Lanuc took them on a tour of the stalls that lined the narrow streets between buildings. Traguh-raj locals called out in broken Nan-Rhouric, hawking their wares: scented oils to daub on the skin or rub into hair; leather sandals encrusted with glittering gems; curly-toed slippers of shiny silk; elaborately carved long-stemmed pipes, dried herbs and fungi to fill the bowls with; pouches containing a reddish powder that was inhaled through the nose.

They passed a man with a grindstone for sharpening knives and a woman selling bulbous and prickly plants, some of which had needle-lined petals that opened and shut like a maw. Much of the clothing for sale was striped with gaudy colors and trimmed with silver or gold—traditional Plains wear, Orix said, though few of the locals wore it. Indeed, most of the Traguh-raj people they saw were dressed in the mainland style—pants and billowing shirts, pleated skirts or plain smocks.

Several of the traders were mainlanders, and there were dark gray-skinned Jargalan nomads plying studded wristbands, leather thongs, and headdresses of wildly colored plumage.

The one Niyandrian they saw was an old woman offering to consult the dead for a silver talent. Anskar was tempted, but Lanuc pulled him away. "Menselas forbids all forms of necromancy," he said.

Anskar already knew that, but he had to know about the shadowy woman who had woken him from sleep—he was drawn to the chance to speak with Queen Talia.

Reluctantly, he moved away from the old woman's stall, but not before she met his gaze with her slitted cat's eyes. She nodded knowingly at him.

They stopped to eat beneath the awning of a stone building in one of the many circular spaces that stood like islands amid the bustle of the market streets.

"Sirra Lanuc!" a sturdy man in an apron cried, wiping his hands on a cloth as he came out of the building's barn doors and hurried over to greet them. He had the ruddy skin of the Traguh-raj and a wispy black beard that curled from his chin.

"Sirra?" Anskar asked.

"A title of respect," Orix explained. "Like the Nan-Rhouric 'Lord.'"

"Is Lanuc a lord?"

"We all are to one another. It's a formality of Plains speech, nothing more."

Lanuc touched a hand to his heart and gave a low bow—Anskar had seen the same gesture countless times among the Traguh-raj in the streets.

"You have been too long a stranger, Sirra Lanuc," the man said. "You are looking thin. They do not feed you well, I think, these knights of Menselas."

"Ah, Utri," Lanuc said, "if I remained here, I would eat your excellent food every day, and pretty soon I'd be too fat to wear my armor."

Utri shrugged. "You could have a bigger mail shirt made."

"Mail is expensive, my friend, and even if I made it myself, where would I find the time?"

"I'll tell you what," Utri said, leaning in for a conspiratorial whisper. "I will provide you with a feast, on the house. Just for you, mind. These young men will have to pay."

"My thanks, Utri. I've missed your food."

Utri seated them on cushions on the ground around a low table. The other tables beneath the awning were all taken by Traguh-raj customers.

"My girls will bring your food," Utri said, "but in the meantime, you would like water, yes?"

Anskar glanced at Orix, who discreetly shook his head.

"Some of your excellent sourberry wine," Lanuc said.

Utri beamed from ear to ear. "Very good. And for your friends?"

"The same," Orix said, and Anskar nodded in agreement.

"You are from the Plains?" Utri asked Orix.

"I was born just outside Atya."

"Your parents?"

"Pael Zugor is my father. Ila Zugor my mother."

Utri rubbed his beard, thinking. "The names are familiar."

"They were musicians. They used to play in the city on occasion."

"Yes, I think I remember them. They played here sometimes. Oh, it was a long time ago. Years. But you ..." Utri indicated Orix's white cloak. "You have gone on to higher and better things, no?" There was an edge to his voice that hadn't been there before. Lanuc was gently shaking his head. "They must be very proud of you," Utri said sourly; then he turned to walk away. "Musicians, yes. I think I do indeed remember them."

Anskar shifted uncomfortably on his cushion. His armor and the padded jacket he wore beneath it were beginning to chafe, and his white cloak was heavy and coated with dust.

"Where do your parents live?" Lanuc asked. "If it's not too far, I'm sure you'd have time to—"

"I don't know," Orix said. "Not anymore."

"But—"

"They moved away when I joined the Order."

"They didn't tell you where?" Anskar asked. "Why? Did you have a falling-out? Didn't they approve of you joining the Order?"

"Like I said, they moved away." Orix turned and made a show of looking around at their surroundings, but Anskar could tell something was wrong. Lanuc met his gaze, gave a subtle shake of his head, and mouthed, "Let it be."

A servant girl came out of the barn doors, carrying a tray upon which were a bottle of wine and three ceramic drinking bowls. The girl could only have been twelve or thirteen years of age. Her hair had been shaved back to the scalp, and she was barefoot. All she wore was a simple black dress, beneath which she appeared stick-thin. Her cat's eyes were glazed and unfocused, and her red skin was dull and scabbed in places. She was a Niyandrian, and Anskar had to wonder if she had been brought to Atya against her will, like the men and women in the hold of the Grand Master's ship.

He met her eyes as she poured his wine, and she smiled, though it seemed to him a lifeless smile, merely what was expected.

No sooner had she gone back inside with the tray than more Niyandrian servants, men and women, similarly shaven and attired, emerged from the building, bearing platters and bowls and baskets of flat, grainy bread, which they set down on the table. Anskar's stomach growled at the aroma of charred and spiced meat as a plate of what looked like lizards was placed in front of him, their skin blackened and crispy, dusted with granules of pink salt. There were green olives, too, stuffed with fried grubs, and the claws of some kind of crab, which Lanuc set about with relish.

"Sand crabs," he said, wiping grease from his lips. "Sautéed in ginger, lemon rind, and rainbow-gilled mushrooms."

"Are they safe to eat?" Anskar asked, wrinkling his nose.

"What do you think?" Lanuc crunched on another claw.

Orix sniffed and turned back round. He visibly shook himself; then his eyes widened at the spread of food. A grin spread across his face as he dove into the bread, which he topped with a white, crumbled cheese, slices of dark meat, and what he described as locusts fried in honey. He rolled the bread around the filling and took a huge bite, chewing vigorously.

"I've not had this kind of food since I was a child," he said, taking a swig of sourberry wine. "My grandmother used to make it for me all the time. Sorry about earlier. Being back in the Plains makes old memories raw, but food brings back the good ones." He looked Anskar in the eye. "No, my parents didn't approve of me joining the Order, but they were savvy enough to know it was better than me staying in the Plains of Khisig-Ugtall. It was bad enough for them, being struggling musicians, but for their tone-deaf son, there was no future here at all. They let me go and then they went away. I think they were in trouble. Menselas knows what they got themselves into, but I can't blame them for it. Music doesn't pay well in the Plains. Probably it was thieving, and the people of Atya don't take kindly to thieves."

"Maybe you'll find them one day," Anskar said.

"Maybe. I'd like that."

"Perhaps once the Order has more of a foothold in the Plains," Lanuc said. "When there's law and order and some semblance of civilization."

Orix stiffened, then took another bite of his bread.

"What I meant—" Lanuc started, but Orix cut him off with a raised hand.

"I know what you meant, sir. No harm done. And, in any case, I agree with you. Atya's a shithole."

"Orix!" Anskar said.

The Traguh-raj lad put a hand over his mouth. Glanced at Lanuc.

"No harm done," Lanuc said with a mischievous smile. "At least nothing that can't be undone by a good confession."

Anskar frowned at the dishes arrayed before him and resolved to try the lizard. He picked off a piece of crispy skin and popped it in his mouth, wincing with anticipation. After a few moments, he began to salivate as his palate absorbed the subtle flavors. He took a sip of sourberry wine, surprised to find it sweet as well as sour, and blissfully refreshing. And then he set about the meal with gusto, trying everything and savoring every last exotic tang. When he'd eaten his fill and pushed his plate away, he poured himself another glass of wine and waited for his companions to finish.

"Do you have coin on you?" Lanuc asked.

Anskar still had the coins Vihtor had given him back at Branil's Burg. He took out his pouch and showed Lanuc. "Will they accept it here?"

"Everyone does these days," Lanuc said, "save perhaps for the Jargalan nomads. Wherever there's trade, our mainland currency prevails. One day—in your lifetime, perhaps—there will be Kailean banks on every continent, and a church of Menselas in every town. Order is coming to Wiraya, Anskar, slowly, a bit at a time. And with it, peace, the Five's kingdom in the world. One day people will be able to walk the wilderness without worrying about dead-eyes, ghouls, and other unholy creatures."

Anskar looked round at the approaching clatter of cartwheels. A cage-topped wagon pulled up outside Utri's restaurant, driven by one of the huge part-blooded Orgol women they had seen at the tavern. There were four Traguh-raj men with clubs flanking the wagon, and inside the cage were half a dozen naked Niyandrian slaves, still with their hair intact. Anskar recognized them from the hold of the *Exultant*.

"The Grand Master's business must be concluded," Lanuc said, without expression. Catching Anskar's look, he said, "It could be worse. Utri's a fair master, if a demanding one."

"But Menselas—" Anskar began.

"Is a god of five aspects," Lanuc concluded, taking a swig of wine and emptying his drinking bowl. "Come on," he said, rising from his cushion. "Settle up with Utri, and then let's go. Like you, there are things about our Order I struggle to understand. Do as I do, Anskar. You too, Orix. Pray to the Elder aspect of the Five. Ask him to grant you understanding. Ask him also for the wisdom to know when to object and when to keep silent. You can't do any good if you're dead and buried."

That night, back at his room in the Cockatrice, Anskar drifted in and out of sleep. He woke once, startled to find he'd been dreaming about Blaice Rancey, the woman who had approached him and Orix downstairs. He could remember no content of the dream, but he was aroused and found it hard to get back to sleep again.

And then he heard it: a gentle tapping at his window, which struck him as odd, given that his room was on the second floor.

He rose naked from the bed, where he had been sleeping on top of the covers due to the dry heat. When he drew back the coarse cloth that served as a curtain, he saw nothing at first save the darkness that lay thick over the city. But then the darkness shuddered. A strip of it began to writhe, pulling substance from the night around it. It became a lithe figure hovering outside the window, serpentine at first, but slowly morphing until it vaguely resembled a woman. A woman of shadow, featureless, as ephemeral as smoke.

Anskar's breath caught as he recognized the visitor from his dream who had awoken him when Colvin had assaulted Orix. He stared at the misshapen head, seeking out eyes but finding none. Darkness, pure and absolute, glared back at him, glared right through him, down to the bone. Anskar was as helpless as the day the golden-eyed crow had led him into the wilderness, all the way to Hallow Hill and the tomb where he had found the vambrace—he lifted the catch on the window and opened it, then stepped back as the shadow woman drifted inside.

She hovered there for a moment, as if she were appraising him. He became aware of a weight inside his skull, within his marrow, and he wondered if he was still asleep and dreaming. The shadow lifted a slender arm. One of its fingers extended, snaking toward him like a tentacle. He shuddered as it stroked his cheek, the touch a chill draft.

A voice sounded in his head, feminine and rasping—a voice from a shredded larynx, or one parched dry, desiccated and long dead. The words sounded familiar, but he couldn't understand them. Niyandrian, he realized. The shadow woman was speaking to him in Niyandrian.

"Mother?" he asked in a trembling voice. "Queen Talia?"

"I ..." the woman said, switching to Nan-Rhouric. "I see you, my child." The pronunciation was off, the words coming out guttural and strained, as if she weren't used to speaking them. "I know ... your desires." Anskar knew she was referring to Blaice, and he immediately remembered snippets of his dream. Images of naked flesh, of grinding and sweating and panting exploded across his inner vision, and he recoiled in shame.

"Menselas," he uttered. "Menselas cleanse me."

But it was too late. The damage was done. He had seen what he should not, and where his imagination went, his desire followed, his body responded.

"It is ..." the shadow woman said, "unseemly. All such ... pleasures fade. Seek only the things that last. Find me and you will be fulfilled. It is your ... duty."

"Mother?" he blurted as the shadow drifted backward, out of

the open window.

She didn't answer. The darkness rippled around her and then she was gone.

Anskar gasped and snapped awake.

Only, he hadn't been sleeping. He was standing before the open window, naked, a gentle breeze caressing his skin. In the crimson light of Jagonath, the one moon visible, he could see the vambrace covering his forearm. It shimmered, reflecting not the red of the moon, but rippling blues and greens and purples.

Anskar closed the window and pulled the curtain across, and immediately the vambrace vanished, though he could still feel its coolness and weight. He took a deep breath through his nose and drew in the scent of sandalwood and something else—loam, perhaps. Maybe mold.

He lay back down on the bed, and the scent lingered in his nostrils. It permeated the entire room, saturated the pillow and sheets.

As if she had really been here. As if she still was. Not just in the room, but inside him, her essence seeping through his pores like sweet-smelling sweat.

When he closed his eyes, there were no more visions of Blaice, of naked flesh; no more feelings of urgent need. Instead, he saw the statue from which he had taken the vambrace in the tomb atop Hallow Hill.

He took no comfort from the vision, and he knew he wouldn't sleep now. He cast wary glances at the curtain, expecting it to part, expecting to see the shadow woman hovering outside his window, rapping at the glass, demanding to be let in.

In the end, all he could do was stare up at the ceiling, reciting the calculations for casting as his ward sphere sprang into existence around him, shimmering silver—the color it should be, not the dark abomination it had previously become. That helped him to relax, knowing he had control of his dawn-tide repository, and that the dusk and the dark were locked safely away behind the barriers he had erected. He dismissed the ward, then cast it again, even quicker this time. And he continued to practice, the ward winking on and off so rapidly it made his head spin, and his eyes grew sore from the silver glare. The ward blinked on and off, faster and faster, till it seemed to blaze continuously around him, and he wondered if any sorcerer had ever developed such speed with casting. It made him consider what more he could do to keep pushing his abilities to their limits.

At least the ones he was supposed to use.

EIGHT

ANSKAR SHOOK ORIX AWAKE and together they went downstairs to meet Lanuc, who was seated at a table in the main room of the tavern.

"I've already ordered for you," the knight said, indicating two plates of eggs, flat bread and sliced green tomatoes.

As they seated themselves, a servant approached and poured a steaming drink into two mugs for them. The liquid had a bitter smell and was cloudy and green.

"Is that ...?" Orix said, lifting his mug.

Lanuc sipped from his own. "Melka. Grown in the shade of acacia trees and harvested at full-dark."

"Fermented?"

"Of course."

That seemed to please Orix, and he sighed as he sipped at his melka. "I used to drink this as a child," he told Anskar. "Good for the blood, the gut, the skin."

"And it cures a host of ailments," Lanuc said. "Scurvy, piles, the hacking cough, even the rot."

"It cures the rot?" Anskar asked skeptically.

"Well, they say it slows its progress."

"So is there anything it isn't good for?" Anskar took a sip of his melka and almost gagged. It was at once musty and vinegary, with a hint of mud and seaweed.

Lanuc laughed. "It's an acquired taste. Now, hurry up and eat your food. We've been summoned."

The room Lanuc brought them to was large, with three arched openings leading off it. The wooden slatted ceiling was hung with diaphanous drapes of pink and purple, the floor festooned with cushions. There were several framed pictures hanging from the walls, but they had been hastily covered with white banners embroidered with the five-pointed star of Menselas—although in one case the banner had slipped to one side, revealing a painting of a naked woman with exaggerated curves straddling a half-beast, half-man with a horned head and glistening fangs.

Three fully armored knights stood around the room, one of whom was the tattooed Ryala Mitredd.

Hyle Pausus sat on a plush couch that had velvet cushions and feet of carved bone. There was a low table before him, upon which was a crudely drawn map showing mountains, rivers, and winding roads. Stooping over the map was a dark-haired woman in a leather jacket and pants, tall boots pulled up above her knees. Anskar recognized her even before she turned to face them: Blaice Rancey.

"It has come to my attention," the Grand Master said, "that

Wiraya has once again disgorged the contents of a meal she consumed in the distant past."

Anskar frowned, glancing at Orix and then Lanuc for an explanation.

The Grand Master waited, savoring the bewilderment his words brought, before explaining. "There was an earthquake a few weeks ago, and after the ground stopped trembling, some locals went to see the extent of the damage. A fissure had opened in the earth, and at its foot lay the entrance to an ancient ruin. How old did you say it was?"

"Millennia," Blaice said. "From before the war against the demon lord Nysrog."

"Blaice here has already investigated for herself," the Grand Master said.

"Just the exterior, the little that's visible beneath the rubble and displaced earth. But there are markings on the door … a kind of proto-Skanuric I've seen before. Several times, actually."

"Blaice is something of an expert in …" The Grand Master hesitated, looking at her for what he should say next.

"I enter ancient sites for a living. Like some of the man-whores." She raised an eyebrow, but no one laughed. Anskar didn't realize it was a joke until Lanuc tsked and shook his head.

"Why?" Orix asked, touching his fingertips to his breast. Everyone knew nothing good came from the ruins that were found all over Wiraya. Those that weren't demonic were from the even murkier past, when strange civilizations desecrated the world with their poisonous lore. It was a period lost to history save for the evidence of the devastation left in its wake.

Blaice rolled her eyes. "As I said, for a living."

"People pay well for relics from the old ruins," Lanuc explained. "Merchants like Yanatos Holdings." He gave Blaice a narrow-eyed look.

Anskar had heard of Yanatos Holdings, one of the major merchant houses in Riem in the Pristart Combine. He'd long ago learned from Brother Tion that Yanatos Holdings was the chief supplier of furnishings and religious paraphernalia to the Order of Eternal Vigilance, and that they also procured precious relics for the Church of Menselas: the toe bones of long-dead saints, skulls, teeth, even entire desiccated corpses for display in the chapels dedicated to the Hooded One—those that remained.

Blaice merely shrugged at whatever Lanuc was getting at. "I've done work for Yanatos Holdings. And whoever's willing to pay."

"Even the Ethereal Sorceress?" Lanuc said, crossing his arms over his chest and looking to the Grand Master for support.

Hyle Pausus, though, was preoccupied with the map on the table before him.

"All finds from the ancient ruins pass through the Ethereal Sorceress's depots one way or another," Blaice said.

"The point is," the Grand Master said, looking up abruptly, "it is the Order of Eternal Vigilance who will be paying Blaice this time, and before there are any objections, it is what Menselas wills. Am I clear?"

He glared at the three knights standing to attention around the room, then at Orix and Lanuc, and finally at Anskar. Lanuc dipped his head.

"Good," the Grand Master said. "I cannot stress the importance of such finds for the Church and our Order. Now, please, Blaice, be so kind as to tell everyone what you told me last night."

Blaice cleared her throat. "Traguh-raj chiefs from the outlying villages led their warriors to within a few hundred yards of the unearthed site during the week. But they're a superstitious people and would go no further. One of the chiefs came to Atya to seek me out." She flashed a white-toothed grin. "My reputation is second to none. The chief offered me copper and slaves and the skins of half a dozen quopoth lizards—giant beasts that stalk the deserts and sometimes take locals as their prey, for those of you new to Atya and the Plains of Khisig-Ugtall—if I would enter the ruin and bring him the treasures that lie within."

"But you turned him down?" Lanuc said.

"I sent word of the discovery to my contacts on the mainland. From the description the chief gave me, they were quite excited."

"You sent a message to the mainland and have already received a reply?" Anskar asked.

"The Ethereal Sorceress," Lanuc explained. "Her depot here in Atya. Don't ask how, but messages and goods pass between her depots with unnatural haste."

"Sorcery." The Grand Master sniffed, though he didn't seem too bothered by the idea.

"But, yes, I turned the chief's offer down," Blaice said. "Only ..."

"You haven't told him yet," Lanuc finished for her.

"What can I say?" She looked coy suddenly. "My mainland contacts offered substantially more, but—"

"But not as much as we did," the Grand Master concluded. He stood and turned a slow half circle, meeting the eyes of everyone in the room. "What I am going to share with you must not pass outside this select group. Discuss it with no one, not even your fellow knights."

Anskar glanced at Lanuc, but the knight gave a barely perceptible shake of his head. Orix was frowning, trying to keep up.

"If we move quickly," the Grand Master said, "we should be able to empty the ruin of its ... contents."

"Content," Blaice corrected, and the Grand Master gritted his teeth.

"Before the chiefs and their people can pluck up the courage to take a closer look," the Grand Master continued, "and before certain interested parties on the mainland—not all of them merchants—can assemble teams and ships to come here."

But why? Anskar thought. Why was the Order offering coin in return for whatever lay inside the ruin?

The Grand Master met his gaze. "This is not about profit," he said, and heat flushed Anskar's cheeks. "There are powers in the world, old powers that have been around since the demon wars, and some even older. They are inimical to the peace and order that Menselas bestows upon Wiraya. They wish for a return to the days of brimstone and darkness, when the demon lord Nysrog rampaged through the world. Others desire a return to the lore of the ancients, a lore that has given rise to cataclysm after cataclysm, and that would see our own civilization crumble into ruin. The Church of Menselas has a sworn duty to protect Wiraya, and our Order is the Church's strong arm. We have good reason to believe there is an artifact of unspeakable power within this ruin. Can you imagine what would happen," the Grand Master asked, and now he was speaking directly to Lanuc, "if such an object fell into the hands of the Tainted Cabal?"

Lanuc remained tight-jawed.

"Neither can I," the Grand Master said. "And so we must do all we can to prevent it. Which is why I've called you all here today. Word of what we are about to attempt must not get out. The *Exultant*'s crew, and most of our knights, will remain in Atya until our regular business is concluded. That gives the rest of us two, maybe three days to pay a visit to this ancient site, get inside, and find this artifact."

"Forgive me, Grand Master," Lanuc said, "but we're expected in Sansor. Further, Anskar is on loan from Seneschal Vihtor Ulnar. He and Orix have been entrusted to—"

"The last I heard," the Grand Master snapped, "Vihtor Ulnar was subordinate to me." He glanced at the three knights in the room. "Or has there been a coup without me hearing of it? No? Then I suppose I must still be in charge."

"But Anskar and Orix are knights-inferior," Lanuc said, "scarce out of training. In the past we've employed sorcerers for such missions. These sites are often warded. An ancient ruin is no place for the young and inexperienced."

"On the contrary," the Grand Master said, "it may be the very place. Menselas does nothing without purpose." He faced Anskar, smiling benevolently. "Vihtor was worried about the rebels' attempted abduction of you. More than that, he was worried about *you*: things he had presumably seen or heard—he wouldn't say exactly what. But then we had that little incident on the ship—Colvin and his unfortunate arm. Don't worry, I'm not seeking to apportion blame, but I am a man who likes to be apprised of the tools in his toolbox. Gadius tells me you have exceptional qualities, Anskar. Isn't that right, Gadius?"

The white-robed acolyte stepped out from one of the archways, where he had been listening in, out of sight.

"Exceptional may be something of an overstatement," Gadius said. "*Promising* is the word I would choose."

"Well, I think you have exceptional abilities," the Grand Master said. "Which is why you are here."

"And Orix?" Anskar asked.

"Vihtor said Orix would protect you. With his life if necessary."

Orix clenched his jaw and nodded.

"Good man," the Grand Master said. "I adore such dogged

loyalty. And besides, Blaice here has a reputation for successfully entering the ancient sites and relieving them of their treasures. I have it on good authority she is one of the best in her line of work."

"*The* best," Blaice said.

"Indeed. Well, let's hope so. In which case Anskar and Orix will merely be along for what could prove a most rewarding experience. I can't see Vihtor objecting to that, can you, Lanuc? No? Then it's settled."

Blaice procured hardy plains ponies for the long ride west, and it seemed to Anskar she had prepared for the trip even before speaking with the Grand Master, as everything was arranged within a matter of hours, and the expedition left Atya by midday.

Lanuc had made it clear he was unhappy about Orix and Anskar coming along, but he seemed even more put out by Blaice's involvement. The manner of their relationship, and why it was now so sour, was a mystery about which Anskar didn't feel it was his place to ask. He didn't know Lanuc well enough, and he knew Blaice scarcely at all.

He rode his pony alongside Orix at the rear of the group, behind Ryala and the other two knights. Lanuc rode next to Gadius Menashin, though neither of them spoke, and at the front, Hyle Pausus and Blaice Rancey. Why someone as illustrious as the Grand Master thought it was appropriate to lead the expedition troubled Anskar. Clearly, he was missing something.

The terrain they rode through was dry and cracked in places, lush and green in others, on account of the irrigation canals that crisscrossed the plains around Atya and that had been there as long as Orix could remember. Longer, given they had been dug before the time of his parents, or even his grandparents. Outside the cities, the Plains of Khisig-Ugtall were arid and devoid of vegetation, much like the Jargalan Desert, apparently. It was an ever-changing, variegated landscape, with mud-baked plains giving way to swaths of tall grasses browned by the heat, oases of palm trees, and miles on end of scrubland that fell away into gorges and valleys, or rose to rolling hills. And there was water everywhere, carried by the canals to reservoirs that had been dug into the parched earth at some time or other.

Seeing so much water, Anskar recalled Orix's warning not to drink it. The waters of the Plains of Khisig-Ugtall had long been polluted by whatever dark sorcery the ancients had unleashed upon the land. At least, that was what Orix believed, and it was interesting to note that the Grand Master had insisted on barrels of rainwater being brought from the *Exultant* for the trip, along with bulging wineskins and a few kegs of beer.

Anskar wore the hood of his white cloak up as protection from the relentless midday sun, but by late afternoon a bank of clouds moved in from the Simorga Sea, bringing some much-needed relief.

Lanuc dropped back to ride with Anskar and Orix, Gadius the acolyte glancing over his shoulder at him. "How are you faring?" the knight asked.

"My thighs are chafed," Orix complained, "and I'm hungry."

"He's always hungry," Anskar said, then realizing his own hunger asked, "When will we be stopping to eat?"

"Soon, I think," Lanuc said. "The Grand Master doesn't enjoy travel. He likes to get to his destination as soon as possible, whatever the discomfort, but I heard him suggest to Blaice that we should take a break soon."

"You know Blaice from before, don't you?" Anskar said.

"I won't deny it," Lanuc said. "But Menselas is merciful, and that chapter of my life is in the past."

"You're sure about that?" Orix said.

Lanuc grimaced. "Less sure than I'd like to be. Menselas also tests us. I'll pray to him that I'm strong enough to endure what he has in store for me."

"Were you—" Anskar started, then hesitated at the sharp look Lanuc gave him. "I mean … you've worked together before, on missions like this, but was there … more? Were you and Blaice—"

"Yes, yes, and yes," Lanuc snapped. "But you will ask no more about it. Please."

Anskar swallowed and nodded.

"What's important," Lanuc said, "is that we get through this alive. It's no laughing matter, entering the ancient places. Blaice knows this, of course. She has something of a reputation for being a survivor, but alas, the same reputation does not extend to her companions. I heard the last expedition she mounted ended in—" He broke off, peering into the distance, where a dark speck had appeared on the hazed western horizon.

"Is that a rider?" Orix asked.

"If it is, and you can see that," Lanuc said, "your eyes are better than mine."

Better than Anskar's too, but as the Grand Master raised a hand to halt the group, the speck became a smudge that steadily grew as it approached, and within minutes he could see it was indeed a rider, a lone man riding a black stallion. The rider wore a broad-brimmed black hat that shaded his eyes, and despite the heat he was dressed in a heavy black coat with silver buttons, dark pants, and knee-length boots. He held the reins in one hand, the other resting on the hilt of a long sword scabbarded at his hip.

The rider drew up a dozen yards from the group and tilted his hat to reveal a dusky, angular face softened by a trimmed box beard, though stubble on his cheeks indicated that he hadn't shaved for a few days. Beneath his coat he wore leather armor of exceptional quality, worked with flat metal rings, each of which was inscribed with flowing script. This close, Anskar could see that the sword hilt was intricately carved and made of a metal he couldn't identify, and on the other side of the sword belt was a shorter blade in a cracked leather scabbard. Long black hair flowed from beneath the hat, falling to the man's broad shoulders. He was tall and muscular, and his eyes, now that Anskar could see them, were a startling green, at once fierce and intelligent, world-weary yet glinting with amusement.

Ryala and the other two knights kicked their ponies forward, but Blaice stopped them with a raised hand. "It's all right," she told the Grand Master. "I know this man."

Blaice rode her pony forward until it was dwarfed by the man's black stallion.

"Well met, Niklaus du Plessis," she said, loud enough for everyone to hear.

"Likewise, Blaice Rancey." Niklaus's green eyes lingered on Blaice for an uncomfortably long moment, drinking in her—if not beauty—striking appearance. Her raven hair perfectly matched Niklaus's own, but her violet eyes were even more exotic than his green ones. "Word reached me you had an interesting find to investigate. I thought I would present myself as a partner in such a noble enterprise." The grin that plastered his face said something completely different.

"Word?" Blaice asked, casting a frown over her shoulder at the

Grand Master. "Who's been speaking?"

Niklaus raised his eyes to the overcast skies. "*She* has."

"Sylva Kalisia?" Blaice said.

The Grand Master rankled at that. "The heathen goddess?"

"The Lady," Niklaus said amiably.

"Does she still haunt your dreams, Niklaus?" Blaice said, drawing herself up in the saddle and arching her back slightly, which had the effect of thrusting out her breasts. "Are you still searching for her likeness in the world?"

Niklaus blinked, then wiped sweat from his eyes. "It is my curse," he said, voice little more than a rasp. "My trial. Speak of it no more. I'll not tell you again."

His words, though delivered casually, caused Blaice to settle back into her saddle and look away.

"One more sword can't hurt us," she said, wheeling her mount to face the Grand Master.

"We need no one else," Hyle Pausus said.

Blaice rode back alongside him and leaned in to speak in a low voice. "I've worked with Niklaus before. He has … skills that may prove useful."

"Please don't whisper on my account," Niklaus said. "I'm sure I'll be more than useful." He must have had exceptional hearing. Either that, or it was some kind of sorcery.

"Do you know who I am?" the Grand Master said.

"I can see from your cloak that you serve Menselas, the God of Five Aspects," Niklaus said. "Someone has to, I suppose. I, however, am the chosen sword of Sylva Kalisia. She has instructed me to accompany you on this … quest. You see, there are things in the ancient ruins that are best left undisturbed, though they invariably come to light and fall into the possession of one faction or another."

"The Church of Menselas is the rightful custodian of ancient relics," the Grand Master said.

"Better that than falling into the hands of the Tainted Cabal," Niklaus said. "So we are agreed on that, at least."

"And you don't seek the relic for the Lady?" Gadius said, riding to the front.

Niklaus studied the acolyte for a moment, jaw working as if he chewed something distasteful. "Sylva Kalisia has no need of trinkets. I'm surprised Menselas has. Perhaps there is something he lacks … not quite a god, after all?"

"How did you learn of our mission?" Gadius asked. "Does the Lady have a church in Atya?"

"She does. But I have come from the mainland."

"Impossible," the Grand Master said. "That's a journey of days, and I only learned of the ruins last night." He gave Blaice a suspicious look, and she shrugged.

"All I know is that the Lady told me to be in this place at this time," Niklaus said. "The ways of the gods are mysterious, are they not?"

The Grand Master exchanged hushed words with his acolyte, ending with a nod.

"Very well, Niklaus du Plessis, you are welcome to join us, to ensure that whatever lies within this ruin does not find its way into the hands of the Tainted Cabal. The relic will, however, remain in my possession until it can be delivered into the hands of the Church of Menselas."

"Of course," Niklaus said, giving a shallow bow and tipping his hat.

NINE

BLAICE LED THE EXPEDITION to an oasis of palms beside a canal choked with sun-dried fronds and murky with dirt from where the banks had begun to erode. After tethering their ponies, they each found a spot out of the sun: Lanuc and the three other knights together; the Grand Master with Gadius and Blaice, all talking in hushed voices; and Anskar with Orix. Niklaus du Plessis left his horse to roam free, occasionally snapping his fingers if it wandered too far. He stood apart, in the shade of a palm, taking discreet sips from a thin metal flask he kept in his boot. Anskar couldn't help noticing a furtive look Niklaus shot Blaice's way. Like Lanuc, Niklaus clearly had a past with her, but in his case, it didn't appear to have been resolved.

Anskar wolfed down some flat bread and hard cheese, and Orix did the same—both of them too hungry and too saddle-sore to talk. When he'd finished his food, Anskar drained his canteen, then, without thinking, went to the canal to refill it.

A shadow fell over him and he turned to see Niklaus stoppering his flask and stooping to tuck it back inside his boot.

"Water's bad," Niklaus said. "Or didn't they tell you that?"

Anskar could have kicked himself. "No, they told me. I just forgot."

"Forgetfulness can get you killed." Niklaus crouched by the edge of the canal and cupped his hands to fill them with water. To Anskar's horror, Niklaus dipped his head and drank deeply from the water in his hands. He glanced up and raised an eyebrow. "Do you believe everything they tell you?" He narrowed his eyes at Anskar's white cloak, the emblem of the five-pointed star on the shoulder. "Of course you do, if you're a devotee of the Five. Personally, I've always found the Church of Menselas to be full of complicated men and women. The kind who'll do many things for silver, and anything for gold."

"So the water's not polluted?" Anskar asked, doing his best to ignore the slight on his religion. There was something about this man that unsettled him … a dangerous gravity.

"The canals feed the palms and anything else that grows out here. They irrigate the crops outside Atya and provide water for the animals the locals eat. If the water was polluted, so would be the meat, the fruit, the vegetables. Why don't you wait and see if I keel over and die, or if I start shitting my pants and puking over my stallion's mane? At a guess, if none of that happens, the water's safe to drink."

"Then why do they say it's not safe?"

"They probably believe that. But ask yourself: who told them the water was polluted? Call it a wild stab in the dark, but I'd say it was the people who stand to make a profit from the sale of beer and wine and whatever else passes for drink in this godsforsaken place."

Anskar knelt by the side of the canal and thrust his face into the water. It was warm from the sun but still refreshing on his skin, washing away the grime of the trail. Emulating Niklaus, he scooped up some water in his hands and gulped it down, then waited for something to happen.

"I feel fine," he said.

Niklaus chuckled. "Ah, but how will you feel later?"

"Your name," Anskar said, refilling his canteen, "du Plessis … I've never heard of a place called Plessis."

"No reason why you should. And you? What do they call you?"

"Anskar. Anskar DeVantte."

"Not a very Niyandrian-sounding name."

"I'm not Niyandrian."

"Curious," Niklaus said, his gaze lingering on Anskar's eyes. "You're going to tell me your mother was a Kailean noblewoman who had a thing for feral cats, I suppose."

Anskar laughed, though he didn't find it funny. But this man intrigued him, carried himself with an air of confidence and something else … as if he'd seen it all before. As if nothing in the world could surprise him.

Anskar reached out with his sorcerous senses but found no trace of a repository. If Niklaus was a sorcerer, he was able to disguise it, which meant he was a powerful sorcerer. Anskar's eye caught the hilt of Niklaus's sword, and there was a brief flash. For an instant, he thought he could see the blade through the scabbard: mottled and shining like a ribbon of moonlight, the first third of the blade etched with runes; and near the hilt was an engraving of exquisite detail—a naked woman, kneeling, wings extending outward from behind her shoulders, her mouth curled in a sardonic smile.

Anskar's senses shuddered and whiplashed back into him, and he barely suppressed a gasp. The sword was … he couldn't say what it was. There was sorcery there, without a doubt, and something else—something brooding, dark, and sentient.

Niklaus cocked his head, and Anskar looked away from the sword. "Recognize her?" Niklaus said, as if he knew what Anskar had seen.

Anskar thought for a moment, and this time he saw the resemblance in the long hair, the shape of the face, the curves … "Blaice?" he whispered.

Niklaus leaned in toward him and whispered back, "Uncanny, isn't it? This blade"—he patted the sword hilt—"carries a representation of the Lady, Sylva Kalisia, my goddess." He swallowed thickly and looked away to where Blaice was deep in conversation with the Grand Master and Gadius. "She …" Niklaus turned back to face Anskar. His eyes had grown haunted, and sweat dripped from beneath the brim of his hat. "The goddess is exquisite."

"You've seen her?"

Niklaus nodded, removing his hat to shake the sweat from his hair.

"In your dreams?" Anskar's heart skipped at the possibility that someone else might have experienced the things he had.

"More than my dreams," Niklaus said. "I smell her, feel her, *desire* her." He shook himself violently and returned his hat to his head. "But she is divine. Beyond my reach. Yet the craving for her never leaves me."

Anskar nodded, thinking about his own haunting visions, and about how they had crossed over into the reality of his life. "So what do you do?"

Niklaus gave a throaty chuckle. "I look for substitutes. But they are never enough. Not nearly enough."

"Blaice?" Anskar asked.

"At one time, but no longer. She didn't live up to my visions of the Lady. No one ever does."

"But you and Blaice are friends?"

"Business associates," Niklaus said. "It's like friendship, only without all the downsides."

"I . . ." Anskar started, then thought better about confiding in this man he'd only just met.

"Yes?" Niklaus said. "You have something to share in return? That's usually how these things work: I tell you a secret, you reciprocate."

"I have dreams. More than dreams."

"Of a woman?"

Anskar nodded, and fire flashed in Niklaus's eyes.

"Describe her? Is she like Blaice?"

"She is dark. A shadow. Her form is only vague, like mist."

"Does she have wings? Violet eyes?"

"Not that I've seen."

"And she speaks to you?"

"Niyandrian mostly, but I can't understand it. A little Nan-Rhouric, but she struggles with the words."

Niklaus drew in a deep breath and let it out in a long sigh. "Not Sylva Kalisia, then. You had me worried there. I thought perhaps she'd decided upon a new Chosen Sword. I've served her a long time. Some would say too long. Do you have any idea who this woman you see is?"

"No," Anskar lied. He'd already said too much.

"You can't even hazard a guess?"

"Anskar," Lanuc said, approaching in a hurry, flicking Niklaus a suspicious glance, "time to go. We're setting off again."

"What were you and Niklaus talking about?" Blaice Rancey asked Anskar. She'd dropped back to ride her pony alongside his. Orix had fallen behind, complaining about saddle soreness.

"Orix's backside," Anskar said. "He's not used to riding so far."

"Want me to check it for him?"

"I think he'd like that."

Blaice grinned, though it didn't reach her eyes. "What else did you talk about?"

"Nothing."

"That was a whole lot of nothing you were discussing."

"Just things," Anskar said. "The water."

"Did he tell you it's good to drink?"

"And is it?"

"Never did me any harm. Perhaps once, long ago, it was bad. Did Niklaus tell you I remind him of his goddess?" She removed her hat and shook out her thick black hair. Anskar's eyes flitted to her chest, where her breasts strained against her sweat-stained shirt.

"He mentioned it."

"What else did he say?"

"Does it matter?"

Blaice looked behind, where Niklaus, astride his dark stallion, was trailing the group at a distance. "Probably not," she added, seemingly as an afterthought.

"Hey!" Orix cried, cantering up alongside, standing in the stirrups.

"Want me to rub some ointment on it?" Blaice said.

Orix ignored her. "What's that?"

At first Anskar couldn't see what his friend was pointing at, but when he squinted, he could make out a hazy smudge ahead and off to the right.

"That's one of the villages," Blaice said, then rode to the front of the group. Within moments, the Grand Master signaled a halt and the ponies drew up in a semicircle facing what was now clearly a cloud of smoke on the horizon.

"Do you know it?" the Grand Master asked.

"Cloefwic." Blaice wrinkled her nose. "It's basically a scatter of huts around a dung pile. And to think of it, the huts are made of dung too. Their elders are weed-smoking dimwits and their chief is a match for the pile of dung the village is built around. Actually, he was one of the chiefs who was trying to get enough warriors together to investigate the ruin, only his warriors are bigger cowards than he is."

"Sounds like you know him well," Niklaus said.

Blaice sneered at that. "I don't. Like most men, in my experience," she said, giving Niklaus a pointed look, "he would no doubt prove a huge disappointment."

"I daresay," Niklaus said. "But you surprise me: I thought huge would be to your liking."

"How would you know?"

Niklaus chuckled and turned to Anskar. "Never get into a dispute with Blaice. She has no rules of decency."

"True," Blaice said. "Which I assumed would be to *your* liking, Niklaus."

"Alas, you know me too well."

"If you two have quite finished," the Grand Master said, though he was smiling, and there was a sparkle in his eye, "we should ride to the village and see what help we can offer."

"I wouldn't," Blaice said. "Like I said, it's a shithole, and if

Chief Parax learns what we're up to, he might grow a pair of balls and mount his own expedition."

"Or tag along on ours," Niklaus said.

The Grand Master rubbed his wispy beard and turned to Anskar. "What would you suggest, young Anskar? What would Menselas wish us to do?"

"It depends on which aspect," Orix answered for him.

"All Five," the Grand Master said, a flash of irritation in his eyes. "And since when did you change your name to Anskar?"

"The Five in harmony," Anskar started carefully, "would demand concern, compassion."

"Go on," the Grand Master said.

"Menselas would want us to go to our brothers and sisters in need."

"Spoken like a true knight of the Order of Eternal Vigilance. Excellent. Then we are decided."

"We are?" Niklaus grumbled.

"It is the will of Menselas."

The stench of smoldering dung and roasted meat was thick in Anskar's nostrils as they approached the remains of the village. Burned and smoking houses sat in a rough circle around a dung heap the size of a hillock at the village's center. Mangled and half-eaten corpses lay all over the place, Traguh-raj men, women and children, all with fire-blackened skin and clothes, some with smoke pluming from melted eyeballs or out of their ears. Broken spears and shattered swords littered the ground, the metal misshapen and charred.

At the Grand Master's command, Ryala and the other two

knights dismounted and tethered their ponies to a low corral that had escaped the burning, then set out across the village in search of survivors.

"There!" Orix said, pointing at a long line of hills in the near distance, where the specks of people could be seen milling about the summit. "Traguh-raj folk. They're watching us."

"They must have fled during the attack," Lanuc said, squinting toward the hills.

"But what could have done this?" Anskar asked. "Sorcery?"

Niklaus climbed down from his stallion and once more let the horse roam free. The stallion seemed skittish, though, prancing and bucking in a tight circle. "Not unless sorcery leaves spoor like this."

Blaice rode her pony closer and peered down from the saddle. "A manticarr?"

Anskar dismounted and tethered his pony so that he could take a look for himself, but Orix remained in the saddle despite his soreness, standing in the stirrups and casting nervous looks around. The acolyte, Gadius, sat rigid on his pony, eyes closed as if he were using other senses. Lanuc steered his mount after Anskar, one hand on his sword hilt. The Grand Master seemed relaxed about the whole situation, as if he were either used to danger or used to being so well protected from it that he no longer took the idea seriously.

Or perhaps he knows something the rest of us don't, Anskar thought.

"Which one's Chief Parax?" the Grand Master asked disinterestedly.

"Oh, he'll be up on that hill," Blaice said. "Probably the first to leave."

Niklaus stood from a crouch when Anskar approached,

gesturing at the tracks he'd been examining. The earth was depressed in numerous places by huge paw prints and deep gashes from monstrous claws. Here and there were curved furrows, which Niklaus explained were from the beast's segmented tail, and craters from where the bulbous tip of the tail had slammed into the ground. The earth around the prints was charred and still smoldering.

Anskar crouched so he could touch his fingertips to the blackened ground. He withdrew them quickly and sucked on them. The ground was scorching.

"Will it be back?" he asked, rising and stepping back from the spoor.

"With any luck," the Grand Master said, "and then we shall avenge these poor people and stop it from terrorizing the neighboring villages."

Gadius's eyes snapped open at that, and he frowned.

"You've not faced a manticarr before, have you?" Blaice said.

"Several," the Grand Master said, puffing out his chest. "I may look a fat fool to you, but I had plenty of experience in the field in my younger days."

"By killing manticarrs?" Niklaus asked. "And I thought lying was against your religion."

"Guard your tongue," Lanuc said, half-drawing his sword and riding his pony between Niklaus and the Grand Master.

"Or what?" Niklaus said. One hand rested on the hilt of his sword.

"Stand down, Lanuc," the Grand Master said. "I'm sure he meant no offense."

"Then you must have misunderstood me," Niklaus said.

"Shut it, all of you!" Blaice commanded. "If there's a manticarr on the prowl, I say we get as far away from here as we can.

Hopefully, it will go after the idiots on the hills and we'll have a clear run to the ruin."

Lanuc relaxed his grip on his sword.

"Pants-pisser," Niklaus muttered under his breath, with only Anskar close enough to hear.

At that moment, Ryala and the other two knights returned from the burned-out dwellings. "No survivors," Ryala said, "save for that lot on the hills. They left their possessions, for the most part."

"Oh?" the Grand Master said, raising an eyebrow.

"Coppers mostly, and poorly minted at that—hammered coins. Wooden bowls and cups, iron pots and pans, badly tanned hides."

"Oh." The Grand Master shut his eyes, nodding, as if he consulted some higher power—presumably Menselas. "Then we should leave the collective wealth of the village for those who might return once the crisis has passed."

"Magnanimous, Grand Master," Gadius said, not a trace of insincerity on his hollow-cheeked face.

"And we found several piles of melted … they looked like crystal eggs," Ryala said.

"With red veins inside?" Niklaus asked.

"Yes."

"Manticarr excrement," Niklaus said. "Fetches a good price at market if you can get it there. The red veins are like lava, and they don't lose their heat. Ever. Back in the day, we used to keep them under the floorboards for heating the houses."

"Back in the day?" Anskar asked.

"I don't recall which day," Niklaus said, looking genuinely confused.

"So," the Grand Master said, "suggestions, everyone. How do

we bait a manticarr?"

"We don't," Blaice said.

"I thought you were the expert in killing them, Grand Master," Niklaus added.

"That is not what I said."

"So you haven't actually faced one?"

The Grand Master sucked in air through gritted teeth. "I do not propose to dignify that question with an answer."

"You haven't faced one," Niklaus concluded. "It was obvious from the outset, because if you had, you wouldn't want to again."

"But you have, I suppose?" the Grand Master retorted.

"I forget when," Niklaus said. "If I'd not been favored by the Lady, I would have long ago been a half-eaten, melted corpse like these poor bastards here."

"And how did you kill it?" Gadius asked, leaning over his saddle pommel.

"I didn't." Niklaus started to pump his arms and run on the spot. "I was younger back then, fitter. Blood and damnation! I ran as fast as a horse. Faster."

Ryala placed her hands on her hips and shook her head. "The beast's tracks lead away to the north," she told the Grand Master.

"Excellent," Blaice said, "because the ruin's to the west. Let's get moving."

"And the people on the hills?" the Grand Master asked. "The survivors?"

"They're nice hills," Niklaus said without any conviction. "And if the manticarr comes back, they'll see it when it's still a long way off."

"Oh, it won't have gone far," Blaice said. "Probably just sleeping off its meal."

"Then I must insist," the Grand Master said, "that we hunt

it down. A beast capable of this"—he glanced around the devastated village—"could ravage the other settlements in the area, maybe even threaten Atya."

"True," Niklaus said with a shrug. "Its lair must have been disturbed by the earthquake that disgorged the ruin. Manticarrs are solitary beasts who prefer the vast open spaces of the Plains, and the caves beneath, where they hunt the other things that live out there … creatures left over from the old world."

"You don't believe that," Blaice said.

"Some of it I do," Niklaus said. "Which part of what I said don't I believe?"

"That the earthquake disturbed its lair. Manticarrs have no lairs, at least not in this world."

"I was trying to keep it simple."

"When the ruin was unearthed," Blaice told the Grand Master, "the nascent wards protecting it would have been triggered."

"Nascent?" the Grand Master said, turning to Gadius for an explanation.

"The wards are brought fully into being by a predetermined set of circumstances, and more often than not they bring other things into being, too, in order to protect the site."

"These ancient metal buildings," Blaice said. "I've seen them before. The sorcerous wards that protect them are potent but not particularly complex. They tend to open portals between the worlds and bring things through. Most of the time it's lesser demons, but occasionally it's worse."

"Worse than lesser demons?" Anskar asked.

"Higher demons," Blaice said. "Or basilisks, wyvern … manticarrs."

"And a manticarr is worse than a demon?" Orix asked.

"Than a lesser demon," Niklaus said. "And some of the lower

higher order demons, if you know what I mean."

"The long and the short of it is, we can't kill it," Blaice said. "Not without a lot more knights and probably a half-decent sorcerer."

The Grand Master looked at his acolyte. "Gadius?"

Gadius in turn looked at Anskar.

"Me?" Anskar said. "But I'm no—"

"Of course you aren't," Gadius said slyly. "I can't vouch for my own meager gift—affliction, or whatever you want to call it—and so I am inclined to agree with Blaice Rancey."

"How far to the ruin?" the Grand Master asked Blaice.

"We could be there by midmorning."

"If we ride through the night?"

"Certainly not," Blaice said. "There are things other than a manticarr out here in the dark. The Traguh-raj are given to exaggeration and superstition, but they're probably understating it about the night prowlers. We'll be fine so long as we find a good spot for a camp and post sentries."

"A fire, too," Niklaus said casually.

Blaice nodded. "A big one."

"And the manticarr?" Anskar asked. "Will the creature stay away from the fire?"

Niklaus guffawed. "As much as a mouse would stay away from cheese."

"Or you from strong spirits," Blaice observed.

TEN

"WE DON'T HAVE TO do nothing, Haijin," Jada said. She lay naked atop the bed in her cabin, big, hirsute, and brutally beautiful.

Carred, perched on the edge of the bed, still hadn't undressed. That alone should have told her she wasn't doing well. A sudden sob rocked her forward and she covered her face with her hands. "I'm sorry, I can't."

"You never was good at sea. I shouldn't have gotten my hopes up."

"It's not seasickness, Jada. And no, it's not you, either."

"Then—"

Carred faced her, tears streaming, chin quivering. Since coming below decks with Jada, she could think of nothing but poor dead Kovin, and Marith, whom she might never see again, and what she'd nearly done back in Ahz … with the thing that went by the name of Count Vasseyli ap Murbian. Vaz.

"What is it?" Jada dragged a sheet across her massive breasts—the first time she'd ever betrayed the slightest self-consciousness in Carred's presence.

"You know I have other lovers."

"'Course I know, Haijin. You've always been honest with me."

"No," Carred said, looking up. "I haven't. Not honest enough to give you my real name."

Jada stood from the bed and started to throw on her clothes. A rare frown creased her forehead, and she wouldn't meet Carred's gaze.

"I wish I'd never lied to you," Carred said.

"Then why did you?"

"Because of who I am. Imagine what all those Order knights would have done if they'd known Carred Selenas was in town."

No reaction. Jada shrugged her shirt on, and Carred's heart lurched then. Their moment of joy had so quickly turned funerary.

"I'm frightened, Jada. Frightened of losing you."

"Well, you did a good job of losing my trust."

"I said I was—"

"But not my respect. Carred fecking Selenas! And my face between your legs, you sly old bitch! Guess that explains the scars."

"You said you liked them …"

"Like them even more now. Carred Selenas, I tell you! What're you doing hanging out with a dog like me?"

"Because …"

"You need a ship, I know."

"Because I love you."

"And all the others?"

"And all the others," Carred agreed. "I really do. It's why I'm acting like such a baby." For an instant she was once more the girl with the blue-eyed doll, screaming in the woods for her mother. "I don't want anything to happen to you."

"You idiot," Jada said with a sigh, slumping down on the bed beside her. "Nothing's going to happen to me. Least, not with you in this sullen mood and cold as a kipper's asshole."

Carred smiled as Jada ran fingers through her hair.

"Is that the slightest bit of interest I detect?" Jada said, brushing Carred's breast through her shirt. "I still can't believe it: Carred fecking Selenas!"

"Maybe."

"And now?" Jada kissed her neck, then gently nipped the skin.

A thrill ran through Carred. Heat bloomed within her. Next thing she knew, she was lying back on the bed, unbuttoning her shirt.

"You know me, Jada: I never like to break a promise."

Just after dawn, Carred stood on wobbly legs at the gunwale. The *Knackered Squid*—Jada had come up with the ship's name herself—had picked up a strong tailwind and was making good time.

"Should be there early," Jada said, handing her a steaming mug of cocoa. "Wind's normally a rancid bitch in these waters, but the fecking sea gods must be happy."

Or Talia, Carred thought. Was she a goddess yet?

"What's that?" she said, pointing with her mug at a black fleck on the horizon behind them.

"That there's the sea," Jada said with a grin. "Ah, that! That there's a ship, if I ain't very much mistook." She hollered up to the crow's nest: "Hillor, you blind fool! We got a floater athwart the prow!"

"Floater?"

"He knows what I mean."

Sailors scurried around the deck, trying to get a look for themselves. Maggow approached Carred, the dwarf-demon Malady in tow.

Up in the crow's nest a young lad called down, "Looks like a merchantman, Captain."

"Sure it ain't no Order galleon?"

"You think I don't know the difference?"

"Well, thank feck for that," Jada said, leaning on the gunwale and glaring across the waves. "Must've set out from Atya. Heading for the mainland, most likely Riem. Tacking against the wind like that, they must be in a hurry."

"Flag shows a balance and a coin stack," Hillor yelled down. He held a spyglass to his eye.

"Yanatos Holdings," Jada said. "Mineral prospectors and dealers in old shit and the like."

"Antiques?"

Before Jada could answer, Malady spoke: "Relics, artifacts. The sort of stuff sorcerers get wet over."

Jada wrinkled her nose at the dwarf. Some people she took an immediate dislike to, no reason given. In Malady's case, Carred could understand why. "And gentry in high places," Jada said. "Ain't nothing unusual. The Plains of Khisig-Ugtall are littered with ruins waiting to be plundered. I thought of setting up shop there a while back."

"Then why didn't you?" Carred asked.

"Couldn't be bothered. Too much digging, dust, sweat." Jada stared in the direction of the merchant ship, but kept glancing at Carred.

"What're you thinking?" Carred asked.

"About this Anskar character, and what you hope to achieve, going up against the Grand Master of the Order of Eternal Vigilance and a galleon full of knights."

"I've got plans."

"You have?"

"Not exactly. I'm waiting for more guidance."

"Guidance from who?"

"Queen Talia."

"I was going to ask you about her," Jada said. "But I had other things on my mind." Jada winked, and Carred felt heat flush her face.

She told Jada about Queen Talia speaking through Noni.

"From the realm of the dead?" Jada swallowed. Despite her great size, she looked like a frightened child. "No wonder the mainlanders call her the Necromancer Queen. And she's Anskar DeVantte's mother? So who's the father?"

"Good question." Carred had given it a lot of thought and was still none the wiser. "One thing's for certain: Anskar's no full-blood Niyandrian."

"Huh," Jada said. "Well, you know what they used to say about Queen Talia …"

"All of it nonsense. She had no demon lover. Talia hated demons. She was terrified of them. More likely it was a bastard mainlander."

"You make that sound worse than her consorting with demons," Malady said.

The old man, Maggow, gave her a warning look. She'd not exactly broken the rules he'd bound her with, but she was starting to push her luck.

"You think it was a knight?" Jada asked.

"No! She would never!"

"What if he defiled her?" Malady said, then flinched as Maggow raised a hand, fingers curled into a claw.

"Back to the cabin with you," the old man snapped. "You need to learn your place."

Malady scowled but put up no resistance as he led her away.

"The midget has a point," Jada said.

Carred shook her head. "I was always with her … or nearby. The Last Cohort protected her at all times. Our barracks was within the palace grounds."

"Maybe she conjured the baby out of her ass?"

Carred slapped her on the arm. "I'm being serious."

"Sorry," Jada said, looking back out to sea. At first, Carred thought she was sulking, but then she saw a smile curl Jada's lips.

"I still can't believe you fucked the Queen!"

"She was cold. Freezing."

Jada shivered and hugged herself.

"One-track mind!" Carred said, finishing her cocoa and tipping the dregs over the side.

"And you're a woman of your word," Jada said, grabbing her hand and leading her back below.

ELEVEN

THEY RODE FOR LONG hours across arid plains. The farther they got from Atya, the more filled with dirt and detritus the irrigation canals. The water had nowhere to go and the patches of lush greenery they had passed earlier were now brown and withered, the mud-baked plains giving way to ocher desert.

Ryala and the other two knights—Anskar heard her call them Hendel and Gaith—scouted ahead, while Niklaus du Plessis was a following speck, holding back to check for signs of pursuit from the manticarr. A beast like that, which had decimated an entire village, could easily slaughter their small group, and the thought of it kept Anskar alert in the saddle, straining his eyes and his sorcerous senses for any intimation of danger.

Orix, riding beside him, was a picture of misery, his thighs so chafed he swore he would get off and walk, even if it meant the manticarr eating him alive. Of course, he didn't, but the moaning and complaining seemed to help him press on.

"Have you ever seen a manticarr before?" Anskar asked Lanuc, who rode on his other side.

"Never, and I'd sooner keep it that way."

"What I don't understand," Anskar said, "is why the Grand Master is risking himself on this expedition? He's the head of the Order. Surely he could have sent someone else in his place, or brought more knights?"

Lanuc clenched his jaw and hesitated before replying. "Discretion in these matters is of the utmost importance. If the Tainted Cabal, or even the local chiefs, get wind of a large group heading out into the wilds, they might mount their own expedition."

"But they still might," Anskar said. "It's not as if we've passed without notice."

"Listen, Anskar, we live in a complex world. There are many shades of good and evil, and challenges that arise that sometimes require the Order to get its hands dirty. The Church of Menselas too. It's a sacrifice we have to make in order to preserve a delicate balance and, more importantly, to prevent the return of the demon lords—especially Nysrog, whom the Tainted Cabal wish to resume his dominion of the world. The Cabalists have been hunted for millennia and are now secretive and hidden, but they're still a threat. For that reason, a select few of our knights have been set aside for the path of sacrifice. We must risk the taint of corruption so that the rest may be preserved pure."

"We?" Anskar said. "You mean you?"

Lanuc nodded gravely. "The Grand Master too. Indeed, it's his function to bear the brunt of any taint."

"And Gadius? Ryala and the others?"

Lanuc nodded. "All have taken the oath to the Elder aspect of Menselas, and all have been instructed by the Elder's priests in the subtleties of the moral law."

"It has subtleties?"

"You think it's all black and white?"

If it was, Anskar was sure he was doomed. "I used to think it was."

"Didn't we all?"

"And do you all have special powers?" Anskar asked.

"Not necessarily powers. Some have the right … inclination for this kind of work. A few have powerful sorcerous marks and an aptitude for the tides most in the Church are not comfortable with."

"You mean Gadius."

"I'd ask how you know," Lanuc said, "but that would be disingenuous. But let's not speak of others so intimately. Perhaps you should ask yourself why the Grand Master saw fit that you should come along."

Anskar's mouth fell open, and he frowned at Lanuc. "Before we left, the Grand Master said—"

"Let's assume it's on account of your unusual aptitude for sorcery that you're here," Lanuc said. "Consider this a test, an examination. The Grand Master has his eye on you, Anskar. Just be careful. It's not always a good thing."

Anskar nodded, mind a jumble of unfinished thoughts. One leaped to the surface, though. "And Orix?" He glanced behind to find his friend had now dismounted and was walking bow-legged, straining to keep up. "Is he just here to keep me safe? Is that all he is to the Grand Master: my bodyguard?"

Lanuc shrugged. "I'm just glad to see that the Grand Master is taking Vihtor's request that Orix accompany you seriously. Perhaps, in his mind, the two of you come as a package."

It was an hour or so before twilight, when Wiraya's two moons hung hazily in the sky above the westerly sun, that Niklaus came cantering up to join the rest of the group. Ryala, Hendel and Gaith had not long returned from scouting ahead to report that they had spotted the escarpment Blaice had indicated on her map as a good place to make camp for the night. It was visible now, a long ridge slightly to the east of their route.

"What is it?" Blaice asked, pulling on her reins.

"It's stalking us," Niklaus said. "Hesitantly. It's still a long way behind."

"The manticarr?" the Grand Master asked. "How long have you known?"

"A couple of hours."

"And you didn't think to warn us?"

"What would you have done?" Blaice said. "Oh, I forgot, you'd have ridden out and slain it by yourself."

"The safety of my knights—"

"Is my responsibility during this expedition," Blaice said. "Or was there some other agreement I wasn't party to?"

The Grand Master turned to Gadius, then, exasperated, back to Blaice. "If I feel you are placing us in unnecessary peril, I will terminate our agreement."

"Probably quite wise," Niklaus said.

"Then we forget about the ruin until I can find another team to open it," Blaice said, picking at her fingernails. "I heard there were a few Tainted Cabalists down south. They're always good for a laugh, and they pay well. Better than you, that's for certain."

"You wouldn't!" the Grand Master said. "Menselas would not stand for it."

Anskar caught Niklaus's eye, noting the mischievous twinkle.

"I have a few contacts among the Jargalan Orgols," Niklaus said. "They always like the ancient relics. It's how they made and enslaved the Undying Ones. Sort of."

"The what?" Anskar asked.

"They don't teach you about the Undying Ones at knight school?" Niklaus asked. "Really, Grand Master, I'm disappointed."

"So what do we do?" Lanuc asked.

"Same as before," Blaice said, suddenly infected by Lanuc's seriousness. "We ride for the escarpment and set up camp."

"But won't it still attack us?" Anskar rested his hand on *Amalantril*'s hilt.

"Probably." Blaice adjusted her hat. "But I'd sooner make a stand on high ground than have it come upon us in the open."

Gadius cast his gaze to the south, and Anskar followed his example but saw nothing of the beast. "You're sure it's stalking us?" the acolyte asked.

"Are you calling me a liar?" Niklaus said.

"The thought never crossed my mind. But it is hesitant, you say? Perhaps it has tangled with armored warriors before and would sooner find easier prey."

"I doubt that," Blaice said. "The easier-prey bit, I mean. The heat coming through a manticarr's hide will roast a person encased in steel, and even if it didn't, its fangs can penetrate armor, and its tail will crush you."

"Then perhaps it senses our sorcerous power."

"Or maybe it's having too much fun watching us squabble and panic and is playing with us," the Grand Master said.

"Do you know," Niklaus said, "I'm starting to believe you *have* encountered a manticarr before."

Orix, who'd been stumbling along behind the main group, leading his pony by the reins, caught up. "I think there's something back there," he said, jabbing a thumb over his shoulder.

"Yes, we know," the Grand Master snapped. "Now shut up."

Anskar placed a hand on Orix's shoulder. "It's the manticarr," he whispered.

"Are we going to fight it?"

"I hope not. But be ready for anything. Keep your blade close, and at the first sign of trouble use your shield." But what good would their wards do against heat?

It was dusk by the time they arrived at the escarpment, a long sloping ridge that Niklaus insisted was man-made. "Alternating layers of soil and crystal," he explained. "From back when quartz was plentiful in the Plains. In fact, the original name was the Plains of Khisgantual, which mutated over the centuries into Khisig-Ugtall. It means 'The Shimmering Plains,' so named for the quartz glaciers that once covered much of the landmass."

"What happened to them?" Anskar asked. No one else seemed interested in what Niklaus had to say.

"Sorcerers is what happened. Quartz was, for the longest time, a fashionable component in their craftings, and there was a lot of sorcery back then. There had to be, on account of the demons constantly crossing over from the abyssal realms."

"So the sorcerers used it all up?"

"Some of it's still there," Niklaus said. "But most of it's buried deep below ground with the ancient cities. Actually, some of the subterranean ruins have plazas formed out of crystal. Buildings, even. Entire roads."

"How do you know all this?" Anskar asked.

Niklaus shrugged. "I read it somewhere. Probably one of my journals."

"You read it in your own journals? Doesn't that mean …?"

"You'd think so, wouldn't you? A journal is meant to be a

record of one's days, a sort of autobiography in episodes. But I can't remember the bulk of the entries I read, though the handwriting is undeniably my own. As is the humor. I can't tell you how many times I've laughed out loud while reading them. I'm not usually so forthright, but I have a good feeling about you, Anskar. And I trust my feelings."

It was a strange thing to say, but then again Niklaus was a strange man.

Dismounting, the group led their ponies up a switchback pathway cut into the scarp face with such exactitude, Anskar had to give credence to Niklaus's theory about the ridge being man-made. Niklaus left his horse at the bottom, slapping its rump and letting it run free.

"Not very bright," the knight Hendel said. "What with the manticarr out there."

"Oh, Nargil can look after himself."

"And I suppose he comes when you whistle," Hendel said.

"He does, and you won't believe how good his hearing is. He'll come from miles away."

Hendel chuckled, but Niklaus looked deadly serious.

Anskar hadn't paid either of Ryala's comrades much attention, but the good humor in Hendel's voice made him take notice. Hendel was short but broad-shouldered. He'd removed his helm when he climbed down from his pony and was completely bald. A long mustache dangled beneath his hook nose. He was bright-eyed and jovial, but the scars on both cheeks and those that crisscrossed his sword arm told a different story. This man was a veteran, a seasoned warrior, but he looked ill-suited to the white cloak and shining mail of a knight. Too rugged, Anskar thought, and his accent was drawling—provincial.

Gaith, the other knight, was much bigger, with arms that

bulged beneath the sleeves of his mail coat. His blond hair hung in greasy strands from beneath his helm, and his braided beard reached his belly. Anskar hadn't heard Gaith speak in all the time they'd been traveling. The man wore a perpetual scowl and looked ready to punch anyone who dared talk to him. Again, he seemed too rough, too unfinished to be a knight, but like Hendel, he wore the white cloak of the Order and was clearly someone the Grand Master trusted. Did they have special skills or abilities? Or perhaps the two were included in the mission for other reasons, perhaps the gray areas of their morality, the laxity of their adherence to the tenets of the faith.

As the path wound higher, Anskar could see that the scarp face was riddled with what looked like blowholes or lava vents—none of them man-made, judging by their appearance. Some were massive, opening onto caves with passageways leading deeper into the ridge.

"One of these caves might be better, defensively, than the top of the ridge," Lanuc suggested.

The Grand Master agreed and sent Ryala and Gaith ahead to explore a cave close to the summit. They returned some time later to report that there was an entire network of tunnels and caves leading right through to the far side of the escarpment, and that some of the tunnels headed down deep into the roots of the ridge.

"So we have options for escape should the manticarr come and be too much for us," the Grand Master said.

"Oh, I'm sure we won't need to flee," Niklaus said. "Not with you leading us."

"What could have caused the tunnels and caves?" Anskar asked.

Niklaus raised an eyebrow but said nothing.

"Volcanic activity?" Gadius suggested.

Several of the others nodded that they thought it was a reasonable theory, but as the group led the ponies into the cave, Niklaus whispered to Anskar, "I heard that they had some big beetles in this part of the world—mandibles that could eat through rock. I'm not saying it's what happened here, but it does get you wondering."

The main cave was indeed pocked with openings, some at ground level but many higher up, perforating the walls and even the ceiling in one or two spots. A natural plinth of rock stood at the center of the cave; it looked like sandstone to Anskar, though the glitter of tiny crystals made him think back to what Niklaus had said about the ridge's artificial construction. Atop the plinth were dried berries, brittle brown leaves, and the bones of a small rodent—probably a mouse. The ashes of a long-dead fire were strewn around the plinth's base.

"Someone's been here," said Niklaus.

Ryala showed them an even larger cave accessed by a massive bore hole to the rear, and that was where they stabled the ponies. In an alcove, an underground spring bubbled up into a basin that had been eroded by the water over years if not centuries, the rock just porous enough for there to be no overflow. The water was dirty brown.

"It's probably caused by iron," said Blaice. "And, as with the waters of the canals, it's likely safe to drink."

"Let the ponies decide," the Grand Master said. "They'll not touch polluted water, and if they do … well, rather them than us."

The animals were too skittish to drink until Gadius incanted some Skanuric words and touched his fingers to one of the cave's walls, leaving a warm illumination in the rock. Then a few of the ponies sniffed at the water and slowly began to drink. Once fitted with their feed bags, the ponies settled and everyone moved back to the front cave.

As darkness drove away the gray of dusk, Gadius moved about the cave mouth, scratching wards into the ground with the tip of a dagger. He chanted Skanuric words continuously, and Anskar sensed the bleed of dawn-tide essence from the acolyte's usually guarded repository. And then he felt something else: the virulence of the dusk-tide.

Anskar could only partially make sense of the cants and the calculations behind them. "What manner of wards are you setting?" he asked. "Do they alert you to anything approaching, or are they triggered when something crosses them?"

"Both," Gadius muttered. "So don't cross the threshold. If you need to relieve yourself, I'm sure there's a suitable cave or alcove back there somewhere. If not, go where the ponies are stabled."

"How far off will the manticarr be when you know it's coming?" Anskar asked, eager to learn. "Will we have time to prepare? And what will happen if it triggers the wards?" He stooped to whisper, "Did you use the dusk-tide for them?"

The acolyte craned his neck to glance at Anskar, eyes narrowed, teeth gritted as he maintained his concentration. "If there is anything you wish to add to my defenses …" He left the sentence unfinished. "Of course there isn't. You're a good knight, aren't you? Exemplary. You'd never sully yourself with the dusk-tide."

Anskar turned at a hand on his shoulder.

The Grand Master stared at him intently, mouth curled into a smile that was meant to be reassuring. "Remember, Anskar, any gifts Menselas has given you, he has given for a reason. Yes, for the most part we are told to stick to the benevolence of the dawn-tide, but Menselas is a god of five aspects. Some must walk the darker paths in order that others may thrive. It is a burden, a sacrifice that some of Menselas's children are fated to bear. The priests of the Hooded One, for example. If you think of anything you can do … to keep your comrades safe, I want you to know you have my full support. My protection."

Anskar was wary of revealing the full extent of his abilities. "Is that why you asked me to come along on this expedition? Because you think I have special talents?"

"I know you do. Gadius sensed them back at Branil's Burg, and I suspect Vihtor knows more than he's letting on. But don't worry. The Church of Menselas and our own blessed Order have always had need of those who would otherwise be condemned as afflicted. Your curse is our blessing. I know this is all new to you, but any time you use your abilities under obedience to the Order is to be considered an act of service, which Menselas will undoubtedly reward, if not now, then in the afterlife."

"But if I use such talents of my own accord?" Anskar asked.

"I wouldn't advise it. The temptations are too great, and there are powers abroad, in this world and in others, who might take undue notice. Trust me, Anskar: obedience is the key to your salvation."

Anskar sat sullenly at the back of the cave while the others ate dried rations and drank the brownish water from the spring in the stable cavern, which they had filled their canteens with. He couldn't stop thinking about what the Grand Master had said to him and wondering if he could do it—use his powers solely in the service of the Order, as an act of obedience. Part of him wanted to, wanted to believe that by so doing he would have found his place within the Order and within the wider Church that they all served.

But he was troubled by something else Hyle Pausus had said: that his curse was the Order's blessing. It made him feel that he would still be considered an oddity, a sinner, but that the Order was willing to make concessions, if only to benefit from the powers that lurked within him. He shook his head. The same way they benefited from the sale of Niyandrian slaves despite slavery being against the will of Menselas. The same way the Order was willing to desecrate a chapel consecrated to the aspect of the Hooded One in order to store wealth from the mainland, no doubt at an enormous profit.

If Menselas himself had appeared and told him to use his talents, he would have had no doubts; but being asked to compromise himself by people who, to his mind, had already compromised themselves and the integrity of the Order … How could he know that what they wanted was indeed the will of Menselas? But, equally, how could he know that refusing to comply wasn't a repudiation of that will? What if he was serving his own needs rather than those of the Order? Brother Tion had impressed upon him the need to regulate his own desires in order to serve the good of all, but Tion had also told him that sorcery was a sin, save for the limited use of the dawn-tide for shield casting and enhancing weapons and armor.

Anskar looked up at the sound of Orix's laughter. His friend seemed to be getting along well with Hendel, the bald knight with the long mustache. The way Hendel was bantering with Orix and chuckling at his own poor jokes made Anskar wonder if there was something stronger than iron-colored water in Hendel's canteen. Despite his laughter, though, Orix continually glanced toward the cave mouth, where Gadius was still fussing over his wards. Were they really that complicated to cast? Judging by the crude symbols Gadius had scratched into the stone and the paltry amounts of dawn- and dusk-tide sorcery Anskar had felt bleeding from the acolyte's repositories, he didn't think so. But maybe there was more to the wards than he currently understood.

Gaith chewed jerked meat while he sharpened the blade of a long-hafted axe he'd unbundled from his pony. Hardly the weapon of a knight, Anskar thought, but perhaps Gaith knew something he didn't about fighting manticarrs. The big man's arm muscles bulged as he worked the whetstone over the already-keen edge of his axe. He still wore a perpetual scowl, and his lips moved as he worked, giving Anskar the impression he was cursing.

Blaice was trying to engage Lanuc in banal conversation, but he was having none of it, ignoring her questions and instead asking the Grand Master his own.

Hyle Pausus looked nervous, casting furtive glances at Gadius as he checked his wards. Once, he caught Anskar's eye, winking and nodding as if to say he had every confidence Anskar would do the right thing when the time came. But would he? Could he? It was one thing being commanded to use his forbidden powers in the name of the Order, but another entirely to actually be able to call upon them at will. What if he froze at the critical moment? What if the powers refused to come, or if Menselas chose to block them?

Niklaus du Plessis was the only other person not eating. He stood, a dark presence in the shadows by one of the tunnel entrances. Perhaps he was getting ready to run away and leave them to their fate. His eyes darted all over the place, often returning to Blaice but never lingering long. All the while there was a sardonic grin on Niklaus's face, as if he found the whole idea of knights holed up in a cave waiting for a manticarr to attack faintly amusing. But why he should be amused seemed strange to Anskar. Niklaus said he had encountered such a beast before, and he had run away.

Outside, a horse neighed. It had to be Niklaus's stallion, Nargil, and it came from a long way off.

Niklaus's fingers curled around the hilt of his sword, but other than that, no one reacted. Anskar glanced at Gadius, but the acolyte seemed oblivious, still checking his wards, adding the odd extra scratch with a knife. So none of the wards had been triggered. Either they lacked sufficient range, or Nargil was just whinnying and there was no threat.

Nargil whinnied again, closer this time, a whinny that turned into a scream, and Niklaus drew his sword, the blade gleaming like a moonbeam even in the gloom of the cave. Hendel and Orix both paused mid-chew. Gaith set down his whetstone and hefted his axe. Lanuc, Blaice, and the Grand Master started to rise.

And then came a roar like thunder, and one of Gadius's wards fizzed and smoked.

"It's coming," the acolyte said.

"You don't say." Niklaus's eyes reflected the sorcerous light Gadius had brought forth from the cave ceiling, making them seem infernal and full of fury. "I liked that horse."

The roar sounded again, and this time it was followed by the pounding of the rock, the shaking of the cave as something huge lumbered up the escarpment trail.

TWELVE

ONE MOMENT MOONLIGHT, SILVERY and red, spilled gently through the cave mouth; the next it was eclipsed by shadow.

Anskar's hand trembled as he reached for the sword scabbarded at his side, *Amalantril*—moontouched. He winced at a blast of fetid breath laced with sulfur. It was accompanied by a low, rumbling growl. And then the shadow roared, a deafening clarion that threatened to split Anskar's skull. His hands flew to his ears.

The shadow erupted into flame, revealing a fiery face that was as human as it was bestial. Ember eyes flared, roving about the cave's interior, marking their prey. Black lips curled back from glistening fangs, a sinuous tongue flicking between them. Steam billowed from the beast's maw, and sparks of crimson flame danced across the skin of its face.

The head lolled forward atop a snaking and chitinous neck.

Beyond that, Anskar glimpsed the blazing conflagration that its gargantuan body had become with that terrible roar. A tree-trunk leg lifted, and a taloned paw crashed down on the cave floor.

Gadius's wards fizzed and popped all around the beast, forbidding its entry—all ignored. The other foreleg came down, and this time lightning forked up from the floor, singeing the manticarr's flame-wreathed hide. Its all-too-human face grimaced, and then it roared again as it lumbered into the cavern, a segmented tail flinging over its head, the tip a gnarly mass of flame-torched cartilage that swayed like the head of a snake.

As if sensing the culprit behind the wards, the manticarr's eyes fell upon Gadius, who backed away, voice trembling as he cried, "Anskar, do something. Do it now!"

Anskar felt the crushing weight of expectation, but he was too afraid to move. His eyes were riveted to the gigantic beast blocking the entrance, all four paws now firmly within the cave. Scorching heat rolled off it, causing him to back away toward the tunnel that led to the cave the ponies were stabled within. Even above the crackling flames that covered but did not consume the manticarr's flesh, Anskar could hear the terrified whinnying of the ponies. Crimson reflected from the steel of drawn weapons. All about him voices cried out in dismay and confusion, mail links chinked, boots scuffed across the floor. In among the chaos he heard the Grand Master's rasping voice in his ear. "Now, Anskar. Don't hold back. Menselas commands it!"

And Anskar was willing to believe him, only he couldn't move, couldn't think. He felt the straining of his repositories, knew they wanted to be unleashed, and still he stood there staring at this magnificent, monstrous, terrifying beast and knowing with all certitude he was about to die.

Orix screamed something in his own language and charged,

his ward sphere flaring to encompass him. A paw crashed down, striking the ward and sending sparks flying. The force of the blow flung Orix against a wall and his ward sphere fizzled out.

Hendel stepped in to protect Orix, weaving his sword in an arc that dazzled with reflected firelight, drawing the manticarr's gaze to him. And while the beast hesitated, Gaith bellowed a battle cry and leaped at it, swinging his axe in a scything arc. The blade bit deep into the manticarr's neck, sending up a spray of steaming blood. The axe haft burst into flame and Gaith cried out, releasing his grip. The manticarr reared and stomped, dislodging the axe head, which fell to the floor, not with a clatter but with a liquid slosh. The steel had melted.

Anskar tried to force his eyes shut, to wrestle his concentration inwards onto his repositories, but he was enthralled by the sheer elemental power of the manticarr; petrified by its heat, its presence, the power of its roar.

All around him was fire and flashing steel, the stomp of monstrous paws. The manticarr's tail lashed at Gaith, but the knight dipped from the waist and the tail's swollen end struck a wall. Rock cracked. Rubble cascaded down through the heat haze and smoke. Hendel rushed in and dragged Orix back. Ryala gingerly advanced on the beast, flailing about with her sword—more a distraction than anything. Gadius stumbled over the words of a cant as he backed away, trembling.

As the manticarr turned its ire on Ryala, Lanuc thrust her aside, yelling and waving his sword, and the beast lunged at him instead. A silver ward sphere sprang into life around Lanuc just as the manticarr's jaws snapped down. Sparks erupted from the ward, which flickered and then died. A huge claw came at Lanuc, but Ryala was beside him, her own ward sphere springing up in time, and unlike Lanuc's, her shield held.

Again, Anskar tried to reach inside for his tidal powers, and again his senses refused to retreat from all that was happening around him.

Niklaus still leaned against a wall of the cave, sword held limply in one hand, a look of faint amusement on his face. And Blaice … Blaice was nowhere to be seen.

Something flashed behind him, and Anskar turned to see the Grand Master surrounded by a ward of golden light. With his sword in hand, Hyle Pausus advanced on the manticarr; then, as it turned to face him, his ward sphere coalesced into a fist of coruscating force that shot out to hammer the beast in the face. The manticarr howled. One of its massive fangs clattered to the floor. Smoldering blood poured from its all-too-human nose. And then the tail whiplashed at the Grand Master, whose golden ward was momentarily down. Hyle Pausus's eyes widened. He started to scream. The club-like end of the tail powered toward him. There was a violent crash. Silver sparks flew. And Gaith, having dived in front of Hyle, was pitched through the air to slam into the wall, his ward sphere fizzling out as he fell limply to the ground.

The manticarr threw back its head and roared. The Grand Master retreated, his ward sphere re-forming around him, though it was silver now, patchy and pulsing on and off. Ryala and Lanuc—his ward restored—stepped in front of the Grand Master, the spheres of silver light that encompassed them merging to form a wall. Gadius, to one side, began to bark a cant as he gesticulated wildly with his arms. The manticarr swung toward him, and the cant froze on the acolyte's lips.

Something like a smirk crossed the manticarr's flame-tinged face, and then it chuckled—a deep, rumbling sound accompanied by a puff of soot and smoke. "Sorcerer," it said dismissively, its voice incongruous: mellifluous, almost feminine. "I thirst for your power."

"No," Gadius whimpered, stepping back until the wall prevented him from going any farther.

The manticarr advanced one slow step at a time, laughing now, full and throaty.

Gadius screamed, and in that instant, the barriers Anskar had placed around his repositories failed. The virulence of the dusk-tide and the poisonous brume of the dark flooded his veins. Pressure swelled within his skull, threatening to burst it apart.

The manticarr turned its blazing eyes on Anskar, and for a moment it looked shocked, confused. Dark flames suffused the skin of Anskar's hands. Wisps of blackness coiled from his fingertips. His whole body shook. His teeth chattered. Acid met fire as the two tides collided within him. And then the manticarr roared and sprang, its massive weight bearing down on Anskar, fangs gleaming, the heat of its crimson fire scorching.

It all happened in a split second, but it was enough for Anskar to realize he was dead. His powers had marshaled themselves into one almighty attack, but he hadn't thought to ward himself. On instinct, he cowered beneath raised arms, feeling the power flood harmlessly out of him. But just before the beast struck, Niklaus shot away from the wall so fast he was merely a blur. Anskar felt himself shoved aside. Glimpsed the flash of silver as Niklaus brought up his sword. Heard the manticarr's shrill and gurgling scream. Saw molten blood shower down over Niklaus, the beast's body fall on him, burying him beneath its crushing weight.

The manticarr writhed and roared and twitched and shuddered; then its mighty head slumped to the ground and it was still, save for the reflex twitches of its tail.

The gore-stained tip of Niklaus's sword protruded from the

creature's spine, no sign of the hand that held it, nor the man flattened beneath the monster's massive body. The flames that wreathed the manticarr guttered and died.

The light in the cave suddenly dimmed as ward spheres were doused. Lanuc warily approached the dead beast, touched its hide with the tip of his sword. The blade didn't melt.

And neither had Niklaus's sword melted when the beast was still alive, still burning with the heat of a forge. But as Anskar had already discerned, it was no ordinary blade.

"You all right?" Orix asked, approaching Anskar, clutching his shoulder and wincing.

Anskar nodded without conviction. "You?"

"Just bangs and bruises."

Anskar turned at the approach of footsteps. Blaice emerged from one of the tunnels. The Grand Master rolled his eyes and shook his head.

"I was trying to draw it off," Blaice said.

"But it refused the bait?" Lanuc asked. "You must be getting old, Blaice. Your charms aren't what they used to be."

She scowled at that, then looked at the beast. "Niklaus?"

"Dead," the Grand Master said. "As is Gaith."

"I beg to differ," a muffled voice said—Niklaus's voice, coming from beneath the manticarr.

"Impossible," Gadius said.

Lanuc, Ryala and Hendel touched their fingertips to their breasts, but the Grand Master merely watched Blaice for a reaction.

"He's a hard man to kill," she explained, though her hands trembled and her eyes were as wide as plates.

Niklaus's sword withdrew inside the beast, and it was followed by the sound of grunting and sawing. Viscous blood, crimson and still smoldering, pooled on the floor beneath the manticarr, and then Niklaus's gore-covered head appeared where his sword had been.

"Blood and damnation! Isn't anyone going to help me out?"

He should have been burned like melted wax.

Every bone in his body should have been crushed.

He should have been dead.

THIRTEEN

CARRED WAS STARTING TO wish she'd brought Noni to Atya. At least then there would be some chance that Talia might speak again from the realm of the dead and tell her what to do next.

The sun outside the eatery was scorching, and she'd sweated so much waiting for Jada to return she felt desiccated. Jada had been to the port a few times in the past and said she knew people—apparently so well that she'd been gone for hours, catching up. Hopefully she was having a better time than Carred. The food was passable, if creepy-crawlies with shells and big claws could be described as food; and the wine was actually rather pleasant—Jada had warned her not to drink the water. But she could barely bring herself to touch the fare, not when the servants who attended their table were Niyandrians. As for the company, Maggow spent more time clucking at birds than he did speaking with her, and the dwarf-demon, Malady, was a sullen presence who ate nothing, drank less, and answered her every question with, "Do I look omniscient?"—which she'd just done again.

"Last warning," Maggow said, opening his hand so the sparrow he'd been talking to could flit away.

"If I knew where Anskar DeVantte was, I'd tell you," the demon said. "Even without the bindings. At least then we could get this over with."

Carred pinched the bridge of her nose. It didn't help. "You have somewhere better to be?"

"You might say that."

"Oh? Important dealings in the abyssal realms?"

"Lost fucking opportunities," Malady said, crossing her arms. "Do you have any idea how degrading the summonings of humans are? You make slaves of us. If I could, I'd kill the lot of you."

"What's his name?" Carred asked.

"*She* is a demon lord with the House of the Black Sun. We were in the middle of negotiating when this shriveled old prick dragged me kicking and screaming through the veil."

"Negotiating what?"

Malady touched a finger to the side of her nose. "Demon business."

"I could compel you ..." Maggow said.

"That won't be necessary," Carred said. "Save it for things we need to know."

Malady raised an eyebrow, then gave a nod of respect and a half smile. More of a sly smile, really, that made Carred wish the demon hadn't smiled at her at all. "Nice to know someone's not a sadistic despot."

Maggow scowled and made a claw of his hand.

"Leave her be," Carred said.

"Give them an inch …"

"I said leave her. So, anything from the birds?"

"They are not trained like my birds back home," Maggow said, "but they tell me white-wings have left the city for the wilds. They could not be specific about who was among them."

"I assume that's bird speak for the Order's white cloaks? Which direction?"

"Headed where the red egg falls from its tree," Maggow said with a little smile. He was enjoying this almost as much as he enjoyed punishing Malady with whatever sorcery made her writhe and scream and try to scratch her eyes out.

"Why can't you just say 'west'?"

"Because he's a toady little ass-face with a stinking loincloth and rancid breath."

Carred turned as she stood. She almost hugged Jada, she was so relieved to see her. Almost hit her too.

"Couldn't have put it better myself," Malady said. "You might be a dismal rebel leader, but I admire your taste in women."

"Well?" Carred asked, but before Jada could fill her in, the nauseatingly obsequious turd—Malady's apt description—who owned the eatery bustled over, kowtowing as if Jada were a queen.

"Utri va Loesp, at your service, madam." He pulled out a chair for her. "Please be seated. Something to drink? Wine, like your friends, perhaps? Water?"

Jada's smile was forced—more of a grimace. She took note of the Niyandrian slaves waiting tables and shook her head.

Utri faltered, suddenly unsure of himself. "The menu, perhaps?"

"Tell him to piss off," Jada mouthed to Carred.

"She won't be dining with us," Carred explained. "Actually,

we're just leaving."

"Ah," Utri said. "Then I shall bring you the bill."

"If you must," Carred muttered at his retreating back.

"I've found us a guide," Jada said.

"Oh?" Carred said. "Who's that, then?"

Jada led them a little outside the city, to where several tents were pitched around a far larger tent with smoke pluming from a hole in its conical roof. A makeshift corral had been constructed from the lashed-together bones of some kind of vast beast. Penned within were a dozen plains ponies and a couple of dog-sized lizards, motionless, basking in the sun. Traguh-raj men and women sat in the entrances of the tents, scouring ringed armor with sand and vinegar, sharpening blades with deft strokes from a river stone, smoking something pungent and sweet-smelling in whittled bone pipes. Several paused what they were doing to watch as Jada led Carred, Maggow, and Malady into the big tent in the center.

Carred shielded her eyes against the glare from inside, blinked, but was still bright-blinded by shimmering colors that seemed to ignite the air. A man's voice, deep and full of grit, said a single word and the light dimmed to a rhythmic, throbbing glow—reds, yellows, greens, and blues that slowly came into focus as tubes of glass that hung down from the tent roof to rest their ends on the floor.

Malady hawked up phlegm and spat it out. Maggow glanced at her; then to Carred he muttered, "Be wary. Tidal forces." He indicated the circle of hanging tubes.

They were suspended from slender chains of silver and formed a circle of what looked like wind chimes beneath the circular opening. Each—there might have been as many as twenty, give or take, with a space of several inches between them—was as long as a spear, and within the glass, colorful liquids seethed and bubbled. Smoke without flames billowed up from the ground encompassed by the tubes, and inside the smoke a dark shape stood, tall and bulky.

"What's going on?" Jada demanded, one hand on the hilt of her cutlass.

"Going?" the dark form within the smoke said. "On?"

The smoke dissipated in thready whorls, revealing not a shadow-woven form but a man, barrel-chested and thick-bearded. His ruddy skin marked him as Traguh-raj, though his eyes glimmered with some orange inner light—and he'd spoken Niyandrian. As Carred met his gaze, though, the light dimmed and the eyes settled into a tawny brown. He wore a leather vest, sewn over which were scales and splints of mismatched armor. His arms were bare save for rings of bronze, gold, and silver around the biceps, and his legs were covered by striped pantaloons of yellow and blue, which might have looked comical save for his grim demeanor. His feet, though, were the most alarming of his features: they seemed carved from obsidian, the toenails plated with gold.

"What's with the lights in the tubes?" Jada asked.

"Nothing to concern yourself with," the bearded man said as he pushed his way clear of the circle formed by the tubes, letting them sway into one another, chinking and chiming before they stilled. "I have simply been consulting." His Niyandrian was fluent, though sounded odd with his Traguh-raj accent.

"Jada …" Carred started. She didn't like the feel of this one little bit.

"He said he'd help us. I know people who know him and say he can be trusted."

The bearded man gave a gleaming, toothy smile.

"But what's he want in return?" Malady asked. "Those tubes don't fill themselves."

"Do not speak without my leave," Maggow hissed, and the demon scowled but closed her mouth.

"Ah!" the bearded man said, widening his eyes and wagging a finger at Maggow. "Good. Very good. I can see we shall have to watch you!" To Carred, he said, "I am Bridnair, Chief of the Kutulki. You likely have not heard of us. We are a small community, wanderers all." Abruptly, he turned to Jada. "You have the beer?"

"Aboard my ship."

"That is not where it needs to be."

"We're in a hurry," Jada said.

"Everyone always is." Bridnair turned to face the circle of glass tubes and ran his fingers across them, eliciting a soft chime. Within the glass there was an agitation of bubbles, and filaments of lightning shot through the different-colored liquids.

"The people we need to find," Carred said, "already have a head start on us."

"Yes, and their destination is the ruins the Plains of Khisig-Ugtall have revealed," Bridnair said, still studying his chimes.

"You can see them?" Carred asked.

Maggow tsked and shot her a warning look.

"I was merely repeating what the Captain here told me," Bridnair said. "But, yes, now that I have consulted, I can see them. I know exactly where they are, and if your intention is to prevent them reaching the ruin, you will have to hurry."

"Or we confront them when they come back out," Jada said.

"If they come back out," Maggow said. "The ancient places are seldom unguarded."

That sent a twinge of panic through Carred's guts. What if Anskar was lost to the ruins? What would that mean for Niyas if the heir was no more? And what punishment would Talia exact for one failure too many?

"Even more reason for us to go now," she said. "They've not reached the ruin yet, right?"

"Correct," Bridnair said.

"Then there's still a chance."

Bridnair shrugged. "Anything can happen out in the plains." Again, his toothy smile. "But without the promised beer …"

"Bridnair's offered to send warriors with us, and ponies," Jada said. "But you know how I feel about riding." She looked to Bridnair. "So send some of your people with me back to the ship. We'll give them half the beer now, the rest when the job's done."

"You're not coming?" Carred asked. Her first reaction was fear of being alone with a bunch of Traguh-raj nomads—Maggow and the dwarf-demon did nothing to reassure her. But then she was relieved she wouldn't be putting Jada at risk.

Jada was still waiting for Bridnair's answer. "Well?" she said.

"Your lack of trust offends me."

"Then be offended," Jada said, turning away from him and making to leave.

"Very well," Bridnair said. "Half now. I will go with you," he told Carred. "But I prefer not to enter the ruins. Don't worry, though, we will get you there and will do as you wish until our arrangement is concluded."

"And we're paying him with beer?" Carred asked Jada. "What else?"

She glanced pointedly at the now fizzing tubes. *Tidal forces,*

Maggow had said. The essence that was drawn into a sorcerer's repositories.

A flash of white teeth as Bridnair again gave his smile. "You are sure you have the agreed amount of beer?"

"'Course I'm sure," Jada said.

"Then nothing else."

Carred only wished she believed him. Still, she'd been wrong about people before—Olana, for instance. Although, thinking about it, she'd suspected Olana of being a turncoat from the start, so not the best example. Talia, then. Bad example number two, she'd begun to think. Fult Wreave … No, she'd definitely been right about him, the pompous, backstabbing little runt.

She manufactured a smile for Bridnair. Swiftly ended it. There was no way her teeth were as white as his, and she could feel fragments of creepy-crawly shell in between some of them.

"All right, let's do this," she said.

Hopefully, for once, her gut feeling was wrong.

FOURTEEN

THEY DUG A SHALLOW grave for Gaith atop the escarpment and made a cairn out of the rubble dislodged by the manticarr to preserve his body from carrion beasts and worse. It had been the impact with the wall that had killed Gaith, according to Gadius. His neck had been snapped, his skull crushed, and several ribs broken.

Hendel openly wept as the Grand Master led the prayers to the Hooded One, and Anskar wondered if those prayers would be heeded, given the desecration of the Hooded One's chapel.

Afterwards, they returned to the cave, the air inside still warm from the manticarr's once fiery body. Pools of its blood smoldered, giving off an acrid stench laced with sulfur.

Anskar went through to the cave behind with Orix to feed the ponies, and the smell there—of dung this time—was even worse. Niklaus joined them, stripping off his clothes and armor so he could wash blood and gore from his body. They left him there and returned to the main cave where the others were settling down in their bedrolls in an attempt to sleep.

As Anskar unpacked his own bedroll and found himself a patch on the hard, rocky floor farthest from the manticarr's corpse, he caught Ryala glaring at him from beneath her covers, and he looked away in shame.

She was right to blame him for Gaith's death. They all were. The Grand Master had ordered him to act, to use his sorcery, yet he'd been frozen with fear. Perhaps he hadn't cared enough, he thought. Perhaps his abilities were purely self-serving. After all, what made him so special, so unique, was the boiling power of the dark-tide within him, a power that was associated with demons or the most notorious Niyandrian sorcerers, like Queen Talia, his mother.

Orix, beside him on the floor, was soon asleep and snoring loudly. Orix had proven himself brave beyond measure when he had attacked the beast. *Brave or foolish,* Anskar thought bitterly, but instantly chided himself. His friend had done better than he had, and he could tell that from the approving looks and pats on the back Orix had received from Lanuc, Hendel and Ryala. Only Niklaus hadn't in some way condemned Anskar's lack of action. Well, Niklaus and Blaice, but she was hardly one to talk.

Anskar didn't dream in the dry heat of the cave, though he did drift in and out of sleep. He was half aware of the rising wind outside, the occasional howling gust that seemed to come from the realm of the dead. Gradually, he became aware of the gentle caress of the dark-tide as it seeped into his already overfull repository, and in response he felt his repository expand somehow, grow deeper, as if it bored into the very depths of his being.

It was still dark when Gadius shook Anskar awake. "It will soon be dawn," the acolyte said. "We are assembling outside the cave to greet the tide."

Anskar grunted that he'd heard, then set about waking Orix. Both of them were stiff from sleeping on the rocky floor in their armor.

Orix winced as he breathed in and complained of pain in his ribs.

"You'll be fine," Anskar said. "Probably just bruised."

"Well, if you could help me out of my mail, I'll have a look," Orix grumbled.

"There's no time. The sky's turning to gray."

Lanuc smiled grimly as they stepped outside the cave to join the others of their Order: Hendel, Ryala, Gadius and the Grand Master. Hyle Pausus curled his lip when he saw Anskar, then quickly tried to mask it with a perfunctory nod. He was unhappy, Anskar could tell. Displeased.

Anskar kept his eyes averted, but he was certain they were all watching him, condemning him.

They partook of the dawn-tide, then returned to the cave, where Niklaus munched on blood sausage and black bread and took long pulls from his canteen—beer, judging by the smell. Certainly not water. Anskar dimly recalled Niklaus leaving the cave at night, presumably to retrieve supplies from his horse. He'd later overheard Niklaus tell Blaice that he'd found poor Nargil mangled, the horse's head half-melted.

Blaice was studying her map and chewing thoughtfully. She glanced up, raising an eyebrow at Anskar, then spat out something slimy and brown, spattering the wall. "Shriv," she explained. "Starts me off on the right foot."

Shriv was a narcotic herb. Anskar had learned as much from

Brother Tion and the other healers, who had warned him of its addictive properties. It was said to sharpen the mind and produce alertness, more even than tea or coffee.

After a bland breakfast of dried rations and iron-water from the stable cave, the group saddled their ponies and led them down the escarpment. Niklaus took Gaith's pony, complaining that ponies were for dwarves or children, and that it would ruin his carefully cultivated image.

As they mounted and traveled west, the Grand Master indicated for Anskar to hold back so that they could ride together at the rear.

"We should talk," Hyle Pausus said. There was tightness in his voice, but if he was angry, he softened it with a smile.

Anskar noticed Gadius looking behind at him, but the acolyte immediately turned back to face the way they were riding when Anskar met his gaze. He didn't trust Gadius. The acolyte had tried too hard to be friendly aboard ship, and he'd sounded irritated by Anskar's questions about his wards. And later, when the manticarr had attacked, Gadius had revealed his hand: yes, he was a sorcerer, but his powers were extremely limited, and he'd panicked, looked in desperation to Anskar for help that hadn't come.

"I wanted you to know," Hyle Pausus said, "that I am not disappointed in you."

Anskar bit down the retort that a servant of Menselas, especially the Grand Master of the Order of Eternal Vigilance, wasn't supposed to lie. It would have been wasted breath. From what he'd observed, lying was part and parcel of governing the Order, and he was sure the Grand Master would have a thousand and one excuses as to why that was necessary. All it showed Anskar was how foolish, how naive he'd been growing up, to take the statutes of the Order so seriously. They were all at it, he supposed, mitigating rules that were inconvenient—the Grand Master, Tion, probably even Vihtor.

"I tried to draw upon my repositories," Anskar said, "but the power wouldn't come."

The Grand Master nodded and chuckled to himself. "Fear will do that to a man."

Anskar remained silent. He was out of his depth, and while he knew he was sinking into a world far more complex and nuanced than any he had known at Branil's Burg, he wasn't certain yet what he was dealing with, what was expected of him.

"Rest assured," the Grand Master said, patting Anskar on the thigh as he rode alongside, "you have nothing to fear from me. Your talents make you valuable to the Order, precious in the eyes of Menselas. It is my function as your Grand Master to nurture those talents and bring them to fruition, but in order to do that, I need your trust. I need your obedience." He gave Anskar a penetrating stare. "Do not hide secrets from me, Anskar, for if you do, how can I help you?"

Anskar started to protest, but the Grand Master silenced him with a raised hand. "We will talk again, but for now, think on what I have said. Contemplate what happened back at the cave. Analyze the fight with the manticarr, how it made you feel, and how you can overcome such ... impotence in the future."

With that, Hyle Pausus kicked his heels into his pony's flanks and cantered toward the front of the group, where Blaice and Niklaus were in animated conversation and sharing the contents of Niklaus's canteen.

As they rode farther from the escarpment, the land continued to fall away into a vast depression. In his imagination, Anskar saw it as the bed of a long dried-out lake, a vast inner sea. The mud-baked ground was riddled with cracks and tufted here and there with spiny grasses and hardy thistles. Now and again he would spot the large conical shells of some kind of sea snail, the insides empty, presumably pecked out by birds long ago, or simply shriveled away to nothing by the sun. He saw fragments of broken rock, some of which displayed the fossilized remains of crab-like creatures and even fish.

By midmorning, with the sun blazing down upon them, Blaice led the group in among a forest of limestone columns that jutted up out of the arid earth—the result of erosion over hundreds, if not thousands, of years, she told them, claiming she had studied the nature of such things at one of Kaile's prestigious academies in her youth.

Anskar couldn't quite work out when that might have been, for Blaice's age was hard to determine. She was hard-bodied and trim, her face striking and angular, yet the beginnings of crow's feet around her eyes told him she was no longer young, if not exactly old. Besides which, she seemed possessed of boundless energy and enthusiasm for their journey, giving Anskar the impression that she would have sooner pressed on until they reached the ruin, rather than put up with the inconvenience of having to stop to eat and rest.

A narrow canal threaded its way between the limestone monoliths, pooling in a reservoir shaded by the stones. They dismounted there and let the ponies drink, and to Anskar's great relief, the Grand Master gave his permission for the knights to remove their armor. Orix winced as Anskar helped him out of his mail and padded gambeson, then lifted his shirt to reveal purplish bruising around his ribs, yellowing at the edges.

In turn, Orix helped Anskar out of his armor, and then they settled down in the shade of a monolith to share out rations before going to drink from the reservoir and filling their canteens.

Niklaus wandered among the limestone pillars, sipping from the metal flask he kept in his boot. He kept glancing toward Blaice until she noticed, and then she strolled over to join him. The two wandered farther from the group, speaking in hushed voices.

Gadius sat sullenly by himself, not eating and barely even drinking. His ward sphere sporadically flashed into existence around him, then winked out again, giving Anskar the impression he was troubled, his confidence shaken by the ineffectiveness of his sorcery against the manticarr.

The Grand Master perused some documents he'd brought with him in his saddlebags, while Lanuc tried to engage him in conversation. Ryala and Hendel remained standing, slowly scanning the area as they ate, neither having removed their armor. Either they expected more trouble, or it was their assigned duty to always be prepared.

When Niklaus and Blaice returned, both chuckling at some private joke, the Grand Master glanced up from his papers.

"How much farther to the ruin?" he asked.

"We'll be there before nightfall," Blaice said, "but only if we leave now."

The Grand Master stood, gesturing with his papers. "Hendel, help me back into my armor."

"Feeling insecure, Grand Master?" Niklaus asked.

"Unless you're offering to carry it," the Hyle Pausus said, "I have no choice but to wear it."

He had a point, Anskar realized. The ponies weren't equipped with hooks and ties for the Grand Master's breastplate and helm, and there was nowhere for the rest of them to drape their mail. With a sigh he caught Orix's eye. "Come on, let's put it back on."

Refreshed but barely rested, they set off again, and gradually the forest of limestone pinnacles gave way to a plain flanked by towering mesas whose flat summits must have been two hundred feet above the floor of the valley between them. In the shelter the mesas provided from the light breeze, the air grew dry, the temperature scorching, and the valley was filled with the background susurrus of copper-colored snakes that Blaice described as "death adders."

"Their venom is quite useful," Niklaus quipped as he rode by one of the serpents coiled about a rock.

"Useful for what?" Orix asked, but Niklaus didn't reply.

An hour or so along the valley, Ryala rode back from the front to inform the Grand Master they were being watched. Anskar followed her gaze to the top of the mesa on the right, where three people mounted on ponies sat, following their progress. Sunlight glinted from tackle and the tips of spears.

"Traguh-raj," Orix muttered.

He was right. Even from this distance, Anskar could make out the tint to their skin—there were two women and a man.

And then he looked again, startled that what had been a vague and blurry impression was now so much clearer, as if the distance between him and the watchers had somehow lessened, or more likely, as if his eyes had adjusted. He'd noticed several times how his vision was growing much sharper over long distances—ever since the kidnap attempt at Branil's Burg.

One of the women atop the mesa wore a conical helm and scale armor. The man was built like a bear, with a beard to match. His armor was cobbled together from mismatches of metal. The other woman was dark-haired and her skin was crimson, not the dusky-red of the Traguh-raj.

"You think they'll follow us to the ruin?" the Grand Master asked.

"Probably ... not," Blaice said uncertainly, glancing at Niklaus.

"The tribes here are superstitious pants-pissers," Niklaus said. "No offense," he added for Orix's benefit. "They won't follow us to the ruin, and if they do, I'll politely ask them to leave." He stroked the hilt of his sword, smiling as he did so, then closed his eyes for a second and shuddered.

Niklaus was right. The three riders didn't move from their spot atop the mesa as the group continued into the west, and when Anskar looked back a while later, the riders were still there, black specks in the receding distance.

But why had they come? The presence of a Niyandrian woman among them had unsettled Anskar. "Are there Niyandrians here in the Plains of Khisig-Ugtall, living among the Traguh-raj?" he asked Orix.

Orix shook his head and laughed in response. "Are you joking? Niyandrians living with my people! Maybe you've not heard, but Niyandrians and Traguh-raj don't exactly have a good history between them. In ancient times, the Niyandrians enslaved the Traguh-raj, and that memory's still raw today."

From what Anskar had seen in Atya, those roles were now reversed.

"But they interbred," he said, referring to the reddish tint of Traguh-raj skin. Orix nodded. "And you seemed to get along fine with Sareya and the other Niyandrians at Branil's Burg."

"Had to," Orix said. "They're consecrated to Menselas. We're all the Five's children." He spat out a wad of phlegm.

"What is it?" Lanuc said, guiding his pony alongside Anskar's.

"One of the riders watching us was Niyandrian," Orix explained.

Lanuc shrugged, though he still cast a nervous look behind, where the riders were no longer visible. "Niyas resumed some degree of trade with the Plains of Khisig-Ugtall after the war, once the mainland blockade was lifted. Probably some merchant who found a better life here." He touched his heels to his pony's flanks and rode up to confer with the Grand Master.

"That doesn't make a whole lot of sense," Orix said.

"No, it doesn't," Anskar agreed. "Why would a merchant watch our progress?"

"Maybe she has a stake in the ruin?" Orix suggested lamely.

Anskar didn't respond. He was afraid that by giving voice to his fear it might translate into reality.

Or maybe she followed me from Niyas.

FIFTEEN

CARRED CLUTCHED THE REINS of her pony so tight they cut into her palms. Already she'd lost sight of the Grand Master's group. But she had seen two other riders with the knights, neither wearing a white cloak—a surprise she'd not expected. One was a woman in a broad-brimmed hat, the other a man dressed in black. By the looks of them, these two were not the sort of people the Order of Eternal Vigilance was supposed to associate with. And, despite being as sensitive as a brick, she'd felt the bristling essence of powerful repositories from one of the two younger knights. It had to be him: Anskar DeVantte. *Melesh-Eloni.*

So close, yet so far! If it were up to her, she'd have galloped down the track that had brought them to the top of the mesa, ridden straight at the Grand Master's band, and …

And what? Whisked Anskar from right under their noses? Cut them all down singlehandedly in a madcap attack? Like she had at Naphor? As defeats went, that was her best yet, but at least then she'd had the choice. Shitty as it was, it had been *her* plan.

She didn't need to look to know that the Traguh-raj bitch Doon Ma'jah still had a death grip on the hilt of her broadsword, still watched her with slitted eyes, daring her to contradict Bridnair. His bodyguard had joined them and never left his side.

"You are too rash, Carred Selenas," the Chief said, scratching his thick beard in a manner that made him seem smug and condescending. "These knights of the Order of Eternal Vigilance ... they are an insufferable curse—pious, pompous hypocrites—but I have seen them fight, and they are not without defensive sorcery."

"I know that." Eldrid DeVantte had demonstrated just how effective knights could be back at Naphor, and here she was dealing with the Grand Master and presumably an elite force.

Bridnair's eyes were glittery and hard, and she wilted under their glare.

Was it just her imagination, or the circumstances? He looked bigger to Carred since the three of them had ridden to the top of the mesa, leaving the rest of their group behind. Without Maggow—and even the demon, Malady—she felt exposed and more vulnerable than she'd allowed herself to feel since she'd run away from home and joined the Last Cohort. Bridnair now carried himself with the air of a man used to getting whatever he wanted, and with the brute strength to take it if necessary. And that didn't account for whatever sorcery he had at his command, because there had been something disturbing about the way he'd apparently communed with the glass chimes back at his tent—chimes Malady said didn't fill themselves ... with the forces of the tides. And Bridnair had brought his chimes with him, bundled up in leather and carried by a spare pony they'd brought for the purpose. It was some slight relief to Carred that he'd left his pack animal at the foot of the mesa with the others.

Alone, against a man like this, she was realistic enough to know she had zero chance of coming out alive. Less with the equally brutish—yet considerably more smelly—Doon Ma'jah on her other side.

She might have been a dismal gambler, but she knew when she had a dud hand.

"Fine. We do it your way."

Bridnair gave his annoying broad smile. Carred indulged the image of shattering his over-white teeth with her sword pommel.

"You will thank me for my prudence later."

"Sure I will."

"Let the ruin weaken them," Bridnair said. "And let them discover whatever lies inside."

"So you can take it for yourself? I thought you only wanted beer."

"I am no mere profiteer, if that is what you mean," Bridnair said. "The secrets of the Plains are a passion of mine."

"You surprise me."

"Hah!" he said. "That is as it should be."

"I was being sarcastic."

"Well, don't," Doon Ma'jah said, leaning across from her saddle.

Carred stifled the urge to fan her hand beneath her nose. Theltek's testicles—they say it wasn't just a hundred eyes he had—her breath stank of rotting mutton. "Thank you," she said. "I always appreciate good advice. And your Niyandrian's really very good. Not as good as Bridnair's, but then again, mine's probably not either, and I'm from Niyas."

Doon Ma'jah scowled.

"Seriously, though, Doon, I can't thank you enough. Left to my own devices, I'm such a simpleton. Honestly, I don't know how I manage to get dressed in the morning."

"One more word out of you—"

"Gentle, Doon," Bridnair said. "Carred Selenas is our employer, remember?"

"Don't worry on my account," Carred said. "It's easy to forget. So, what now?"

"Now we follow," Bridnair said. "At a distance. And then we set our trap."

"Which is?"

"That remains to be seen."

He turned his pony and rode for the far side of the mesa. Doon Ma'jah gave Carred a nod full of warning and went after him.

"I'll bloody kill you for this, Jada," Carred muttered as she wheeled her pony and followed.

SIXTEEN

THEY RODE ON, STICKING to the shade of one of the mesas, given that the center of the valley exposed to the sun was sweltering. At one point they were forced to find a ford of accumulated detritus across a narrow canal that split the valley in two. The canal presumably flowed through the roots of the mesas, which begged a number of questions Anskar tried not to dwell on. Likely, only Niklaus knew the answers, but how reliable was he, a man who could scarcely remember the things he'd written in his own journals?

An hour beyond the crossing, Ryala, riding at the front now, held up a hand for the company to halt. There had been rockfalls on either side of the valley, the walls of both mesas here sloping banks of rubble that converged in the center, making the route impassable.

"We dismount here," the Grand Master said, "and proceed on foot. We must be near now."

Blaice nodded her agreement and climbed down from her saddle. "Damage caused by the earthquake. The fissure containing the ruin is on the far side of the landslide."

"Hendel, stay with the ponies," the Grand Master said. "Lead them back to the canal we crossed and wait for us there."

Hendel glanced at Ryala, the merest of frowns crossing his face, but he quickly buried it beneath an expressionless mask. "Grand Master," he said with a salute.

"On second thoughts …" the Grand Master said—he had noticed Hendel's hesitation, followed by the iron-clad act of obedience. Hyle Pausus looked over the other companions, his gaze eventually settling on Orix. "You stay behind instead. Ruins are dangerous places, and we may have need of Hendel's strength and experience."

"But—" Orix said, glancing at Anskar for support.

"Vihtor sent Orix to watch over Anskar," Lanuc said.

"Yes, I know." A tight smile crossed the Grand Master's face. "And he asked you, his old friend, to look out for Anskar, too. Because, of course, the rest of us are incompetent. Or is it that Vihtor Ulnar does not trust me with his special charge?"

Lanuc swallowed thickly before replying. "I'm sure that is not the case, Grand Master. Vihtor is your loyal servant, as am I."

"Good, then you won't mind staying behind with Orix to take care of the ponies."

Lanuc's mouth hung open before he eventually mustered a reply. "I … Grand Master, I …"

"Conflicted loyalties?"

"No, Grand Master."

Hyle Pausus rolled his eyes at Anskar. "See what I have to put up with? Now, Anskar, we will soon arrive at the ruin. Let us hope you are better able to perform this time."

"I'll do my best, Grand Master."

"Indeed you will. Of course, it may be that we will simply stroll into this ruin and walk out with that which we seek."

"The relic?"

"You want to know what it is? Blaice can explain."

She whipped off her hat and used it to fan her face. "According to my contacts—and this is just a theory based upon the historical records and the proto-Skanuric writing I discovered on the outside of the ruin—we may be looking at a portal stone."

The Grand Master gave Anskar a knowing look, while behind him, Niklaus shook his head and took a swig from his flask. "You see why this is so important now?"

"No …?" Anskar had no idea what they were talking about. Though presumably a portal stone opened a portal. But to where?

"Historians believe that the ancient people," Blaice said, "those who still haunt the old places, may have devised a way to travel between the worlds. A portal stone is thought to create a doorway from Wiraya to another plane."

Ryala and Hendel pressed in closer to listen. Gadius tucked his hands inside the sleeves of his robe and affected a bored expression. It gave Anskar the impression the acolyte was still smarting from the failure of his wards back at the cave, and he was now trying to look superior, as if portal stones were nothing special to him. Orix and Lanuc had already moved away to tether the ponies together in preparation for leading them back to the canal that crossed the valley.

"What plane?" Anskar asked.

"The only one, other than our own, we have any knowledge of," Gadius said, as if an idiot should have worked it out by now. "The abyssal realms."

"It is believed," the Grand Master said, "that the ancients

devised portal stones in an attempt to colonize other planes of existence, but instead the other planes—or rather, the abyssal realms—decided to attempt to colonize our own."

The demon wars, thought Anskar. Tion had regaled him with the stories when he was a child; tales that were intended to make the listener draw back from wrongdoing.

To Anskar's surprise, it was Niklaus who replied. "Demons came. Sorcery repulsed them, but not without cost. In my travels, I've seen the evidence of countless civilizations that rose from barbarism to make the same mistakes as their predecessors, either in how they fought the demons or in how they emulated them."

"You've explored the ruins before?" Anskar asked.

"Many times." Niklaus shrugged and took a sip from his flask. "Wiraya is riddled with them. Most from after the struggle with Nysrog, but the really interesting ones are those from long before."

"Like this one," the Grand Master said, eyes flashing with irritation, as if he thought it supremely impertinent that Niklaus had spoken.

"So the portal stones were responsible for the horrors of the past?" Anskar asked. "Without them, there would have been no demons invading Wiraya? No wars or the cataclysms that followed?"

Wiraya, as far as he could gather from his lessons, had endured many such cataclysms, during which entire civilizations had been reduced to pockets of survivors scrabbling out an existence amid the barbarous wastelands. Each time, people had rebuilt, uncovering the secrets of the past and progressing in the same direction as their ancestors, only to one day make the same devastating mistakes.

"There have always been demons," Niklaus said with a scowl before tilting his head and taking a long pull from his flask.

"The portal stones just made it that much easier for them to cross the veil between worlds," Blaice said. "Usually there's need for a summoning."

Gadius snorted. "Do you have any idea of the power a sorcerer would need to wield to effect the summoning of a demon from the abyssal realms?"

"More than you'll ever have," Niklaus said.

"A single portal stone can open the floodgates to the abyssal realms," Blaice said. "Hundreds, if not thousands, of demons could come pouring through. Thankfully, at the end of the demon wars, the ancient people destroyed the portal stones."

"Save for one," the Grand Master said. "If Blaice's contacts are to be believed, and this ruin does indeed contain the sole surviving portal stone, then just think of the repercussions if it should fall into the wrong hands."

"Depends how you define the wrong hands," Niklaus said.

The Grand Master shot him a black look. "Any that are not ours. Only Menselas can ward us from the evils a portal stone might unleash. Which is why such relics must be delivered to the Church. You said you agreed with me when you so conveniently turned up. Are you telling me you've changed your mind?"

Niklaus took a swig from his flask. Cursed. Upended the flask. Empty.

"So the Church will destroy this portal stone?" Anskar asked.

The Grand Master hesitated before answering, "Of course."

"The really troubling question," Niklaus said, "is why the ancient people left one of the portal stones. Why didn't they destroy it with the others?"

The Grand Master shrugged. "That is not relevant."

"Let's hope not," Niklaus said.

"We can stand here and speculate all day," the Grand Master said, "or we can get on with the task at hand." To Lanuc he said, "Wait for us until this time tomorrow. I will send you word before then should we need longer in the ruin. If you hear nothing from us, do not come looking for us. Return to Atya, and send word to Bishop Rowasoth in Sansor via the Ethereal Sorceress. He will decide what to do."

"Don't look so worried," Ryala said to Anskar, a fake smile plastered over her face. "I'll look after you. We both will, won't we, Hen?"

Hendel clapped Anskar on the arm. "You'll be fine, son. I've got your back."

Anskar watched Lanuc and Orix lead the ponies back down the valley. He felt exposed, alone without them. And with the Grand Master's expectations weighing heavily upon him, he felt a fraud.

The vast piles of rubble sloped down from the mesas on either side of the valley, at their highest points a good fifty feet above the valley floor, at their lowest, where they met in the middle, just the height of two grown men. It made sense that the group should climb over the landfall where it dipped, and that was just what the Grand Master commanded them to do. It meant stepping away from the shade of the mesas, but thankfully the piled rubble provided a little shade of its own.

Blaice went first, scrambling over the rock bank with effortless grace, and Anskar thought how much easier it would be for him without the armor the Grand Master insisted all his people wear.

Niklaus went next, as sure-footed as a mountain goat, then the Grand Master and Gadius. Anskar followed them, with Hendel and Ryala bringing up the rear.

As Anskar climbed, he frequently had to stop to wipe stinging sweat from his eyes. His fingers and palms were abraded by the rocks, and once or twice his sword became tangled between his legs and he had to pause to resituate it.

Some of the rocks had split open to reveal the fossilized forms of strange birds and lizards and shells within. As he reached the summit and began to crab-crawl down the far side, he caught sight of what appeared to be a fragment of the fossilized jaw of some monstrous beast, the fangs as long as swords.

When he reached the bottom, he took a swig from his canteen as they waited for Hendel and Ryala to catch up, then the group followed Blaice's lead across the rubble-strewn floor of the valley.

A spiderweb of fissures had fractured the ground between the mesas and for as far as Anskar could see in front. On one side, the cracks terminated at a sizable rupture in the rock face. Below this, the ground had fallen away into a deep cleft that must have opened up during the earthquake.

Blaice led them to the edge of the ravine and stood peering down into the depths, where dust motes glittered in the failing light of day. At the bottom, some thirty feet below, an alcove had formed beneath an overhang that protruded from the mesa's exposed roots, and in the gloom within, a metallic surface glinted.

"That's it?" the Grand Master said uncertainly. "That's a door?"

He was right to be perplexed. To Anskar's eyes, all the earthquake had revealed was a large metal panel—door-sized, he had to admit—fused with the rock face.

"Peculiar, isn't it?" Blaice said. "You'd have thought the ruin would be high above ground, given that a mesa is formed by the erosion of the ground around it."

"Unless it was there before the mesa was formed," Niklaus suggested, "and the erosion brought it to light. Either that, or the mesa's not natural. Perhaps it was deliberately built on top of the ruin—if, indeed, 'ruin' is the appropriate word for whatever lies beyond that door. And yes, to answer your question," he said to the Grand Master, "it is a door, albeit a particularly tricky one, most likely difficult to open."

"To those without the know-how," Blaice said, then started off down the scree bank.

At the bottom of the fissure, the group reassembled in front of the metal panel. It was orange-tinted—probably orichalcum—and it was square, the bottom edge still hidden behind the limestone of the mesa that cladded it. It must have been ten feet by ten feet, and it struck Anskar as an odd shape for a door. Either it was that shape and size so that wagons or whatever transport the ancients had used could pass through, or the people themselves had been giants, as wide as they were tall.

There were symbols and sigils engraved all over the panel—some letters that were recognizable as Skanuric, but twisted together to form new and composite forms. Other symbols he didn't recognize: they were more linear—cuneiform—than the typical swirling Skanuric script. He could make no sense of the arrangement of letters and symbols, nor how they had been made. For though he'd at first thought they had been engraved, he now saw that they stood out in relief from the surface of the orichalcum, yet some cunningly employed use of light and shadow made them appear cut into the metal. When he peered closer, he saw that the letters were transparent, and that within each a viscous fluid speckled with what looked like crystal dust oozed in perpetual motion. Where the crystal dust caught the sun's light, it sparkled as if on fire.

"Would you care to open it?" Blaice said in a voice of saccharine sweetness to Gadius.

"Just get on with it," the Grand Master said. "It'll soon be dusk, and I for one don't want to risk a night in the open."

"What about Orix and Lanuc?" Anskar asked, suddenly afraid for his friend.

"I'm sure they'll cope," the Grand Master said. "Now, get this so-called door open, if indeed you can."

"Oh, I can open it all right," Blaice said. "Only, it might take some time."

The Grand Master rolled his eyes—a mannerism that struck Anskar as all too frequent for the pious head of a holy order.

"Don't worry about the others," Hendel whispered in Anskar's ear. "Lanuc is highly skilled in such matters."

"What matters?" Anskar asked, and though he kept his voice low, Gadius turned a glare on him.

"Surviving the things that stalk the dark," Hendel said. "The Plains of Khisig-Ugtall have their unique challenges, but nothing Lanuc hasn't faced before."

"Save the manticarr," Ryala said, having been listening in.

"That was unforeseen," Hendel said, and for a moment his eyes looked haunted by the loss of Gaith. "But didn't they say it was summoned by the wards of this ruin, which were activated during the earthquake?"

Ryala glanced at Niklaus and then Blaice, who was running her hands over the script on the orichalcum panel while muttering under her breath—Anskar assumed it was a cant, but he could sense no repository within her.

"Those two say a lot, but not much of it's true," Ryala said.

"How do you know?" Anskar asked.

"I don't know. I just feel it. Call it a talent, if you like, but watch your backs, both of you."

Long shadows fell over the fissure as the sun dipped lower in the sky, and Anskar began to worry that, if Blaice didn't get them inside the ruin soon, he would be exposed to the dusk-tide in front of his comrades. Not that it should matter, he told himself, given that the Grand Master already knew about his forbidden talents. But even so, the prospect of absorbing the dusk-tide in company made him feel sullied, ashamed. Years of being told that all but the dawn-tide was evil in the eyes of Menselas had left its mark.

He became aware of Niklaus conferring with Blaice, translating one or two symbols for her as the Grand Master stood by impatiently and Gadius shook his head and tsked. Niklaus stepped back, crossing his arms and watching as Blaice resumed her muttering, this time touching her fingers to a sequence of letters. When nothing happened, she threw a look over her shoulder at Niklaus.

"Trochaic substitution?" he suggested, and Blaice thought about that for a moment—whatever it meant—then commenced her chant and the touching of the letters again.

And once more nothing happened, though this time Anskar heard Niklaus humming to himself and tapping out a rhythm on the pommel of his sword. "There was some interruption of the meter," he told Blaice, "at the other ruins of this kind I entered. A wise man got them to open up for me, but I can't for the life of me recall his name."

"You've been inside ruins of this period before?" Gadius said disbelievingly.

"Several times," Niklaus said, then resumed his humming.

"When?" Gadius pressed. "Surely the Church would have heard of it."

"Ah, but back then the Church of Menselas was but a twinkling in the eye of the charlatan who invented her," Niklaus said, and before anyone could react, he exclaimed, "Pleiham Ponsair!"

Blaice frowned, then squinted at the symbols on the door. "I don't understand," she said. "Which letter?"

"Not the letters," Niklaus said, "the wise man who got me into the ruins. His name was Pleiham Ponsair. Poor bastard's probably nothing but dust by now."

"He's dead, then?" Blaice said.

"I killed him. Several times, actually."

"So what was the point in mentioning him?"

"No point. Just old memories rising to the surface like bog gas. Ah!" he said, stepping to Blaice's side and jabbing a finger at three of the letters. "Omit those ones and substitute a pause of equivalent length."

"Why?" Blaice asked, confused.

"*Indir, Yanuk, Nadyroth,*" Niklaus said as he touched the letters. "All negative consonants—proto-Skanuric is a weird language, to put it mildly. It's a kind of code, a recipe, if you like, for which there are customs to let you know what to keep in and what to leave out."

"And this Pleiham Ponsair told you that, did he?" Gadius said.

"I think so," Niklaus said as Blaice began her muttered chant again, once more touching the symbols with her fingertips. "Probably. I can't remember."

Gadius shook his head and turned to the Grand Master. "Perhaps I should have a go after all. This pair are clearly quite—"

"Got it!" Blaice said, stepping back from the door as it juddered and shook, then started to sink into the ground.

SEVENTEEN

THE EARTH BENEATH ANSKAR'S feet shuddered as the door descended and finally disappeared below ground. In its place, a square of darkness remained. It both called to him and repulsed him. His guts clenched at the thought of entering that absolute emptiness, and it was all he could do to stop himself manifesting his ward sphere.

Blaice stepped back from the threshold and shot Gadius and the Grand Master a triumphant grin.

"Don't mention it," Niklaus said. He had been the one to provide Blaice with the clues that enabled her to open the door. Niklaus appeared to be taking it all in his stride. He leaned against the rock face beside the opening and reached into his boot for his flask, then apparently remembered it was empty. "Blood and damnation!"

"Gadius, a light," the Grand Master said with a snap of his fingers.

The acolyte stepped up to the entrance and held out his palm. A sphere of golden light burgeoned there, but when he thrust it into the darkness, it went out. Gadius tried again, and again his light was swallowed by the dark. He glanced helplessly at the Grand Master, who sighed and glared at Anskar.

"Suggestions?" the Grand Master said.

Anskar stared back at him blankly. What was he supposed to do?

"No, of course you don't."

"If I might …" Niklaus said. He stepped inside the entrance, where he was instantly lost to sight. A moment later, the darkness dissolved as motes of silver sprang to life, flaring ever brighter until they merged into a stark and shimmering light.

Anskar shielded his eyes from the glare, but when they adjusted, he could see the blurry outline of Niklaus standing in the entrance, facing the right-hand wall and fiddling with something there. Gradually, the intensity of the light diminished, leaving only a steely glow that was easy on the eyes.

"There," Niklaus said, rubbing his hands together. "I'll bet you're glad you have me along, aren't you?" The question was aimed at the Grand Master, who merely sniffed and set foot into the passageway the strange light had revealed.

Anskar bit down on his bottom lip, angry at himself for his hesitation, for the fear that had paralyzed him back at the cave and that threatened to unman him again now. He strode forward, intending to follow the Grand Master inside, but bumped into Ryala. She snarled and shoved him back. Hendel caught him by the shoulders, gave him a reassuring smile.

"After you," Niklaus said to Gadius.

The acolyte scuttled inside behind Ryala.

Blaice approached Niklaus and they exchanged hushed words.

Niklaus nodded, then pinched her buttock as she entered the ruin next. Blaice spun round, and Anskar thought she was going to slap Niklaus; but instead she grabbed his crotch and squeezed. When she let go and went inside, Niklaus grinned at Anskar, but it was a forced grin. Sweat beaded Niklaus's brow, and his eyes were feverish and haunted.

"Shameless, good-for-nothing hussy," Niklaus said.

"You started it," Hendel observed.

"I don't deny it. But am I to be blamed for the fact that she looks so much like Sylva Kalisia?"

"You'd pinch a goddess's backside?" Anskar asked.

"I'd do much more than that, given half a chance," Niklaus said bitterly; then he turned and walked across the threshold.

Anskar went inside next, followed by Hendel.

They entered a corridor that stretched away endlessly before them. The walls, ceiling and floor were comprised of black stone—obsidian maybe—that glistened in the gray light Niklaus had somehow effected. There was no visible source of the light; it just seemed to effuse from the stone of the corridor. Distorted images of each of the companions were reflected in every surface and repeated into the diminishing distance, carried there by some clever sorcery.

There was a circle of crystal on the right-hand wall where Niklaus had stood earlier when the darkness had lifted. Anskar covered the circle with his hand, and the light went out.

"Oh, for Menselas's sake!" the Grand Master exclaimed.

In the dark, fingers nudged Anskar's hand aside. He heard several dull taps, and the steely light returned.

"It's a neat trick," Niklaus said, his breath stale and smelling of alcohol.

"Sorcery?"

"Isn't everything, when it comes down to it?"

"What is this place?" Hendel asked in a voice hushed with awe. "A tomb?"

"Why is it everyone assumes ancient ruins are tombs?" Niklaus said.

Blaice cast a look over her shoulder and said, "This is merely the entrance to something much bigger."

Niklaus chuckled and gripped the hilt of his sword, as if to reassure himself it was still there. After a moment his fingers uncurled and brushed against the first third of the blade, where Anskar had seen the engraving of the naked body of a winged woman—Sylva Kalisia, the Lady.

"Are there likely to be traps?" the Grand Master asked as he surveyed the way ahead.

"Collapsing floors? Poison darts? Pressure pads?" Blaice said.

"Or sorcerous wards?" Gadius asked anxiously.

"Pants-pisser," Niklaus said. "At least if they're anything like the wards you set back at the cave, we'll have nothing to worry about."

"Well?" the Grand Master demanded.

Blaice glanced at Niklaus, who shrugged. "Probably not this far up, but just in case, Grand Master, you go first."

"This far up?" the Grand Master said. "What's that supposed to mean?"

"This is merely the approach to the … site," Blaice said. "The main bulk of it is even deeper below ground."

"How deep?"

"Seven cities deep," Niklaus said, "but don't worry, there's usually a shortcut."

"After each of the cataclysms that devastated Wiraya," Blaice explained, "new settlements were often built atop the buried wreckage of the old. But they are all still down there somewhere, the ancient cities, some still waiting to be dug out of the earth that has smothered them, others preserved intact somehow by the lore of the ancients. This entrance is a later addition, probably between ten and twelve thousand years old. It's during that period that proto-Skanuric was in common usage. The cities buried beneath it are even older, and the one we're interested in—Yustanwyrd—is believed to have disappeared from the face of Wiraya more than thirty thousand years ago."

"And the portal stone is down there?" the Grand Master asked. "In a city? Buried beneath six other cities? How can you possibly know this?"

"Education. You might try it some time."

"Blaice claims she was sent to the finest academies on the mainland," Niklaus said, "by insanely wealthy parents. I've always assumed they disowned her for failing miserably at her exams; otherwise why did she end up in this line of work?"

"I failed nothing," Blaice said, though Niklaus had clearly touched a nerve. "But back to the real world: There are scholarly papers that say much about the lost city of Yustanwyrd, though none said anything about how to find it. We know that it was the seat of power in the prehistoric world, that it was intentionally sunk beneath the ground—don't ask me how. And we know of the treasures it's purported to contain."

"Treasures?" the Grand Master said. "I thought there was just the one."

Blaice frowned and then corrected herself. "I meant treasure, if you can call it such. The portal stone."

"I don't know about this," the Grand Master said. "I was led to believe that an ancient ruin had surfaced, but now I learn it is only some kind of access tunnel, and that the ruin we seek is an entire city … buried deep underground, beneath six other cities. No, we'll not take a step farther. The entrance needs to be cordoned off until we get help. Hendel, you must return to the canal, tell Lanuc and the lad to ride for Atya. Bring the rest of our knights here. And laborers—carpenters and the like. Tell them they'll be well paid. We should erect a palisade to protect the entrance, and man it until the Church can send a full expedition."

"Good idea," Niklaus said with altogether too much enthusiasm for Anskar's liking. "This task is too big for our ragtag little band. I'll head back with Hendel. Clearly, the goddess was mistaken in sending me here. Whatever was she thinking?"

"Niklaus …" Blaice growled. Then to the Grand Master she said, "What do you think will happen if we sit around and wait for a full-scale expedition? I can assure you, we're not the only ones who know about the portal stone. The Tainted Cabal are bound to have heard about it by now. What if they get here before the Church? They're sorcerers, or have you forgotten? Real sorcerers. Who among us could possibly stand against them?" She glanced pointedly at Gadius. But when her eyes fell on Anskar, she shrugged, then widened them suggestively. Heat rushed to Anskar's face and he looked away.

"Ah, the Tainted Cabal," Niklaus said. "Yes, I'd quite forgotten about them." He sighed and gave the Grand Master a stern look. "I don't envy you the decision you're going to have to make. The fate of the world may depend upon it," he said with a theatrical flourish. "And what if Menselas disapproves of your decision? Five is a lot of aspects to get on the wrong side of."

The Grand Master clenched his jaw and looked off down the interminable corridor flanked by the ever-receding reflections of the group. After a while he gave Niklaus a considering look.

"There's a shortcut, you say?"

"Maybe. Probably."

"And you have experience of such buried cities?" the Grand Master asked Blaice.

"I've explored several, but Niklaus is the real expert."

The Grand Master rubbed his beard, thinking. "A happy coincidence, don't you think, that the two of you met up on the way here?"

"No coincidence," Niklaus said. "My path is determined."

"By a heathen goddess," Gadius pointed out.

"Shut up, Gadius," the Grand Master snapped, visibly annoyed. "Do something useful and scout ahead down this corridor."

"Grand Master?"

Hyle Pausus bunched his hands into fists. "Useless. Utterly useless. Ryala, you go first."

Gadius glowered at the Grand Master's back. It looked to Anskar as though he'd like to plunge a knife in it.

"So you're decided, then?" Blaice asked. "We're continuing?"

"We can't have the Tainted Cabal getting hold of the portal stone," the Grand Master said. "It would mean disaster. Though I won't pretend I like this one little bit. And no, before you ask: I don't trust you. Either of you."

"Then you're not as stupid as you look," Niklaus said. "I wouldn't trust me either."

As the group started down the corridor, Ryala in the lead, Anskar's eyes were repeatedly drawn to his own reflection in the dark surfaces of the floor, walls, and ceiling. His distorted image was repeated endlessly ahead of them, but when he glanced behind, there was nothing: the surfaces were blank. Even more disconcerting was the fact that their footfalls on the glimmering black floor made no sound. Anskar's heart skittered in his chest. What if the steely light went out? The thought of being plunged into impenetrable blackness, coupled with the unnatural quiet, made him think of oblivion, of the endless night of space, of the seething essence within him that roiled and strained against the barriers of his dark-tide repository.

It came as a relief when they passed another of the crystal circles set into the wall and Niklaus demonstrated how to increase the illumination by tapping the upper portion, or reduce it by tapping the lower.

Little by little, the passage began to angle downwards, a gentle gradient that was, at first, not easy to discern. It brought them at last to a spherical chamber of the same obsidian-like stone as the passageway. Gems bedizened all the interior surfaces save the floor, winking with amber, lime and crimson light. There was a circle of brass riveted to the floor, perhaps thirty feet in diameter. All around the perimeter, proto-Skanuric letters had been etched, some of them aflame with reflected light from the gemstones. The atmosphere within was pregnant with some unreleased pressure, the air thick with sulfur and something astringent that irritated Anskar's nostrils.

"Dead end," Ryala said, eyeing the blinking gems suspiciously.

The Grand Master stood, hands on hips, surveying the chamber. "Gadius?" he asked. "Thoughts?"

The acolyte made a show of inspecting some of the gemstones, then turned his attention to the brass circle on the floor, stooping to peer at the inscription.

"Stop pretending you can read it," Niklaus said, taking off his hat and using it to fan his face.

"It looks like some kind of summoning circle," Gadius said, standing and turning to the Grand Master.

Blaice made a scoffing noise, and Niklaus slapped her with his hat.

Anskar sent out feelers of awareness to stroke the brass circle. If Gadius was right, surely there would be some sort of sorcerous residue. His feelers recoiled, whiplashing back into him. Something about the circle had repulsed them, but he had no idea what. Not sorcery, though: there had been no trace of that.

"You all right?"

Anskar jumped at the voice beside his ear. It was Hendel, twiddling with the end of his mustache.

Ryala folded her arms across her chest and cocked her head to one side so she could glare at Gadius. "So what now?"

"You're asking me?" Gadius said.

"There's usually a clue in the proto-Skanuric," Blaice said, "but this is gibberish to me, and this chamber's a little different to anything I've seen before."

"Same here," Niklaus said. "Maybe try singing the gibberish . . ."

"Be my guest."

Niklaus coughed, then returned his hat to his head. "I don't have the voice for it."

"What about these crystals?" Gadius said. He went to touch one, but Niklaus grabbed his wrist, causing him to squeal.

"Not a good idea," Niklaus said. "At least, I don't think it is. Do you, Blaice?"

"Let him go ahead. See if I care."

The Grand Master tapped his foot impatiently. "I was under the impression you two knew what you were doing."

"Usually I do," Blaice said. "And I will again. Sometimes these things need a bit of working out."

"Anskar?" the Grand Master said. "Thoughts?"

"I don't think the circle's for summoning," he said.

"Oh?" Gadius said. "And why's that, then?"

"I could be wrong," Anskar said carefully, "but it reminds me of the circle the kidnappers used back at Branil's Burg, when they spirited me away to the street outside."

Niklaus raised an eyebrow, and Blaice blew Anskar a kiss.

"The kidnappers chanted something," Anskar said, "but there was more to it than that."

"How do you know?" Blaice asked, interested now.

"I don't. I just … feel there was."

"Well, of course they would have needed to do more than utter a cant," Gadius said. "The circle would have needed an infusion of sorcery, and not the kind most of us are familiar with, thanks be to Menselas."

"It's all right if you want to try something," the Grand Master said.

"Go ahead," Blaice said. "I can't see any harm coming of it so long as no one touches those crystals. I'll recite the gibberish. Maybe it's the sound that's important rather than the meaning."

"But I don't know what to do," Anskar said.

"Then allow me," Gadius said.

The acolyte turned to face the brass circle and closed his eyes. He took a deep breath, and as he released it, Anskar sensed the flow of dawn-tide energy from Gadius's repository. The eldritch essence infused the brass, flaring golden for an instant, then died out. Dirty smoke rose from the letters inscribed in the circle, and there was a smell like heated metal.

"It rejected me," Gadius said.

"Nothing you're not used to, I'm sure," Niklaus muttered.

"Perhaps the dusk-tide?" Anskar suggested.

Gadius cast a furtive look at the Grand Master.

"Go ahead," Hyle Pausus said. "There are no secrets here."

"Apparently not," Gadius said.

Again, the acolyte shut his eyes and took a deep breath. This time, when the vitriol of the dusk-tide washed over the brass circle, the letters blackened, and a ghostly howl echoed around the chamber. Everyone went still, scarcely daring to breathe, until the howl slowly died down to a whispering susurrus, and then it was gone.

Gadius was pale-faced and sweating profusely.

"Next?" Niklaus said, a wry grin on his face.

"There is no next," Gadius said. "At least not for me. I have only the two repositories, not like some people I could mention."

"Anskar?" the Grand Master prompted.

Anskar licked his lips. Hendel clamped a reassuring hand on his shoulder. Opposite, Ryala smirked. Blaice still didn't seem to be taking things seriously, instead giving Anskar a seductive raise of her eyebrows. He gave her a look that he hoped told her she was old enough to be his mother. The thought instantly soured his already deteriorating mood. His mother. Talia, the Necromancer Queen of Niyas. The woman from whom he'd presumably inherited the dark-tide.

He glanced at Niklaus, expecting to be met with mockery or more foolishness, but this time Niklaus held his gaze with an inscrutable look. Anskar felt exposed then, weighed and tested, as if Niklaus were working out if he were of any value, if there was some way in which he could be used.

With a flare of anger, Anskar turned to the brass circle, not needing to shut his eyes to concentrate, as Gadius had done.

He could see clearly in his mind's eye the bindings he had constrained the dark-tide with, the virulence that bubbled within its repository. Bunching his hands into fists, Anskar dipped into the seething miasma within, steeled himself against its corrosive touch, and then opened himself to let it course through his veins, scouring, scalding, boiling. With a gasp, he uttered the words of a cant and flung the dark-tide at the circle. Shadows flowed from his fingertips, swirling around the brass and flooding the grooves that made the letters. No rejection this time. No rebuttal of his sorcerous senses. Black flames roared into existence around the circle's rim, setting the inscription ablaze, not with dark flames, but with every conceivable color, until the chamber danced with the spray of their prismatic brilliance.

Blaice began to chant barbarous words, reading from the proto-Skanuric inscription around the circle. Her voice was soft, scarcely more than a mumble, yet the resounding echo was deafening, rising to a sonorous wail of overlaid sound, a macabre, shuddering dissonance. The atmosphere bristled. Pressure built until it felt explosive. Blaice's chanting became stronger, faster, more confident, and with it the echo screamed into an earsplitting cacophony.

And then the center of the circle dissolved into an inky well of blackness.

Blaice ceased her chanting, and Anskar took that as the cue to douse the flow of his dark-tide energy. The tide withdrew reluctantly, oozing like sludge through his veins, dripping back into the repository that contained it. Swiftly, he refashioned the barriers around his repository, then clutched his shoulders, hugging himself against the sudden cold that engulfed him.

"You're sweating," Hendel said, wiping the moisture from Anskar's brow.

And then it struck Anskar. He turned to the Grand Master and asked, "Did you know? Did you know we would need the dark-tide for this?"

The Grand Master was staring at Blaice, almost imperceptibly shaking his head.

"The little you told me," Blaice said, "I thought Anskar might come in handy."

"But you could have done this without him?" Hendel asked.

"Without a doubt," Blaice said. "There's more than one way to skin a cat. This was just the most efficient and cost effective. Do you know how much it costs to hire a dark-tide sorcerer these days? And most of the time you'd be killed just for trying to find one. We should count our blessings. Menselas must be on our side."

Niklaus guffawed, and the Grand Master flashed him a murderous glance.

"Anyhow, we're in now," Blaice said. "So let's not hang around."

With that, she leaped into the void at the center of the brass circle.

EIGHTEEN

ANSKAR STARED INTO THE void at the center of the brass circle. He could feel the empty dark tugging at him, willing him to plunge into its embrace. He tried to take a step back, but his legs refused to obey him. Niklaus glanced at him and grinned before leaping into the circle and disappearing.

"I don't know about this," Gadius said, but the Grand Master shoved him in the back and the acolyte squealed as he stumbled into the black hole and vanished.

"You next," the Grand Master said.

Anskar nodded, then inched closer to the edge of the circle. He reached out with his sorcerous senses but was instantly overcome by nausea and dizziness. He stumbled back from the brink, but Hendel was there, supporting him by the elbow, uttering reassuring words. And then Anskar shut his eyes and stepped into the dark.

Chill winds buffeted him. Behind his eyelids lightning

flashed. His stomach lurched. Bile hit his throat. The stench of sulfur and burned metal assailed his nostrils. Sand blasted his skin where it was exposed—at least, it felt like sand. Gossamer feelers prodded the inside of his skull, probed the barriers he'd set around his repositories, forced their way inside, hissing, whispering, cackling. Something stronger coiled about the vambrace on his forearm, tightening, wrenching. He lashed out at it with his free hand, but there was nothing there. He opened his eyes onto a kaleidoscope of colors streaming upwards in a blur. He glanced down at a ball of flame, iridescent and many-hued, racing toward him. He opened his mouth to scream but lacked the breath.

His knees buckled as he struck solid ground. Not hard, as he had expected. Softly. It was the anticipation of a crushing impact that had made him land in a crouch.

He was in the center of an identical circle to the one he had entered, though the surroundings were very, very different.

Niklaus and Blaice stood outside the circle, their backs to him. Gadius knelt, body racked with spasms as he retched.

The air above Anskar's head grew suddenly heavy. A shrill whistle sounded, growing louder and louder. At the last instant, he flung himself clear of the circle just as the Grand Master appeared out of thin air, staggered, and then steadied himself.

"Well, I'll be—" the Grand Master started, but Anskar lunged for him and pulled him clear of the circle before Hendel could appear.

Anskar stiffened in anticipation of the chastisement that was to come for manhandling the Grand Master, but to his surprise Hyle Pausus merely nodded his thanks before turning his attention to their surroundings.

They stood within a ring of silver pillars, each as tall as a man. They were fluted and capped with spheres of blue stone veined with gold. Tongues of dark flame licked over the pillars, and black lightning leaped from pillar to pillar in a continuous circuit. The air was oppressive, thick with the threat of something terrible about to happen. In the center of the ring of pillars, the inscription around the brass circle flickered with guttering black flames, which slowly died down until the letters they had sprung from smoldered red.

Beyond the ambit of the pillars Anskar saw buildings without end, stretching into the distance, bathed in a soft, bluish glow. There were looming edifices, towers, sprawling tenements with row upon row of windows that sparkled with reflected blue. He saw colonnaded walkways and ornate stone balustrades. Deep trenches threaded their way between clusters of buildings with overhanging balconies, flying buttresses and arches spanning them. To his mind, the trenches looked as though they had once been canals, but they had long since dried up, and many were piled high with dust. They had been filled at one time, he assumed, by water flowing along the arched aqueducts that loomed over everything, as tall and vast as mountain ranges.

Broad avenues of gleaming, dark-veined stone intersected the city—for that was what it was: a vast underground city that dwarfed even Dorinah back home in Niyas. The stone of the roads shimmered with reflected blue light, making them seem like frozen rivers.

It was odd to Anskar that the city wasn't shrouded in gloom, or even absolute darkness. He looked up and saw the source of the strange blue glow. What he at first took for a clear blue sky was in fact a vast dome that hung overhead, seemingly as endless as the city it covered. An artificial sky, then, and a barrier between the city and the mountains of earth beneath which it was buried, and that, without the dome's protection, would come crashing down to bury the ancient structures once and for all. Blue light suffused the dome, radiating down to the buildings and roads below.

"The ruins of six other cities are stacked above us," Blaice said, following Anskar's gaze. Her voice trembled with awe. "It's hard to believe we're actually standing here. Yustanwyrd," she breathed. "This has to be the fabled lost city."

The streets, the roads, the bridges, the buildings—all empty. So very empty. Silent. Whatever glory Yustanwyrd had enjoyed in its heyday, however illustrious its past, it was all gone now. All that remained was a monument to whichever dead race had constructed it, a footprint in time to mark their existence in the world, a record of their passing. Yustanwyrd was a city of ghosts.

Gadius stood with a groan, wiping drool from his bony chin. He cast a look around that was more despairing than awed. "How do we get back up top?" he asked miserably.

"Same way we came down," Niklaus said. Even he looked amazed by the spectacle of the underground city.

"So what next?" the Grand Master asked, eyes still roving the magnificent scene that surrounded them.

Blaice fished about in her pocket and produced a crumpled-up piece of parchment. She unraveled it and studied its contents. Niklaus moved to her side and peered over her shoulder.

Just then, a shadow passed overhead, and Anskar looked up to see something dark swoop by on enormous wings. He had the impression of feathers and scales, a sinuous neck and a curved beak, though the thing lacked substance, as if it were formed from smoke or cloud.

"What was that?" Gadius asked nervously.

Niklaus tracked the creature's flight until it drifted behind one of the aqueducts. "We should probably get moving," he said. "Find better cover."

"Agreed," Blaice said, cramming the parchment back in her pocket. She made a show of looking around and then pointed toward one of the broad avenues. "That way, I think."

"You think?" the Grand Master said. "You mean you don't know?"

"Hard as it may be to believe," Niklaus said, "she's just being modest."

Blaice struck out for the avenue with Niklaus in tow, the Grand Master and Ryala striding purposefully behind them, Gadius scurrying to keep up. Anskar was about to follow when realization struck him and he asked the question no one else had thought to ask:

"Where's Hendel?"

"Oops," Niklaus said.

"Ah . . ." Blaice said, offering a shrug, as if to say, "These things happen."

The Grand Master glowered at the brass circle they had each appeared in. "He'd better not have deserted, because there will be ramifications if he has. Painful ramifications."

Ryala's eyes flashed with anger, but when she spoke, her voice was calm. "Hendel would never desert. None of us would."

"Then what's he waiting for?" Gadius asked.

"Perhaps he was too late?" Anskar wondered aloud. "Maybe the circle's sorcery abated before he entered it."

"A likely story," the Grand Master muttered.

"Sounds feasible," Niklaus said, exchanging a look with Blaice that was difficult to read.

Blaice puffed out her cheeks and sighed. "Nothing we can do about it right now. We'll find out when we go back."

"If not sooner," Niklaus said.

Blaice narrowed her eyes at him. "Just … we'll find out."

Anskar was already reaching for his dark-tide repository. "Redo the cants," he told Blaice. "I'll go back and fetch him." He couldn't suppress the worry that something had happened to the knight. Something terrible.

Irritation flashed in Blaice's eyes. She fiddled with her nose rings, then realized she was doing it and dropped her hand to her side. "The brass circles need time to recharge—an hour or more. We'll find Hendel later."

"Or sooner," Niklaus added again.

This time Blaice gritted her teeth and turned back to the avenue she'd been about to take. "Coming?" she growled.

Another shadow passed overhead—a vast scaled bird with the consistency of smoke once again. It opened its curved beak and cawed, the sound grating yet strangely distant, as if it came from another place, another time.

"Let's go," the Grand Master snapped, and the group moved off.

Reluctantly, Anskar followed.

The avenue proceeded for what felt like miles, flanked on either side by looming buildings of tightly mortared stone that reflected blue in the light from the crystal dome that covered the city. Insubstantial birds scudded overhead, casting fleeting shadows on the road.

Blaice held the group up beneath one of the arches of an aqueduct so she could refer to her scrap of parchment. Anskar could see over her shoulder that it was a crude map of the city.

He recognized the shapes of some of the larger structures, and with difficulty was able to get his bearings. Some of the buildings on the map were marked with proto-Skanuric letters, and Blaice scanned them with her fingertip before scrunching up the parchment and returning it to her pocket.

"I like you being so close," she muttered so that no one but Anskar could hear. She paused, head tilted in expectation of a reply, but when Anskar said nothing—for he could think of nothing to say—she chuckled and once more led the way.

"Like a bitch in heat," Niklaus whispered in Anskar's ear as they walked side by side. "Never satisfied." He wrinkled his nose and grimaced, as if he'd swilled something rancid about his mouth; then he shook his head. "But neither was I, truth be told."

"But you still like her?" Anskar whispered back. He could tell from the way Niklaus stared at her when she wasn't looking, and from the way the two of them interacted.

"Her resemblance to the Lady is … striking." Niklaus gazed wistfully at Blaice, then turned his head to the side. "But she mars her gift with piercings and tattoos. And, of course, she has no wings. And those are just the physical differences."

"You told me you'd seen your goddess," Anskar said. As far as he knew, no one had ever seen Menselas—any of his five aspects.

Niklaus coughed to clear his throat. "Oh, I've seen her, right enough. Sometimes—seldom, if I'm honest—she visits me at night. She is … exquisite." He closed his eyes and raised a hand, as if stroking something invisible. But then he tripped on an uneven paver and cried out as he stumbled. The only reason he didn't fall flat on his face was because Anskar caught him by the arm.

Niklaus sighed and nodded his thanks. "Women!" he said. "Goddesses! My advice to you …" He shook his head and gave

Anskar a wry grin. "My advice to you is never to listen to my advice."

"Grand Master!"

It was Ryala who cried out. She'd wandered away from the road, taking a parallel course, weaving in between the buildings. She appeared now a little way behind them, gesticulating.

"What now?" the Grand Master grumbled.

"I think she's found something," Gadius said, already starting toward Ryala.

"We don't have time for this," Blaice protested. "Whatever 'this' is."

"Now, now," Niklaus said. "Patience was never your strong point, was it, Blaice?"

"In my profession, time is gold."

"I knew a courtesan who said pretty much the same thing," Niklaus replied. "Or was that you as well?"

They followed Ryala down a tributary street lined with crumbling tenements until they came to a plaza. There were overturned tables and chairs, all made from some black, grainy substance that could have been metal, could have been stone, or neither.

On the far side of the plaza was a massive stone edifice—some kind of basilica, perhaps. It was capped with an enormous spire that came close to touching the underside of the city dome. The pitched roof of the building was coated with silver tiles that shimmered blue in the dome's light. They looked like the scales of some exotic lizard. Anskar's eyes were drawn to the gable, where eight crossed swords had been hung to form a rough circle, the tips of their blades pointing outward. They must have been huge swords to be visible from so far below, and the blades had flamboyant edges that gave the impression of uniform waves.

It was toward the basilica that Ryala led the group, and once there she stood in front of double doors of cast bronze and pointed.

There, in the center of one of the doors, was what Anskar at first took to be a blister, a lump, some kind of imperfection in the bronze casting; but as he drew nearer he saw that he'd been mistaken. It was no lump. It was a human head, eyes wide open in shock, mouth agape.

A bald head, the face badly scarred. A long mustache hung below the hook nose.

"Hendel," the Grand Master breathed.

It looked as though Hendel's head was growing out of the bronze door.

"But how …?" Gadius started, then turned away to retch.

"How did he get here?" Niklaus approached the head. "Blaice?"

Blaice shifted from foot to foot. "He must have followed Anskar through the brass circle. Only …"

"Only what?" Ryala said. Her hand tightened around the hilt of her sword. The Grand Master saw and wagged a finger, and Ryala relaxed her grip.

"I've seen it before," Blaice said. "The brass circles form the poles of some kind of sorcerous transport …"

"Teleportation," Gadius said. "Which goes to prove this place is demonic. Only demons using the dark-tide are capable of …" He dried up when he saw Anskar watching him.

"My point is," Blaice said, "that sometimes these transport circles go wrong. Maybe too many of us passed through in quick succession. I don't know."

"So Hendel entered the brass circle but reappeared here rather than where he was supposed to?" the Grand Master asked. He sounded more fascinated than upset.

"His head did," Niklaus quipped. "The rest of him could be strewn all over the place."

"We should …" Anskar started, glancing at the Grand Master. "We should pray for him."

Hyle Pausus looked about to refuse, but then nodded. "Quickly, though. Gadius, a few lines from scripture, and then we press on."

After Gadius's rushed prayer, they hurried back to the avenue, but Anskar couldn't stop looking out for any more bits of poor Hendel's body fused with the surroundings. He thought he might have glimpsed a leg sticking up from the ground of an alleyway in the distance, but he couldn't bring himself to say anything. What would be the point? Hendel was gone, and that made him sad. Hendel had been a reassuring presence. He only wished he could say the same about anyone else in the group.

Blaice guided them away from the densely packed buildings and through a wide open space populated with fossilized trees. The ground climbed at a steady gradient toward the base of a hill, atop which was a long, tall building with a single row of what looked like embrasures all around its center.

As they approached, Anskar could see that the hill had been formed from tightly packed rock, and that a flight of iron steps had been set into the bank facing them.

"This is it?" the Grand Master asked. "This is where we'll find the portal stone?"

"If my map's correct," Blaice said.

"Why wouldn't it be?"

"The man I acquired it from is sometimes trustworthy."

"Which is another way of saying not at all," Niklaus said. "A bit like someone else I could mention."

"Then why are you here, Niklaus?" Blaice snapped. It was the first time Anskar had seen her angry. The first time he had seen a chink in her usual self-control.

Niklaus didn't seem to notice. "Like I said, *she* came to me."

"Pathetic," Blaice said.

"Perhaps. But even so, I am here, and I would not have been for any other reason."

"The heathen goddess seeks the portal stone for herself?" Gadius said.

"Now that I sincerely doubt," Niklaus said. Then, with a penetrating look, he added, "What do you think, Blaice? Does the Lady desire the portal stone? Has she any need of one? Do they even exist?"

"Of course they exist," the Grand Master said. "Don't they?"

Blaice started up the iron steps toward the building atop the hill. "Let's find out."

The Grand Master, Ryala and Gadius followed Blaice. Niklaus gestured for Anskar to go next.

"Fodder. That's all we are to her," Niklaus whispered.

"The Lady?"

Niklaus paused, a frown crossing his face. "I meant Blaice. Do you know how many people she's lost on her expeditions into the ancient ruins?"

Anskar shrugged.

"A lot," Niklaus said. "And we've already added to the tally."

"You're worried?"

"Not me. I'll come to no lasting harm. And besides, she needs me."

"As much as you need her?"

"What? Oh, you mean carnally. That's all in the past. Mortals can never live up to gods and goddesses, no matter how closely they resemble them. I don't think poor Blaice has ever gotten over the fact that I was disappointed. You see, she likes to be the one in control, the one who has impressionable young men fawning all over her. The idiots find her exotic—it's the nose rings and the other piercings you've not yet seen. The violet eyes. And the tattoos, of course."

At the top they came to a flat floor of gravel that shimmered every imaginable color. Not gravel, Anskar realized as he stooped for a closer look. Granulated crystal. They stood upon a hill topped with ground quartz.

Blaice's boots crunched over the surface as she approached the building. Before she reached it, a section of the wall parted with a rush of air, revealing a vast space beyond, illuminated by a soft, silvery glow that resembled moonlight. She turned and caught Niklaus's eye.

"Is that usual?" the Grand Master asked.

"It's rare," Blaice said. "But nothing to worry about."

Niklaus chuckled. "This is the part where she asks someone else to go first."

"Be my guest," Blaice said, but Niklaus ignored her, pretending instead to be interested in the panoramic view of the city.

"Is it warded?" Gadius asked.

"If it were, I'm sure you'd know," the Grand Master replied.

Gadius swallowed. "I can check, use a few cants of detection I know."

"Waste of time," Blaice said. "The wards on these ancient sites are subtle, probably beyond anything you've encountered."

"But not you?" Gadius asked.

Blaice grinned, then crouched down at the doorway's threshold, running her palm over the floor there and whispering.

Ryala shifted nervously behind Anskar. He turned to see her glowering at the cityscape. "Yes?" she said.

"You were thinking about Hendel?"

"We were friends."

"I …" Anskar dipped his eyes, not sure what he should say.

"Go on," Ryala said.

"I liked him. He seemed a good man."

She stared at him for a long while, then finally nodded. "Thank you. He was that. And so much more."

Anskar wanted to ask if they had been lovers, but that was a question loaded with accusation. The Order of Eternal Vigilance didn't permit romance between its knights. But if he could have asked her, maybe she could have advised him. His own relationship with Sareya had transgressed the Order's rules, and he'd been forced to break it off. But if Ryala and Hendel had found a way, perhaps there was something he was missing, some hope for him and Sareya.

Blaice yelped and fell on her behind. Lightning sparked across the entrance, leaving the air charged and smelling of burned metal. It quickly abated, leaving in its wake an inky black vapor that slowly dispersed on the breeze.

"Did you disarm it?" Niklaus asked.

"Let's hope so," Blaice said, climbing to her feet and brushing herself down.

"I have every confidence in your abilities," Niklaus said, gesturing toward the entrance. "After you."

"No, no, after you," Blaice said.

"Oh, for Menselas's sake," Ryala said, and pushed past them both to step across the threshold.

She turned back to face the group with a "What are you waiting for?" expression, and at the Grand Master's nod, the rest of them filed inside.

At first, Anskar couldn't see the floor, ceiling, or walls of the space they entered—everything was awash with a silvery glow. As his eyes adjusted, he saw that they stood within a massive hall, the ceiling and walls curved like the inside of a gigantic egg, the floor composed of the same reflective material, yet perfectly level and flat. The space was uncannily quiet, the floor beneath his feet soft, though it had the appearance of steel; it elicited no sound as he walked on it.

He became aware of a gentle warmth on his forearm and drew back his shirtsleeve a little way. The vambrace he wore invisibly beneath now glowed a brilliant cobalt blue. He instantly covered it, checking to see if anyone else had noticed. They were all still taking in their surroundings, too rapt by the mesmerizing surfaces of the hall.

Suddenly, the floor shuddered. From somewhere beneath their feet came a succession of resonant clunks, a droning whir. The floor began to blister in places; then lumps started to grow out of it, swiftly resolving into domed heads with long, angular faces. They were carved—or fossilized—from dark stone grained with glittering specks of gold. The features were humanlike, though only just: the eyes were hollow cavities; the noses flat, barely protruding; mouths thin slits. The heads rose above the floor, followed by robed bodies with slender limbs, hands clasping the hilts of upturned swords, black blades wavy like those they had seen on the gable of the basilica. Each of the statues—there were eight surrounding the group—was at least six feet in height. They settled into place with a final clunk from below, staring blankly; still, yet with the semblance of movement from their golden glitter and the interplay of the chamber's silver light.

Save for the faces, they resembled the cowled wraithe Anskar had encountered atop Hallow Hill, when he'd found the vambrace. He glanced behind at the entrance. He would have to pass between two of the statues to reach it, and just the thought made his legs grow as heavy as stone.

"What are they?" the Grand Master said in a hushed voice.

"An ancient race," Blaice said. "No one knows what they were called. There's nothing in the historical records about them, save for their abandoned buildings."

"But you've seen this sort of thing before?"

"Once or twice," Blaice said. "Niklaus?"

"I've run into them several times on the surface, where they haunt the ancient sites."

"Wraithes?" Anskar said, then regretted speaking when everyone turned to look at him.

"That's what we call them," Niklaus said, an interested glint in his eye.

"You have something to add, Anskar?" the Grand Master asked.

Anskar shook his head. "No, nothing, Grand Master. I just wondered. They used to tell us stories about the wraithes back at Branil's Burg. The priests, that is." And he wasn't lying. Brother Tion had loved frightening the children with tales of the ghostlike beings that haunted the old places of Wiraya. But it was a sin of omission, Anskar knew, failing to reveal that he had met a wraithe that fateful night the crow had led him away from Branil's Burg, and that even now he wore the vambrace it had told him to retrieve from the tomb.

"You think this is a trap?" the Grand Master asked Blaice.

"Probably."

"The swords look real," Ryala pointed out.

"Are they?" the Grand Master asked.

"Probably," Blaice said again. She didn't appear to be listening, her focus on her parchment map. She frowned as she mouthed the sounds of the words inked there beside the crude map of the city: words in a language Anskar hadn't realized existed until the last few days: proto-Skanuric. Even the Skanuric that had presumably evolved from it was impossibly ancient, the provenance of scholars and sorcerers, and those who had penned the holy scriptures—if that wasn't Menselas himself, as some theologians among the priests of the Elder taught.

Ryala approached one of the statues and reached out to touch the sword it held.

"I wouldn't," Niklaus said.

Ryala drew back her hand. "Why not?"

"Oh, you're probably right," Niklaus said. "Don't mind me. Go ahead."

Ryala glanced at the Grand Master, who shook his head, and she withdrew to the center of the circle to stand with the others.

"So what do we do now?" Niklaus asked. "I assume the statues are going to come to life and fight us if we make the wrong move."

Blaice rolled her eyes. "You've been listening to the bards too much." She looked around at the group. "I was hoping …"

"That you had more fodder?" Niklaus said.

"Perhaps we should have brought more knights," the Grand Master said. "Despite the risk of alerting the Tainted Cabal or others to our expedition."

"I'm starting to think you're right," Blaice conceded. "I hadn't expected to run into a manticarr back there, and what happened to Hendel …"

Ryala tensed.

"It's not something that happens often," Blaice quickly added. "So it wasn't something I could have foreseen."

"Keep telling yourself that, and maybe the rest of us will start to believe it," Niklaus said. "But the reality is, we're here now and there are only six of us left. To my mind, that should be enough, so long as we are all willing to share the risks. I know the Grand Master here is, and this fine strapping woman," he said, indicating Ryala. "The young man will either find his courage or he won't." He dismissed Anskar with a shrug. "But it's you who concerns me, Blaice. How many expeditions have you led? How many times were you the only person to emerge unscathed?"

"The others were fools. Amateurs."

Ryala advanced a step. "Those that died?"

"Ryala!" the Grand Master growled. "It was not Blaice's fault that Hendel didn't make it."

The wall opposite the entrance shimmered, drawing Anskar's gaze. A massive reptile's head had appeared there, molded or carved so that it stood out from the wall. Its fanged jaws opened upon a dark stretch of tunnel where its gullet should have been.

"We should probably leave now," Niklaus said.

Blaice flashed him an anxious look. "We have an agreement, remember?"

"What agreement?" the Grand Master asked. "You mean your meeting wasn't a coincidence, after all?"

"The agreement we made after we met," Niklaus said. He raised his eyebrows suggestively at Blaice.

Her face tightened, and she sighed. "Niklaus thinks I look like his goddess," she explained.

"Merely a passing resemblance," Niklaus said.

"But enough to get him excited."

"Barely."

"I fail to understand …" the Grand Master started, then clearly did understand. "Oh, I see." Anskar expected him to touch his fingertips to his breast, but instead the Grand Master said, "So she taunts you, does she? Sylva Kalisia, I mean. Some of these lesser so-called gods are terribly capricious, don't you think?"

"No," Niklaus said. "I do not think. And yes," he said to Blaice, "the resemblance is a poor one and growing weaker with every new wrinkle you acquire, every new tattoo or piercing. Carry on at this rate and I doubt I'll be able to perform."

"Well, that'll be a change from last time, when you might say you overperformed. It was over in a flash," she told everyone. "I was quite disappointed."

"Not as much as I was," Niklaus said. "Like fool's gold, it was. And I was the fool."

The warmth of the vambrace grew suddenly into a scalding heat. Anskar clutched his arm, wincing, not daring to look beneath his shirtsleeve. The vambrace was heavy now. It shivered above his flesh, then tugged him, almost imperceptibly at first, but with increasing urgency, toward the lizard's maw. Before anyone registered the fact, he'd passed between two statues and continued toward the reptile's gaping mouth.

"Anskar!" Ryala called. He heard her footsteps behind him.

"No!" the Grand Master commanded, and Ryala stopped. "Anskar!" he cried. "I order you to come back!"

Anskar hesitated. He could have obeyed. Whatever it was that tugged at him was more of an invitation than a compulsion. He could have resisted it and turned back to his companions, but the burning heat of the vambrace conveyed excitement, and a curiosity that was in its own way compelling.

"Anskar!" the Grand Master called again.

"I wouldn't . . ." Niklaus said. Then added, "Oh well, don't say I didn't warn you."

Sweat dripped from Anskar's brow into his eyes. He could feel the frantic beat of his heart within his rib cage. His guts clenched, and every instinct told him to turn about and flee. But the vambrace was heavy and hot and straining forward like a dog on a leash. He gritted his teeth and stepped into the reptile's maw.

Almost at once a new succession of clunks and whirs from below struck up. He turned to see the statues gliding across the floor, collapsing the circle they had formed and making a line in front of the lizard's mouth, their backs to him, facing his companions.

Ryala took a step forward, but the statues flowed closer together until they made an impregnable barrier between Anskar and the others. To his left, he saw another doorway open in the wall of the chamber, an invitation for his companions to walk through. They each saw it but remained hesitant.

Again Ryala called to Anskar, and again she took a step forward. As one, the eight statues raised their wavy-edged swords.

And then the reptile's teeth snapped down, plunging Anskar into a darkness so black he could see nothing save the faint glow of the vambrace beneath his shirtsleeve. He gasped, then started to roll up his sleeve, but the floor tilted. He cried out as he pitched forward and plummeted into the void.

NINETEEN

BRIDNAIR SPLIT THEM INTO two groups. The first, he instructed to tail the Grand Master's expedition from a distance, and the rest came with him: six warriors, Carred, Maggow, and the demon Malady.

"The Plains of Khisig-Ugtall are riddled with tunnels," Bridnair said as he led his pony by the reins toward a mound of fine earth.

"All right," Carred said. "So how does this help us?"

"You will see."

Bridnair nodded to a couple of his warriors, and they left their ponies and set about clearing the earth with their bare hands.

"The moles must be big in the Plains," Maggow said.

Malady scoffed and shook her head. "Moles, my ass!"

"Do not be concerned, old man," Bridnair said. "They will smell us long before we see them, and keep out of our way. But they are most definitely not moles."

"Oh?" Carred asked, but Bridnair wasn't listening. Instead, he removed one of his glass rods from the bundle on his pony and held it up so that it reflected the sun's rays. Within the tube, golden fluid bubbled and sparkled.

"What's that for?" Carred asked.

"Be silent, he's concentrating," Doon Ma'jah said. She'd been breathing down Carred's neck ever since they came down from the summit, her hand seldom leaving the hilt of her broadsword.

Carred took her pony to one side, where there was still a little shade from the mesa. She gazed back toward Atya, thinking she'd have been better off coming alone. She jumped as a shape emerged from the shadow she entered. Well, not quite alone …

"Makes you wonder who's the master and who's the slave," Malady said.

"How'd you slip your leash?" Carred said, glancing round to see Maggow hobbling in pursuit of his charge. The old man led Malady's pony as well as his own.

"I forbid you from shadow-stepping," Maggow said.

The dwarf woman gave a mock bow. "But of course. You only needed to ask."

"I do not ask, demon," Maggow said. "I command."

"And people wonder why summoners always end up with a knife in their backs, sooner or later. Is it so hard to show a modicum of courtesy?" Malady turned her nose up at the state of the old man's loincloth. "I suppose we shouldn't expect manners from the unsanitary."

"You're thinking of leaving?" Maggow asked, ignoring the demon.

"Wish I had the choice. But I'm starting to regret …" Carred didn't complete her sentence. Doon Ma'jah was watching her. Not Bridnair, though: he was still communing with his glass rod, or whatever it was he was doing.

At length, the two warriors finished clearing away the earth to reveal a massive hole in the ground.

"Not moles, you say?" Carred said. "Giant bunnies?"

Bridnair laughed, though it sounded insincere. "You amuse me, Carred Selenas. You all amuse me. Come now. The bulk of the Grand Master's group has passed beyond my ..." He twirled the glass rod in his hands, considering. "Let us say 'my senses.'"

"Great," Carred muttered.

"But two of them are closer by," Bridnair said. "Half my warriors will follow them but remain out of sight. We will take a faster route"—he indicated the hole in the ground—"and get in front of them. If they try to flee, they will run into the warriors behind."

"And one of these two is Anskar?" Carred asked.

"I detected only the dawn-tide."

"So, no, then."

Bridnair pressed his face up close to hers. His breath smelled of something sweet. "Why do you think they let two of their group lag behind?"

"No idea," Carred said. "I'll just offer up a quick prayer to Theltek of the Hundred Eyes, see if he knows."

"Hah!" Bridnair said.

"To guard the ponies?" Malady suggested. She gave Maggow an insolent look. "Sorry, wasn't I supposed to say that ... Master?"

"Indeed," Bridnair said. "Which means the rest of the group will rejoin their two companions at some point, if they are able."

"Callous bastard," Malady said. "You mean to kill the stragglers and eat the ponies? Because I know I would."

"I have something else in mind for them," Bridnair said. "And then I plan to use them as bait."

Following Bridnair, they led their ponies into the hole and down a steady gradient. It smelled of loam and something Carred couldn't quite put her finger on, vinegary and at the same time cloying. Behind her, Maggow made a series of clacking noises, which she took to mean disapproval, or caution. She turned to find the old man examining streaks of glistening mucous on the dirt wall of the tunnel.

"Like I said," Malady remarked, "not moles and definitely not bunnies."

"Bridnair . . ." Carred said in a hushed voice, but the Chief had already rounded a bend, and all she could see was the golden glow of his glass rod reflected on the walls.

"Move it," Doon Ma'jah said, "else we'll be stumbling in the dark."

The warriors trailing Doon exchanged nervous looks.

"You've not entered one of these tunnels before?" Carred asked.

As if she were reminding the warriors of what would happen if they backed out, Doon said, "What Bridnair commands is law."

They both nodded.

"And if Bridnair commands you to jump off a cliff?" Malady asked.

Maggow shushed her with a glare.

"Then we jump," Doon Ma'jah said.

As they passed the bend, the ponies grew restive. At a commotion from behind, Carred turned to see one of the warriors struggling to restrain his mount. Bridnair greeted

Carred with a beaming smile in the light of his glass rod. He waited for them in a massive circular burrow with dozens of tunnels leading off it.

"I hope you know the way," Carred said.

Bridnair shook his rod, and the golden fluid within sparkled and bubbled. He touched his forehead to the glass, then let out a long sigh. "They've stopped moving," he said as he strode for one of the tunnels, his pony following.

"How does he know that?" Carred muttered as she went after him.

"The rod is imbued with the dawn-tide," Maggow said. "And it seeks out such energy like a magnet."

"Handy," Carred said.

"Thirsty is how I would describe it," Malady said. "These kinds of rods are outlawed even in the abyssal realms—which isn't to say they are not still used by those with the guile and the means."

"Is Bridnair a demon?" Carred asked.

"He is not."

"Must you make so much noise?" Doon Ma'jah said. "You should not speak so much. Not about Bridnair."

"Sorry," Carred said. "We intended no disrespect."

"No, it's not that …" Doon Ma'jah grimaced, as if she couldn't find the right words to say. "Come on," she eventually said, "best keep up."

Bridnair led them through a warren of tunnels, some ribbed with dead tree roots, others scabbed with fungi. Several tunnels had caved in, and Bridnair had to consult his glass rod in order to find an alternative route.

"We are getting close," Bridnair said when he paused at a junction. Again, he consulted his rod by pressing the glass to his forehead.

A flash of red drew Carred's eye to the other rods bundled together in leather and strapped to the back of Bridnair's pony. At her shoulder, Malady let out a hiss.

Bridnair turned, and his eyes settled on where one of the rods—glowing an angry crimson—had come partially unwrapped. With a sly look at Malady, and a smile at Carred, he covered it with its bindings, then turned back to the junction.

"This way," he said, taking the left-hand tunnel.

About twenty feet along, Bridnair stopped again. In front of him, the way was blocked by a flimsy curtain that hung down from the tunnel ceiling. Bridnair stepped aside and held his golden rod up for her to see by. Not a curtain: it was some kind of translucent membrane webbed with thready veins of black. Mucous dripped from it to collect in gelatinous piles on the ground.

"Let's hope you're right about them smelling us and keeping out of our way," Carred said.

Bridnair frowned and drew in a deep breath. "The question is whether it shed its skin and proceeded along the tunnel the way we are heading, or whether it went the way we came and has gone deeper into the warren."

"You're assuming there's just the one," Malady said.

Bridnair chewed his bottom lip, nodding thoughtfully.

Behind them came a scream—one of Bridnair's warriors. A sound like pulped fruit, then hissing, scuffing, dragging.

"No!" the man cried. "Help meeeeeee!"

It was too dark back there for Carred to see. Doon Ma'jah started toward the noise, but Carred put a hand on her shoulder to stop her.

"Follow me!" Bridnair yelled, and then they were all running, the ponies skittish and whinnying.

Up ahead, the walls flickered with light—and not from Bridnair's rod. A little farther and the tunnel mouth came into view, beyond it some kind of cave.

Two figures stood in the entrance, silhouetted by the campfire behind them. First one drew a sword, then the other. Shimmering wards of silver sprang into existence around them.

Bridnair extended his glass rod and shouted barbarous words, and both ward spheres went out. The two figures backed out of sight into the cave.

Bridnair let go the reins of his pony and barreled through the entrance. Carred was next, then Maggow and Malady, Doon Ma'jah and the remaining warrior.

Carred caught sight of two white cloaks disappearing outside. A fire still crackled on the floor, and tethered together against one wall were half a dozen ponies with their heads in feedbags.

"Well, that didn't exactly work," Malady said.

"Is that what you think?" Bridnair said, pursuing the two knights outside. Carred started to go with him, but then Bridnair backed into the cave once more, chuckling as the two white cloaks reappeared in the entrance, swords in hand. Before Carred could fathom what was going on, she heard the clop of hooves, and soon after, Traguh-raj warriors mounted on ponies came into view—the other half of Bridnair's group.

The knights, though outnumbered and surrounded, prepared to fight. Doon Ma'jah and the other warrior stepped in front of Bridnair, swords drawn. Behind the knights, half a dozen mounted warriors crowded them, leveling spears. With their ward spheres, the knights might have stood a chance. Carred rushed forward, waving her arms. One of the knights was scarce out of boyhood and looked Traguh-raj himself. She started to speak Niyandrian, caught herself, and said in her seldom-practiced Nan-Rhouric, "No harm … Calm."

The older knight frowned at her, looked her up and down. He was quite handsome. The lad was trembling, and his knuckles were white where he gripped his sword too tight. But he was a fighter, she could tell that from his narrowed eyes.

"We look …" Carred grimaced and started again. "We looking … *Melesh-Eloni.*"

The knights exchanged baffled looks.

"Anskar DeVantte?" Carred said.

"What do you want with him?" the older knight said.

"What do you think?" Bridnair interjected in fluent Nan-Rhouric. His glass rod effused golden light, and sparks danced along its length. He pushed between Doon Ma'jah and the other warrior to face off with the older knight.

The lad stepped in front. "Back off, goat-face," he said. Carred was starting to like him.

Bridnair leveled the rod at the young knight. The lad stiffened, then arched his back and dropped his sword. Bridnair's rod begun to pulse. A rhythmic thrum sounded from it, then changed into a sound like slurping. The lad shuddered, letting out a whimper. Carred could feel the dawn-tide essence leaving him, flowing into the rod.

The older knight lunged at Bridnair, but Doon Ma'jah parried, then countered with a slash at his throat. He swayed back, reset, and came at her with a fury. She blocked once, twice; then her sword flew from her grasp and clattered across the cave floor.

The young lad groaned. His hands clutched his temples. "He's my friend!" he shrieked. "Anskar's my friend!"

Riders dismounted behind the knights, but they were too late. The older knight sheared through Bridnair's rod with his sword. For a second, all went still, and then there was an explosion of light. An unearthly wind skirled around the cave, howling, merging with Bridnair's scream of rage.

Carred blinked her eyes into focus and saw Bridnair rush to his pony and pull out the crimson rod from its wrappings. Steel met steel as the older knight fought with the other warrior in the cave. Doon Ma'jah ran across the floor to retrieve her sword. Warriors with spears pressed in from behind. The young knight was on his knees, trembling, still clutching his head. Bridnair, crimson rod aflame in his hand, strode toward him.

Carred caught Malady's eye. Then Maggow's. Nodded to the old man, then indicated Bridnair with a flick of her head.

"Kill!" Maggow whispered, and a grin split the dwarf-demon's face.

Bridnair raised his crimson staff overhead with both hands. The older knight staggered. The young knight slumped to the ground. Red flames streamed from the rod, snaking toward them both.

And then Bridnair jerked. Blood spurted from his mouth. His rod shattered into smoldering fragments as it struck the cave floor. Carred blinked. She couldn't tell what had happened. Blinked again, and this time she could see a ribbon of shadow—a dark and insubstantial spear—that passed through Bridnair's back and exited his chest.

"Impressive, huh?" Malady growled, her eyes narrowed in focus, the shadow spear sprouting from her open hand. She clenched her fist and the spear vanished.

Bridnair collapsed to the floor, unmoving.

Doon Ma'jah roared and started forward. Warriors edged into the cave.

Carred drew her sword.

Maggow crouched, his hands curled into claws. "You will

fight, demon," he said. "You are bound."

"No need to remind me," Malady said. "I'm enjoying myself."

"Think before you take another step, Doon," Carred said. "Or are you telling me you liked working for that bastard?"

Doon Ma'jah hesitated, looking down at Bridnair's bleeding corpse. "No, I didn't. And neither did they."

The other warriors nodded, then one after another knelt to her.

Doon Ma'jah shrugged. "I lead now."

"And you'll honor our agreement?" Carred asked.

Doon Ma'jah glanced between Maggow and Malady. "It is a point of honor. But beer? Is that the best you could offer?"

"For now," Carred said. "Let's see what they bring from the ruin."

"Yes," Doon Ma'jah said. "Let's see." She sheathed her sword as she approached Bridnair's pony, running her hand over his bundled-up rods.

"You plan to use them?" Carred asked.

"Sell them, most likely. I've no need for the stolen essence of sorcerers—even poor sorcerers like these knights. You know, you and the old man were to be next, and that … thing."

"I'd like to have seen him try," Malady said.

"What happens to us?" the older knight said as he helped his young comrade to stand.

Carred appraised him. Evaluated the younger knight too—nothing much to look at, but she'd seen his grit, and he had youth on his side. But then she remembered why they had come here, and she remembered Bridnair's plan.

"Does anyone have any rope?"

TWENTY

"WELCOME," A VOICE SAID out of the darkness.

Had he stopped falling? Anskar didn't know at first. But then he felt the solid floor beneath his feet. He didn't remember landing. He'd felt nothing, known nothing save that first terrifying moment of his plunge into blackness.

The darkness dissolved into motes of gray that blossomed and brightened, expanding, touching, weaving a tapestry of silver that caused Anskar to blink until his eyes adjusted to the harsh light.

Within the brightness that surrounded him, he could make out the blurry forms of three robed and hooded figures.

"Welcome," the figure in the middle said. "Child of the Queen who would be a goddess."

As they flowed closer, he could see their features: black cowls of some thick-weave cloth, armored boots beneath their cloaks. Each had a sword scabbarded at their waist, the cross guard studded with gemstones that winked rapidly. He could see no faces beneath the cowls, just empty blackness.

Was he supposed to respond to their greeting? How? What should he say? He'd encountered a wraithe before and felt inadequate then, a child in the face of the knowledge of ages.

"I met one of your kind at Hallow Hill," he said.

No response.

"In Niyas."

Nothing.

"Did you know that?" They seemed to know who he was, after all.

"Show us," the wraithe on the right said, its voice a grating rasp, "what you wear on your arm beneath your shirt."

Anskar glanced at his forearm, where brilliant blue light bled through his sleeve. Feeling he didn't have much of a choice, he tugged up the sleeve and extended his arm.

The blue radiance from the vambrace hurt his eyes. It had never blazed so brightly before. The metal it was forged from no longer burned. If anything, it had grown cold.

The wraithe on the right glided forward to inspect the vambrace. Although it didn't touch Anskar, the chill coming off the creature made him flinch. And there was a smell, too—graveyards and old tombs.

"Some," the wraithe said, "have ascended by this method, but not many."

"A paltry form of godhood," the wraithe on the left said.

"What method?" Anskar asked.

His question was greeted with silence.

"Am I to become a god?" he asked. *Melesh-Eloni*, the leader of the rebel kidnappers had called him. *Godling*.

"Is that what you desire?" the wraithe in the middle asked.

"No! I serve the Five."

"So we see." And now it was difficult to discern which wraithe was speaking as they flowed into one another, exchanging positions, drifting around him in a slow and predatory orbit.

"This vambrace," Anskar asked. "What is it? Who made it?"

"We are under no obligation to answer," one of the wraithes said.

"We fulfilled our part of the bargain at Hallow Hill," said another. "What happens next is none of our concern."

"But you knew about the vambrace," Anskar pressed. "You used it to lead me here."

Silence.

"Why, if it's none of your concern? Or were you just curious?"

The wraithes ceased their circling and stood motionless, one in front, one behind, one to the side.

"We have questions of our own."

Anskar spun around to face the speaker.

"What brings you here?" another asked.

He turned back. "The Grand Master of my Order."

"He brought you here?" the wraithe on Anskar's right asked. "Why?"

"This place … I mean the entrance …" Anskar glanced up, trusting they would understand that he meant on the surface, above the ruins of six cities. "It was exposed, following an earthquake."

"We know." All three spoke in unison.

"Did you cause the earthquake?"

"We will ask the questions," one of the wraithes said. "Your Grand Master seeks something?"

Anskar nodded. "An object of power. A portal stone that opens a doorway into the abyssal realms."

The wraithes glanced at each other, their faces shrouded in darkness.

"Why seek it here?"

"They said … Blaice, the woman guiding our expedition, said …" Anskar checked himself. The wraithes weren't exactly forthcoming in answering his questions. "Why should I tell you?" Within, his dark-tide repository shivered and writhed.

The wraithes began to circle him again, slower this time. Warily.

"You will be judged by your words," one said.

"Say nothing," another said, "and you will be judged on appearances."

"And they do not look good," the third wraithe said.

Slender, pallid fingers curled around sword hilts. Gemstones flared upon cross guards.

"Contacts," Anskar blurted. "Blaice said her contacts on the mainland knew what this city contained. That they knew from the old texts or something."

"Ah," one of the wraithes said. It let out a loathsome, gurgling cackle.

The other two wraithes emulated the noise, as if they shared some private joke.

"What's so—" Anskar started, but stopped himself. "Sorry. You don't want me to ask questions."

"There is no portal stone," one of the wraithes said.

"But—"

"Someone has misled you. Misled your Grand Master."

"Blaice?"

The wraithes stood still, watching him.

But was it Blaice who had misled the Grand Master, or had she been misled herself, by her contacts? Or perhaps the historical texts had gotten it wrong? Or—and he had no way of knowing—what if the wraithes were misleading him now? Why? To protect the portal stone? But why misdirect him if that was the case? Surely they had the power to kill him, kill the entire expedition, and anyone else foolish enough to come here?

"Tell your companions there is no portal stone," one of the wraithes said. "Tell them also that, by coming here, they have seen things they should not have seen. All of you have."

The silvery light began to fade.

"Are you going to kill us?"

One by one the wraithes swirled away into the encroaching shadows.

The floor beneath Anskar's feet shuddered and shifted. He stumbled and flung his arms out for balance. There was a rush of air as a gaping black hole appeared in the wall in front of him. The floor pitched, and he fell into the opening.

The next he knew, Anskar was swaying on his feet. Stark light hurt his eyes. His stomach clenched, and he bent double, a stream of vomit issuing from his mouth.

And there was a sword at his throat, the blade a silver moonbeam.

Just for an instant, and then Niklaus removed it. He waited for Anskar to stop being sick before asking, "How did you get here?"

Anskar straightened up, wiping his mouth and chin with his shirtsleeve.

Ryala stood behind Niklaus, her sword also drawn. The Grand Master was on her left, a look of puzzlement on his face, golden motes swirling around him from where his ward sphere had been about to spring to life. Blaice stood from a stoop to frown at Anskar, then returned to whatever it was she'd been examining. Someone was missing … Anskar turned and almost groaned. Gadius stood behind him, eyes narrowed.

They were in a large, low-ceilinged room with smooth walls, no sign of any mortar joins. The walls, ceiling and floor gave off a soft, lavender glow. The center of the chamber was stacked with square boxes of what looked like clear crystal, and it was into these boxes that Blaice was peering.

"How did I …?" Anskar started, then turned a full circle, looking for the dark opening he must have come through. It wasn't there, but there was an archway to his left, illuminated by silvery light, and on the right the outline of a second arch, its solid center indistinguishable from the rest of the wall. "How did I get here?"

Niklaus watched him patiently.

"I don't know," Anskar said. "I started to fall, and then I was here, throwing up."

"You appeared out of the air," Ryala said.

"By your own means?" Gadius asked.

"How would that make you feel if I had?" said Anskar.

The Grand Master raised an eyebrow.

"What's she doing?" Anskar asked.

Blaice was pressing her fingertips against the side of a crystal box. Indentations appeared in its surface at her touch, and as she pressed harder, her fingers passed through the crystal as if it were water.

"She thinks this is where the portal stone is kept," the Grand Master said.

"There is no—" Anskar started, then edged forward to see

what Blaice was reaching for.

In the other boxes stacked above and to the sides, he glimpsed the inert bodies of strange and exotic creatures—crab-like things with long, coiled tails; scorpions the size of a small dog; a man's head—Traguh-raj—perfectly preserved, the neck cleanly severed and trailing filaments of brass. There was a hand too, the skin black like that of the Orgols. He saw something that resembled a gigantic woodlouse, only its carapace was formed from segments of silver, and it had two tiny rubies for eyes.

As he came to stand behind her, Blaice curled her fingers around a severed hand with crystalized droplets of blue blood beaded around the stump of the wrist. She pulled it out through the wall of the crystal box, eliciting a faint plop. There was an ebony ring on the hand's index finger, a glinting emerald set into its broad band.

A subtle look passed between Niklaus and Blaice. Anskar thought he might have been the only person to have seen it, because the others were so focused on the grisly relic.

"Is that—" the Grand Master asked "—it?"

"It's a ring," Blaice said dryly.

"And a hand …" Niklaus added.

"I can see that," the Grand Master said. "But the ring has a stone. Or are you going to tell me an emerald's not a stone?"

"It's a stone," Niklaus said. "I'll grant you that."

"But not the one we're looking for," Blaice said. "Agreed?" She tossed the hand to Niklaus.

Niklaus caught it deftly and turned it over, inspecting every inch of it. He began to fiddle with the ring on the dead finger.

"There is no portal stone," Anskar said.

"What?" Gadius said. "How would you know?"

"You saw something, didn't you?" Ryala said. "What happened

when you disappeared?"

"Wraithes," Anskar said. "I met a group of them."

That got everyone's attention.

"And they didn't kill you?" Blaice asked. "Interesting."

The Grand Master smirked. It was his chance to get his own back. "I would think the evidence is against that," he said smugly.

Blaice rolled her eyes. "What did they want?"

"To talk."

"About what?" Gadius asked, but the Grand Master waved him to silence.

Anskar hesitated, wondering how much he should say. *Someone has misled you.*

"Well, Anskar?" the Grand Master prompted.

Anskar glanced at him, still trying to figure out what was going on here. Still trying to piece together what Blaice had to gain by misdirection and false promises? Coin, presumably. Who was it she worked for? Yanatos Holdings. Perhaps she'd told the truth about her mainland contacts knowing what the ruin contained—something of great value that they, or some other contact of hers, wanted. Something they would be willing to expend the lives of others in procuring.

Because if he was right, and Anskar was starting to suspect that he was, Blaice Rancey had used the portal stone as a ruse to entice the Grand Master and the rest of them on this madcap quest. She'd couched it in terms of a religious necessity so that the servants of Menselas could prevent the portal stone falling into the wrong hands and ushering in a new demon war.

Blaice was staring at him now, either bemused by his hesitancy in answering the Grand Master's question, or suspicious that he was on to her.

"They asked what brought us here," Anskar said. "I told them about the portal stone. They said it doesn't exist."

Niklaus tossed the severed hand over his shoulder. "Moldering rubbish," he said.

"But the ring ..." Gadius said.

Niklaus shrugged. "Go fetch it yourself if you like ancient-world jewelry. Personally, I find it a little too effeminate, but that might be to your liking. I've heard about the kinds of things you devotees of the Five get up to in your perverse rituals."

"Be careful," the Grand Master said.

"Or what?"

Ryala took a step toward Niklaus, but the Grand Master held up a hand to stay her. Golden motes spangled the air around him.

"The important thing to ask," the Grand Master said, "is are we in any immediate danger?"

"I think so," Anskar said.

"From the wraithes?" Gadius asked.

"They said we'd seen things we shouldn't have."

"We should leave," Blaice said.

"And the portal stone?" the Grand Master asked.

"Anskar says it doesn't exist," Niklaus said helpfully.

"The wraithes told him that," the Grand Master asked. "And do you believe them, Anskar?"

"Why would they lie?"

"So that we would give up the search," Gadius said. "I'd have thought that was obvious."

"If this place is protected by wraithes," Niklaus said, "do you seriously think anyone else will be successful in retrieving the portal stone? Even the Tainted Cabal aren't that stupid."

"If the stone exists," Blaice added.

"You told me it did!" the Grand Master said. His tone implied there would be consequences if he believed Blaice had lied to him. Maybe not now, when he was vulnerable, but later, once he had returned to Atya, or perhaps Sansor, from where he could mobilize the considerable resources of the Order of Eternal Vigilance to exact any punishment he thought Blaice deserved.

"I'd still like to take a look at that ring," Gadius said, starting toward where Niklaus had tossed the hand.

There was a muffled boom from somewhere below, and the floor juddered.

"We should leave," Blaice said again. "Now."

A succession of whirs and clunks started up. Blaice turned to face the direction the noise was coming from, then set off through the entrance.

"The ring …" Gadius said, glancing from Blaice's retreating back to the severed hand.

"Leave it," the Grand Master said. "Withdraw."

"But …"

Gadius protested as Ryala grabbed him by the back of his robe and dragged him toward the entrance. A resonant clang came from the direction Blaice had taken, and the whirring and clunking stopped.

And then they were running, following Blaice down one silver-lit corridor after the next.

"With me!" Blaice urged periodically, as time passed in a blur, until somehow, short of breath and lungs burning, they arrived back at the entrance hall.

The doorway that led onto the hilltop outside was still wide open.

"That's odd," Blaice panted. "I must have disarmed whatever sorcery opens and closes it when I tackled the wards."

But their way out was blocked nonetheless. The eight statues armed with swords were now arrayed in a semicircle between the group and the entrance. Only, they were statues no longer. They were wraithes, hooded, no sign of the long faces and flat features of the statues. Cloaks rippling in some unseen wind, the wraithes raised their wavy-edged swords and flowed toward the group.

Anskar spoke a cant and his ward sphere blazed into life around him, dazzling silver. He could feel the discharge of essence from his dawn-tide repository, and though the dusk- and the dark-tide strained at the barriers that contained them, they didn't break free.

A sphere of perfect gold appeared around the Grand Master, then one of silver around Ryala. Gadius's ward sphere materialized a split second later, though it wavered, as if fear undermined his casting.

Niklaus's sword seemed to sigh as he drew it. Blaice stepped beside him, something glinting in her hand, but Anskar didn't see what it was.

Ryala met the ghostly charge of the wraithes. Sparks flew from the clash of blades, but as she parried one wraithe, another thrust at her, and its sword tip slid through her ward sphere as if it were nothing but a pretty aura. Ryala managed to twist aside at the last instant, though she took a step back, shocked by how easily the wraithe had penetrated her defenses.

The Grand Master turned a wraithe's blade with a deft parry, his speed belying his appearance. Another wraithe slashed at him, but at the moment of impact, the Grand Master's ward flashed blue and the wraithe's blade lodged in the eldritch sphere. The wraithe thrust out its palm and the Grand Master shrieked, falling to his knees and dropping his sword so he could cover his ears. His ward vanished, and the wraithe raised its sword.

Anskar leaped at it, at the same time drawing *Amalantril.* The blades clashed and a jolt ran up Anskar's arm. The wraithe swung again, and Anskar went to block, but it had been a feint. But then Niklaus was there. Steel met steel, and a blade shattered. Not Niklaus's. The wraithe stood frozen for a moment, clearly stunned.

From somewhere out of Anskar's line of sight, Gadius spoke a cant.

A wraithe swiped at Anskar from the left, another lunged from the right. He parried one blade, slipped away from the other, pivoting to slash his sword into the wraithe's cowled head. The blade passed through the wraithe as if it were made of mist.

A column of flame erupted—the result of Gadius's cant. The wraithe it struck was consumed by the conflagration, but then the flames died down and the wraithe was still there, unharmed, not even smoldering. It surged toward Gadius and, with a brutal cut, severed the head from his shoulders.

Anskar started to cry out, then blocked a sword thrust on instinct, ducking beneath another.

Ryala batted aside a hack that would have disemboweled her, but then a second wraithe ran her through from behind. Blood sprayed from her mouth. She grunted as she dropped her sword and pitched to her knees. Anskar screamed as he tried to reach her, but already the first wraithe was swinging. Ryala's head spun through the air, a look of shock on her face, the stump of her neck spouting crimson as her body toppled to one side.

Without pause, the two wraithes who had been fighting Ryala came at Anskar, the two he had already been fighting closing in from the other side. He twisted and turned, keeping his foes in sight, not letting any of them get behind him. The Grand Master was suddenly beside him, sword back in hand. As the wraithes attacked, the Grand Master's ward sphere reappeared, then punched out at them like a fist of light. One of the wraithes shot backward under the assault, but it immediately recovered, and the Grand Master's golden force disappeared as he staggered with exhaustion.

Three blades came at Anskar, and without thinking he unleashed his dark-tide energy. His ward sphere turned from silver to black, and when the blades struck, they bounced off. But Anskar felt the force of those blows, as if his flesh had been struck by heavy clubs. He cried out in pain and backed away, the Grand Master coming with him.

Niklaus danced about like a madman, avoiding the strikes of the wraithes, always keeping himself between them and Blaice. Sweat poured off him, and each time he found a gap in a wraithe's guard, he struck only air. The wraithes had learned from their first attack on Niklaus. None of them swung at him. They merely thrust and jabbed so that their blades would not shatter against his; and where they got through, Niklaus bled from a score of tiny nicks and cuts. The wraithes resembled a pack of wolves, darting in, nipping at their prey, letting it bleed out its strength, letting it tire so they could move in for the kill.

The four attacking Anskar advanced slowly, as if they knew there was nowhere for him and the Grand Master to run. Anskar glanced at Hyle Pausus and was surprised to see no trace of fear, only fatigue and a jaw set with grim determination. Whatever else he was, the Grand Master was no coward.

His ward a glistening sphere of darkness, Anskar stepped in to meet the wraithes, trusting he could weather a few more blows while striking one of his own. Not a mundane blow, though, for what would be the point? Two more blades bounced off his shield and pounded his bones. He endured a slash from a third sword, a thrust from the fourth, and as he lunged *Amalantril* with all his might into the empty space beneath a wraithe's hood, he spoke a cant and unleashed the full virulence of his dusk-tide repository along the length of the blade—forbidden sorcery, outlawed by the Order, an offense to Menselas and his Church. And yet …

A colossal boom rocked the chamber. *Amalantril* blazed with white fire. And the wraithe screamed as it burst into flame. It thrashed and flailed, shrieking as it dropped its sword and streaked into the air, orbiting the room like an angry fly. The other three wraithes attacking Anskar paused to watch, and then the burning wraithe let out a final, keening moan and fell to the floor in a pile of soot.

So they weren't just ghosts.

They could be killed.

In the distraction, Anskar saw Blaice fling something that glinted golden toward the wraithes fighting Niklaus. There was a blinding flash, and when Anskar's eyes recovered, he saw Niklaus and Blaice fleeing through the entrance to the hilltop outside, the wraithes pursuing them to the doorway but no farther.

"Blackguards," the Grand Master growled. "Spineless, traitorous cowards."

Slowly, one by one, those four wraithes turned to face Anskar and the Grand Master, who now stood back to back, surrounded.

Anskar probed his dusk-tide repository but found it empty. He'd used up all the vitriol he could muster in one colossal attack, and what had it gotten him? Merely a moment's reprieve.

"Any other powers you have," the Grand Master said, "I command you to use them. With Menselas's blessing," he added.

The dark-tide seemed to hear him, and it swelled within Anskar. He had no idea how much more of its essence his repository contained, how long it could sustain his black sphere.

But he did know that he couldn't take many more hits on his ward sphere. Beneath his clothes, his body and limbs throbbed with bruises.

As the remaining wraithes closed in around them, Anskar altered his calculations and cant, extending his dark-tide ward to encompass the Grand Master. He glanced frantically about for any shadows he might disappear into, as he had when he'd saved Vihtor Ulnar from the dead-eyes by entering one pool of shadows and reappearing in another. But the silver luminescence that bathed the chamber was too uniform, too perfect. There were no shadows.

The wraithes swooped in from every side. One after another, swords hammered against Anskar's ward sphere. The Grand Master cried out, clearly also feeling the bludgeoning impacts of the blows. Anskar's head rocked back. Bright light exploded behind his eyes. His legs gave out, and he slumped to his knees, dazed. He felt the Grand Master's grip on his arm, heard the terror in his pleas.

Vision hazed, Anskar saw not seven but dozens of blurry wraithes, blades moving with unnatural slowness as they slammed down into his ward sphere. He grunted under the force. Tasted blood on his lips. The black sphere protecting both him and the Grand Master dissolved into nothingness. The dark-tide shriveled inside him. Its flow ceased.

The swords came again, and this time there was nothing between them and his flesh. He closed his eyes, no strength left for anything else.

And then the vambrace on his forearm burned with such ferocity, Anskar screamed. He could feel the skin beneath blistering, melting. Pain flooded his limbs, burned deep in the marrow of his bones. The chamber dissolved into blackness. The floor he was kneeling upon lurched …

And Anskar opened his eyes upon another place. A place of mist and gloom. A place of twilight. A place of shadows.

Yustanwyrd.

Spectral forms wafted around him. Beside him on a floor of rocks that were as insubstantial as smoke, the Grand Master lay unconscious, hand still clutching Anskar's shirtsleeve, a knot the size of an egg on his forehead, which he must have sustained during that last savage assault.

The assault that had killed them.

For there was no doubt in Anskar's mind that they hadn't been teleported away to safety. Tattered rags that resembled people fluttered past in the unnatural wind. Voices shrieked and howled and whispered. Phantom faces leered down from charcoal skies, bathed in the dark light of a black sun.

Yet, upon his forearm, the vambrace blazed brightly, silver and gold, blue and green, violet and crimson—rays of multicolored light that stood out like an offense against the crepuscular gray.

The vambrace no longer burned.

It was, once more, cold.

The icy chill of the grave.

And yet …

A shadow coalesced out of the teeming shapes in the gloaming.

Tall, slender, swathed in a diaphanous gown of soot and spiderweb. A hollow face, dark-eyed and haunting, the skin no more than desiccated flakes clinging to bone. A high-pronged crown sat upon the skull, threads of gray hair streaming from beneath it, fanned out by the roaring gale.

And Anskar recognized the bearing from the visitation in his dream. He breathed in the stench of rot and mustiness and decay. A crow clung to one shoulder of the apparition, talons digging into the gown. A crow with golden eyes. A crow that Anskar had seen crushed.

"Mother?" he whispered, despising the quaver in his voice. "Queen Talia?"

The specter reached toward him with bony fingers. Not him: the vambrace. But before the dead Queen touched the eldritch metal, she withdrew her hand.

"No," she said, her voice a loathsome rattle. "The vambrace alone is not enough. There is more, fool. Much more before you come here!"

The Queen flung out her hand and the light of the vambrace vanished. Shadows swirled about Anskar. His stomach lurched. Bile filled his mouth, and next thing he knew he was running. Running for his life down the side of the hilltop in the buried city, the Grand Master panting and gasping beside him, hand still clutching Anskar's sleeve, Niklaus and Blaice somehow still with them, but running ahead.

Anskar glanced behind, to where wraithes were pressed in around the entrance of the building on the summit, watching but not giving chase.

At the foot of the hill, Anskar paused to catch his breath. There was a relentless pounding in his skull. His limbs felt bruised and heavy. There was a sharp pain in his ribs, a fierce ache in his back … the results of blows that would have killed him if not for his ward sphere.

"Look," the Grand Master gasped. He was a mess of bruises and welts, and he looked ready to collapse. Somehow, he still held onto his sword with his free hand.

Anskar followed his gaze to see Niklaus and Blaice turn back to face them, gesturing frantically for them to keep up.

Dark shapes wheeled above their heads, beneath the radiant

ceiling of the dome. Anskar looked up and saw dozens of the ghostlike birds circling them. An echoing caw sounded, followed by another, and another.

"Run!" he yelled, freeing himself from the Grand Master's grip and sprinting after Blaice and Niklaus, who were almost in among the shelter of the buildings.

He could hear the Grand Master's panting breaths, the muffled thud of his boots behind.

And then with a cacophony of shrieks and caws, the ghost birds swooped toward them.

TWENTY-ONE

PROBABLY, HE COULD HAVE made it. If he was by himself. If he had no honor. But he wasn't alone, and despite Niklaus and Blaice yelling for him to catch up, Anskar turned back and ran toward the Grand Master.

"What the bloody darkness are you doing?" Blaice cried.

Anskar thought her words were intended for him, but a glance over his shoulder showed Niklaus running after him, sword in hand.

Blaice yelled again, raised her hands in frustration, then fled in among the buildings.

And the smoke-birds struck.

The Grand Master gave up trying to run and stood his ground, flailing above his head with his sword. Steel clove through a wing, yet it might as well have struck mist. Talons raked the Grand Master's breastplate, scoring the metal, before the creature veered away.

One came at Anskar, and while he knew it would do no good, he swung *Amalantril*. The bird passed through the blade and thrust its beak at Anskar's face. He ducked and pivoted, then stumbled as another bird hit him in the back, its talons turned by his mail.

The Grand Master delivered futile hacks as he backed toward Anskar. Blood streaked his face from a cut beneath his eye. His cloak was a shredded mess, his chest plate a latticework of scratches. Without it, Anskar thought, he'd already be dead.

Anskar flailed above his head with his sword—no more than a distraction—then side by side with the Grand Master, retreated toward the buildings.

From the corner of his eye he saw a flash of silver. One of the bird things squawked, then disintegrated, speckling the ground with its black remains. Niklaus had arrived, and his sword—the sword that bore the image of his goddess—clove spectral flesh as if it were solid.

Claws came at Anskar's face, snagged in his hood when he ducked. He tried to swipe the bird away, but his hand passed straight through it.

Not Niklaus's blade, though, which sent the smoke-bird to the ground in a pile of soot. He slashed overhead, and more black dust rained down; then he took the last of the birds assailing Anskar with a vicious swipe across its belly.

"Put your sword away and run," Niklaus said. "Get back to the circle of brass."

"But the Grand Master ..."

"Leave that to me."

"Why are you doing this?"

But Niklaus was already in among the birds that were attacking the Grand Master. He cut about him with controlled ferocity, weaving and dodging, thrusting and slashing, soot piling up on the ground around him. He shoved the Grand Master toward Anskar, and Hyle Pausus would have fallen had Anskar not grabbed his arm. As they fled, dark clouds scudded beneath the domed ceiling that covered the city. More smoke-birds. Hundreds of them.

Niklaus staggered as a bird slammed into him. Blood trickled down his arms and face. "Run!" he cried.

And then he disappeared beneath a mountain of cawing and clawing birds, still fighting, still spitting and cursing, as Anskar ran for cover, dragging the Grand Master with him.

More and more smoke-birds swarmed beneath the dome, yet not one of them came at Anskar or the Grand Master. They passed overhead, streaking toward Niklaus. They smelled blood, Anskar reasoned. Saw Niklaus as the easier prey. Only they were wrong about that. He continued to hack into them, slaughtering them by the dozen.

When Anskar and the Grand Master reached the ring of pillars and the brass circle, Blaice was there waiting for them.

"Niklaus?" she asked coldly.

"A good man," the Grand Master said, panting for breath. "Acted like a knight. Sent by Menselas to save us."

"Don't tell him that," Blaice said. "Not if you want to live."

"We should go back for him," Anskar said.

"And do what?" Blaice said. "Die?"

"Then what do you suggest?" the Grand Master said.

"We leave."

"Not without Niklaus," Anskar said.

Blaice sneered. "As the Grand Master said, he's a good man. Don't let his sacrifice be in vain."

Anskar glanced at the brass circle. It still danced with black flames and exuded the smell of molten metal. "My repositories are empty." All but the dawn-tide, but what good would that be here?

"Don't worry about that," Blaice said. "The circle still holds a charge, by the looks of it. Hopefully enough for us all to return to the surface."

"And if it's not?" the Grand Master asked. "Will we end up like Hendel?"

"Either take the risk, or stay here below. Forever." And with that, Blaice stepped into the brass circle. At first, nothing happened, but then she made an incantation from the proto-Skanuric lettering engraved into the brass. The black flames flared and flickered. Still canting, Blaice disappeared.

Anskar looked at the Grand Master, who sighed and gestured for him to go first.

With a quick prayer for Niklaus, Anskar stepped into the circle.

They reappeared in the identical brass circle in the egg-shaped chamber, its concave walls and ceiling encrusted with winking gemstones of amber, green and red. Black flames burned around the circle, the same as they did around the one below, and something occurred to Anskar as he followed Blaice and the Grand Master toward the chamber's exit.

"Why couldn't we all have entered the circle together and made one trip?" Maybe then Hendel would still have been alive.

Blaice hesitated on the chamber's threshold, as if the thought hadn't occurred to her. She shrugged. "I suppose we could have done if you wanted to run the risk of our bodies being fused together." She raised an eyebrow. "Actually, that might not be such a bad idea. With you, at least."

Anskar felt heat rush to his cheeks and looked away.

"Harlot," the Grand Master muttered.

Blaice laughed. "You mean to tell me you haven't thought the same? Or isn't Anskar your type?"

"Impudent woman!" The Grand Master stormed ahead of her and started to ascend the sloping corridor outside.

"Shouldn't we wait awhile?" Anskar called after him. "In case Niklaus makes it back."

The Grand Master turned, caught Anskar's eye and swallowed.

Before he could answer, Blaice said, "He won't."

"How can you be so sure?"

"I saw him go down … while you two were running. He didn't get up again."

"But … After the manticarr he was alive. He survived," said Anskar. He wanted to go back if there was even a slim chance Niklaus was still alive …

"Face it, Anskar," Blaice snapped. "He's gone."

A confusion of emotions crossed the Grand Master's face. He still looked chagrined by Blaice's goading, but it was mixed with concern, indecision, and maybe a tinge of guilt.

"He was my …" Blaice started, voice strident, face flushed with anger. She paused and sniffed, then wiped her eyes with the back of her hand. "He was my friend. More than a friend. If I thought there was any way he could live through that, I would go back down there and find him."

Of course you would, Anskar thought bitterly.

Blaice looked from him to the Grand Master, tears tracking down her cheeks. "He's dead, I tell you. My Niklaus is dead."

Your Niklaus? The bitch was acting, Anskar was certain of it.

Putting on the tears to get her own way. Or was she? When Blaice began to sob uncontrollably, the Grand Master came back into the chamber and placed a hand on her shoulder.

"Forgive me, Blaice. I am tired. We all are. I … I mourn for your loss."

Anskar felt suddenly guilty. Had he been too quick to judge her? And by what standards? By the way he acted himself, the way he lied and cheated and did what he needed to get by? For he was no saint, of that he was certain. How many times had he lied to Vihtor? Or, if not lied, how many times had he held back the full truth?

Awkwardly, he inched toward the sobbing Blaice. "I'm sorry too," he said. He still didn't trust her, but perhaps he had been too harsh.

"You mean that?" Blaice said through sniffles as she wiped away her tears.

Anskar nodded, and she threw her arms around him. He could feel the heat of her body pressed up against him, smell her sweat and musk and something that reminded him of roses. He patted her back, embarrassed. She wriggled and moaned, shoving her face into his chest as she sobbed.

Anskar glanced at the Grand Master, who merely shook his head. He gently pushed Blaice back from him, holding her at arm's length. His eyes were transfixed by the serpent tattoo that wended its way between her breasts, its head adorning her throat. She arched her back slightly, thrusting her chest toward him. Anskar shifted his gaze to her tear-streaked face. The violet of her eyes captivated him. They still glistened with wetness, but he saw something else there now: a neediness, a desire that found its echo in his mounting arousal.

The Grand Master coughed into his fist. "Sorry to rush you," he said, "but perhaps we should be going."

"Agreed," Blaice said, giving Anskar a sly grin. Her sobbing ceased at once, and she wiped away the last of her tears. "If we linger, the wraithes may send something else after us. Or they might come themselves."

"But down below," Anskar said, "they didn't follow us from their building."

"That doesn't mean they couldn't if they'd wanted to," the Grand Master pointed out. "Blaice is right to be cautious. Come on, let's go."

They followed the passageway's gentle gradient upwards, their reflections in the illuminated surfaces of the walls disappearing into the distance ahead of them. When they came at last to the square doorway they had entered the ruin by, it stood open, as they had left it.

"What?" Blaice said to the Grand Master's expression of surprise. "You think it would close itself?"

A spiny, red-crested lizard the size of a cat had come to explore within the entrance. It gazed at the group as they approached, long tongue flicking out, then it turned and crawled away at its own lazy pace.

It was night outside, the twin moons hanging overhead. Anskar felt the tickle and prod of the dark-tide as it dripped and oozed into his empty repository. By the time they reached the lip of the ravine and rested for a moment beneath the looming face of the mesa, Anskar could feel his dark-tide repository swelling with potency. It writhed within him, boring deeper and deeper into his core, expanding. He'd pushed his dark-tide reserves to the limit, emptied his repository, yet here it was restoring itself and growing stronger than before. He wondered if there was a limit to the dark-tide's expansion within him, some cut-off point beyond which he couldn't go. Or would his abilities continue to grow until he came to rival the greatest sorcerers Wiraya had ever known? Or perhaps surpass them? Would he exceed even the power of the demon lords of the abyssal realms? The gods?

He winced, his head full to bursting with possibilities, none of which he was sure he wanted. If anything, the idea of infinite power frightened him. All his life he had wanted to serve, to increase in the virtues demanded by Menselas. But ever since the sorcerer Luzius Landav had embedded the crystal catalyst beneath the skin of his chest, Anskar had felt different inside. It was supposed to be a catalyst for the use of sorcery, yet he couldn't help thinking it had proven a catalyst for something else, some inner change, or perhaps the unveiling of a hidden latency.

He became aware of the low exchange of voices. The Grand Master was confronting Blaice about the portal stone, accusing her of using the idea as a lure to bring him and his knights along … as fodder. It was Niklaus who had first used the term.

"Paranoia," Blaice said. "You really think I would bring you all the way out here just to have you and your knights face the dangers and leave me free to steal the loot?"

Silence was her answer.

"I feel I have been maligned," she said. "Denigrated. Has Lanuc of Gessa being saying bad things about me? I could tell you one or two things about him if you like. Did you know that Lanuc enjoys—"

"I don't need to know!" the Grand Master snapped. "It is dishonorable to speak about someone who is not present to defend themselves."

"Bet you never told Lanuc that while he bad-mouthed me."

"This is fruitless," the Grand Master said. "First, we need to get back to Lanuc and Orix. Once we return to Atya, we can address the ramifications of this disaster of an expedition."

"Ramifications?" Blaice said. "Is that a threat?"

The Grand Master's sword sighed and scraped as he drew it from its scabbard. "This is a threat, woman. Don't think I won't use it if you continue."

"You're telling me to shut up?"

"Shrewd of you to realize. But before we set off, tell me this: did you salvage anything from the ruin? I can't believe a woman like you would have gone to all this trouble and come away with nothing."

Blaice emptied her pockets. "Satisfied?"

The Grand Master nodded and sheathed his sword.

"Anskar," he said, "can you light our way for the return journey to the canal where we left Orix and Lanuc?"

Anskar reached into his dawn-tide repository, which was virtually unused. He drew upon its essence and spoke a cant. His silver ward sphere sprang into life around him. Then, slowly, with fierce concentration, he altered the calculations and his cant, forcing the sphere of light outwards, away from his body. It floated a few feet in front of him; then he willed it to contract. When it was the size of an egg, radiant with compacted light, he reached for it and held it in the palm of his hand.

"Did they teach you that at Branil's Burg?" the Grand Master asked.

Anskar shook his head. "It's the first time I've thought of doing such a thing." In truth, he'd been inspired by the way some of the other knights had used their ward spheres as weapons, condensing the light into fists of force that they could slam into their opponents; Vihtor had given him and Sareya the cants to do the same thing themselves. What Anskar had just achieved was an even simpler matter, and it took considerably less power. At the rate his dawn-tide essence was trickling from his repository, he could probably sustain the silver sphere for hours—enough to see them through the night, if necessary.

Just before they got underway, Blaice touched the Grand Master lightly on the arm.

"If I were you," she said, "I'd organize a full expedition when I got back to Sansor, with the backing of the Church of Menselas and the resources of your Order."

The Grand Master studied her for a long, uncomfortable moment and then said, "For what reason? An imaginary portal stone?"

"I wasn't lying."

Yes, you were, Anskar thought. Nothing Blaice Rancey said sounded like the truth. Was her name even Blaice Rancey?

He could see the Grand Master mulling over the same questions. Of course, there was the remote possibility that she believed what she said about the portal stone. Perhaps her contacts really did think it was hidden somewhere in the lost city of Yustanwyrd, a secret jealously guarded by the wraithes. And there was also the very real possibility that the wraithes had lied about it not existing.

"Gaith, Hendel, Ryala, Gadius," the Grand Master said, punctuating each name by driving his fist into his palm. "Those are the names of your accusers. The Order has lost four good people because of you. The only consolation: Menselas has gained four new saints. Perhaps I will discuss what you say with the bishop in Sansor. Perhaps there will be a properly organized expedition. You, however, will not be a part of it. Furthermore, there will be a reckoning, Blaice Rancey. You will be summoned to a tribunal in Sansor to answer for your crimes."

"Crimes?" she said. "How is anything I've done a crime?"

"Maybe not here in heathen Atya," the Grand Master said, "but in Sansor you will be harshly judged for your actions."

"Then remind me not to go to Sansor."

"Justice will be done, whatever you decide."

"How?"

"You will see."

It didn't sound an empty threat to Anskar. The Order's reach was long, and he'd already seen that the Grand Master was not averse to bending its rules when the need arose.

"I can't believe you're doing this to me," Blaice said, the tears starting to fall on cue.

Anskar loathed her at that moment. Despised everything about her. Like the Grand Master, he held her accountable for the deaths of their companions, Niklaus among them. As she once more began to tear up and protest her innocence, Anskar turned his back on her and her games. Catching the Grand Master's eye, Anskar set off along the trail between the mesas, back toward the canal where they had left Lanuc and Orix. Anger seemed to have restored some of the Grand Master's spent energy, and he walked briskly at Anskar's side. After a while, Blaice's footsteps followed as she scurried to catch up.

The air in the valley between the mesas was cool and refreshing, but it did little to allay Anskar's fears of being out in the open. Neither did the shrieks of night birds, the distant growls of predators. It was hard not to think of the dead-eyes and other abominations that preyed on those foolish enough to travel in the dark.

Once the initial thrill of their escape from the ruin wore off, Anskar's exhaustion clawed its way back, leaving his limbs leaden and making each step along the trail torturous. He could see from the way the Grand Master swayed as he walked that he was faring no better now that his anger had run its course, and even Blaice, who had hardly expended any energy at all during the fights with the wraithes and the smoke-birds, could barely stop herself from yawning.

After an age, they came once more to the landslide that blocked the path between the mesas and, weary beyond belief, Anskar led the way to the top, where he could see a flickering orange glow on the far side. It had to be Lanuc and Orix, waiting for them by the canal.

"Thank Menselas," the Grand Master said when he reached the top of the rockfall. "I think I'll sleep for all eternity once we stop."

Blaice muttered something as she came up behind him.

They half-climbed, half-slid down the far side, then hurried toward the warmth and comfort offered by the fire. Even from a little way off, Anskar could make out the silhouettes of two figures seated by the flames, facing away from them.

"Where are the ponies?" the Grand Master asked.

"Probably found them shelter in an alcove or a cave in the rock face," Blaice suggested.

"And left them unattended?"

As they drew near, Anskar saw that the two figures were indeed Orix and Lanuc, though something seemed wrong. Their heads were bowed and their arms were behind their backs. Too late he realized what that meant. They had been taken captive.

Orix looked around, eyes reflecting the silver light in Anskar's palm. "I'm sorry," he said miserably.

Without conscious thought, Anskar caused the light to expand and encompass him—a dazzling ward sphere of silver.

Lanuc turned his head to face the Grand Master and cried, "Flee! Back the way you came!"

Blaice didn't need telling twice. She was already turning to run when lightning streaked down from the darkness atop the mesa. It struck the ground with a deafening boom mere feet from her, sending up a shower of rock and dust. Blaice swerved aside from the blast, but before she could take another step, a second blast of lightning exploded in front of her, even closer this time. She threw up her arm to shield her eyes, then turned back toward the fire, blinking furiously.

Effortlessly, Anskar altered his cant and extended his ward sphere to encompass the Grand Master; then, after a moment's hesitation, he stretched it to include Blaice as well.

"They're on the mesa," Orix told him. "And more behind . . ."

Orix's warning trailed off as there came the slow clop of hooves from the other side of the fire, and then, a few dozen yards down the trail, the darkness thickened as shapes began to emerge from it: riders on ponies. Six riders, five of them hard-looking Traguh-raj, four men and a woman. The sixth was a woman in boiled leather armor, a sword hanging at her hip. She heeled her pony ahead of the group, her cat's eyes blazing with reflected argent from Anskar's shield, her skin a vibrant red.

The Niyandrian.

Then Anskar saw that someone else sat in the saddle behind the woman—a child perhaps. Not a child, he realized as the second rider climbed down from the pony and stood glaring, a malevolent glint in her eyes. A dwarf in motley attire.

"How's the catalyst, boy?" Malady asked, following her question with a cackle.

She appraised him with narrowed eyes. Perhaps she was assessing the changes that had taken place in him, measuring his growth as a sorcerer. He sought to deflect her with the only thing he could think of to say.

"I'm sorry about Luzius."

"I'm not," Malady said. "A demon never forgives the one who binds her. The only good slaver is a dead slaver. Think about that, Anskar, and how it pertains to your precious Order."

Malady made a claw of one hand, vapors the color of fresh bruises pluming from her fingertips. They wafted over the fire, coalescing into a poisonous brume that roiled toward Anskar, Blaice and the Grand Master. Instinctively, Anskar took a step back, but then the mist surged over them, coating Anskar's ward sphere. Dawn-tide energy bled from Anskar's repository as the sphere faded and flickered. He tried to stem the flow, but essence continued to drain from him until, with a stutter and a pop, the ward went out, leaving them in the orange glow coming off the fire.

Instinctively, Anskar reached for the dark-tide, but at the last instant he stopped himself. The evil vapors the dwarf had sent roiling over them had vanished along with his ward sphere. There was no need to do more, not yet. Better to let them think they had already won.

"*Melesh-Eloni*," the Niyandrian rider said, leaning over the saddle pommel. She had a striking face, cast into shadow by the dancing flames. Angular, high cheekbones, a hawkish nose. A long jagged scar ran from beneath her left eye to her chin. Her black hair showed signs of gray and was bound at the nape of her neck. She was a tall woman, almost ludicrously large for the pony she was riding. Lean and hard-bodied.

She raised her right hand in a placating gesture, the effect lessened by the fact that two of her fingertips were missing. Battle scars crisscrossed her forearm. "Do not fear me," she said in Nan-Rhouric, heavily accented and not at all confident. "I am Carred Selenas."

TWENTY-TWO

CARRED'S HEART THUDDED IN her chest. The young man was glaring at her. *Melesh-Eloni.* He had his mother's depthless eyes, though they looked out of place against his dusky skin hue—that of a mainlander, with only the merest blush of red. She was overcome with the need to say something else, something momentous, but she despised the way her speech came out stilted—even to her own ears. She'd learned enough Nan-Rhouric to get by over the years, but she so seldom practiced, and every foreign word felt a betrayal.

Beside Carred's pony, the dwarf-demon sniggered. That, as much as the young man standing before her, made her even more self-conscious.

"Carred Selenas?" Anskar turned to the Grand Master. "The rebel lead—"

"I know who Carred Selenas is, Anskar. On top of her numerous crimes, she is the woman who wanted you kidnapped."

"Slow down," Carred said, her understanding lagging as she worked a translation. "It was not like that. Well, it was, but … your mother …"

"My mother is dead."

"I know." Carred's throat tightened. Theltek's eyes, she almost sobbed. She looked away from him so she could stop seeing Talia in the lines of his face. She found herself meeting the gaze of the woman beside Anskar—mussed-up black hair, but rather striking olive skin. And her eyes! Violet. The effect was somewhat ruined by the ear and nose jewelry and the way she was dressed like a mainland privateer in leather boots and black pants. Her shirt was open-necked, revealing deep cleavage threaded by a serpent tattoo.

"Blaice," the woman said with a slight widening of her eyes. "Blaice Rancey." In Niyandrian, she added, "You might have heard of—"

Carred wrenched her eyes away. "No, I …" *Get a grip,* she told herself. She was getting flustered.

To Anskar, she said, "Your mother was …" And immediately dried up. She couldn't tell him what Talia had been to her, what they had done together. Couldn't tell him how she felt, either, because she no longer knew. "I was—how do you say?—Captain of the Last Cohort. Her personal bodyguard. When Naphor fell, I saw her die."

"The Necromancer Queen was your mother?" the Grand Master asked. "But that's … that's …" He glanced at the older of the two knights Carred had captured earlier, but the man—his name was Lanuc or some such—was staring at Anskar, open-mouthed. "That's preposterous," the Grand Master finally concluded.

"Anskar?" the younger captive—Orix—said. Like Lanuc's, his

hands had been tied behind his back.

Doon Ma'jah edged her pony closer to Carred's.

"*Melesh-Eloni,*" Carred said, forcing a tentative smile for Anskar. Extended her hand. Withdrew it when he noticed the nubs of her severed fingertips. She covered it with her other hand—an old habit she'd forgotten till now. Theltek, she was acting like a lovestruck maid. It had to be the resemblance to Talia, or the enormity of what was taking place—the end of a decade and a half of waiting.

"I didn't know," Anskar told the Grand Master. "I still don't know if it's true. How could it be? Queen Talia had a daughter, not a son."

"Oh, it is true," Carred said. She was getting better, the foreign words coming easier now that the rust was flaking off. "I had my doubts, but not now I have seen you."

"Then who is my father?" Anskar demanded. "Tell me! Or did the Necromancer Queen make me with sorcery? Am I inhuman? Am I damned?"

"I did not know the Queen had a child until after her death. I was told …"

"Told by whom?" the Grand Master asked.

"I was told there was a child. As were the Order of Eternal Vigilance."

Lanuc nodded, still staring at Anskar. "A daughter, they said."

"Did you just come here to wag your pretty little chin, or are we going to take what we want and go?" Doon Ma'jah said. She had spoken in Niyandrian. Of a sort. It made Carred's Nan-Rhouric seem fluent.

"Pretty?" Carred unconsciously touched the scar that ran beneath her eye. Marith said she liked it. Jada too. Kovin had never been much interested in her face.

"Time is coin," Doon said, sticking to Niyandrian.

"I thought we were paying you in beer."

"You were paying Bridnair in beer. I require coin."

"Then you'll need to negotiate a new contract," Carred said, "and this is hardly the time."

When Doon opened her mouth to say more, Carred looked down at Malady, then glanced up at the top of the mesa, where Maggow stood with a couple of warriors. "You think your new master will permit you to kill her?" she asked the demon.

Doon's eyes widened then swiftly narrowed. She'd seen what Malady could do.

"He didn't forbid it …" the demon said.

Anskar was watching their interaction with intelligent eyes. Could he follow what they were saying? Clearly the others couldn't. The Grand Master tried to look nonchalant, but he was an open book to Carred, weighing the cost of attempting to free his comrades against that of making a run for it. Neither option seemed to fill him with much confidence.

"I am sorry we had to meet this way, *Melesh-Eloni*," Carred said, "but I could not risk losing you a second time."

"You're the one who tried to kidnap Anskar?" Orix said. Not the sharpest arrow in the quiver.

Malady snorted.

"It was my people who came for him," Carred said. "My people who died in the attempt. *Your* people, Anskar."

He swallowed as he stared at her, mouth working in a reply that refused to take shape.

"Yes, *Melesh-Eloni*," Carred said, "*your* people."

"Don't call me that. Ever again." His hand went to the hilt of his sword.

"Anskar, then," Carred said. She smiled, but that only seemed to increase his tension. "Anskar DeVantte. The family name … Eldrid is your father, yes? Your—what is the word?—uncle? Elder brother?"

"None of them," Anskar said. "I don't know who my father is." He glanced at the Grand Master, who shook his head and shrugged.

"He will not give you … answers you need," Carred said. "The Knights of Eternal Vigilance have …" *Blathoev* was the Niyandrian word. In Nan-Rhouric, it was … pay … poy … "They have poisoned your head … your brain … since you were a baby. Come with me. Let me aid you in understand."

"And if I refuse?"

Carred sat tall in her saddle and studied him for a long moment. Bluish light bled from beneath his shirtsleeve. Anskar noticed, covered his arm, glanced up at the sky. Carred looked too. The two moons hung overhead like gigantic eyes, one white, the other bloodshot.

"What is that?" Carred asked. No response. "Do you want Doon here to undress you?"

Anskar raised his arm and rolled up his shirtsleeve.

Blaice Rancey edged closer so she could see. The Grand Master let out a gasp.

Upon Anskar's forearm, a vambrace shone cobalt and silver.

"Where did you get this?" Carred asked. What did it mean? Was this part of Talia's scheming?

"Is that divine alloy?" Blaice Rancey said, reaching out to touch the vambrace.

Anskar pulled back his arm and tugged down his shirtsleeve.

"What do you know of divine alloy?" Carred asked.

"Not a lot," Blaice said. "But you hear things … you know, from necromancers and the like."

"What things?"

"I'm not sure I want to remember."

"The heathens," the Grand Master said, with a pointed look at Carred, "say it is a path to divinity. To becoming a god."

"And what do the holy Knights of Eternal Vigilance say?" Carred asked.

"That it is the ore of the abyssal realms."

"Idiot," Malady said.

"That those who possess it are no better than demons." The look Hyle Pausus gave Anskar was both angry and full of concern. "Remove it, Anskar. In the name of Menselas, take it off."

"I can't," Anskar said.

"I command you."

"I can't, I tell you. I've tried, but …"

"I could have a look if you like," Blaice offered.

"Enough!" Carred Selenas said. "You and you," she said to Blaice and the Grand Master, "back away. Do not interfere, or you will be killed."

"I had rather assumed you were going to kill us anyway," the Grand Master said.

"Why?" Carred asked. "Because heathens are … *kulau amork* … bloodthirsty killers?"

"Well … yes."

"Then thank your god with the five faces that I am not at all like you and your Order of torturers and murderers. Now, do as I say and back off. Last warning."

The Grand Master stepped away and, with a shrug and a smirk, Blaice Rancey went with him. Beside the fire, Orix and Lanuc exchanged worried glances.

"Remember this small mercy, Hyle Pausus," Carred said. "And learn from it. Learn never again to do what you did to my people at Branil's Burg."

"They got what they deserved," the Grand Master said. "It is what's generally known as justice, at least among those familiar with the concept."

"Is it justice to steal away our babies?" Carred asked. "To raise them as if they were mainlanders? To test them with the trials of your Order, then to throw away—discard? Is it a word?—those who are not what you are looking for?"

"It was necessary," the Grand Master said. "We needed to prevent people like you from finding the Necromancer Queen's child, from rallying around ..." He glanced at Anskar. "We needed to stop the heir to Niyas from being the focal point for your irritation of a rebellion."

"Oh, he is so much more than that," Carred said. "The *Melesh-Eloni* is the one who goes before, the one who will bring about the return of the Queen."

"But he won't, will you, Anskar?" Orix said from his place by the fire.

Anskar said nothing, merely met Carred's gaze with his tawny eyes. Talia's eyes. How much did he know? Had Talia communicated with him, the way she'd spoken to Carred through Noni? And the vambrace ... Anskar's idea, or part of his mother's plan? *You don't need to keep me in the dark, Talia. I'd be more help to you if you didn't. Maybe I'd trust you more, want whatever it is you really want.* Or maybe she wouldn't—a thought that was increasingly troubling her.

Lanuc was watching Anskar intently, the bunch of his shoulders indicating that he was straining against the ropes that bound his hands behind his back.

"Anskar," Orix persisted, "you won't bring the Necromancer Queen back, will you? Tell her you won't."

Carred looked round at the sound of stomping. The ponies were growing restive, their Traguh-raj riders hard-eyed and impatient. Doon settled them with a glare. Perfect control. They had accepted her leadership without hesitation. They were also getting belligerent, and even the threat of Malady might not be enough to hold them back if Doon gave the word.

"Bring a spare pony," Carred commanded a sullen-looking man. He grunted something in his own tongue but then obeyed, leading one of the ponies they had taken from Lanuc and Orix.

"Get on," Carred told Anskar.

"I'm not going with you."

"And I refuse your refusal." Carred drew her sword.

"She won't kill you, Anskar," Orix said. "She needs you."

Carred gritted her teeth with frustration and, guiding her pony with her legs, one hand grasping the reins, she rode closer to Orix and leaned over the saddle pommel to point the tip of her sword at his throat. "But I do not need you."

Doon Ma'jah edged forward. Behind her, the other Traguh-raj warriors started to follow. *Dumb cow,* Carred muttered—against herself, not Doon. Orix was Traguh-raj. They were protecting their own.

"Don't forget," Carred told Doon in Niyandrian, glancing up at the dark-shrouded heights of the mesa. "I still have a sorcerer."

The Traguh-raj riders stopped where they were. Doon gave an almost imperceptible nod. Having served under Bridnair, she was used to the threat of sorcery. She'd behave herself.

"Last time," Carred said to Anskar. "Get on the pony."

Anskar met Lanuc's eyes. The knight had given up struggling against his bonds and sat, head bowed, by the fire.

"I have no dawn-tide energy left," the Grand Master muttered.

Anskar's eyes flicked left and right, alighting on the pooling shadows.

"That won't help your companions," Malady said. "And, in any case, wherever you flee, I will follow. Your dark-tide tricks are no match for a real demon's."

Anskar's fists clenched and unclenched. His chest swelled with a deep breath, then deflated as he let it out.

"Promise you'll not harm my companions," he said.

Carred sheathed her sword. "You have my word."

Anskar mounted the pony, and Carred took the reins, leading it behind her own. Malady climbed up behind her once more, sending a shudder up Carred's spine.

"I'll find you, Anskar," Orix called out.

Such loyalty. It was actually rather touching. It made Carred wonder what she was doing, whether it was right. But second-guessing accomplished nothing, and too many had died to bring her to this point.

"Try anything," she cast over her shoulder, "and you die. If I even set eyes on you again, you die."

TWENTY-THREE

THREE OF THE TRAGUH-RAJ riders with Carred Selenas backed up their ponies to allow Anskar's into the middle of the group, then the other two set off, leading the way. The three at the back followed, bringing with them the remaining four ponies of the Grand Master's expedition. Carred Selenas rode alongside Anskar, the demon Malady clinging on behind her. Anskar's hands were unbound, and something inside him saw that as a dare: Carred Selenas didn't think he had it in him to attempt to escape. Either that, or she was confident in Malady's ability to stop him. Part of him strained to be unleashed, wanted so much to show her she was wrong. Another part counseled patience: wait until the opportunity presented itself. Still another part was afraid, though it chafed to admit it. Anskar doubted Niklaus would have been so indecisive. It felt like a curse, not being able to act when he knew he should—and it wasn't the first time. All these sides to him! Was that an effect of worshiping a god of five aspects? Of course it wasn't. Menselas was one. Five in one, but still one.

And besides, maybe Carred Selenas had another reason for her confidence, Anskar thought, when the sky above the left-hand mesa was suddenly streaked through with ribbons of sunlight, even though it was still the middle of the night. The sorcerer Carred Selenas had mentioned. In the unnatural blaze atop the summit, Anskar could see the silhouettes of half a dozen riders, and with them, at the head, a figure hunched over a pony, sorcerous light effusing from his raised hand. The group riding along the mesa took a parallel course to Carred Selenas's riders below. As the mesa began to drop away in gigantic steps and sheer slopes, the sorcerer and the other riders made their descent. Once into the foothills, they picked up their pace, finally crossing the flatland at the bottom at a gallop. Carred Selenas's group slowed to allow them to catch up.

As the two groups merged, Anskar saw the sorcerer was an ancient-looking Niyandrian, naked save for a grimy loincloth. The old man looked at Anskar and grinned. He only had one tooth, a vile, brown stub of a thing.

Malady dropped from the saddle behind Carred Selenas and climbed up behind the old man. Carred Selenas spoke to the newcomer in Niyandrian. The only thing Anskar recognized was *Melesh-Eloni.* She also used the word "Maggow," which Anskar took to be the sorcerer's name.

The old man nodded, then fixed Anskar with a penetrating stare. Invisible feelers probed and prodded at Anskar's repositories, weaving their way through the boundaries he had erected around them. For a moment Anskar struggled to ward himself against the old man's intrusion, but he quickly realized it was a losing battle. Instead, he relaxed his guard and sent his own sorcerous senses into the old man. What he found was a profound shock: tangles of wrongness. Distortions. Jagged shards of potency that formed a twisted amalgam of the dusk, the dawn, and something else—though it wasn't the dark-tide. There was no recognizable repository as such, just a clumping of disparate powers, an indelicate growth of malformed sorceries that resembled a tumor to Anskar's *sight*. It was as if the sorcery were a parasitic mass within the old man, feeding off him, growing, until one day it would consume him.

The old man's lips tightened into a thin line as he withdrew his senses. Something like a shadow passed across his eyes and he nodded sagely, as if he'd seen the power Anskar possessed and was now wary, like a man who had cornered a poisonous snake.

Anskar withdrew his own senses, but what had he learned? There was nothing within the old man that he could properly read or understand.

When Carred Selenas gave the order for the riders to move on, Anskar kicked his heels into his pony's flanks, and they resumed the long ride west.

They rode hard through the night, their path illuminated by the golden glow coming from the sorcerer's hand.

"I am sorry for what happened at Branil's Burg," Carred Selenas said as they rode. "I am sorry for the kidnap attempt. But I do not know what else I was supposed to do. I was charged by Queen Talia, I think, to find you, so that you can restore her to the world."

"You think?" Anskar asked.

Carred glanced at him then looked away into the far distance.

"A wraithe told me who you were, the same wraithe that spoke with me atop Hallow Hill the day of Queen Talia's death."

"At Naphor," Anskar said. "You were there." It wasn't a question. Everybody knew Carred Selenas had been with the Queen at the end. Somehow, she had survived. *Did you abandon my mother?* he wanted so badly to ask. *Did you flee like a coward?* He could almost hear Tion's voice in his head, cautioning him not to offend her, telling him the Healer aspect of Menselas approved only of words that built others up. Not that Tion had always followed that advice to the letter. But what else could he ask her? Her mention of Naphor had roused a host of warring images in his imagination: scenes of glory, the part of him who had been raised by the Order wanted to believe; but they were overlaid with scenes of terror.

"Naphor…" he asked. "At the end… What…?"

"What was it like, the last battle?" She looked off into the distance, remembering. When she faced him again, she opened her mouth to say something, then seemed to choke on the words. He couldn't work out if it was grief he saw in her cat's eyes, or anger.

Anskar's mind raced, searching for what else he should say. "I too …" he started, then decided not to share the rest of his thought with her: *I too spoke with a wraithe atop Hallow Hill.*

He found himself wanting to trust her—trust the woman who had taken him captive! He wanted to share what he knew and have her piece it together for him. But he had been formed by the Order of Eternal Vigilance, by Brother Tion, by the tenets of the Church of Menselas. To their way of thinking, Carred Selenas was a fanatic, an outlaw, a dangerous woman with aims that were at best misguided, and at worst evil.

It didn't help knowing that she revered his mother. The

realization of who he was and who had spawned him was a still-open wound, a wound he wanted sutured, healed and forgotten.

But that could never be. Unless he had been deceived in some way, he had to face the fact that he was the Necromancer Queen's son and heir, but that didn't mean he had to be happy about it. Nor did it mean that he had to meekly comply with his dead mother's wishes.

"It must have—what is the phrase you use?—turned your world upside down when you came to realize who you were," Carred Selenas said, as if she could read his thoughts. "What your purpose was in the world. But I need you to trust me. The knights who raised you are not good people, Anskar. They seek only to … *quolth* … to pervert your mind, blind you to the truth."

"That's funny," Anskar said, "because I'm sure that's exactly what they'd say about you."

She didn't seem to have an answer to that. She clamped her lips shut and turned her gaze once more to the west, toward Atya.

The Traguh-raj warriors spoke in low voices to one another, leaning out of the saddle the better to hear. Occasionally they would chuckle at some shared joke, but every now and again they would grow deathly quiet in response to a distant growl, a shriek from the pitch skies, the rasp of something slithering.

All the while, the dark-tide pitter-pattered against Anskar's skin, pooled within his repository, filling it to the brim, stretching it, increasing its capacity.

Several times Anskar caught Carred Selenas watching him. Each time, she looked away into the night. Anskar couldn't quite work her out. She was clearly a strong woman, physically at the very least, and she was dedicated to her cause. Fanatically so. But there was a fragility to her, a clinging sadness that was conveyed through her eyes, the way she dipped her head when lost in thought. Not exactly the treacherous demon the Order of Eternal Vigilance portrayed her as.

This time it was Carred Selenas's turn to catch him watching, and Anskar's turn to look away. He hadn't realized he was doing it, but as he thought about the riddle of her personality, he had been staring at the curves of her breasts, admiring the sharp lines of her face, the knotted tautness of her muscles. He felt a pang of guilt for looking at her that way. Tion would have chastised him for it, although all the evidence suggested Tion was no better himself.

"What is it, Anskar?" she said. She seemed to grow in confidence with her Nan-Rhouric the more she used it, though her accent made listening an act of supreme concentration. "I know this must be hard for you, but I will do whatever I can to help you understand."

"What if I don't want to understand?" He knew he was being childish. Of course he wanted to understand. No good ever came from ignorance—an aphorism attributed to the Elder.

Carred Selenas offered him a smile—of reassurance? Kindness? Whatever it was, he felt uncomfortable with the way she appraised him with her eyes. Probably, she'd felt the same when he'd been watching her.

"What was she like?" Anskar suddenly blurted out.

"Your mother?"

They rode on in silence for a while, but Anskar could see she was thinking. Finally, with her eyes focused on the darkness ahead, she said, "She was a strong leader. A great queen."

"I meant as a person."

"As a ..." Carred Selenas looked at him, Maggow's sorcerous light giving her cat's eyes a feral glint. "She was my queen. I ... loved her." She quickly added, "As every subject should love their ruler."

Anskar couldn't imagine any of the knights he knew professing love for Hyle Pausus. The idea brought a smile to his lips.

"You find that amusing?" Carred asked.

"No, I—"

"Queen Talia was the one who was supposed to lead us all to immortality," Carred said. "Her life was one long sacrifice for her people. Even now, even in death, she strives to return and fulfill her promises."

"How can you be sure?"

For a moment, Carred's expression told him she wasn't sure, but she quickly masked it. "You have been too long under the influence of the Order of Eternal Vigilance. How could you possibly understand?"

Carred Selenas had a ship waiting when they passed through the deserted streets of Atya in the gray predawn light and came at last to the harbor. It was a carrack, a big-bellied trading ship with three masts and raised decks aft and stern. As they approached, the sails were being unfurled from the yards, and there was a flurry of activity on deck.

Anskar could just about make out the *Exultant* through the half-light and the haze. The Grand Master's galleon was berthed at a wharf a few hundred yards from the carrack, her yards naked and creaking in the breeze. There was no sign of movement on deck, but he caught sight of a handful of armored knights patrolling the jetty in the shadows cast by the galleon's hull.

Shadows.

The demon, Malady, was in conversation with the old sorcerer she rode behind—not a particularly friendly conversation, either.

He might never have a better chance.

Carred Selenas spoke with the leader of the Traguh-raj—Doon—while the ship's captain, a massive woman he at first mistook for a man—supervised the unloading of barrels.

When he was sure no one was looking, he slid from his pony and poured himself into the shadows.

He emerged in the dark beneath the *Exultant*'s hull, on the wooden walkway beside the galleon's berth.

"What the—!" a knight said, fumbling for his sword.

Anskar raised his hands in a placating gesture even as three ward spheres blazed into existence.

Three knights.

"What in Menselas's name do you think you're doing?" one of the knights—a woman—demanded.

The man beside her touched the tips of four fingers and a thumb to his chest in the sign of the Five's protection.

The other man had by now fully drawn his sword. "Anskar?" he said. "Where is the Grand—?"

Before he could finish the question, the knight jerked violently and his eyes almost burst from his head as they stared down at the clenched fist protruding from his chest.

Malady emerged from the shadows behind the knight and wrenched her arm free with a sharp plopping sound. No blood, no gaping hole, yet the man still collapsed to his knees and keeled over onto his side. He twitched a few times, then grew still.

The other male knight's silver ward flickered erratically, its light reflecting in his wide eyes. The woman attacked, her sword coming down in a vicious arc. It struck only air, and Malady reappeared behind her, having slipped from one shadow to the next. The dwarf leaped and punched the woman between the shoulder blades. Once more her fist passed through flesh and bone and armor. The woman shrieked, then gargled, then fell trembling to the walkway. Malady turned on the remaining knight, but he was already running for the gangplank up to the ship, yelling at the top of his voice.

Malady vanished, but before she could reappear, Anskar stepped into a shadow close to the gangplank. Needles of hot pain pierced his skull. A wave of nausea rose from his guts.

The dwarf reappeared where he had been standing, then located him with her eyes. She shadow-stepped again, and again Anskar did the same, this time re-emerging behind her. It had been a guess but a good one. He staggered under a fresh wave of nausea.

As Malady turned, Anskar punched her in the face, rocking her head back. The demon spat out a tooth. Anskar's hand flew to his sword, but before he could draw it, Malady leaped at him, outstretched hands wreathed in black flame. Anskar's black ward sphere sprang up to cover him, and the dwarf rebounded from it, cursing as she hit the ground and rolled.

She came up swiftly and advanced on him more cautiously now. Sweat poured into Anskar's eyes from the effort of using so much dark-tide essence. He glanced around frantically, seeking some other avenue of escape, shivering as if he had a fever. He'd not be able to maintain the ward sphere for much longer.

Malady reached out with her fingertips. Where the black flames effusing from them met the surface of Anskar's ward, they fizzed and burned and corroded. First one fingertip came through the ward sphere, then another, then the entire hand. Anskar backed away, but Malady stepped with him, bringing her other hand to bear on the sphere, widening the hole she had made in it, then ripping the ward apart like a curtain.

With a lunge, she grabbed Anskar's wrist. If not for the vambrace, he feared she would have snapped his arm, so strong was her grip. He tried to draw *Amalantril*, but she caught his other wrist as she glanced behind at the shadows around Carred Selenas's ship.

Reeling with nausea, Anskar drew upon the dawn-tide, forming his silver ward sphere into a fist of force, which he slammed into Malady.

Only, it never touched her.

Inky black vapor surrounded the dwarf, swallowing the dawn-tide fist and snuffing out its power. Anskar lurched as his dawn-tide repository deflated; then he stumbled as Malady yanked on his arm. Shadows washed over him and he felt himself pouring into the darkness, but before he was fully gone, he heard a man bellow strange and barbarous words.

The tug of the demon's shadow-step abated, and Anskar glanced up as the voice came again, the words foreign sounding and guttural, but the man leaning over the gunwale of the *Exultant* to deliver them was instantly recognizable:

Captain Hadlor.

He was clutching his pendant, holding it out toward the demon below: the Axe of Juagott.

Hadlor shouted again, prayers to his god, thrusting the axe pendant with each word. Malady spat and hissed and let go of Anskar's arm.

Men and women poured down the gangplank—knights roused from their beds. None had taken the time to put on their armor. A few were even naked.

Malady slung threads of blackness up at the deck, causing Captain Hadlor to duck beneath the gunwale. Where the sorcery struck, timbers blackened and smoke plumed into the iron skies.

Malady sprang at Anskar. He threw out a punch, but she was too fast, ducking beneath his blow and pivoting behind him. A punch to the kidney dropped Anskar to his knees. An arm wrapped around his neck. He felt again the tug of the shadows. Silver flashed—the knights' swords as they came streaming along the wharf, bellowing prayers of warding.

But they were too late. Anskar felt himself slipping away, drawn into the pooling shadows. He strained against it, held onto his form just long enough to see the first ribbon of red cresting the horizon.

And in that instant a gale blasted through him. He made no attempt to tame it, to corral it within his repository. Instead, he gave himself to it, let it immolate him, make of him a conflagration.

Malady screeched and released him. Golden flames wreathed her flesh. Smoke plumed from her motley clothes.

The dawn-tide had come.

The dwarf cavorted around the walkway, dancing a mad caper, screaming and cursing, and then, consumed by flames as brilliant as the rising sun, she flung herself into the waters of the harbor. Anskar saw her briefly beneath the lapping waves—a clumping of darkness in the midst of a ring of fire. But then she dissolved into a thousand specks of blackness and the fire fizzled out.

Anskar collapsed to his knees as the first of the knights reached him—a woman in a nightgown, her hair wild and unkempt, long sword gripped in one hand.

"Are you all right?" she asked, glancing across the wharves to the carrack, where two of the Traguh-raj who had accompanied Carred Selenas were riding away from the harbor toward the city, leading the stolen ponies behind them, laden with barrels brought from the ship. The rest formed a semicircle around Doon Ma'jah as she exchanged words with Carred Selenas and the old sorcerer. And then Doon Ma'jah led her warriors onto the ship.

That struck Anskar as strange.

"They're leaving," another knight said, a bare-chested man. He reeked of beer and pipe smoke.

Anskar squinted at the carrack, where crewmen were untying ropes from the mooring posts, and the mainsail bellied with captured wind.

"Captain!" the woman hollered up at the ship. "Can we catch them?"

"The *Exultant*'s nowhere near ready to sail," Hadlor shouted back.

Anskar started at a loud hiss that came from the water. He hurried to the edge of the wharf to see.

Where Malady had dissolved into soot, the waters boiled, then something dark and snakelike formed beneath the surface and streaked off after the carrack.

TWENTY-FOUR

AS THE SUN CAME up, Anskar stood at the gunwale of the *Exultant* with Captain Hadlor, looking down at the six mounted knights and four spare ponies heading away from the wharves to go to the Grand Master's aid. The knights had commandeered the ponies from one of the harborside stables, compensating the owner with silver talents for the inconvenience.

Anskar sipped hot tea, then took another bite of the toasted bread and salty butter the Captain had ordered brought up for him from the mess. It helped fill the void in his stomach, but not elsewhere. His dark-tide repository felt turned inside out, and it was too late to refill it now that the night had passed. He still had a trickle of dawn-tide he could draw upon in a pinch, though his repository was far from full. Something had happened when Malady had tried to shadow-step away with him. The dawn-tide had surged over him, and it had erupted with violence. Whatever he had done to cause such an uncharacteristic effect had been purely instinctual. But the dawn-tide behaving like the dusk … He'd never before considered such a thing possible. Neither had anyone else, as far as he was aware.

As the knights passed from sight amid the city's buildings, Anskar turned so that he could gaze across the harbor and out to sea. Already, Carred Selenas's carrack was no more than a speck receding into the east.

"Looks like she's heading back to Niyas," Captain Hadlor said. "Unless that's just what she wants us to think. Do you think they'll try again?"

Anskar clamped his jaw shut as he thought about that, then remembered to chew the bread in his mouth. Once he'd swallowed, he nodded. "They'll come again." They weren't running away, he was sure. They'd regroup.

How could they not? Without him, Carred Selenas believed there was no future for Niyas.

She was delusional, he thought.

He wished.

The knights returned by the middle of the afternoon the next day, and to Anskar's relief, Lanuc, Orix, Blaice and the Grand Master were with them. As Orix headed up the gangplank, Anskar ran to embrace him. Orix stank of sweat and ponies, and there was a few days' growth of fluffy stubble on his chin.

Lanuc was next up the gangplank, long hair speckled with dust from the trail, black bags under his eyes and face drawn from exhaustion.

"I'm sorry I failed you back there," Lanuc said.

"It wasn't your fault," Anskar replied. "I should have known

Carred Selenas wouldn't give up so easily. I just ... maybe I didn't want to believe what was happening was true."

"But here, in the Plains of Khisig-Ugtall?" Orix said. "She must be desperate."

"You're not wrong there." Almost two decades chasing Queen Talia's heir and keeping her rebellion alive. Carred Selenas must have possessed an inner core of strength he could barely imagine. Either that, or she was obsessed to the point of insanity.

Raised voices reached his ears from the wharf below, and Lanuc shook his head.

"They've been arguing all the way back here," he said. "About who's to blame for the disaster of an expedition. The Grand Master believes Blaice misled us about the portal stone, that she used us as muscle to get what she wanted."

"And he's probably right," Anskar said. "But what did she want?"

"She's a ruins scavenger, that one," Orix said. "I remember my parents talking about such people when I was growing up—they used to sing a song about the scavengers. They steal from the old sites and sell whatever they can on the mainland."

"That about sums Blaice up," Lanuc said. "Though there's no need for her to go to the mainland now that the Ethereal Sorceress has a depot in Atya. Of course, Blaice is complaining that she lost out, too, so I have to assume that whatever she was looking for is still down there somewhere, buried with the city. She even had the audacity to ask the Grand Master for compensation. Apparently, Yanatos Holdings, or whoever it is she works for these days, will want the gold back they paid her in advance."

"But paid her for what?" Anskar asked. "It must have been something valuable, given the risks, and the wraithes told me there was no such thing as a portal stone."

Lanuc clapped him on the back. "Well, whatever it is, it's Blaice's problem now. Hers and hers alone. The Grand Master isn't the least bit tempted to go back to the lost city, and I doubt he'll mention anything to the bishop when we arrive in Sansor. He finds the whole episode rather embarrassing."

Anskar wasn't so sure. "If only that was all it was," he said, glaring down at the wharf, where Blaice was storming away from the Grand Master, heading toward town. "But we lost Ryala, Gaith, and Hendel, all because of her greed."

"And Gadius," Lanuc said. "Don't forget Gadius."

"Oh, yes." It was hard summoning up even an iota of grief for the acolyte, a fact that caused Anskar yet one more pang of guilt he'd have to pray about. "Him too."

That evening, Anskar returned with Orix and Lanuc to the Cockatrice. All three of them wanted one last night on land before the sea voyage that awaited them in the morning. It was a long haul to Sansor from Atya, Captain Hadlor had warned Anskar: around two thousand miles.

They drank beer as if it were water, and it amazed Anskar how quickly his companions started to recover from their ordeal. When local Traguh-raj musicians struck up some jaunty reels and jigs, Orix got up and cavorted around the tavern like a lunatic, all to the cheers and claps of the locals.

Anskar was feeling much better too. He had taken the time to replenish all three of his repositories, the dawn and the dusk at their respective times, allowing the sorcerous winds to wash over and through him, no longer caring if he was seen. The dark, even now, was a steady trickle collecting within. It came as a shock to him when he realized he found it comforting.

Still, his secret was out, and though the other knights were wary of him, Anskar knew he had their grudging acceptance. Lanuc explained it to him before they left the *Exultant*: "You're one of us now, Anskar. One of the Five's chosen. Your past is just that: past. Your current actions are what matters."

He felt no pride being told that. Instead, he felt like a tool of the Order's, tolerated simply because his powers—his forbidden sorcery—might prove useful at some point.

As he watched Orix dance, Anskar cast furtive looks about the tavern.

"She's not here," Lanuc said, taking a long pull on his beer. He'd taken the time to shave and wash his hair before they left the ship. "Don't suppose we'll see Blaice again. Till the next time."

"Can't say I'll miss her," Anskar said as Orix rejoined them at the table and immediately downed what was left in his mug.

"Miss who?" Orix said.

"Blaice."

Orix snorted. "Never trust a woman with tattoos and piercings, my ma used to say."

"Oh?" Lanuc asked. "And why's that, then?"

"They're the marks of sorcerers," Orix said with a sniff. He glanced apologetically at Anskar then added, "The bad kind, you know, witches, warlocks … shamans."

Anskar looked round as the tavern door swung open, admitting a chill blast of wind from outside.

It wasn't Blaice. It was one of the obsidian-skinned Orgol women he had seen the other day.

"I don't know about you two," Anskar said, "but I'm getting tired. I think I'll head upstairs to bed."

"Sounds good to me," Lanuc said, draining his mug.

"Thank the Five for that," Orix said. "I didn't want to be the one to break up the party, but I think I'm going to sleep for a week."

"You'd better not," Lanuc said. "We set sail in the morning."

The creak of the bedroom door woke Anskar. He'd been in a deep and dreamless sleep, but he grew instantly alert. Opening his eyes a crack, he tried to see who had entered the room in the dark. He cursed himself for leaving his sword on the chair at the foot of the bed. Instead, he sent his senses inwards, where they gently unbound the constraints on his dusk and dark-tide repositories.

A floorboard squeaked, and Anskar's heart raced at the thought it might be Malady come to snatch him away again.

Another muted footfall, closer this time. He caught the scent of something familiar … sandalwood.

And then she was there, plonking herself on the edge of his bed, pressing a finger to his lips, chuckling to herself.

Blaice Rancey.

Her breath stank of wine.

"What are you doing here?" Anskar said. "Get out."

"Don't be like that. I thought I'd see you off before you leave for Sansor." She held up an open bottle of wine. "I didn't bring glasses, but I'm sure you don't mind. We can share."

She slipped beneath the sheets beside him, propping herself up on one elbow so she could drink from the bottle.

Anskar couldn't think of anything to say. He shifted toward the far side of the bed, heart hammering in his chest, pressure building in his groin.

"You're naked," she said, running a hand along his thigh.

"It's hot."

"Poor dear," Blaice said. "Have a slug of wine. It'll cool you down."

"I don't want—" he started, but Blaice upended the bottle and wine splashed his face and mouth. He swore and tried to sit up, but Blaice tossed the bottle aside and pushed him back down.

"Here," she said, undoing the front of her shirt and guiding his hand inside. "What do you feel?"

Anskar swallowed. His mind screamed at him to get out of bed and run, but the heat flooding his groin had already grown almost unbearable.

What did he feel? Skin, warm and soft. Firm roundness. His thumb pressed against a nipple and he swallowed. Metal. One of her piercings.

"Do you approve?" Blaice asked.

Anskar cupped her breast, then reached for the other, where he found another ring.

"I have them everywhere, you know," Blaice said. "Would you like to see?"

She pushed away from him and sat, swinging her legs off the edge of the bed. She stooped over the nightstand then struck a fire-stick, using its flame to light the oil lamp beside the bed. When it was aglow, Blaice shook out the fire-stick and stood, facing Anskar as she shrugged out of her shirt.

In the lamp's glow, he could see the tattoos covering her torso: the snake that wound its way between her breasts, its tail encircling her navel. There were Skanuric words above her breast, on her belly, the insides of her forearms. Piercings glinted at her navel, both nipples. He let his eyes drop to the crotch of her pants, which she was in the process of unfastening.

"Oh," Blaice said, holding up her hand. She displayed a ring upon her middle finger, and when Anskar frowned, she edged closer to give him a better look.

Set within a broad ebony band was a large, faceted emerald.

Before he could stop himself, Anskar rolled out of bed and grabbed her wrist.

"This ring …" he said, meeting her gaze. Her eyes twinkled, and a smirk tugged at the corner of her mouth. "It was on the severed hand we found in Yustanwyrd."

"Ten points for observation," Blaice said. "Or rather nine."

Anskar frowned. "But Niklaus tossed the hand away. He said it was effeminate jewelry."

"The reason you only get nine points is that you obviously didn't see Niklaus pocket the ring before he threw the hand away."

"But why would he … Wait … This ring is what you two were after all along?"

"Does that make me naughty?" Blaice said. She pulled her hand away from him and held the ring to her eyes, pouting at it. "I really shouldn't be wearing it, but I couldn't resist. It'll fetch me a goodly sum when I take it to the Ethereal Sorceress."

"I thought you'd already been paid."

"Half up front," Blaice said. "That's how Yanatos Holdings always work. The rest on delivery to the Ethereal Sorceress. I really should thank you and those idiot knights. You've done me an enormous service."

"Wait a minute," Anskar said. "When did Niklaus give you the ring? When you ran from the wraithes?"

"Just now," Blaice said. "Downstairs in the tavern."

"Niklaus survived? He's downstairs?"

"He was," Blaice said. "But he's a busy man. Always doing his goddess's will. At least that's what he thinks he does. In truth, Sylva Kalisia is a sadistic bitch who has Niklaus by the balls. He's her slave, every bit as much as the Niyandrians are the slaves of the Order of Eternal Flatulence."

"But he was smothered by those smoke-birds. We left him for dead."

"And he was crushed by the manticarr," Blaice said. "Niklaus du Plessis is a difficult man to kill. Some might say impossible." She dropped her hand to fiddle with one of her nipple rings.

Anskar couldn't take his eyes from her hand on her breast. He drank in once more the sublime art of her serpent tattoo, the swirling Skanuric script on her skin. He swallowed and tried to focus. "So you did use the Grand Master. You used all of us."

"Not all of you," Blaice said, touching her fingers lightly to his cheek. "I prefer to think of you as a partner in this venture. Perhaps in future ventures as well. You have such useful abilities."

Anskar brushed her hand away. "But the rest of them—Gaith, Ryala, Hendel, Gadius—Niklaus was right: they were just fodder."

"It's an honorable profession. What else would you describe them as?"

"People. Companions. Friends." That last was a stretch, but he had a point to make.

"Ah, yes," Blaice said, and now it was her turn to grab his wrist—the one upon which he wore the invisible vambrace. "But there are people and then there are people." She raised her eyebrows. "Interesting. In Yustanwyrd, it glowed beneath your sleeve, yet now I see only the flesh of your arm."

"It reveals itself in moonlight," Anskar said.

"I'd expect nothing less."

"The light in the lost city must have been similar."

"Indeed." Blaice let go of his arm. "You know what it is?"

"You called it divine alloy before."

She wrinkled her nose. "A joke, like fool's gold. Ancient junk. I could probably persuade the Ethereal Sorceress to take it off my hands if you're interested in selling it."

"I can't take it off."

"The Ethereal Sorceress will know how."

Anskar stared at the skin of his forearm. It still felt odd to him—the weight of the vambrace but nothing there to see. "It's not for sale," he said. He couldn't get the vision of the spectral Queen Talia out of his mind, her hand reaching for the vambrace.

"Just make sure, if you change your mind," Blaice said, pushing him down on the bed, "you give me first refusal."

She straddled him and guided his hands to her breasts.

Anskar tried to put up a struggle, but it was a feeble one. What was happening to him? He had noticed how he could scarcely keep his eyes off women, and despite his conscience yelling at him that lying with them was sinful, an affront to Menselas, he knew he was powerless to resist.

He was vaguely aware of Blaice shifting position, moving down the bed.

Something had changed within him. Changed the day he'd been fitted with his catalyst. And not all the changes involved the awakening of latent sorcery. Something else had been awakened, something he feared was a far more powerful master than any of the three known tides.

All he could think about was the burning need in his groin, and Blaice no longer seemed interested in talking.

Blaice was gone by the time Anskar awoke. He swung his legs out of the bed and checked his forearm. The vambrace was still there.

Then he noticed something atop the rumpled sheets: a folded piece of paper with his name on it. As he opened it up to read what was written inside, he could smell sandalwood. Her perfume, scenting the paper. Presumably so he would remember her. As if he could ever forget!

He shook his head and read, "I hope you enjoyed our depravity as much as I did. Don't be too harsh on yourself. Penitence is for the slaves of other people's ideas. And don't forget, the offer's still open on the vambrace. You know where to find me if you change your mind. Safe sailing. Love, B."

TWENTY-FIVE

THE SKY WAS THE color of ash the next morning as the *Exultant* left Atya's port and reached the open sea. A fierce wind bellied the sails, driving the ship onwards with great surging gusts. Waves broke over the prow, spraying the deck with saltwater. Swollen clouds gathered overhead, and thunder rumbled far off to the north.

Teams of sailors scurried about deck, bailing water with buckets. Captain Hadlor encouraged them with hearty shouts in between bites of cheese and bread. Half a dozen crewmen were in the bilge, laboring under the pump to stop the ship from flooding.

Anskar emptied his bucket over the gunwale, then bent to fill it again. Orix was green-faced and groaning, not just from the movement of the ship this time, but from the heavy night's drinking at the Cockatrice. Lanuc was the only other knight on deck. The rest had complained about the sea spray rusting their weapons and armor, although none of them had been wearing armor at the time. "Stuck-up, good-for-nothing bastards," Orix called them. They were also sullen, as if the Grand Master's sour mood had infected them.

Hyle Pausus hadn't surfaced from his cabin since they left the harbor. That Blaice Rancey had tricked them into helping her festered like a wound that had contracted the rot. The Grand Master and his knights had been no more than fodder, as Niklaus du Plessis had warned them. Not that he was any better. Niklaus had been conspiring with Blaice all along.

"What are you grinning at?" Orix asked.

"Niklaus," Anskar said, though in truth he was thinking of Blaice and her tattooed flesh.

"Bastard."

Anskar laughed as he tipped another bucket of water over the side. "Is that your word of the day?"

Orix scowled, then staggered as the ship lurched.

"You have to admit that Niklaus was good, though," Anskar said.

"For a bastard."

"You think I should tell the Grand Master?" Anskar had already told Orix what Blaice had told him: that Niklaus had slipped the ring from the severed hand they had found in the buried city, and he had later delivered it to Blaice. While there was still no portal stone to retrieve from the ruin, it would have gone some way to softening the Grand Master's mood, having a valuable artifact to bring back to Sansor.

"What's the point?" Orix said. "By the time we catch up with her, Blaice will have sold it."

"I think she planned to take the ring to the Ethereal Sorceress's depot in Atya," Anskar said, "which means it could be anywhere in Wiraya by now."

"Bitch," Orix said. "Bastard bitch."

"Mind your language!" Lanuc chided from where he was bobbing up and down, bailing water far faster than Anskar and Orix were. It shamed Anskar into matching his pace. Orix, though, seemed incapable of speeding up his efforts. He returned to grumbling and clutching his guts, only occasionally filling his bucket and dragging it to the gunwale.

"You should try to be more discreet," Lanuc said, looking over at Anskar.

"Sorry?"

"We all have needs," Lanuc said, "and everybody's doing it, but the Order has rules. At least give the impression of obeying them."

Anskar felt his cheeks redden. Blaice hadn't exactly been quiet. Neither had he, truth be told.

Orix nudged him on the arm. "So, what was it like?"

"Just focus on bailing unless you want to swim all the way to Sansor."

Orix chuckled, then emptied his bucket over the side with far more vigor than he'd previously shown. "Filthy bastard," he said as he bent down to collect more water. "Me personally, I'd sooner have a turn at that Carred Selenas. Now that's what I call a woman."

"She captured you, Orix, or have you forgotten?"

"And she can capture me again any time she likes."

Days later, gray clouds had grown black as the *Exultant* sailed into a growing storm. The skies churned, driven by violent winds. Cold rain sheeted down, sending ripples through the water flooding the deck. The prow rode steep peaks and troughs, climbing above surging waves and plunging down the other side. Lightning forked across the sky, chased by ever-nearing booms of thunder. Captain Hadlow gave the order to abandon the bailing. Last thing he needed was crewmen over the side.

But the Captain knew these waters well, knew when to risk their ire and when it was ill-advised. Relying on a sodden chart and past experience, and the hollered cries of a boy crazy enough to remain in the crow's nest, the Captain brought the beleaguered ship at long last to a sheltered cove on the leeward side of one of the many small islands that studded the Simorga Sea between the Plains of Khisig-Ugtall and Kaile on the mainland. The wind still howled angrily around them, skirling about the bay, and lightning flashed sporadically across the black skies. The waves were merely choppy here, the ship bobbing and swaying, but no longer careening dangerously. They dropped anchor a few hundred yards from shore—a strip of white sand, beyond which Anskar could see the thrashing tips of trees buffeted by the strong winds.

"The Komolan Jungle," Captain Hadlor told him, slapping Anskar on the back as he bustled past, yelling for sails to be furled and yards to be stowed. When he'd finished shouting at the crew, Hadlor turned back to Anskar and said, "Not a place you would want to visit. A ship was wrecked off the coast here some years ago. Sharp-tooths ate most of the crew, but those who made it to shore … well, let's just say they should have stayed in the blood-swilled waters."

"What happened?" Orix asked, listening in.

Captain Hadlor stared at him. Wide-eyed and trembling, Orix swallowed, and when the Captain took a step toward him,

Orix backed away to the gunwale.

Hadlor let out a rumbling belly laugh that rivaled the booms of thunder now moving away to the south. "Ah, lad, if we're going to make a sailor of you, you'll have to know when your leg's being pulled."

"You were joking?" Anskar said. "There was no shipwreck?"

"Now, that I didn't say," Hadlor said, suddenly serious. "Where do you think I got this?" He rolled up the leg of his pants to show them a ridged scar just beneath the knee. It had been badly stitched at some point, the white dots of the needle's path still visible around the old wound.

"You were bitten by a sharp-tooth?" Orix said, fascination drawing him back from the gunwale.

"I didn't say that, either," the Captain said, then with a good-natured shake of his head and a ruffling of Orix's hair, he left them alone as he strode toward the quarter deck, chuckling as he went.

Anskar went with Orix to their cabin so they could get out of their wet clothes. Orix didn't even have the energy to get dressed again, falling into bed instead. Within minutes he was snoring fitfully.

Anskar threw on some dry pants, a cotton shirt, then stuffed his boots with the rags he kept in his pack for the purpose, to help them dry out. His stomach growled, and he'd intended to visit the mess for something to eat, but he made the mistake of lying atop his bed first—just a few minutes' rest for his aching limbs.

He knew he was dreaming by the ashen haze that swirled around him. At least, he thought he knew. He had his feet under him, though he could feel no solid ground. He was light as a feather. Lighter. He had no sensation of any weight at all. And he was moving, drifting slowly through the swirling mist, and it was cold, so very cold.

Up ahead, a shadow grew steadily larger as it approached. At first Anskar panicked, tried to turn around, find some way of propelling himself through the mist. But then the shadow was upon him, over him, within … Hands the consistency of smoke stroked his face, and he felt their touch as if they were solid. As if he were solid now too: the only two real things in this gloomy limbo.

The shadow resolved into a woman, dark-haired, and with eyes at once tawny and aflame. The pupils were slitted like a cat's. She wore a clinging robe of emerald green, open to the navel, revealing crimson skin and the cleft between her breasts. Her full lips were painted a deeper red than her skin, giving the impression she had been drinking wine … or blood. And though she hadn't appeared in such lucent detail to him before, and never quite in this form, he knew her and she knew him. She was the crow who had visited his rooms. She was the shadow woman who had come to him previously, vaguely formed, as if the world of the living rejected her. Queen Talia of Niyas. The Necromancer Queen. His mother.

"Anskar," she said, voice no more than a sibilant hiss. "Anskaaaaar."

Even here, even in this twilight dreamscape, she struggled to maintain any semblance of form. She faded once more to shadow, the green of her robe now indistinguishable from the dark. At the same time, her voice strengthened, though it was not his name she uttered now; it was a word he didn't recognize.

Then another word, followed by a spectral finger touching his chest. Yet more words, and now she touched his hand. And then Anskar knew what she was doing: speaking phrases in Niyandrian and urging him to understand.

She was teaching him.

Anskar awoke to an empty cabin. Orix must already have gone up on deck. His stomach growled. By the Five, he was starving. He went to throw off the sheets, then realized he'd fallen asleep on top of them, fully clothed.

And then he recalled the visitation in his dream. His hand where his mother's shade had touched him began to itch. He raised it so he could see. There, the merest discoloration of the skin, no larger than a drop of rain. No larger than the tip of a finger. Even now, though, it was starting to fade.

So it had been real, then? A dream and yet somehow more? When Queen Talia had come to him before, she'd been little more than a ghost, struggling to make herself known; but this … her occupation of his dreams … What else had she said and done when the unconsciousness of deep sleep had settled over him? How long had her lessons in language endured, without him being an active participant? He swallowed, his hunger pangs giving way to a crawling dread beneath his skin.

And why was she teaching him Niyandrian as he slept? So that she could communicate with him more effectively in the future? It seemed reasonable for a mother to want to speak freely with her son. Until he reminded himself she was a dead mother, a mother he had never really known. And he still wasn't sure he wanted to know her, either.

"You're dead, Mother," he uttered under his breath. "Accept it. Move on." He almost added "Leave me alone," but some niggling concern at the back of his mind wouldn't let him. He wasn't certain if the concern was his or hers.

Instead, he prayed for his mother to Menselas. Prayed that she would find peace in death. And he prayed for himself too, that the God of Five Aspects would grant him discernment, enable him to decide between right and wrong. He prayed that Menselas would protect him from the threats of the afterlife, and at the same time deliver him from the perils of the world about him, threats like Carred Selenas, who had come so close this time.

Up on deck the storm had passed. A light drizzle continued to fall, cool and refreshing. The waters of the Simorga Sea were still churlish, but they were no longer violent. Captain Hadlor was hollering for the sails to be unfurled, and sailors were scurrying about deck, climbing the rigging in a flurry of activity.

Not the Knights of Eternal Vigilance, though. Now the storm had abated, they were loitering on deck, doing nothing useful.

Anskar found Orix sweeping residual water overboard with a stiff broom. Lanuc was speaking with a sailor hanging low down in the rigging, then the knight started to climb, tentatively at first, but with the sailor's encouragement he grew in confidence. Anskar watched, expecting at any moment that Lanuc would plunge to the deck and break his neck. Within a few anxious minutes, Lanuc reached the broad yard of the mainsail and shared a joke with the sailor.

"Lazy bastards," Orix said as he swept. He flicked a look at the knights leaning against the gunwale.

Above the chopping of the sea, Anskar could hear them grumbling as they shook their heads. From what he could gather, the knights were hungry. The galley hadn't started serving breakfast, Orix told him, because the cook and his aides were helping out on deck.

Anskar found himself a broom and joined Orix driving the water overboard. With the sun now breaking through a rent in the clouds, his mood lifted somewhat, and the specter of his dream evaporated along with the morning mist.

At some point, Captain Hadlor brought them hot tea and pastries filled with fruits and sugar he'd picked up in Atya. Lanuc dropped down from the rigging and hurried over to join them. As they ate on a bench at the gunwale, they drew envious looks from the knights.

"Those who don't work don't eat," Captain Hadlor said. He took another bite of his pastry and wiped sugar from his lips.

But the knights did eat, eventually. Anskar caught the smell of cooking bacon and roasted coffee coming from the mess. The cook must finally have taken pity on them.

Briefly, the Grand Master popped his head out of his cabin door. He was swathed head to toe in a white robe cinched at the waist with a rope belt. There were dark rings around his eyes, and he yawned as he instructed one of the knights to fetch him breakfast. He glanced Anskar's way, nodded, then went back inside and shut the door.

When they had finished eating and drinking, Orix collected the plates and asked if anyone wanted anything else from the mess. Captain Hadlor's eyes lit up, and he was halfway to ordering himself some toasted bread and bacon, when a sailor yelled down from the crow's nest.

"There's a ship, Captain, off our starboard bow."

"I'll get something from the cook later," Hadlor said, standing and brushing crumbs from his shirt.

Orix took the plates back to the mess, but Anskar went with the Captain and Lanuc to see this ship for himself.

"It's adrift," Hadlor said.

Anskar squinted across the intervening water. The ship's sails were furled, its decks empty. Yet it bobbed slowly in their direction, a ghost ship carried by the tide toward the cove.

"Is that ...?" Lanuc said.

"The carrack that was docked in Atya's port," Hadlor said with a nod of certainty. He glanced at Anskar, stuck out his bottom lip and widened his eyes.

Carred Selenas's ship.

So she hadn't returned to Niyas. She was still following him.

"It's a trap," Hadlor said in a bored voice, as if it were patently obvious. "Oldest one in the book."

"What will we do?" Anskar asked. He turned, suddenly aware of the press of sailors around them, listening to what the Captain had to say, sternly nodding their heads.

Captain Hadlor grinned. "We take the bait."

TWENTY-SIX

"FINALLY, THEY ARE MAKING themselves useful," Captain Hadlor said as knights began to come up on deck armored in mail, sword belts buckled around their waists.

Lanuc was organizing men and women into units and directing them to various points around the ship. The bulk were gathering on the main deck, but reserves were placed on the forecastle above where Hadlor stood with Anskar and Orix, both of whom had fetched their armor and swords from below. A handful of knights were directed to the aftcastle.

The Grand Master emerged from his cabin in his white cloak and gleaming cuirass, which shone so brightly it must have been freshly scoured with vinegar and sand. He strode across the deck to them.

"You're sure it's her, Captain?" he asked, reaching the gunwale and staring out at the carrack drifting inexorably closer.

"I'd stake my plums on it," Hadlor said. "Begging your

pardon, Grand Master. But that's her all right. There aren't too many carracks nowadays. Old design, see. And you can tell from the broad belly and high prow she's of Niyandrian design. Built for trade, not war. And those strakes are Niyandrian redwood, not oak like the *Exultant*'s."

Lanuc approached the Grand Master and they stepped aside to exchange words.

Captain Hadlor barked instructions to the steersman, and the *Exultant* started to turn away from the prow of the coasting carrack, heading alongside its flank instead.

And still the decks of the approaching ship were empty.

"Ready," the Grand Master called to the assembled knights standing in staggered lines, shoulder to shoulder, swords drawn. Motes and sparks shimmered around them as they tested their ward spheres.

"Wait for it," Lanuc said. "Wait."

The *Exultant* slid past the carrack's prow and scraped along its strakes. Sailors rushed to the gunwale, slinging grappling ropes over the side, snagging the carrack and pulling the two ships into a tight embrace.

And then chaos broke loose.

Aboard the carrack, men and women who had been crouched behind the gunwale threw off the cloaks that had covered them. Most were Niyandrian, but there were Traguh-raj among them. They screamed battle cries and surged toward the *Exultant*. But the Grand Master's galleon was a larger ship than theirs, its gunwale higher, meaning the enemy had to climb.

Lanuc gave the command, and the decks of the *Exultant* suddenly blazed with scintillant wards of silver. The knights on the main deck formed up in tight lines, their ward spheres overlapping, doubling their density where they met. They advanced in unison, three staggered lines six knights wide. Lanuc signaled for the knights on the forecastle to join the assault, while the six on the aftcastle were kept in reserve.

The first line of knights jumped down from the *Exultant* onto the carrack's deck, plowing into the disordered Traguh-raj there, swords stabbing with merciless efficiency.

The Traguh-raj fought back savagely, but their blades failed to penetrate the overlapping ward spheres, and as the second line of knights dropped to the deck of the carrack, followed by the third, it became a slaughter. Blood slewed across the planks, along with gore and entrails. One Traguh-raj man ran in tight circles, screaming, his skull cleft and spilling brains. Another slipped in blood, pitching into the man behind and blocking his swing. A Niyandrian woman started to shout a cant, but Lanuc punched out his shield, bludgeoning her from her feet. Lanuc staggered from the excessive use of his dawn-tide essence, and his ward flickered on and off.

The Grand Master glanced at Anskar, staring wide-eyed from the higher deck of the *Exultant*. "Are you ready?" he asked. "Whatever you can do."

Anskar licked his lips and nodded, scanning the enemy ship for the old sorcerer and the demon. He saw Carred Selenas fighting furiously. She hacked uselessly at a knight's ward sphere, sending up showers of motes, then retreated as the line of knights came on, yelling at her warriors to fall back with her. None of the enemy had shields, and they were helpless before the relentless advance of the wall of ward spheres.

Anskar felt a growing pressure in his skull—the tingling presence of sorcery. There was an answering ripple in his dusk-tide repository; then he followed some hidden instinct to pinpoint the cause of the disturbance on the carrack's aftcastle.

There, the old man was weaving his hands through the air, fingers curled into claws. Dark whorls surrounded his hands, leaving misty spirals in their wake. Spirals that began to knot together, gaining in density, swelling ...

"Do something!" the Grand Master cried, his golden ward sphere springing up around him.

Attack or defend? Anskar couldn't decide, and he knew he didn't have much time. Attack or—

A cloud of dark vapors rolled out across the carrack. The Traguh-raj and Niyandrians threw themselves face-down on the deck, letting it pass over them ... toward the knights.

"I said do something!" the Grand Master yelled.

Anskar could only watch, his mind churning with ideas that wouldn't come fast enough. He drew upon the dark-tide, began to throw up his black ward sphere, intending to send it punching into the old man's roiling brume, but some instinct told him that wouldn't work, that the old man would have expected such a move.

Abandoning the cant, he began another, in his mind's eye seeing the old man ripped to shreds by a colossal blast of dusk-tide force. He had no idea if it would work; all he could do was unleash the full virulence of his dusk-tide repository and hope. But the old man must have sensed something: a shimmering sphere of crimson sprang into life around him, causing Anskar to second-guess himself.

And in that moment the dark cloud struck the front line of knights. Where vapor touched each ward sphere, the sphere guttered and went out. Screams rent the air as flesh sloughed from bones, and one after another, the front line of knights slopped to the deck in puddles of gore.

In a scream of frustration and failure, Anskar threw out feelers of awareness at the old man, probing, seeking vulnerabilities.

The dark cloud rolled on. The remaining two lines of knights separated to avoid it, fanning out around the deck, where they were easier prey for the Traguh-raj and Niyandrians starting to stand now the cloud had passed over them. Fighting resumed, the clash of steel on steel, shouts and screams. But it was a chaos of individuals hacking and slashing at each other now. Towering above the fray was the carrack's captain, whom he'd seen at the harbor in Atya, a huge Niyandrian woman with wrestler's shoulders and a massive cutlass, which she swung with measured ferocity.

The knights had lost the advantage of their disciplined advance. But still, many of their ward spheres held, and sparks flew from them at every impact.

Anskar's tendrils of awareness made contact with the old man's crimson sphere. He expected them to recoil, but whatever it was, this strange sorcerous protection that warded the old man, it was designed for something else, perhaps a full-on assault using the dusk-tide. Anskar's senses passed right through, and then he was in the old man's head, feeling what he felt, thinking his thoughts—a jumble of fear and anticipation, and single-minded focus on his sorcery.

And he didn't know.

He didn't know Anskar was in his mind.

Anskar's ears pounded with the clangor of battle. He screened out the demands of the Grand Master, the screams, the curses, the ring and scrape of steel. And he felt the torrent of dusk-tide pouring from the old man's repository to fuel his roiling sorcery. Felt it and traced it to its source. And as he had done with his own repositories—the dusk and the dark—he wove a forbidding barrier around it, a dam against the corrosive tide. The old man gasped and stumbled, and his dark cloud evaporated.

Anskar felt a sudden chill behind him.

He whirled to see the dwarf, Malady, emerge from the shadows beneath the main sail. Her motley coat was open to reveal a baldric crammed with silver knives. She grasped one in her childlike hand, the slender blade dripping vitriol.

The old man's attack had been a ruse, a distraction.

The dwarf-demon shot toward him like lightning. He tried to raise his ward sphere but was too late.

And then Orix was there, swinging his sword in a vicious arc. It took the dwarf in the stomach, slinging her to the deck. Her dripping blade skittered away across the timbers, coming to a halt in a puddle of gore. The wound Orix had slashed across her belly was devastating, a gaping rip, a disemboweling blow that should have killed her. But there was no blood and no entrails, just a cascade of black sand spilling across the deck. And then Malady struggled to her feet, staggered, and came once more at Anskar.

Dropping his sword, Orix dove at the demon, tackling her to the deck. She thrashed and squirmed beneath him, but Orix was heavier than her. Veins stood out on his neck as he held Malady down. She tried to reach a blade, but Orix controlled her bicep with his hand and his weight. She spat and cursed and bucked beneath him. Orix looked at Anskar, panic in his eyes. "What do we—?" he started, but he never finished the sentence.

In a blur of light and shadow, Malady disappeared, and Orix vanished with her.

The din of battle rose to a crescendo in Anskar's skull: ringing blades, clinking mail, strangled screams, cracking bone. He saw the big Niyandrian woman go down, her cutlass skimming across the blood-slick deck. Heard another woman scream. Could have sworn it was Carred Selenas.

The knights were winning, that much he knew without having to look. It was as if the battle raged on the periphery of his awareness. All he could do was stand and stare at the spot Orix had vanished from.

But where had the demon taken him?

Anskar scanned the decks in front and behind. There! In the shadow of the carrack's mainsail, a warping of the air, then the dwarf-demon appeared, cradling the unconscious Orix in her arms, as if he weighed no more than a baby.

Without a thought, Anskar shadow-stepped after them, feeling the gush of dark-tide essence leaving his repository. He lurched when he reappeared beneath the sail, suppressed the urge to vomit.

But Malady was already running for the gunwale, Orix now slung over her shoulder.

"*Melesh-Eloni!*"

Anskar whirled at the cry to see Carred Selenas running toward him out of the fray, sword spattered with blood, free hand raised in placation.

Amalantril sighed as Anskar drew her from her scabbard and stepped in to meet Carred Selenas, veins on fire with rage. "Back off," he commanded her, casting a glance over his shoulder, where the demon had climbed atop the gunwale with the Orix.

"Please," Carred Selenas said, lowering her sword and continuing toward Anskar. She'd been weeping. "Come with me."

"Never!" Anskar snarled, rushing at her, swinging his sword in a wild arc.

She stepped back as she parried, but Anskar struck again, this time hitting her blade with all his strength. She yelped, and her sword spun away to the deck. Anskar thrust the point of *Amalantril* at her face. She stumbled and pitched to her backside.

Behind her, a wall of blazing silver pressed in—the re-formed knights, all resistance overcome.

Anskar glimpsed the Old Niyandrian sorcerer lying on the deck, a jagged wound in his chest bubbling froth and crimson, a gash across his throat that had almost severed the head from his body.

"Please," Carred Selenas said, extending her hand as she stood. "Please."

"Maggow is slain," came the demon's voice from behind Anskar. "But he passed my bindings to you, Carred Selenas. Think of a command if you can."

"Take the *Melesh-Eloni*!" Carred said.

"Impossible!" the demon replied, then leaped from the gunwale, taking Orix with her. There was a loud splash, then the sound of something huge thrashing in the water.

But the demon had been right. Lanuc and a dozen knights spread out in a semicircle behind Carred Selenas. If Malady had come against Anskar, she would have been struck down in an instant, assuming it was possible for mere blades to slay a demon who had black sand for blood.

Carred Selenas turned to face the knights, holding up her hands in an attitude of surrender. Knights either side of Lanuc looked to him for direction, but before he could tell them what to do, the Grand Master pushed his way to the front. A look of desperation crossed Carred Selenas's face. She glanced pleadingly one more time at Anskar, and then she sprinted for the gunwale. Anskar moved too late. Before he could grab her, she vaulted over the side.

No splash of water this time. Had she somehow clung to the strakes and ended up suspended above the sea?

He rushed to the gunwale, aware of the others crowding

around him—Lanuc, the Grand Master, several of the knights.

A gigantic serpent undulated through the waves, its tail held aloft, coiled around the prone form of Orix. And on its back, as if she were riding a horse, Carred Selenas, hair slick with sea spray, pants drenched from where her legs trailed through the water.

TWENTY-SEVEN

AFTER THE LOSS OF Orix, Anskar retreated to his bed. He'd never felt so alone, not even at Branil's Burg when Brother Tion had left for a new life on the mainland. Not even when the Order's strictures had forbidden him to be with Sareya, his first love and, he had hoped, his last.

Anskar would have lost count of the long hours he languished below decks, were it not for the comings and goings of the sailors he shared the dorm with, and Lanuc checking on him at intervals, bringing food that he couldn't eat. At some point, he smelled smoke. Maybe the ship was on fire, but the thought caused him no alarm. He simply didn't care.

He fancied he could feel the steady crawl of the dark-tide through his veins. It wove strands of blackness throughout his mind, smothering any sense of hope, of purpose, of life. He drove it back with uttered prayers to Menselas, but always the dark regrouped and closed back in again. He sipped water when his mouth became too dry, but other than that he sat on his bed, or lay there unable to sleep. Sat and brooded, or lay and pondered: who he was, where he came from, where he was going.

Because it wasn't just to Sansor and the Mother House of the Order he was traveling. There was another vector to his life, an invisible thread that tugged him relentlessly toward someone else's goal.

"We've separated from the carrack," Lanuc said on his way out, carrying the tray of untouched food he'd brought earlier.

"And the bodies?" The stench of all that blood clung to Anskar's nostrils.

"The Grand Master ordered the carrack burned."

Whenever he fell asleep, Queen Talia's shade visited him, teaching him to speak Niyandrian in his dreams. Each time he awoke, his head swarmed with new ideas, alien thoughts that couldn't be expressed in Nan-Rhouric.

Speculating about his role in Queen Talia's schemes did nothing to allay his melancholy. He knew that his anxieties about what was happening to him were the underlying cause of his depression. The loss of Orix had merely been the removal of the balm of friendship that had covered over the real issue like snow on a dung pile.

An added complication was that, no matter how much he denied it, he was fascinated by the burgeoning powers within him. His gift from his mother. His inheritance. The pity was he had still lacked the power to save Orix.

On the third day since the sea battle with Carred Selenas, Anskar's mood started to improve.

He sat for a long while, listening to the seethe of the waves, rocked gently by the sway of the ship. Up above, yards creaked, and every now and again a sail would whip and snap as it caught the wind. Boots tramped the deck, sometimes hurried, mostly plodding. It occurred to him that he had no idea what the conditions were up top, whether it was night-time or day, sunny or overcast, dry or raining. And the strange thing was that he cared.

As he began to move around, feeling a growing sense of boredom, he made an inspection of his repositories. The dawn-tide one had somehow drained dry, as if all its unspent essence had evaporated like a puddle beneath the morning sun. His dusk-tide too was all but empty, and when he sent his senses questing into the dark-tide repository, it was more of a ditch of stagnant water than the brimming well of vitriol it had been before. He knew it was an effect of languishing so long below decks, shielded from the tides.

He perched on the edge of the bed.

The tides. It seemed so obvious a question, but it had never occurred to him to ask it before, and Frae Ganwen had never once spoken on the subject: What exactly were the tides? Where did they come from? Who sent them, and why? Or were they simply natural phenomena, like the ocean tides, the rising of the sun, the phases of the two moons? And why were there three tides and not just one? Was it possible there were more?

He was startled by a knock at the door.

It was Lanuc once more, and again he had brought food. This time Anskar managed a smile, and he accepted the food with nodded thanks.

Lanuc sat himself down on the edge of Orix's empty bed, watching with a combination of bemusement and relief as

Anskar devoured the meal—eggs and ham and hunks of hard black bread spread with salted butter.

"Chef will be happy," Lanuc said. "The sharp-tooths, less so. They'll be going hungry today. How are you feeling? Any better?"

"Much." The food was certainly helping, but Anskar had already felt a profound shift in his mood since waking. He only hoped he wasn't getting used to the fact that his friend had been taken and there was little or nothing he could do about it. "Are we still looking for Orix?"

Lanuc sighed. "The Grand Master's impatient to return to Kaile. He's in an ill temper and has managed to reduce the knights and the crew to nervous wrecks."

"Did he even look for Orix at all?"

"A little. But even if we could have kept up with that serpent thing the demon became, what's to stop it spiriting Orix away by some other means?"

"You're assuming it has such power."

"There's little any of us knows about demons for certain, especially the higher order ones."

"And that's what Malady is, a higher order demon?"

"I'd have to assume so," Lanuc said. "The lower demons are little more than beasts, driven by hunger and other insatiable lusts. This Malady showed clear intelligence and a grasp of sorceries forbidden by the Five."

"Dark-tide," Anskar said.

"No one knew that Luzius Landav had taken a demon for an apprentice. Or more likely his slave. Some sorcerers over the centuries have been known to bind demons unwillingly to their service."

"And yet Luzius Landav was in the service of the Order,"

Anskar pointed out.

"You will find," Lanuc said, "the further you progress in the life of a consecrated knight, that things are seldom black and white. Compromises have to be—"

"No," Anskar said. "I don't accept that."

"Are you going to tell me you've not made compromises? Moral ones?"

"I …" Anskar started, but he saw at once the lie in what he was about to protest.

"Remember, I heard Blaice Rancey's moans and cries that night at the tavern, and Vihtor informed me about the girl. Sareya, wasn't it? Attractive young thing … for a—"

"For a Niyandrian? Have you seen my eyes?"

Lanuc chose that moment to look away. "Are they yours? Vihtor told me about the change that came over them. Forgive me, Anskar. I'm being insensitive. My only point was that we all make compromises in this life, even those of us who profess to be holy. And there are precedents in scripture for this. Many were the patriarchs and bishops who took too rigorous an approach to the Five's teachings. Our history is steeped with intolerance and condemnation. Just look at the years of bloody persecution for those who didn't live up to the ideal."

"Better that than what Menselas would do to them at the end of their miserable lives," Anskar said.

"You believe that?"

"No," Anskar said. "I don't."

Lanuc smiled and shook his head. "Well, that's a relief. I thought I was doomed for sure. Why don't you join me up on deck?" He stood and picked up Anskar's tray.

"I will," Anskar said, suddenly aware of how badly he must smell, how unkempt he must look. "I'll freshen up and change my clothes first."

"Thank the Five for that!" Lanuc nodded and smiled. "It's good to have you back, Anskar," he said as he opened the door and slipped outside.

Idiot.

The unbidden thought almost had volume, it was so strong. Was it even his own?

But then he realized to his shock that the thought hadn't been in Nan-Rhouric.

It had been in Niyandrian.

TWENTY-EIGHT

UP ON DECK THERE was a bite to the wind, and the sky was the color of slate. A ceiling of swollen clouds pressed down heavy, but ahead gray light slid through a widening breach.

Anskar tugged his cloak around him and pulled up the hood against the spit of freezing rain. With a nod, he acknowledged Lanuc standing at the gunwale, then moved toward the front of the ship where a raised voice called out directions.

Captain Hadlor stood on the forecastle, glaring out at the choppy channel between two craggy headlands into which the *Exultant* was moving. Whitecapped waves frothed where dark patches shadowed the surface—rocks that would ground the ship or punch through the hull if the surging tide or the slightest error by the helmsman brought them too close.

The *Exultant* moved slowly, riding the current, only the one sail bellied with the wind, the others furled on their yards. The decks were dotted with anxious-looking knights, cloaked and armored, as if they expected a fight.

The ship rounded a rocky headland, and in the distance to the east, the channel widened into a great bay. As they entered the mouth of the bay, Anskar was confronted with miles upon miles of coastland shrouded by fog.

The Captain hollered more commands, and the *Exultant* hugged the southern coastline, riding a patch of lighter sea just shy of the whitecaps and brooding dark of a reef. There was a forest of masts ahead of them, and beyond, a sprawl of towers set back from the shore in the far southeast, where the coastal cliffs sloped away to a basin that met the lapping waters of the bay. He realized then that it wasn't the expectation of a fight that had the knights dressed in their battle gear; it was for more ceremonial reasons. It was because they were coming home.

"Anskar!" Captain Hadlor called down from the forecastle. "Come up here and join me."

When Anskar made it up the slick wooden steps, the Captain beckoned him to the prow.

"Sansor," the Captain said. "The only approach is by sea, and the waters of the bay are perilous indeed." He pointed out the blackened ribs of ships that had strayed too close to the reef. There were dozens of them, all along the coastline, some still with masts and tattered sails, a few hulls jutting above the white horses, but most just the skeletons of carracks, galleons, and smaller fishing vessels. "Not hard to realize why Sansor has never been invaded from the Simorga Sea, eh? The fortunate city, they call her. Not only is her west side protected by the hazards of the bay, but she is surrounded by hills, each with its own fort and garrison. A good place to build, the old people of Kaile chose. It is the reason for Sansor's wealth and flourishing."

Beyond the city, to the north, Anskar could just about make

out a looming spire. "What's that?" he asked.

"The Abbey of the Hooded One." Captain Hadlor rubbed the axe pendant around his neck.

Far to the north, and traveling in the opposite direction to the *Exultant*, Anskar saw a broad-bellied ship under sail, fighting against the current on its way to the open sea.

"Trade ship leaving Kyuth to the east of here," the Captain said. "Probably on her way to Thessalika. A pirate's dream, a ship like that."

"There are pirates here?"

"Notorious ones."

Anskar studied the Captain's face, trying to work out if he was joking. Hadlor's eyes widened and he stuck out his bottom lip, but then he clapped Anskar on the shoulder and turned back to the prow, resuming his calls to the helmsman.

After watching for a while, Anskar backed away and returned to the main deck. The last thing he wanted was to distract the Captain's concentration and have them strike a reef or rocks. The thought of the *Exultant* becoming another casualty of the treacherous bay waters was not one he wanted to entertain.

The *Exultant* glided into Sansor's vast harbor, where stone wharves kept the churlish waters at bay. More than a score of long piers jutted out to sea, providing berthing for hundreds of vessels, most of them small fishing boats, but in among them fat-hulled traders that were, even now, disgorging their wares into carts pulled up on the piers, or being loaded with merchandise packed into crates, sacks and barrels.

A fair way to the north of the harbor was another pier, isolated and aloof from the rest. At this pier were moored a dozen or so sleek-hulled yachts. In among them were two great war galleons, their decks alive with sailors making sure they were seaworthy. The smell of pitch drifted over from the warships on the gusting wind. Cloaked men and women, their faces obscured by white masks, patrolled the boardwalk approach to the ships.

"Officially, they're members of the City Watch," Lanuc said, leaning against the gunwale beside Anskar.

"Officially?"

"Coin talks here in Sansor. It's sometimes hard to differentiate between those who work for the city council and those who are privately contracted by the noble elites. It's rumored the Watch have been endowed with special powers by Zihanna, the goddess of justice and mercy." Lanuc hawked and spat overboard. "Wear your Order cloak at all times, and they'll leave you alone."

"Do they have an arrangement with the Order?"

Lanuc wrinkled his nose, looked as if he was going to spit again, but evidently thought better of it. "It's complicated. Just don't do anything you shouldn't be doing and you'll be all right."

"It's so big," Anskar said, shifting his gaze to the city beyond the wharves.

There were properties perched over the waterfront on stilts or purpose-built jetties. Planked walkways connected them, and many were multistoried, with winding staircases leading to flat roofs where brightly dressed people could be seen lounging and taking their lunch. Servers in black flitted among the tables, bowing obsequiously as the patrons handed them coins.

"Looks like the weather's shifting," Captain Hadlor said as he approached. "This stiff breeze off the mountains is blowing the clouds back out across the bay. It's shaping up to be a warm day, if I'm not very much mistaken."

The helmsman brought the *Exultant* to a broad berth between two fishing boats, their crews already aboard, unraveling nets, shaking their heads and cursing at the big ship coming in and blotting out what little sun they had been enjoying.

Captain Hadlor roamed the deck, bellowing commands, and soon traps were thrown open and crates and barrels were hauled up from the hold.

So the *Exultant* had been carrying more than Niyandrian slaves, and judging by the eagle-eyed way Captain Hadlor monitored the preparations for unloading, it was his own cargo rather than the Order's. No doubt it would fetch a tidy profit in a city as rich as Sansor.

The Grand Master emerged from his cabin in his full finery. Someone had washed his cloak and pants, and his breastplate had again been polished to mirror brightness. He carried his shiny helm tucked under one arm as he made an inspection of the remaining knights formed up in neat rows on the main deck.

"Should I?" Anskar asked Lanuc, feeling suddenly conspicuous in just his pants and shirt.

"The Grand Master has given me instructions to go on ahead and show you a glimpse of the city on our way to the Mother House. You might want to put your mail on to save you carrying it, and the white cloak to keep the Watch off our backs."

Anskar hurried below to his cabin, where he put on his armor and cloak, hung *Amalantril* in her scabbard from his belt, then crammed his spare clothes into his pack. He paused in the doorway, then went back inside, this time gathering Orix's clothes and possessions. There were a few of Orix's personal effects in the bottom of his pack—a gaudy necklace of beads, a painted ceramic mug, and a pouch of some brittle, dry herb with a pungent smell.

Carrying both packs, Anskar returned to the deck, where the gangplank had just been lowered. Lanuc gestured him ahead, and with a backward glance at the Grand Master and his immaculately presented knights, and a wave at Captain Hadlor, Anskar tramped down the gangplank and onto the pier.

"Welcome," Lanuc said, failing to disguise the sardonic edge to his tone, "to Sansor."

Captain Hadlor had been right. Even before Anskar and Lanuc left the wharf, banks of cloud scudded out across the bay and the sky turned a brilliant blue.

As they came off the boardwalk and approached the eateries and taverns that skirted the harbor's edge, a trio of white-masked City Watch started toward them, then stopped at Lanuc's waved greeting. They were all clad in black woolen pants and long gray coats. Telltale bulges beneath the coats hinted at concealed weapons.

Anskar could feel their eyes on him as he and Lanuc walked away. He wouldn't have wanted to arrive in Sansor alone, without the protection offered by the Order's colors.

A chill wind blew from the east, down the slopes of the Great Southern Mountains of Ealysia. But it was a merciful wind, Lanuc informed him, without which the dry heat of the Kailean summer would have been unbearable.

They threaded the narrow alleys between the shoreside eateries, and Anskar's stomach grumbled at the scents coming from the rooftops and the open windows of the kitchens—the yeasty smell of fresh-baked bread, the aroma of ground coffee. All those smells were permeated by the odor of fish—recently caught and fried in a mixture of tangy spices, honey and sweet herbs.

"Tempted?" Lanuc said. "I would be too if I didn't know how much they charged so close to the water."

When they emerged from the narrow alleys onto a paved street flanked by tall brick tenements, Anskar was startled by the sound of squealing from somewhere off to the left.

"Pigs," Lanuc said. "There's a slaughterhouse a few blocks back."

The farther they walked from the sea, the more Anskar began to notice the stench that soured the air, which Lanuc informed him came from too many peat fires belching smoke from houses, and manufactories burning coal.

Lacquered wood carriages clattered past them, drawn by shaggy horses. Either side of the road, where sludge oozed through blocked gutters, men and women in stained and patched clothes glanced hopefully at the carriages rattling by.

"I thought you said Sansor was a wealthy city," Anskar said.

"It is," Lanuc said, glancing up at an elevation toward the east, where huge mansions stood over and above the city, surrounded by swaying palm trees and elegant gardens spangled with color. "For some. There's more wealth up there among the few than in the whole of Niyas."

"And the Five permits this? Surely the Patriarch doesn't approve."

"You'd think so," Lanuc said. "Of course, you'll be able to visit the Patriarch's basilica every day while you're here. It has a chapel for four of the five aspects of Menselas arrayed around a great central fountain where people cast coins in return for a blessing."

"Four? Why not all five aspects?"

"I'll leave that to you to find out. The Mother House of

our Order is situated within the basilica's estate. The Order of Eternal Vigilance was originally founded to protect the pilgrims coming to the basilica. Before then, pilgrims were assailed by the devotees of the other faiths, or their offerings were stolen by rogues and bandits."

"But now they're safe to come?" Anskar asked.

"Their offerings are safe, which I sometimes think is all that matters."

"You don't approve of the Patriarch?"

"I wouldn't go so far as to say that," Lanuc said. "For all I know, the fault may be my own. I have a tendency to simplify the spiritual path into black and white."

"I do the same," Anskar said, then added after a moment's thought, "Though recently …"

"You've started to admit shades of gray? We all do, sooner or later. Wisdom, my confessor calls it. I'm not convinced."

"So," Anskar said, "the Mother House stands within the basilica's estate, you say. Where is that?"

Lanuc pointed. "Up there, with all the other wealthy folk."

It was easy for Anskar to forget the conflicts raging inside him, the growing disillusionment with the Order that had been creeping up on him even back at Branil's Burg, the forbidden forces growing within, the nocturnal lessons while he slept. Easy, because of the awe-inspiring scale of the city, the all-pervasive opulence, the varied and exotic attire of the people—the affluent ones who flocked all around Anskar and Lanuc now that they had passed the wharves and entered upon a district heavy with traffic. There were carts, wagons, laden mules, and silk-dressed women on thoroughbred stallions, waving at all and sundry, wanting to be seen. Glass-fronted stores lined both sides of the street, gaudy signs above the entrances shouting the names of the businesses, chalkboards in the windows displaying their wares—no mention of the prices.

"If you have to ask the cost here," Lanuc said, "you can't afford it."

The people themselves were the greatest source of wonder to Anskar. The majority were dusky-skinned Inkan-Andil, the dominant race of Kaile and the neighboring City States, but moving freely among them, and judging by the way they were dressed in luxuriant garments and sparkling baubles, enjoying their own share of the wealth, he saw gray-skinned San-Kharr, who originated in the south; wide-eyed Charral; a smattering of Soreshi—nomads from the region beneath the Ymaltian Mountains to the far north; and people with a greenish tint to their skin.

"Ilapa," Lanuc said. "From the jungles half a world away. Nature-worshiping smokers of hallucinogenic fungi. Probably brought here for their exotic value, or maybe they have something rare to sell. This is Sansor, after all. The rich merchants here will pay a fortune for desiccated goat turds if they think they can sell them at a profit."

"My ancestors . . ." Anskar started, then trailed off.

Lanuc glanced at him askance. "Which side?"

"My father's . . . I think he was from Kaile, maybe even from Sansor. At least that's what I was told."

Lanuc paused in the street, and a middle-aged woman bound neck to toe in shimmering silks sewn with glittering gold thread cursed him when she nearly bumped into him. "Did Vihtor tell you that?"

"And others."

A frown worked its way across Lanuc's face, but then he laughed. "Then you should soon start to feel at home here. And you might as well, as there's no telling how long the Grand Master will want you to stay."

"So I can't return to Niyas?"

"No," Lanuc said, serious once more. "No, you can't. At least not for the foreseeable future. Come on, I'm getting as hungry as your stomach sounds."

"Where will we eat? The Mother House?"

"Bread and water? I don't think so!"

Anskar set down his packs, his own and Orix's, on the floor beneath the tall table and lowered himself onto a stool. He coughed again—the irritation in his throat had started the moment they entered the Card and Coin gambling house, and already it was becoming intolerable.

A server in a long cream coat and pantaloons came over to their table. Lanuc ordered them both drinks. What, Anskar couldn't say. He couldn't hear over the sound of his own coughing.

"It's the cravv desiccant everyone seems to be smoking these days," Lanuc said, gazing about the gambling house's interior. "The latest fad, apparently. Some entrepreneur brought the idea back from the Jargalan Desert and made a fortune selling it to the nobles, the merchants, and the cartels—if they're not one and the same."

It was hard to believe this was a mere gambling house. Anskar would have expected such an establishment to be sleazy, run-down, but the Card and Coin was anything but.

They were seated on padded leather stools at a polished round table in a bustling room with a circular bar at its hub. The Card and Coin had four levels, and Lanuc suggested they remain on the ground floor, where there was slightly less gambling and more of an emphasis on dining and drinking. "You need to earn your way up, in any case," he said. "This is where new patrons start out."

Alchemical globes hung from the high ceiling on slender chains, wavering in the flow of air coming through the open clerestory windows situated above the far larger windows that were shuttered against the world outside. Swirling banks of cravv smoke glowed in the rose-tinted light.

If not for the raucous outbursts from the upper levels, and the background hubbub of conversation, the atmosphere would have been warm—tranquil, almost.

Guards patrolled the floor. Others went up and down the wide marble stairs that connected the Card and Coin's four levels. They were dressed in white uniforms, and each had a truncheon and a short stabbing sword hanging from their belts.

Behind the circular bar, on the broad pillar that rose like an axle at its center, a sign read, "No sorcery."

The odd thing was, Anskar had been troubled by a scratching beneath his scalp since they had entered the gambling house. He'd come to recognize the sensation as his new senses reacting to something they had detected without him being aware of it. His abilities, he was coming to understand, had a life of their own. But the scratching sensation implied someone close by bore the mark of sorcery, so he sent out feelers of awareness. Several patrons had at least some degree of dusk-tide stored within them. One woman in particular, with a pile of tokens stacked up in front of her on the gaming table, seemed to be doing quite well for herself. He probed deeper and started to get a taste of something else, but before he could discern what it was, the woman flicked a look his way and Anskar lowered his eyes.

The server returned with their drinks. "Pearlescent alchemical brandy. You, sir, have impeccable taste," he told Lanuc. "You know, of course, where such fine brandy comes from? Or rather, where it is found. Because no one can figure out how to make it any longer. Secrets of the ancients," he said to Anskar as he passed him the glass. "Will you be eating?"

"We will indeed," Lanuc said, lifting his brandy glass and sniffing the contents.

As the server shuffled away to fetch the menus, Lanuc said, "Don't believe a word of it. They call this stuff 'pearlescent' but it's just the regular kind with some cheap flavors they've thrown in. The real stuff is so rare, it's impossible to buy, and you certainly wouldn't find any in a place like this."

"Then why did you order it?" Anskar asked, taking a sip and wrinkling his nose. "It burns!"

"I ordered it to show you how wary you need to be in Sansor. Everyone is trying to sell you something, trying to persuade you it's the best that coin can buy. There's a simple rule to follow if you're going to get by in this city: assume everyone's a liar."

The menu, when it came, was as exotic as the fake brandy, and Anskar immediately wondered what the fare would really be like. He took his time reading the descriptions of the available meals: pickled butterflies dusted with crystalized honey, sharp cheese writhing with velveteen maggots, braised horse meat with ginger and red onions, crab eggs accompanied by slivers of bread, and bowls of something called a Nimbras caterpillar, lightly spiced and topped with crystals of pink salt.

Lanuc ordered them sample plates of several dishes, instructing the server to put it on the Order's account.

They made the ascent to the upper city by foot, drawing disapproving looks from the rich folk in their two-wheeler cabs pulled by pairs of well-groomed horses with ribbons in their manes.

Anskar looked in awe at the manicured lawns, the cultivated trees, many with streamers of gold and silver hanging from their branches. They passed the high walls of estates guarded by hired soldiers.

"Many nobles," Lanuc said, "have their own private armies."

Anskar winced at a twinge in his stomach. He stopped and belched, and an aftertaste of sharp spice hit the back of his throat.

"Something I said?"

"Just the food from the Card and Coin repeating on me."

Lanuc laughed. "It was certainly rich and varied fare. I thank Menselas every time I eat there for blessing me with a cast-iron stomach."

The spire of the basilica came into sight above the top of palm trees that had been planted in neat and tidy rows. As they walked beneath the fronds, enjoying the shade, Anskar marveled at the sheer scale of the basilica. They emerged from the palms onto a flagstone courtyard that led to a covered portico. Below the five-sided spire that terminated in a sphere of glinting amber, the main structure of the basilica was a massive pentagon constructed from blocks of dark stone that held a greenish tint. The entrance they approached was an arched opening with wide-open doors of blackwood. Above the stonework arch, a woman's serene face stood out in bas-relief: the Healer.

There were carved stone benches in the courtyard outside, grouped around a tinkling fountain. Golden-scaled fish darted about the crystal-clear waters. Armed men and women patrolled the perimeter. Three wore the white cloak and mail of the Order of Eternal Vigilance; the other four were white-masked members of the City Watch.

A few of the benches were occupied by white-robed priests of the Healer, who looked up as Lanuc and Anskar approached. A man stood and rushed toward Lanuc, drawing him away and engaging him in enthusiastic conversation. They smiled and laughed like old friends.

A young woman approached Anskar. She seemed hesitant, making the effort out of politeness or duty, the cowl of her robe thrown back to reveal tightly bound fair hair and striking eyes of gray. She held out a slender hand to Anskar and he shook it.

"You're new here," she said, at the same time glancing over his shoulder. Anskar craned his neck to see Lanuc waggling his fingers and smiling at the young woman.

"Yes," he said. He coughed before going on, but not from cravv smoke this time. "I'm from Branil's Burg in Niyas. Anskar DeVantte."

"I know of Branil's Burg."

"You've been there?"

"I haven't. Perhaps one day, the Five willing."

"You'll like it," Anskar said, not sure why he said that. He felt awkward, tongue-tied, and he was trying his best not to belch. The spicy aftertaste hadn't left him, and he thought he was going to be sick. The woman's eyes widened with amusement. "Perhaps when I return to Niyas," he added, and she bobbed her head in encouragement, "it will be my honor to show you around."

"Oh …" she said, her expression suddenly troubled.

"Not like that!" Heat prickled his cheeks. "I meant …"

"Of course," she said. "That would be kind of you, Anskar."

"Do you have a name, sister?"

"Gisela," she said. "Gisela of Gessa."

"Gisela," Lanuc said, approaching with his arms open wide and crushing her in an embrace.

"Father!"

"Gisela is your daughter?" Anskar said. "But …"

"I know," Lanuc said. "I don't look old enough."

"You're married?"

Lanuc and Gisela shared a glance. "I was."

"Menselas took my mother when she gave birth to me," Gisela said.

"The loss of my wife was devastating at the time," Lanuc said, "but slowly the Five lessened my grief and then restored my faith and hope with this beautiful girl."

"Woman, Father," Gisela chided.

"But still my girl."

"Would you like me to show Anskar around the basilica?" Gisela asked.

"I don't think there's time," Lanuc said. "The Grand Master will be expecting him for the official welcome home to the Mother House this evening, and we both need to bathe and change our clothes."

"You're not wrong there," Gisela said. "Perhaps some other time, then," she said to Anskar.

"I'd like that."

Slut. The thought came unbidden to Anskar's mind as Lanuc led him away toward the houses beyond the basilica. *Ripe little bitch. Wasted in the service of her insipid god. Use her and leave her. It's the best thing you could do.*

Anskar flinched and faltered in his steps.

"Are you sure you're all right?" Lanuc asked.

Anskar pinched the bridge of his nose. "I think so. Probably just tired from all the traveling, the excitement of coming to a new place. And that bloody food!" He clutched his stomach as it tightened. It felt as though it were full of sludge, and he fought against a wave of nausea.

To the rear of the basilica there was a veritable village of brick houses with tiled roofs. "Where the priests live," Lanuc said.

There were certainly a lot of priests on the basilica grounds, but that was on account of there also being a seminary here, Lanuc explained, with separate schools for four of the five aspects.

"No school for the Hooded One?" Anskar asked, remembering the strife caused back in Branil's Burg when the Grand Master had ordered the Hooded One's chapel turned into a banker's vault.

"Not on the basilica grounds," Lanuc said. "The seminary here is relatively new, whereas there has always been a school of the Hooded One at the old abbey, just shy of the city. The Abbess was invited to relocate her school here but chose not to, so the chapel built for the Hooded One within the basilica stands vacant, although I believe the other priests use it for storage space."

Beyond the priests' houses there was a cloister for contemplatives—a long, low building in the shape of an "L." Unlike the brick houses of the priests, this one was constructed from wattle and daub, and its roof was thatched with black-mottled straw.

Around the cloister were fenced-off strips of cultivated land where vegetables had been planted in neat rows, and gardeners in smocks and broad-brimmed hats moved among them, here and there watering their crops, but one or two harvesting potatoes, leeks and broccoli and collecting them in wicker baskets.

Three fat sows lazed in the mud of a pigpen, the stench so ripe it had Anskar holding his nose and picking up his pace. There were goats roaming free—no doubt the reason for the fences around the vegetable patches. Their incessant bleating was grating to the ears. Within a fenced-in acre of pasture off to the north, a flock of sheep grazed, the odd piebald cow in among them.

"The Church here likes to be self-sufficient," Lanuc said. "Though donations are always gratefully accepted."

At last they came to the compound of the Order of Eternal Vigilance. The buildings here were old, though not as old as the cloister. There was a large, two-story manse with a tiled roof. A broad chimney stood at either end, and the gable facing Anskar and Lanuc as they approached displayed a five-pointed star. This largest of the buildings—the Mother House, Anskar assumed—stood at the center of a circle of smaller dwellings, each built from the same green-tinted dark stone that the basilica had been constructed from.

The smaller dwellings, Lanuc explained, were for the officers among the knights, or those with special abilities or duties. Behind them were five long buildings with embrasures in place of windows—the barracks for the regular knights. Little more than a monk's cell with a cot bed and a nightstand for each knight stationed there.

Lanuc led Anskar to one of the smaller buildings and they entered through a sturdy wooden door, for which Lanuc had the key. The house within was divided by a narrow corridor into two rooms, each with a bed, nightstand, and a closet.

"This one's yours," Lanuc said, gesturing to a bed. "Mine's

the other."

Anskar tossed his and Orix's packs on the bed, wincing at a needle stab of pain in his guts and the growing need to break wind. "And the latrines?" he asked.

"There's a communal block out front of the barracks."

Anskar didn't need to be told twice. He ran from the house, clutching his stomach.

TWENTY-NINE

"JADA'S DEAD." CARRED'S FIRST words to Vilintia when she reached the new hideout in Rynmuntithe.

"Jada?" Taloc said.

Carred shut him out by refusing to meet his eyes. It was all she could do to address Vilintia without collapsing into a bawling heap. She'd seen Jada fall during the fight at sea. Been too far away to protect her. Screamed until her throat was raw. Some guardian she was. All she seemed to do was fail those she loved.

Vilintia acknowledged the news with the clench of her jaw. "We set you up a shelter. Sleep. We can talk later."

Carred nodded and let out a ragged sigh. All she wanted to do was get out of her clothes, which were crusted with salt and still damp from crossing the sea on the serpent's back. And, Theltek's nipples, her thighs chafed.

She caught sight of Noni sitting forlorn beneath a tree, muttering to herself.

"Been like that since you left," Vilintia said. "Not that it's any great change."

"Do the others … talk to her?"

Vilintia shook her head. "She makes them uncomfortable."

"I'll see her later," Carred said. "Once I've rested."

"What about the others?" Taloc asked, indicating Malady—back to her motley-clad dwarf form—and the Traguh-raj lad, Orix.

"There's a spare shelter?"

Taloc glanced at Vilintia. "Could use mine, I suppose."

Carred raised an eyebrow, and Vilintia, bless her, remained stony faced.

"Watch over the knight, Orix," Carred told Malady. "Don't let him out of your sight." Then to Vilintia, "He'll need to clean up, and something to eat." He must have been starving. As was she, but despite the twisting of her stomach, she couldn't face food.

"There's a brook on the edge of camp," Vilintia said. "He can scrub his clothes there, take a dip."

"Malady …" Carred said.

"You've already told me to watch over him. Or don't you trust the bindings that stinking old fool passed to your control?"

"Don't worry," Taloc said, "I'll keep an eye on them both."

Well, that was reassuring.

Carred caught Orix watching her. He quickly lowered his eyes. She reappraised him then. Dull-witted and duller featured. But, still …

Stop it, Carred. You're too tired. And old enough to be his mother.

In Nan-Rhouric, and harsher than she meant, she said, "Go with Malady. Clean yourself up. Eat and sleep. Give me a few hours and then we will talk. Understood?"

Orix spat at her feet.

"Confessional material?" Carred asked.

He almost smiled.

Pity. It would have suited him.

"Carred!"

She moaned beneath the blanket that covered her and Orix. He'd washed, she'd rested, they'd had their talk, and then things had progressed. Several times. Orix was as inexperienced as he was dumb, but he was young and teachable. And warm.

"Carred!" came the voice again, echoing through the shroud of sleep. A man's voice. Sounded urgent.

Orix stirred, gave a lazy smile as he rubbed tired eyes, then looked at her like a doting dog.

"See," she said, "Niyandrians aren't so bad."

"This one's not," he said, stroking her breast. Theltek, he was hard again! Did the young have no limits?

"Carred!"

She slung off the covers. "Sorry," she told Orix. "Maybe later."

As she stepped into her pants, Taloc poked his head inside the tent, withdrew it again when he caught sight of her naked breasts. "You're needed," he said from outside.

"I'll come with you," Orix said, rolling out of bed.

Carred didn't wait for him as she followed Taloc to the heart of the camp, still buttoning her shirt.

"She's doing something weird," Taloc said. "Vilintia thought you should know."

Vilintia waited with a group of rebels, watching Malady, who was squatting on her haunches, writing on the ground with a stick. She'd formed a circle of crude symbols about herself. As Carred approached, the dwarf-demon scratched out one of her runes, muttered something, and started to draw another.

"What are you doing?" Carred asked.

"Oh, do I need your permission?"

"Maybe."

"I'm trying to help."

Carred crouched beside her. "Is that Skanuric?"

"No."

"Proto-Skanuric?"

"No."

"And you say you're being helpful?"

"It's Nazgrese, if you must know. The language of demons. We're not savages. We have language, culture, architecture …"

"But not manners."

Malady spat on the ground. "Never had any use for them."

"How does this help?" Carred said, scanning the circle of symbols.

"Your aim is to get Anskar DeVantte back in your clutches, is it not?"

"To be honest, I've given up—"

"And mine is to go home, minus the shackles of a slave."

"What shackles?"

"You don't have to see them to know they're there. I'm bound to you. I don't like being bound."

"So you get me Anskar and I set you free?"

"Do we have a deal?"

Carred could imagine Maggow warning her: *Don't make bargains with demons.*

"The bindings: they give me the power to compel you?"

"Yes, but …"

"Then just do it."

Someone giggled—Noni, seated beneath a tree, staring blankly into space.

"It won't be easy. I may need some time to perfect the summoning circle."

"You can do that? You can conjure him here?"

"I got the idea from Luzius Landav—the sorcerer you beheaded. I'd have killed him myself, only …"

"Only, you were bound."

"Bastard summoned me from the abyssal realms at a bloody inconvenient moment. After he died, I returned there and started to set things right, then that toothless old man brought me back."

"At my request," Carred said. "So I guess you'd like to kill me as well now?"

"I was considering slitting your throat. Maybe a knife in the back. Tell the truth, I've given a lot of thought to impaling you via the quim."

Carred smiled. At least the demon was honest. "This thing you wanted to set right, was it business?"

Malady swallowed and shook her head. Agitated now, she scratched out another symbol in the earth.

"Love?"

A sigh this time. Malady shut her eyes and gave the slightest nod.

Carred stood, wincing at the pain in her hip. "We have a deal. Bring me Anskar, and you can go home."

THIRTY

ANSKAR WAS GIVEN TIME to settle into his new life, and he began to hope that his stay at the Mother House wasn't as temporary as he'd first believed. He tried telling himself he missed Niyas, and indeed part of him still yearned for Sareya. But other than that, he couldn't think of a reason to go back.

Despite his reservations about the knights on board ship, despite the Niyandrian slaves they had transported below decks, life in the compound surrounding the Mother House was every bit as he would have expected, before his callow vision of the Order had started to fray at the edges. Knights and priests gathered at dawn each day to greet the tide, congregating on the lawn between the cloister and the priests' houses. There was communal prayer at the basilica afterwards, a priest of the four represented aspects taking it in turns to lead the service; and the entire community met again at noon, dusk, and in the middle of the night.

The shared piety, the rigorous daily discipline, made him feel a part of something greater than himself, but with the new sense of belonging came a clawing self-chastisement. All the while he had been criticizing others for failing to adhere to the Order's rules, he had indulged in forbidden sorcery—it didn't help that he'd been ordered to. He had consorted with wraithes in ancient ruins, and he had slept with … not just Sareya, but Blaice.

And so he sought out a confessor among the priests. At first he lacked the courage to approach any, but on the third day since his arrival, while he ate breakfast in the refectory, he saw Gisela sitting with a group of white-robed priests of the Healer, sipping tea and eating only sparingly from a plate of sliced fruit. He caught her eye, and she smiled before looking away.

As Gisela got up to leave, Anskar headed her off at the door. Lanuc looked up from where he had just started his breakfast with a trio of knights he'd introduced Anskar to the day before—Borik, Nul and Rindon, who had fought with Lanuc in the south, where Jargalan pirates had been harrying the coast.

"Gisela," Anskar said, and she turned back to face him. He thought he detected worry in her eyes. Her glaze flicked over his shoulder, acknowledging her father's frown.

"Anskar." She tucked her hands inside the sleeves of her robe. "You're settling in well?"

"I think so."

"I've seen you at the daily prayers."

"There was no routine of community prayer at Branil's Burg."

"Really?"

"It was a different life," Anskar said. "Full of training, and the knights were constantly out on patrol."

"A frontier citadel," Gisela said. "My father says it's tough there, as it is most other places he's sent. He's always relieved to spend time at the Mother House." She smiled past Anskar's shoulder and removed a hand from her sleeve so she could waggle her fingers at Lanuc. "I think he is worried about your intentions."

"My … No, there's no need to … By Menselas, I give you my word."

Gisela smiled. "I know that, and I'm sure my father does too. He's just overprotective. It's been good talking with you, Anskar."

"I was going to ask you …"

"Yes?" There was a flash of irritation in her gray-blue eyes. "Oh, yes, I was going to show you around the basilica properly. Forgive me, Anskar, I've been so busy. There are a lot of sick to attend, and—"

Anskar looked down at the floor. "I need to make my confession."

"And you thought I would be a lenient confessor?"

"No! I just … You were friendly when we met the other day, and I find these things …"

"Difficult? We all do, Anskar, even us priests." She glanced around the packed refectory. "Especially us priests. Come to the basilica after morning prayer, to the Healer's chapel."

"Thank you, I will," Anskar said as she turned away.

"What was that about?" Lanuc asked as Anskar joined him and the others at the table.

"Spiritual guidance," Anskar said.

"Oh, aye?" Rindon said, nudging Nul.

"I need to make my confession."

"Don't we all," Rindon said. "Eh, Lanuc?"

"That we do, Rindon. But a young man like this, there can't be much to confess. Isn't that right, Anskar?"

The east door of the basilica opened onto a widening passageway with roseate marble flooring and walls frescoed with scenes of sunlight, lush greenery, and flocks of brightly colored birds. The clever use of hooded alchemical globes highlighted the details of the paintings. Here and there the frescoes showed signs of fading, but in other places fresh paint had been painstakingly applied by an expert in restoration.

As Anskar approached the chapel at the end of the corridor, he breathed in some kind of sweet incense. When he reached the arched opening, he simply stood there, absorbing the tranquility of the chapel, the harmonious lines and soft tints, the silence—save for the mumbling of penitents and the uttered blessings of the priests.

Opposite where he stood, another, darker, corridor led deeper into the heart of the basilica, and he could hear the faint tinkling of a fountain. Atop a stone dais in the middle of the floor stood a replica of the fabled restorative cauldron in which the Healer was said to renew all the life of Wiraya. Set around the chapel were screens stretched between rectangular frames of varnished wood. The screens themselves were mostly white, veined and wrinkled with imperfections that gave the impression of vellum, but might have been some kind of plant fiber. Rushlights burned behind the screens, where the silhouettes of kneeling penitents and seated priests were visible. Only one such penitential space was vacant, and from behind its pale screen stepped Gisela. Anskar could tell it was her despite the white cowl obscuring her face. It was in the posture, the bearing, her slender body beneath the white robe.

"Have you come to unburden your heart to Menselas?" she said in the standard greeting of the confessor.

Anskar was taken aback by the formality. He chastised himself for being a fool. He was nothing to her. Besides the fact that her father had been charged with his protection, they had no connection.

"If it is the will of the Five," Anskar mumbled the ritual response.

Gisela beckoned him behind the screen and he followed, waiting as she seated herself in a carved blackwood chair, and then lowering himself to the cushioned kneeler before her.

"You have smirches on your soul, Brother?" Gisela asked. "Barbs you would have dissolved by the healing balm of Menselas?"

"I do, Sister."

"Then unburden yourself, and know the mercy of our god."

And so he told her. Told her about Sareya. About Blaice. Told her about his sickness after his catalyst had been fitted, about the dreams that had haunted his convalescence, his fight with the dead-eye, the golden-eyed crow leading him to Hallow Hill.

"These last are not sins," Gisela interrupted. "They were not under your conscious control."

"But there is more," Anskar said. "And it only gets worse."

There was a palpable change in the atmosphere between them when he told Gisela of the sorcerous abilities that had begun to grow within him, and how he had used the forbidden tides of dusk and dark. He spoke at length about the kidnappers back at Branil's Burg, how they had called him *Melesh-Eloni*—godling. The atmosphere chilled even further. He revealed what the Niyandrian sorcerer had done to his eyes—either changed them or revealed their true appearance.

"I had noticed the eyes," Gisela said quietly.

"Their leader, Carred Selenas, told me I was the heir to Niyas," Anskar said. "The secret child of the Necromancer Queen." He looked up into the shadows beneath Gisela's cowl but could see nothing of her expression. "The Grand Master knows, as does your father, but I feel … I mean … Am I cursed? Hated by Menselas?"

"I …" Gisela started.

"And there's still more," Anskar said. He told her of the knight, Colvin, aboard ship. "I used dark-tide sorcery on him. It withered his hand."

"What else?"

He swallowed, then told her of the thought that had come unbidden to his mind when he had first met her. *Ripe little bitch.*

"And the thought was your own?" Gisela sounded distant, distracted. Perhaps she was disturbed.

Wasted in the service of her insipid god.

"I don't know. I don't think so. It's not something I wanted to think. It … appalls me."

Use her and leave her. It's the best thing for her.

"And the thought was in Niyandrian, you say?"

He nodded.

A long silence ensued, during which Gisela angled her cowl away from him, as if she were thinking about what to say next. He felt certain she wanted to get up and leave, refuse him the words of absolution.

"Such … thought intrusions," Gisela said, still not looking at him, "come from one of three possible sources. Often it is the hidden part of our own minds, our instincts, our … bubbling nature buried beneath the surface of our awareness."

The heat of shame prickled Anskar's cheeks.

"Other times it is Menselas himself speaking to us, but given the evil nature of the thoughts in this case, we have to rule that out. That leaves the intrusion of a malign influence … a demon, a sorcerer, or"—and now she angled her cowl back to face him—"those who should be dead. Something foul clings to you, Anskar. I will pray that Menselas casts this evil from you. Promise me you will block out all such thoughts and grant no admission to this … thing. If it speaks within you again, refuse to listen, and never act upon what it says."

"I promise."

She peered deeply into his eyes for a long moment, and then she pronounced the formula of absolution.

As he knelt, head bowed, Anskar's eyes moistened. A tremor started up somewhere along his spine. It radiated out through his body, growing violent as he shook. He clenched his fists and tautened every muscle he could in an effort to stifle the physical reaction to his cleansing, but all he achieved was an involuntary moan.

"Anskar?" Gisela said. "Are you all right?"

"Fine." He nodded and gritted his teeth. "I'm fine."

And then it passed.

His shoulders slumped, his fingers uncurled from the fists they had been bunched into, and he drew in a long and shuddering breath. He felt scoured inside and out, scourged clean by the boundless mercy of the Healer. He had felt something similar before, the many times he had confessed his childish sins to Brother Tion, but nothing as intense as this.

And with forgiveness came a new sense of clarity. He had been slack, halfhearted in his adherence to the rules of the Order, the tenets of his faith. He had allowed the enemy to get inside him, and now his job was to cast it out. Her. His mother.

"Thank you, Sister," he said as he stood to leave.

Gisela pulled down her cowl. Her soft and beautiful face was stern, her eyes frosty. "Anskar," she said, her voice at first hesitant but swiftly growing in confidence, "I would like you to find another confessor."

Anskar swallowed a half-formed protest, nodded, and strode from the chapel.

As he left the basilica, Anskar heard the familiar clangor of a forge carried on the morning breeze. After Gisela's rejection, it made him nostalgic for Branil's Burg. Contentment, he found, not altogether to his surprise, was a fragile thing.

He approached the blacksmith's through a copse of willow that he supposed must have been left to grow as a barrier to the din of the forge. As he came to the edge of the trees, he heard the hissing rush of steam from a slack tub, and he could smell coal smoke and hot metal. The hammering had ceased for the moment, presumably so the blacksmith could plunge whatever he was beating into the cooling waters of the slack tub.

Or rather, she, he corrected himself as he drew near and saw a woman emerge from the cloud of steam that was, even now, dispersing through the open side of the smithy. A big woman, with muscled arms and broad shoulders. A grubby headscarf kept her gray-flecked hair out of her face—a face marred by old burns and blackened with soot. She had a brow like thunder and dark pebbly eyes that squinted out between cheeks reddened by the forge's heat. She wore a patched leather apron that seemed too tight for her prodigious breasts. Sweat stained the armpits of her smock, and on her feet, iron-banded boots.

"Who the fuck are you?" she said, lifting a dagger blade from the seething slack tub in a pair of tongs and carrying it to a bench beside the forge.

"My name's Anskar," he said as he came to stand in the entrance to the smithy—which was little more than a metal-roofed pole barn with a sand-covered floor. Tools and half-finished weapons hung from hooks screwed into the beams beneath the ceiling. The space within was cluttered with offcuts and twists of metal, bent nails, broken hammers and the like. There were barrels filled with bolts and rivets set around a rusty lathe. In among the junk was a half-buried grindstone, and there was a pitted anvil, atop which lay a heavy hammer.

"I didn't ask your name."

"You said—"

"Who the fuck are you. I know what I said, and I don't need a spavined sack of goat shit to tell me otherwise. I was being polite, you stringy piece of offal seeping from a pig's ass."

The afterglow of confession was perilously close to dispersing along with the slack tub steam. Anskar fought back an angry retort. With a silent prayer, he manufactured a smile.

"Don't you smirk at me, you louse-infested weasel," the woman snarled, dropping the dagger blade she'd been working onto the smoldering coals of the forge. She turned it idly with the tongs.

"I'm sorry, I didn't mean to smirk."

"You still here?" She turned a glare on Anskar, and he half-expected her to laugh and tell him she'd been pulling his leg. But she didn't. Her ill-temper, it seemed, was in deadly earnest.

"I …" he stammered, then coughed and started again. "I was looking for a smithy."

"Congratulations," she said. "You found one. Now piss off."

You fat, insolent—Anskar squashed the thought before it caught fire. "I'm a knight of the Order of Eternal Vigilance."

"Good for you." The woman spat onto the coals and watched the resultant hiss of steam with a look of grim satisfaction.

"The Grand Master brought me to the Mother House from Niyas."

"I feel sorry for you, lad, I really do."

"I was hoping I could continue my learning in metalwork."

"I'll bet. And you was expecting a man, was you? Is that why you're so bloody surly?" She sniffed and rubbed her thumb into the corner of her eye.

"Surly? Me!"

"Don't you play the innocent with me. All the same, you are, you jellied pieces of cat puke. Just because I ain't no man don't mean I can't smith."

"I never said it did."

The woman growled then spat again.

"You ain't the first. My ma was a blacksmith. Took over my pa's forge when she ripped open his guts with a kitchen knife and pulled out his heart through his stinking asshole."

"She murdered your father?"

"Had it coming. Used to beat her senseless, but the final straw was when he got one of the priestesses pregnant. Plump little tart, they say she was. Ripe where it mattered."

"What happened to the child?"

"You might well ask." She cocked her head and gave him a warning look.

A sudden change in the direction of the wind brought with it the smell of leather and urine. The woman saw the face he made and scowled.

"I ain't pissed myself, if that's what you're thinking. That's the tanning pits you can smell."

Anskar grasped his shirtsleeve at the wrist, felt the hardness of the vambrace underneath. A forge like this, open to the moonlight ... he could make a study of the vambrace, maybe work out how to remove it. Or how to emulate its design. "As I was saying, I'd like to continue my studies in metal craft—"

"Down in the lower city. Didn't they tell you that, the good-for-nothing chicken-shaggers? The Order has its own smithy down there. Seven forges they got, or maybe even eight. I don't know for sure and I don't care, so long as they leave me in peace to get on with my work."

But whose work? Anskar wanted to ask. Why was there a smithy within the Order's compound if not for the use of the knights? He thought better of asking. He'd been insulted enough for one day.

"Sorry to have disturbed you," he said. "I won't do so again."

He heard a snort in response, but he'd already turned to leave. He'd barely taken a step when the woman spoke.

"Braga," she said.

Anskar turned back to face her. "Sorry?"

"My name, you ignorant piece of fetid dung, seeing as you didn't have the manners to ask." She softened the insult this time with a crooked smile. "It's Braga."

She lifted her dagger from the coals and carried it over to the anvil, where she resumed beating it with a hammer.

Anskar stood watching her for a moment until the clangor became too much for him, and then he made his way back to the house he shared with Lanuc.

Anskar was surprised to find the door to Lanuc's room open, a fragrant, spicy smell coming from within. When he poked his head inside, he saw the knight changing into fresh clothes, his recently oiled mail lying atop the bed beside a stained and frayed gambeson.

"Ah, the penitent returns," Lanuc said. "I had expected you sooner. Here, help me on with my gambeson and mail, would you. Just been for a wash at the communal bathhouse. You might want to too, if there's time."

"Time?"

"Settling in is over. The Grand Master wants to see you."

"Now?"

"You have a couple of hours. I have knights to inspect first, hence the armor."

"Should I wear mine?"

"Probably best if you do. The Grand Master sets a lot of store by appearances. So, that was a long confession."

"I went to the blacksmith's afterwards."

Lanuc shook his head as Anskar laced up his gambeson for him. "Don't tell me you met Braga and lived to tell the tale."

"I don't think she likes me," Anskar said. "She insulted me constantly."

Lanuc laughed. "Then you're in a whole heap of trouble. That means she does like you. A lot."

"Oh … Anyhow, I thought the knights would have had their own forges, like we do at Branil's Burg, but Braga said we have to use the forges in the lower city."

"And she's right, but there's scarcely any need of it. Most of the knights stationed here have crafted all the armor and weapons they'll ever need. Braga's father was a knight before he retired, and ran the little forge as a way to stay part of the Order. When he … passed away, his wife continued the work, and Braga after her. She repairs tools the priests and their grounds folk need, and she sometimes makes weapons for the Watch down below. There was a time we knights brought her armor and weapons to fix, but we've learned it's easier to make the repairs ourselves at the city forge."

"Yet she's still here?"

"Would you want to try to remove her?"

"No!" Anskar laughed as he helped Lanuc into his mail. "No, I wouldn't."

"Listen, Anskar, Gisela spoke with me after you went to the chapel."

"She did?"

"Thank you," Lanuc said, tugging down the skirt of his mail and taking his cloak from the closet beside his bed. "I owe you an apology."

"What for?"

"I thought at first, the way you looked at her … Never mind." Lanuc fastened the cloak around his neck. "And don't worry, Gisela didn't reveal the contents of your confession."

"I knew she wouldn't." Confession was confidential, between the penitent and the priest of the Healer. "She was helpful, but I have to find a different confessor."

"Now that she did tell me."

After Lanuc left to inspect the knights under his supervision, Anskar scoured his mail with sand and vinegar, working away at stubborn blemishes that ran the risk of turning into rust if untreated. When he finished, he applied a coat of oil before inspecting *Amalantril* for nicks and rust spots. He found neither. He'd made her too well.

He re-sheathed the blade, then headed to the bathhouse. When he returned a little later, clean clothes had been laid out for him on the bed—one of Lanuc's servants—and while it was something he was used to from Branil's Burg, he was discomfited by the thought that someone had been in his room.

He made a cursory inspection of his and Orix's things and decided nothing had been taken or tampered with. He was about to start getting dressed in preparation for his meeting with the Grand Master when a pain stabbed inside his skull. He winced and clutched his head until it passed. Only, it didn't pass, it just softened into a tugging sensation, which he attributed to his nascent senses.

He started at a broken fragment of speech that seemed to come from a long way off: words repeated in a language he'd never heard. Darkness began to pool in front of the closet. As he stepped back, the shadows coalesced into a malformed shape that swiftly resolved into a motley-clad dwarf in a tricorn hat.

"Malady!" he gasped.

She wasn't fully present, merely a ghostlike image devoid of color. Her lips moved, but he could hear nothing other than a harsh rasping sound. The dwarf shut her eyes in concentration, mouth working in what looked like barbarous cants. Her form rippled then grew more substantial. Behind her, where trees lined the background, he saw Carred Selenas, and beside her, Orix, nodding, smiling, apparently unharmed.

"Can he hear me?" Carred Selenas asked in Niyandrian—and Anskar understood her perfectly.

"He can now," Malady replied. She flashed Anskar a grin.

"It's all right," Orix said. "I'm all right."

"There's not much time," Carred Selenas said in Nan-Rhouric. "Take Malady's hand. Join us."

Anskar retreated another step until he was backed up against the bed.

"Trust me," Carred Selenas said. "Trust Orix."

Malady began to lose substance. Behind her, Carred Selenas and Orix were no more than blurs.

Malady narrowed her eyes. "What is happening ? Who are—?"

And then the vision disappeared and Anskar was left staring at the closet door.

Never consort with demons, Queen Talia said inside his head. *There, my first motherly advice. You feel a bond developing?* She spoke in Niyandrian, and, as with Carred Selenas just now, Anskar understood every word.

"What did you do?" he asked in the same tongue, the words awkward on his lips but springing to mind as naturally as breathing.

Something as simple as closing a door.

"But Orix … my friend …"

Patience, child. All is unfolding better than I planned.

"What did you plan? My childhood in Branil's Burg?"

Silence.

"My becoming a knight of the Order of Eternal Vigilance? Did you plan for me to come here to Sansor?"

Nothing.

"What next, *Mother*? What next?"

No answer.

"Then let me tell you what next," he said, and he reached within, drawing from his dawn-tide repository. Fearing that might not be enough, he took also from the dusk-tide, then the dark. He made calculations, spoke cants on the fly, wove invisible threads together, following some hitherto unsuspected instinct. He made nets and barriers, which he spun around his mind, a fortress of wards with only one explicit aim:

To keep his mother out.

THIRTY-ONE

"INTERFERING BITCH!" MALADY CRIED as she reappeared within her circle of Nazgrese runes back at the camp.

"Who, me?" Carred asked.

"Did you interfere?"

"No."

"So how could I be referring to you?"

"I assumed, from the word 'bitch.'"

Malady whipped off her hat and glowered at it before putting it back on. "I sensed a woman, but she stank of demon."

"Like you?" Orix asked. "Like rotten eggs?"

"Funny. No. Not an olfactory scent. Something too subtle for a dullard like you to perceive."

"So you failed," Taloc said, rolling his eyes for Vilintia's benefit.

"I was thwarted."

"By a woman," Carred said. "And you didn't see her?"

"What do you think, genius?"

"Was it Queen Talia?"

"How should I know? But what I do know is I tried my best. We had a deal, remember?"

"Is Anskar here?" Carred asked, pretending to look around.

Some of the rebels gathered to watch chuckled.

Malady turned on them. "Which one of you cunts wants me to pull their guts out of their asses?"

"I command you to do nothing without my leave," Carred said.

Malady opened her mouth.

"Not even to speak!"

The demon shook with suppressed rage, and tears glistened in her eyes. She had left someone behind in the abyssal realms. Someone special. Carred knew all too well what it was like to lose a loved one. She couldn't help herself. She felt a pang of sympathy.

"I will release you," she said. "I promise. But not until we have Anskar again."

She became aware of someone muttering—the same words, over and over. There, by the smoldering embers of last night's fire. Noni.

Carred approached until she could hear what Noni was saying.

"Carred, my love. Talk to me. Carred. Can you hear me? Carred, my love …"

"Talia?" Cared breathed, drawing wide-eyed looks from the men and women standing around.

"Carred? You can hear me?" Noni said, eyes staring into space.

"I can hear you."

The rest of the camp knelt on the dew-damp grass, as if the dead Queen were really and physically present in their midst.

"I've failed," Carred said.

"No, my love, you haven't failed," Noni said, her voice mellifluous yet somehow rasping, as if every half-sung cadence came at a great cost. "I'm pleased, Carred."

"Pleased by failure?"

"There has been a change of plan," Noni said. "I didn't anticipate Anskar being taken to Sansor. It may work to our advantage. In the meantime, you must do what I had intended for him."

Orix chose that moment to shamble over to Carred. "What's going on?" he asked.

"Who is this?" Noni turned her vacant eyes on Orix, then squinted as if she couldn't see him clearly.

"No one," Carred said.

Orix actually looked hurt by that. Theltek's nipples, the dunce was besotted.

The hint of a smile curled Noni's lips. "Do you miss me, Carred?"

"Of course I miss you." But the words were hollow, a lie.

Something had changed, and she wasn't sure what. All these years had eroded her certainties. All her losses. And the thought that Talia might rise from the dead and resume her bed made Carred shudder.

"I miss you too," the Queen said.

"So what is it you want me to do?"

"Before you entered my service, after I learned of the threat from the mainland, I journeyed to Mount Phryith."

"The site of the Necromancer Tain's ascension?"

"I found it, Carred. I found him."

"He didn't ascend?"

"He is vague on the matter. But he returned from *somewhere*. He had made mistakes. His Armor of Divinity was imperfect.

Only part of him came back. He had his theories as to why. Tain agreed to help me with my own attempt, on the understanding that I would help him in return. A process was begun. New armor was to be created. I had agents in the Kingdom of the Thousand Lakes, a smith in the royal forges, the only ones hot enough to work with divine alloy. We made a start—"

"The vambrace Anskar now wears?"

"All there was time for."

"Because the war began?"

Noni nodded. "But Tain always insisted there was another way, if we couldn't access the forge in Thousand Lakes. Others had created their own Armor of Divinity in the past. Some might have succeeded—they vanished and never came back. Tain discovered a half-finished suit of armor, which he used for the basis of his own design. He told me there might be more, that if we could not forge a new suit, perhaps we could modify an old one."

"And you did this? You searched for old pieces of Armor of Divinity? Did you find any?"

"I did not. Tain knows all the likely sites, but he and I had a falling-out while I still lived. Later, I tried speaking to him from the realm of the dead, but he mistrusts spirits. The man has a morbid fear of death. Probably why he dedicated his life to overcoming it. He told me he would speak only with the living. I planned to send Anskar when he was old enough."

"But now you want me to go?"

"You could do this, Carred. I know how persuasive you are. Earn Tain's trust, and he will tell you where to look for the pieces."

"I don't understand. Why doesn't he find them himself?"

"As I said, only part of him returned. He needs us, Carred, as much as we need him."

"Needs us why?"

"To become whole again. To learn from his mistakes and make a new Armor of Divinity for himself. To ascend once more and live forever."

"And this is possible?"

"Tain believes so. I'll instruct Noni, and she will tell you the promises you must make Tain as you travel."

"Mount Phryith, you say? That's some journey, and much of it by foot." The approach to the peak through jungle and foothills was said to be impassable for horses. Which was why no one ever went there.

"I remember," Talia said through Noni. "I still feel my blistered feet, even in death."

Carred smiled, though her emotions were all over the place. But for a moment she was reminded of the Talia before the invaders came. Could they ever go back? Drive the mainlanders out and restore the old Niyas? Would it really be so bad if Talia returned from the dead? Experience told her not to get her hopes up. An inner voice warned her to be careful what she wished for. Sounded a lot like her mother.

"Will you go, Carred? Do this for me, please."

"What about Anskar?"

"I'll work on him," Talia said. She sounded distant now, Noni's voice a mere whisper. "He will come back, and when he does, the armor will be waiting for him."

"And then what happens?"

Noni keeled over onto her side and curled into a fetal ball, sobbing and shaking. Carred knew from the timbre of those cries that the girl was herself once more, that Queen Talia had returned to the realm of the dead.

At least for now.

THIRTY-TWO

LANUC BROUGHT ANSKAR TO a large room at the heart of the Mother House, the walls paneled with dark and grainy wood, the faltering light of an alchemical globe suspended from the ceiling, augmented by dozens of rushlights on iron stands. Gray-clad servants melded with the shadows, each clutching a handful of fresh rushes soaked in pig's fat—the crude lights quickly burned down to nothing and needed frequent replenishing.

"Ah, young Anskar," Hyle Pausus said. He was seated upon a blackwood throne engraved with images of each of the five aspects of Menselas. "I trust you have acclimated?" He turned his head to address one of the priests flocking around his throne, jostling for position, vying for his attention. "That is the correct word, Brother Gordiz, is it not?"

"Most apposite, Grand Master. An exquisite choice."

"Brother Gordiz is our scholar of languages. I forget how many he speaks and writes. Is it seven, Brother?"

"Fluently, nine, Grand Master, and several others are familiar to me."

Judging by the frayed and patched robe, his sallow look, and the carefully cultivated white beard that hung to his waist, Brother Gordiz was a priest of the Elder.

"Thank you, Grand Master," Anskar said. "I've settled in. It's tranquil here. Disciplined. Everything a knight could ask for."

Hyle Pausus gave him a tight smile. "Everything? I'm sure Brother Sidus would beg to differ." He glanced at a spindly man in a black hooded robe.

"There is an imbalance in the aspects." A rasping voice came from beneath the hood.

"You mean the absence of the Hooded One from the basilica?" Anskar winced as Lanuc nudged him in the ribs.

The Grand Master interlaced his fingers and met Anskar's gaze, as if daring him to go on. Anskar looked away.

An armored priest of the Warrior said something to the knight standing beside her. Three priests of the Mother bent their heads together, sharing whispers. Two were men, which surprised Anskar. Back at Branil's Burg, the only priests of the Mother he had seen were women.

The remainder of the priests in the room were seven white-robed healers, by far the best represented of the Five's aspects, as they always seemed to be. It perfectly illustrated Brother Sidus's remark about there being an imbalance among the aspects of the Five, an imbalance that Anskar had been told on several occasions could result in catastrophic perversions of the faith.

"Tell us, Anskar," Hyle Pausus said, leaning forward out of his throne, "how are you coming along with your burgeoning abilities?"

The room immediately hushed at that.

"There are no secrets here," the Grand Master encouraged him. "Well, there are, but there is no need for you to fear revealing your unique qualities to this august company." Again, a look to Brother Gordiz. "That is the right word, is it not, Brother? August?"

"Indubitably, Grand Master."

"In-dubit-ably," Hyle Pausus sounded out. "Very good, Brother. I like that one. I shall have to see if I can use it. Brother Gordiz is teaching me, Anskar. Improving my vocabulary, aren't you, Brother?"

"Not an easy task, adding to your already overwhelming lexicography, Grand Master. It is undeniably a most salutary challenge."

"Remind me again of the meaning of 'sycophant,'" Hyle Pausus said. "And that other word you were so kind as to teach me a while back: 'obsequious,' wasn't it?"

"I … uh …" Brother Gordiz said. "Would you like me to …"

"No." The Grand Master waved Gordiz to silence. "What I would like is for Anskar DeVantte here to answer my question. Or do I need to repeat myself?"

"My abilities, Grand Master," Anskar said. "You asked me how I'm coming along with my abilities."

"Your *burgeoning* abilities, if we are going to be pedantic about it." The Grand Master glanced at Brother Gordiz, who was looking thoroughly miserable and didn't react. "Not one of your words, Brother? Pedantic. I managed that all by myself."

"I made my confession," Anskar said. At that, the seven white-robed priests of the Healer exchanged looks.

"You answer like a politician," Hyle Pausus said. "Go on."

"I've done things. Ever since my catalyst was fitted, I've been drawn to the use of forbidden sorcery. I was led to believe there was no choice, that I used my powers for good, but each time the temptation grew, to do more, to go further."

"That is the nature of temptation," said one of the women who served the Mother. The Grand Master shushed her with a raised finger.

"I was taught at Branil's Burg that Menselas abhors all but the use of dawn-tide sorcery." Anskar glanced at the priests now gathered around him in a loose semicircle, trying to gauge their reactions. Some among the healers nodded their agreement, but by and large the others remained unreadable. "And so I have promised the Five that from now on I will only do as he wills. I will restrict my sorcery to the dawn-tide, for the purpose of casting a ward sphere."

The Grand Master nodded slowly, one hand rubbing his chin. "Does not Menselas demand obedience of us, Anskar? Obedience to our rightful superiors?"

"He does, Grand Master, but—"

"You yet lack wisdom. You lack faith, and, most serious of all, you lack humility. That much I observed on our recent adventure in the Plains of Khisig-Ugtall. And how is humility developed? Through obedience. Listen to me, Anskar, and listen carefully. As the others in this room will testify, I am not a man given to repeating myself. When I speak, is it not Menselas who speaks through me? And if that is so, then whatever I desire of you, the Five also wishes. That is how all followers of Menselas are taught to consider their superiors: as the god's mouthpiece, the conduit through which we know his will on Wiraya."

"Menselas permits this?" Anskar said despite Lanuc's whispered warning in his ear. "One of his own using sorcery that he himself has forbidden?"

"There are some priests—indeed the Patriarch himself—

who would say not," the Grand Master conceded. "Their interpretation of the scriptures would have you slain as a heretic, a demon, an abomination. Perhaps you would prefer that?"

Anskar swallowed a lump in his throat. He ignored Lanuc's hand on his elbow, urging restraint. "Is there some way to contain the power within me, to cut it off from the tides? To eradicate it?"

"That is not what I wish for you," the Grand Master said. "Think of it as a sacrifice, if you must, but it is a sacrifice for the sake of obedience. And rest assured, if there is any sin involved, the sin is mine, not yours. It is no sin to obey the command of a superior."

"You're commanding me to use the dusk-tide?" Anskar asked. He looked around the room for support but saw none. The seven priests of the Healer wouldn't meet his gaze, and the others all watched him impassively. "And the dark?"

"I'll leave that to the Abbess, who is wiser in such matters than I am," the Grand Master said.

"The Abbess?"

"Anskar ..." Lanuc cautioned.

"I'm sending you to the Abbey of the Hooded One," the Grand Master said, "to further your training. You are, after all, still only a knight-inferior. There are a good many things you still need to accomplish before you can go forward for solemn vows. While there, I would like you to entertain the possibility that the Patriarch and his supporters are wrong in their interpretation of Menselas's will. What if the Five wishes you to learn how to harness your gifts and channel them in the service of the Order? Does not Menselas himself use evil to bring about good? Just think of the redress of natural balances brought about by plague and flood and tempest. Not all is as it seems at first. The Abbess once made a remark to me that has forever lodged in my mind, and I'm still not sure I understand it. 'What if,' she asked me when I was but a young man starting out on the consecrated life, 'the three extant tides are at essence one? What if they all come from the same ineffable source?'"

"Menselas?" Anskar said.

"Ask her when you meet her, though you'll probably be just as baffled as I was by her answer. How about you, Brother Sidus? Do you know what she meant?"

"I cannot speak for the Abbess, Grand Master."

"But you frequently do. Why else does she send you here in her stead and refuse to attend herself?"

"She is old, Grand Master."

"Old? She's bloody ancient, but that never seems to stop her doing whatever she sees fit. Well, tell her, when you get back to the abbey, that I am sending her a very talented young man. I would be eternally grateful to her if she would offer Anskar her incomparable guidance as it pertains to his unique gifts. Don't worry yourself about the details, I will give you a letter to take to her."

Brother Sidus nodded beneath his cowl.

"Grand Master," Lanuc said, "will I be permitted to escort Anskar to the abbey?"

"You will not. Brother Sidus, would you care to explain?"

"Those who come to the abbey seeking the wisdom of the Hooded One must do so alone. You," he said directly to Anskar, "must make the journey without assistance, without a guide. There must be no crutches in the service of the Hooded One. Either you will survive or you will not. You will either find your way or grow lost in the wilderness and end up as prey for the beasts, maybe even the dead-eyes. It is of no concern to the

Hooded One. Death is her provenance."

"It is a journey of several miles only," the Grand Master said, "though there is scant shelter from the sun, which will be blazing by the time you leave. You've not yet experienced the severity of Kaile's weather, have you? Four seasons in one day, they say, and not without a modicum of truth." He glanced at Brother Gordiz and whispered, "Modicum. See, I squeezed it in." Then to Anskar he said, "Just be sure to take plenty of water."

Anskar could see there was no point in arguing. Suddenly, his newfound resolve to be an exemplary knight was hanging by a thread. "How long will I be there?" he asked.

"The Abbess will inform you when you are ready to return."

THIRTY-THREE

A MILE AWAY FROM Sansor, the heat was sweltering. Another mile, and it was deadly. Anskar stopped at the banks of an irrigation canal to refill his canteen and splash his face with water warmed by the sun.

Visibility was good for miles in every direction. East was uniform red earth dotted with stunted trees and vividly colored cacti. The emerald waters of the Simorga Sea rolled away to the west until they were lost in the haze on the horizon. Behind him, to the south, Sansor had retreated until only its tallest towers could still be seen.

He surveyed the countryside for the landmarks Lanuc had marked on the crudely sketched map, judging direction by the position of the sun in the sky. Lanuc's map said nothing of the peaks and troughs of gorges and ravines, the huge banks of scree that slid underfoot as Anskar climbed them. And there were ruins too, the burned-out shells of stone dwellings, an ancient lookout tower that was overgrown with hardy brown creepers and skirted by piles of masonry that had fallen from the upper levels. He entertained the idea of resting inside the tower's base, but was afraid of what he might find inside—a nest of dead-eyes, ghouls, a Kailean lion.

And so he pressed on.

He walked for hours, and the sun came directly overhead as he reached the flat summit of an escarpment that gave him a clear view of the way before him.

To the north, the Abbey of the Hooded One was a looming presence, perched atop a granite promontory. Gray-barked trees with washed-out green leaves skirted the edifice.

Anskar lost sight of the abbey as he entered the copse and dragged his feet up a steepening incline of shale. Cackling cries and muted hoots rose from the undergrowth, but whenever he looked around, there was nothing. *Birds*, he told himself, *or some kind of monkey.*

Licking his lips and trying to make spit to moisten his throat, he paused beneath the shade of a tree. Tall grasses rustled just shy of the trail, and he caught a glimpse of something half the height of a man bounding into cover.

Anskar pressed on up the path, sucking in each panting breath. The air was so hot and heavy, his lungs seemed to shrivel up and refuse it. He stopped three more times, gasping against the trunks of trees, but when he came out of the copse's cover, the shadow of the abbey walls plunged him into a coolness that, if not quite refreshing, was enough to spur him on.

The trail took him up a twisting gully until it emerged atop the promontory that formed the abbey's foundations. From thereon in, the pathway was flagged and lined with unlit braziers.

Anskar came at last to an iron gate set into the outer walls.

Lizards darted away from his boots. He went to grasp the bars so he could look through, but they were thick with cobwebs. Dozens of bulbous black spiders clung to the underside of the rails, vivid red stripes on their backs. Careful to avoid touching them, he lifted the latch and pushed. Hinges squeaked in protest, and when he shut the gate from the inside, there was an answering clang.

A narrow strip of brown lawn led to a cloister that enclosed the central structure in a quadrangle. The body of the abbey proper was veneered with blind arcades. Above the faux arches built into the masonry, the second story was punctuated with clerestory windows, and perched along a tiled roof were all manner of grotesque carved figurines with horns and fangs. Behind the central structure, the bell tower rose from a sheltered arcade, and upon its flat roof stood a statue of the Hooded One, although this had to be an earlier depiction, from before the time that name had been adopted: a skull could be seen peeking from beneath the cowl of the robe. A grinning skull with dark garnets for eyes. A representation of Death.

Anskar crossed the lawn and entered the quadrangle. The abbey grounds were empty save for a solitary white bird atop one of the arches, watching him with an unnerving tilt of its overly large head. When it let out a ululating cry that terminated in a mocking cackle, he knew he'd found the source of the noise on his way up the slope.

He made a circuit of the building until he came to a covered portico that sheltered a heavy door of some reddish wood, studded and banded with black-painted iron, more suited to a fortress than an abbey.

Scents from the herb garden off to one side wafted to his nostrils—lavender, sage, marjoram, if he wasn't mistaken. For an instant, it took him back to the Healer's herb garden at Branil's Burg, to simpler days when all he had to worry about was Tion's chastisements... and the snide remarks about the reddish tinge to his skin. By way of contrast, the abbey's herb garden was a drab affair, ill-kept, overrun with weeds and brittle, brown leaves. Citrus trees bordered it, fallen fruit moldering on the ground. About the only thing thriving was a single olive tree, heavy with fruit that looked long overdue for picking.

Anskar ran his eyes over the cloister one last time. The place had the feel of a cemetery.

He began to wish he hadn't left Branil's Burg and the securities it offered. But then again, he'd not exactly been given a choice.

When he knocked on the door, he didn't expect a response. Part of him hoped there wouldn't be one.

He waited, then knocked again. This time, he was answered by the metallic shriek and clunk of a bolt being drawn back. The door creaked open with an almost audible gasp of stale air from inside. Dust motes rose in swirls above the threshold. Pale fingers curled around the edge of the door, then pulled it fully open.

A cowled figure stepped into the entrance. He was covered head to toe in a black robe, cinched at the waist by a leather girdle. The lower half of the priest's face was washed with shadows from the hood: a narrow chin, cracked lips, pocked skin peppered with blemishes.

Anskar waited for the man to say something, but he was met with silence. Unseen eyes scrutinized him; he could feel their probing appraisal. When he could take no more discomfort, he broke the stalemate.

"I'm here to see the Abbess. I'm expected, I think." The Grand Master had sent a letter with Brother Sidus. "Anskar DeVantte. From the Mother House?"

The priest stepped aside and gestured for Anskar to enter.

The vestibule was shrouded in shadows, but before Anskar's eyes could adjust to the gloom, the priest walked on ahead, sandals slapping on the tiled floor.

Anskar followed him along a corridor flanked with closed doors, and into a circular chapel ringed with choir stalls. A statue of the Hooded One stood in an alcove behind a granite altar. The Death's head atop the altar was carved from obsidian, its blood-red eyes cunningly faceted to reflect light and convey the impression of movement.

Two priests looked up from a hushed conversation they were having in one of the stalls. Their cowls were down, and both had shaved heads. The Elder sported an unkempt beard, and he nodded sagely as the other, a young man of no more than twenty, spoke what was on his mind. Judging by the wild look in his eyes, the tears streaking his face, it was nothing good.

The cowled priest who had answered the door nodded to them, then led Anskar across the chapel and into a narrow passageway.

Candles in brackets flickered along the walls and cast wavering shadows across the floor. The doors on either side were ajar, affording Anskar glimpses of food stores, hanging robes, and cellared wines.

The corridor ended at a blackwood door. The priest knocked three times, gestured for Anskar to wait, then walked back up the passageway like a ghost.

"Come," a woman's voice said from within. It sounded brittle, wheezy, the voice of someone very, very old.

Anskar turned the doorknob.

He entered a cell barely wide enough for a tall man to lie down in. A gilt-framed painting dominated the opposite wall, depicting skeletons rising from their graves, around which the dead, flesh hanging in strips from their bones, cavorted in a macabre dance. There was a desk before it, the lone guttering candle atop it providing a wavering ambit of light. Propped up in one corner was a frayed and stained bedroll. Hunched over the desk, scrutinizing a handwritten letter, was an elderly woman in a black robe that starkly contrasted with her iron-gray hair.

"You're letting a chill in."

Anskar shut the door behind him. "My lady Abbess?"

The woman set down the letter and swiveled on her chair to face him. Her skin had the appearance of mildew. Her eyes were wintry, her lips slivers of slate. The impression was of a woman with all the moisture leeched out of her, yet she was in no way shriveled. If not for the unhealthy pallor, Anskar would have taken her for forty, at most.

The Abbess fingered a wood-carved Death's-head around her neck. Its eyes glimmered orange in the candlelight.

"Coincidence is a fickle beast," she said, picking up the letter and making a show of scanning it. "I felt an inexplicable yearning to have another look at Hyle Pausus's missive, and lo and behold, I had barely reached the end when there was a knock at my door. I assume it was Brother Canus who let you in. He was civil?"

Anskar was stuck for words, acutely aware he was being appraised, even while her eyes were on the letter.

"Tell me," she said, "is Hyle Pausus a good man these days?"

"I believe so," Anskar said. It wasn't a complete lie. People were complicated, he'd begun to learn.

"He says the same of you. He tells me you are special. Gifted. He also tells me you are disillusioned with the Order of Eternal Vigilance."

"He does? I have doubts, as most do, I assume. Menselas tests us."

"Whatever masks you might employ elsewhere," the Abbess said, "they are useless here. If longevity has granted me anything, it is the ability to see right into the soul of others. You are serious in your vocation, I'll grant you, but a vocation is not all about seriousness. Sometimes, it is about clarity. Unbuckle your sword and set it upon my desk."

Anskar lowered his hand until it covered the pommel beneath his cloak. He had made *Amalantril* from folded steel, imbued her with sorcery, named her ...

"As I thought," the Abbess said. "It is no easy thing for a warrior to cease being what he is. A knight does not simply lay down his sword and become ... something else. Violence once tasted is an addictive drug, is it not?"

Anskar removed his sword belt and lay *Amalantril* on the desk.

"You take that as a challenge?" the Abbess said. "Good. That gives us a place to start. But I have to tell you ..." She glanced at the letter. "Anskar ... I am not at all convinced this is such a good idea. Hyle Pausus has done his best to persuade me, and he has not been entirely successful."

Anskar reached for *Amalantril*. "Then forgive me for wasting your—"

"Nonsense." The Abbess lay her hand over the hilt of his sword. "What is the first thing a child of Menselas is taught?"

"The first ...? For the Five, all things are possible."

"Indeed. Your armor, too, if you don't mind. And your white cloak."

Anskar removed his cloak, mail, and padded gambeson, and at a gesture from the Abbess left them in a pile on the floor. He stood only in his plain shirt and pants and the dust-caked boots that had brought him here. He feared for a moment she was going to demand those few clothes as well, but instead she stood and embraced him. She smelled of must and off-meat.

"Welcome to the Abbey of the Hooded One, Anskar. Just remember, you are not to leave the abbey building without my express permission, and that permission will not come quickly. You must be acclimated first, tried and tested. And you must not speak, not to anyone save myself when we meet. I will send for you from time to time, so you need not concern yourself about when.

"Silence, then, and time alone in which to contemplate the mysteries of death and let the air of the abbey pervade your very being. For you it will only be temporary, but there are many among us who, once having entered the abbey, have never left. The walls of this building are as much a part of us as the skin that holds in our bones. Think about that while you are among us. Think and learn, but more than that, when you are alone in your cell, and that is where you will be most of the time, contemplate your own mortality. Imagine yourself as a stinking, festering corpse, putrid with rot, riddled with worms. Make this the basis of your meditation day and night. It will open you up to the truths embodied by the Hooded One.

"Oh, and I almost forgot." She shuffled off into a darkened corner. A few moments later she returned clutching a black robe with a cowl. "Wear this while you are with us. The abbey hides you from the life of Wiraya, and this robe will hide you from yourself. You are dead with us, Anskar. Entombed."

THIRTY-FOUR

ANSKAR WAS LED TO his cell by a faceless priest, indistinguishable from all the other black-robed devotees of the Hooded One they passed on the way. He couldn't even tell if it was a man or a woman.

He felt naked without his sword, as though he had left a part of himself behind on the Abbess's desk, and with it the cherished memory of hard work in the forges, of Sned Jethryn and Orix. In one fell swoop, the Abbess had severed him from the parts of himself that served the Warrior and perhaps the other aspects too. Everything he had learned as a child of the Order, everything he was, had gone into the crafting of that sword. And the name, *Amalantril*, had come from Sareya.

His cell was a windowless box, perhaps ten feet square, dark, cold, and damp. The only light came from a crimson stone set into the ceiling—not enough to read by. The cowled priest closed the door behind him, leaving without uttering a word.

Heart hammering in his chest, Anskar checked to see if he was locked in. He wasn't. The door opened onto the retreating back of the priest.

So, Anskar reasoned as he shut the door and set his pack in a corner, he wasn't a prisoner. At least not of the cell. But he had been told not to leave the abbey. Still, he was used to confinement. He'd not left Branil's Burg all his life until that first time Vihtor had taken him beyond the walls to enjoy food and beer at the Griffin's Rest.

Nevertheless, he quickly plummeted into a state of melancholy and sat there brooding on the cold stone floor, which he supposed was going to have to serve as his bed. He tried to pray but experienced only absence. Like a man buried alive, he felt totally cut off from the tides of dusk and dawn, and he could almost feel the stored essence within his repositories ebbing away.

He pondered the seething pit of the dark-tide, picking at the bindings he had set to contain it. He prodded and poked at its essence, only drawing back because of the promise he had made to Menselas.

At some point, there was a knock at his door. Anskar rose stiffly and opened it onto a hooded priest—it could have been the same one who had first brought him to the cell. With a gesture that he should follow, the priest turned and walked away.

Anskar realized it must be dusk outside, due to the dirty spears of gray light that came through the clerestory windows. He felt the remnants of the dusk-tide as a thin and ragged breeze, as if it broke upon the rock of the abbey and dispersed without filling him with its essence. Glowing stones like the one that partially illuminated his cell were everywhere, washing the corridors in red.

The priests they saw were all headed in the same direction with scuffing, shuffling steps. Anskar had the sense that these men and women never varied their pace, never hurried for anything. To their minds they were dead already, interred within the abbey in service to the Hooded One.

The priest brought him at last to a refectory, in which cowled figures lined up for slops and hard bread served by a one-eyed girl with a twisted spine. Anskar sat beside anonymous priests, hidden beneath his own cowl, and ate without enthusiasm, washing down the bland and tasteless fare with sips of chalky water from a wooden bowl.

He remained seated until the priests had all finished and begun to file out, this time heading toward the heart of the abbey, where he guessed the chapel was located.

Anskar cleared his place at the table and then started to follow the long line of priests, but one at the back turned and made a forbidding gesture with his hand.

He returned to his cell along the same gloom-shrouded corridors, surprised at how easily he found his way.

Muffled by the stone walls, he could hear snatches of some ritualistic chant echoing down long corridors from the chapel. He strained to listen for words he might recognize, either in Nan-Rhouric or Skanuric, but could distinguish none. It could have been the barks and growls of wild animals for all he could tell.

Days went by, long, lonely, oppressive days, measured only by the shifting light beyond the clerestory windows of the corridors whenever he was taken to the refectory.

In all that time, Anskar received no summons from the Abbess. He began to worry she had forgotten him, that he really was in some way buried, lost to the world.

He took to roaming the corridors alone, unremarkable in his cowled robe. He passed other robed figures, who never acknowledged him. He felt like a ghost haunting the passageways of the abbey, unseen by anyone living. Menselas, he felt like a wraithe. When he wasn't roaming, he was seated on the cold stone floor of his cell, muttering the words of prayers like a madman, teeth chattering from a chill he wasn't sure was real.

And, as ever, Menselas kept his silence, left Anskar teetering on the brink of a void. When the despair grew too much and he felt himself drawn back to the fathomless depths of his dark-tide repository, he would get up and leave his cell, wander once more through the labyrinthine ways of the abbey, always skirting the heart, where he wasn't permitted to tread.

He ceased to notice the changing light outside the clerestory windows. For the most part he prowled the corridors with his head bowed beneath his cowl, a nobody like everyone else.

Sometimes he asked himself how long he would wait before he decided enough was enough and returned to the Mother House. If that time came, would he be allowed to leave? If he resisted, could the priests here stop him?

And there it was: the rearing of temptation's head. For implicit in the thought of a struggle between himself and the abbey's priests was the suggestion that he'd need all his talents in order to prevail, not just a ward sphere powered by the dawn-tide.

And so he walked the passageways, he sat in his cell contemplating the darkness at his core, and he slept, only to awaken stiff and cold from lying on the floor.

Then, at last, the summons came. A knock at the door, an indistinguishable priest, and the first words he'd heard in a very long time:

"The Abbess will see you now."

"A demon, you say?" the Abbess said, her face a fossil, betraying nothing, dark eyes glinting in the ruddy hue of the single luminous stone set into the ceiling.

"A dwarf," Anskar said. "Though I saw it turn into a gigantic serpent."

"A shapeshifter." She hesitated, mouth working as if she lacked the spit to finish her sentence, or as if she were gauging how much she should say. "It had a name, this demon?"

"Malady."

The Abbess elicited a noise like the draining of a ditch. "A joke, no doubt, probably a contrivance of the one who bound the demon."

"Luzius Landav," Anskar said. "The sorcerer I told you about."

"The man who fitted your catalyst, yes. Luzius is not unknown to me."

"He's dead."

"Aren't we all, ultimately? But that does raise an interesting question. If Luzius Landav died before you left Branil's Burg for Atya, who was in command of the demon? Someone, it seems, must have summoned and re-bound it."

"There was an old man with the rebels, some kind of sorcerer."

"A Niyandrian?"

"Yes," Anskar said. "But he's dead now too."

"And the demon did not return to … wherever it came from?"

"It took Orix," Anskar said. "Which is when it turned into a serpent and leaped into the sea. Carred Selenas rode on its back."

The Abbess closed her eyes, lips working as if she spoke to herself, or to someone not present. "The old man must have passed its bindings to Carred Selenas upon his death. Unless of course she is a sorcerer of some ability."

"She's Niyandrian …" Anskar said.

"Even among those with innate sorcerous talent, proficiency to command demons does not come easily. And if she had the ability, why the need for the old man? No, it is loosely bound to her. There will be many loopholes the demon could exploit. She will need it to perform its tasks quickly so she can be rid of it."

Anskar nodded, all the while wondering how the Abbess had acquired such knowledge of demons. No one save initiates really knew what secrets were revealed by the Hooded One, but he'd not expected one of them to be the lore of the abyssal realms.

"Malady appeared to me at the Mother House," Anskar said. "And I could see Carred Selenas in the background with Orix. They wanted me to go with them."

"Through a portal?"

"I don't know. I suppose so. I think they were back in Niyas."

"But you did not go. Why? Were you not tempted?"

He'd given that a lot of thought during the days on end of gloom. Yes, he had been tempted, but he'd also been afraid—of it being a trap or, worse, a sin. Side with the enemies of Menselas, and he could expect an eternity of pain. So Tion used to say.

"The demon's power was blocked. It faded away."

The Abbess nodded and steepled her spindly hands on the tabletop. "The presence inside you?"

"My mother."

"Yes, the Necromancer Queen. Now there was a woman of rare talent."

"You knew her?"

"We knew of each other. All that potential, incinerated by the light of goodness and truth. Do you think the Order of Eternal Vigilance and its allies were right to stamp out your mother's rule?"

"I don't know," Anskar said. "I was a baby at the time."

"Yes or no. It is a simple enough question."

"Yes, then." He steeled himself against a protest from within, but his mother didn't stir. His wards seemed to be working.

"And you do not wish to rule in her stead?"

Melesh-Eloni.

Was she testing him? Testing his loyalty to the Order? "No," Anskar said, "I don't want to rule."

"So," the Abbess said in an amiable tone, "you are a loyal child of the Order of Eternal Vigilance? A son of the Church? A faithful servant of Menselas?"

"I am."

A shadow passed behind the old woman's eyes. "And what do you know of Menselas?" she said. "Your tutor was a healer, did you not say?"

"Brother Tion," Anskar said. "A good man."

"A good man who renounced the priesthood?" Anskar had told her perhaps more than he should have. "Don't think for one minute that I am being critical. If anything, I wish you to confront this idea of goodness, what it takes to be good."

"I don't understand."

The Abbess's eyes sparkled with renewed vigor, and she leaned across the table toward him. "Tell me, do you think imbalance in the five aspects is a good or a bad thing?"

"Bad," Anskar answered without hesitation.

"How so? Enlighten me."

"Because the aspects are like the branches of a teetering tree that only stays upright if all five are perfectly balanced."

"Not the pat answers of others, Anskar. It is your answer that interests me, the one you have cut for yourself from the fabric of your own unique experience."

He thought and he thought, but he could come up with nothing better.

"Take the aspect of the Hooded One," the Abbess said. "In isolation from the other four, what would you say are its excesses?"

"I don't know."

"Then think! No, don't think, feel. Close your eyes and tell me what you see, hear, taste, and smell. Focus on the Hooded One ... upon Death ... at the exclusion of all else."

"Rot," Anskar said. "Decay. Emptiness. Nothing."

"Yes ..." the Abbess prompted. "A return to the nothingness whence all things came. What else?"

Anskar thought of the long dark hours in his cell. "Sorrow," he said. "Despair."

"Yes," the Abbess said. "And suffering. And these things, which are reviled by the sheep who comprise the masses, lead us to buried and unexpected doorways."

Anskar opened his eyes. "What doorways?"

"Things we must disinter," the Abbess said. "Things that have lain hidden within our kind so long they have almost ceased to be."

"What things?"

"Think upon it," the Abbess said. "Take your time and ponder. That is enough for today."

"When will we speak again?"

"Soon, Anskar." The Abbess worked her lips into a tight smile. "Very soon."

THIRTY-FIVE

"WHAT IS YOUR NAME?" Anskar asked the very next day when he was summoned to her cell. During a lull in the conversation, it occurred to him that she'd not told him, and he'd only ever heard her referred to as "the Abbess."

"A name defines a person, don't you think?" she said. "But a person subsumed by their role has no need of one. I am the Abbess. Of the abbey. Which is dedicated to manifesting the will of the Hooded One. I am her representative on Wiraya. I am *her*. I am."

"You claim to be a god?"

The Abbess chuckled, and again Anskar was reminded of a draining ditch. "The Hooded One is but one aspect of a god. You were the one, after all, who spoke so earnestly about the need for balance."

"And you are that aspect? You manifest the Hooded One?"

"It sounds like heresy to you? Blasphemy?"

He nodded, and still the Abbess held his gaze, searching him, sifting his thoughts.

"Black is black and white is white?" the Abbess said. "Is that how you view the world?"

"For most things it is the truth."

"There are no other truths? No shades of gray?"

Anskar started to say no, but he hesitated.

He felt a sudden tension in the air between them, and he had the irrational fear that the Abbess was going to spring at him, but she didn't move. After a long stillness, she relaxed back in her chair, eyes shining with warmth.

"Go, Anskar," she said, surprising him. "You have much to meditate upon."

The Abbess met with Anskar more frequently after that. She probed him and challenged him about all manner of things he had been taught as a child growing up in Branil's Burg, and just when he thought he understood where she was going with her arguments, when he could start to accept the reasonableness of her position, she would pull the rug right out from under him and send him back to his cell in a tempest of confusion. They were bleak days, and there were times he could almost feel his skull splitting as he labored to grasp concepts or hold together his fraying world view as the Abbess pulled it apart thread by painful thread.

And when he wasn't with the Abbess, he was alone in his cell, where, despite his resolution, he continued to dip his toe in the fathomless darkness that seethed at his core.

One day during their meeting, the Abbess surprised Anskar

with a question:

"You think Hyle Pausus holds the five aspects in balance?"

"No," Anskar said. "I don't."

"He came here once," the Abbess said. "A long time ago, to round out his training. He did not do well in the dark, alone. He spurned the Hooded One, and his imbalances sought relief in unnatural vices. I tried to warn the Patriarch when Hyle Pausus was nominated Grand Master, but like so much in the Church of Menselas these days, the choice was politically motivated, not based upon merit or piety, and most certainly not upon balance. You know Hyle Pausus wants you for your talents? You are merely a tool to him, a weapon in his war."

"Which war? Against Niyas?"

The Abbess shook her head. "That battle was won long ago. Against rivals within the Order of Eternal Vigilance, within the Church of Menselas. Against powerful lords in Sansor. Against other lands, other kingdoms. Ultimately against fear itself. That is the destiny he plans for you, Anskar, and for others he has sent to me previously. You will fight his battles for him, bolster his defenses, enact his will, until such time as you cannot, and then you will be cast aside with scarcely a thought. But I will say to you as I said to the others: there is a higher calling. All it requires is your freely given assent."

"What calling?" When she didn't answer, Anskar tried another question: "What happened to the others who were sent to you?"

"Some of them stayed."

"And the abbey will be their tomb?"

She laughed, and her laughter bubbled up into a productive cough. She spat a wad of phlegm to the floor.

"And the rest?" Anskar asked.

"They returned to the Order, of course. Enlightened or

otherwise. Balanced or off-kilter. A few are serpent's eggs, waiting to hatch—something I'm sure you understand, as the son of the Necromancer Queen."

Later, the Abbess showed Anskar a book with brittle, brownish pages speckled with mildew. It contained diagrams of circles and swirling sigils. There were unfamiliar letters inscribed around the perimeters of the circles, and the same letters within, only bound and twisted together, combined into complex patterns.

"Have you seen such diagrams before?" she asked.

"Never."

"Luzius Landav didn't show you anything like this?"

Anskar shook his head. "He came to Branil's Burg to fit our catalysts and test us in our use of the dawn-tide, but these diagrams are something else, aren't they?"

"You are no one's fool, Anskar," the Abbess said. "But Luzius Landav did not encourage you in the pursuit of your other talents?"

"Not really. A little perhaps, but he showed no interest in teaching me. I thought about asking him to, but by then he was already dead."

"Ah, the paradoxical approach. He does not offer to train you but sows the seed that ensures you will ask him to. And then he has the defense that he was only doing what you pestered him to do."

"I hadn't thought about it that way," Anskar said, but he knew she was right.

"What do you think of the idea that, to effectively defend ourselves, we must understand our enemy, inside and out?"

"When we fight in the squares," he said, recalling the day of the first trial that had eventually led to him being elevated to the rank of knight-inferior, "I watch the preliminary rounds with great care, studying the moves, the feints, the inclinations of my potential opponents. It allows me to plan for them, should we meet later on in the tournament."

"So to kill an enemy, it is necessary to study how he fights?"

"Not necessary, because that's not always possible. But it is desirable. If I ever achieve command, I'll make use of scouts, and I'll pay spies to infiltrate the enemy's lands, to learn as much as I can of their ways and customs, their methods of making war."

The Abbess smiled, but her eyes remained dark as she scrutinized him. "And is that the will of the Five, that you excel in warfare? What about the throne of Niyas?"

Anskar slumped in his chair, and his head began to pound.

"What was it Carred Selenas called you? *Melesh-Eloni*. Godling. I assume that is your destiny."

With anger he'd not realized he was harboring, Anskar said, "That's what my mother planned, but it is not my destiny."

"So she is manipulating you, your mother? I guess that is a necromancer's prerogative, to pull the strings of the living from the realm of the dead."

"Not any longer," Anskar said. "I've shut her out."

The Abbess raised an eyebrow. "Impressive." She turned her attention back to the open book on the table between them. "These words around the perimeters of the circles …" She thumbed through the pages, revealing a circle on each of them, but with differences in the letters and the central sigils. "Is the language familiar to you?"

"It's not Skanuric," Anskar said.

"Obviously," the Abbess said. "Skanuric is an old language,

and proto-Skanuric is impossibly ancient. This," she said, jabbing a dirty-nailed finger at a letter on the page, "is infinitely older."

"Nazgrese?" he breathed.

The Abbess held his gaze steadily.

Anskar's heart thumped against his rib cage, and the pounding in his head grew so severe, the dim light of the Abbess's room was blinding to him. He put a hand over his eyes and squinted against the pain.

"Too much for one day?" the Abbess said, closing the book. "You must not run before you can walk. Return to your cell and think about all that we have discussed."

As Anskar stood on shaky legs and turned toward the door, the Abbess said, "Remember the fight squares, Anskar. Know your enemy."

He nodded and stepped across the threshold into the corridor outside. As he shut the door behind him, he almost missed the Abbess's parting words. Almost, but not quite.

"And learn to love them."

Anskar was out of his depth and he knew it. His mind buzzed with new ideas, warnings, condemnations, but he was incapable of a single coherent thought. He craved old certainties. He craved the company of friends. He missed the security of Branil's Burg. He missed Brother Tion. And most of all he missed Sareya. He'd not thought about her much since leaving Niyas, but now he could almost smell her mint breath, her floral scent, her musk. Images of what they had done together tantalized his aching flesh. He paced his cell incessantly in an effort to banish them.

Gradually his need for Sareya, his crushing sense of loneliness, gave way to a growing anticipation, and he was shocked when he realized what it was.

He was looking forward to his next meeting with the Abbess.

He couldn't wait.

"Lower order demons must be submitted like dogs," the Abbess said, drumming her fingers on the book atop her desk. The red glow of the single stone set in the ceiling found its reflection in her eyes. "The principle is the same for the higher demons, too, only the methods are more complex and the severity of the coercion is exponentially greater."

"Why are you telling me this?" Anskar was starting to grow concerned that this wasn't just about knowing his enemy.

"Malady, the demon you told me about, the shapeshifter bound to the will of Luzius Landav, then the Old Niyandrian, and now, we must assume, to Carred Selenas … how do you suppose her compliance was achieved? Did Luzius win her over with his charm? Did he pay for her services? I think not."

"In the stories, they say that demons must first be summoned," Anskar said.

"And the stories are correct in that. But to summon a demon, the summoner must know the demon's name. Its true name, not the false one this Malady goes by."

"But how would Luzius Landav have known her true name?"

"Perhaps the same way I have been able to discover it."

She held Anskar's gaze and his cheek began to twitch. Drool glistened at the corner of her mouth, and fleetingly, she seemed to shiver.

"Demons are ranked according to their power," the Abbess continued. "According to their awareness, their ability to self-regulate their innate savagery, their progress toward some semblance of order amid the chaos that defines them. What we tend to think of as demonic—evil, unbridled lust, eating human flesh, the need to slaughter and rape and work all manner of defilements—pertains only to the lesser demons, who are on a level with the dead-eyes. But the higher up they rise in the pecking order, the more refined demons become, the more self-controlled. The more like us."

She left that last thought hanging in the air.

"Until at the highest levels, the level of the demon lords, they surpass us in every way. They are more cultured, refined, more powerful, more intelligent … and more benevolent."

Anskar's chair scraped on the floor as he stood and raised a finger in warning. What she said was blasphemy. "I'm leaving," he said through clenched teeth. "Don't try to stop me."

"Hear me out, Anskar. This is knowledge not easy to come by. When I am done, decide for yourself whether I am right, or whether I deserve to be condemned. If the latter, no one will stop you if you wish to leave and report what you have heard from my lips to the Grand Master, or even to the Patriarch himself. Please, sit and let me finish."

He sat back down and folded his arms across his chest.

"Thank you," the Abbess said. "I'm just trying to help. Now, Malady. That is the name Luzius Landav's demon gave you, but as I have already said, it is not her true name. In the order of demons, those above know a good deal about those below. I have made enquiries, and I have for you a name: Yashash-na-Agarot, a demon of the Thirty-Third Order. A powerful demon indeed, but not as dangerous as a demon lord."

Anskar's mind was still racing, trying to keep up with what he was hearing, trying to connect all the inferences. "You got this information from a higher order demon?"

"Know your enemy, Anskar. Isn't that what we've been talking about these past few days?"

"But—"

She waved him to silence. "And is that not what I have just given you? Knowledge of your enemy? Knowledge of the demon who took your friend?"

Anskar swallowed. Looked at her. Looked away. Back again. "How does that help?"

"That depends," the Abbess said, "on how far you are willing to go."

"You can help me find this demon and get my friend back?"

"I can teach you how to summon the shapeshifter, how to bind it, and how to punish it for the merest hint of disobedience. You see now what I am getting at? Evil is only evil if you give it its head. Bind a demon to your will so tightly that it cannot breathe without your consent, and you have harnessed evil to good, have you not?"

"Menselas can bring good from even the foulest evil …" Anskar recited the axiom Brother Tion had long ago taught him.

"Exactly."

"And it won't damage my soul?"

"Oh, Anskar, you see now the harm done by neglect of the Hooded One's lore? The Church makes do with a four-chapel basilica in Sansor, and now our chapel at Branil's Burg has been turned into a banker's vault! Do you honestly believe such an imbalance in the Five can be brought about without perversions in the true knowledge of Menselas? Without ignorance? Without dire and far-reaching consequences? If we abandon what the

Hooded One teaches us about the abyssal realms, then will we not fall behind in the race for influence in those realms? Will we not cede control of the demonic to those who would use it for their own ends?"

"Who?" Anskar asked. "And why?"

"The Tainted Cabal. As to why—they desire a return to the times of blood and screaming not seen since the mad demon lord walked the surface of Wiraya."

"Nysrog?" Anskar had heard the tales of shadow and slaughter from a bygone era. Everyone had.

The Abbess raised a trembling hand, and there was a quavering rasp in her voice when she spoke. "Do not speak that name so irreverently again. Not here. Not anywhere. Forgive me, Anskar, I should not have said so much."

For the longest time, Anskar stared at her face, appraising every twitch and frown and movement of her eyes. Something about the Abbess told him that she never said anything she didn't mean to.

"All right," he said, and the accompanying feeling was like plummeting down an endless shaft toward some innominate pit. "Show me how to bring Orix back."

The Abbess studied him for a moment, one corner of her mouth twisted into the semblance of a smile. She spoke a cant.

And then the pain struck.

Anskar's hands flew to his temples. But the agony was not just in his head: it was in his arms, his legs, his belly, his back. His knees buckled and he hit the floor hard, bucking and writhing. Fire and acid and lightning scourged his veins. Froth bubbled from his mouth. He tasted blood. Screams welled up inside him, but he had no control over his lungs, his throat, his tongue in order to give them voice. And then the world collapsed in on him and he was buried in a blackness so absolute he knew he must be dead.

It took a while before he realized the pain had stopped. He cracked open his eyes onto an infernal glow.

He waited a moment for his eyes to adjust, then widened them to find himself staring at the glowing red stone set into the ceiling. The Abbess stooped over him, staring with a mixture of concern and amusement on her face.

"Before you beat a dog into submission, you should always have some idea of what it is like to be beaten. It is no different with sorcery, especially the kind you will need to enforce compliance in a demon."

"What did you do to me?"

"It is called the Wracking Nerves. And now that you have experienced it for yourself, it should be that much easier to learn. Especially with your capacity for the dark-tide."

"Dark?"

"Oh, Anskar, don't play the ignoramus with me. The dawn and the dusk will not serve us on the paths we must walk if you are to learn the ways of summoning. And you have used the dark-tide before—the scars are gouged into the very fabric of your repository. And what a repository! A seething, boundless ocean. In his letter, the Grand Master asked me to help you tame it, direct it, bend it to his purposes. He is such a fool."

THIRTY-SIX

THE ABBESS INSTRUCTED ANSKAR to copy out by hand one of the circles from her ancient book, substituting letters she provided for the inscriptions around the perimeter and the sigils within.

"For your own protection," she told him. "The diagram is a focus for the wards you will need to erect around your mind. The symbols are words of forbidding tailored to the shapeshifter's nature, its rank within the abyssal orders, its name."

"Yashash-na-Agarot," Anskar said. "Did I say it right?"

"Like a man who wants to die. 'Rot' not 'row.' The vowels are short, the consonants, hard. What is her Order?"

"Thirty-Third."

"Good."

She also showed Anskar how to prepare the rushlights that would illuminate his circle—reeds stripped back to their pith and dipped in tallow so they would burn more slowly. For each of the seven rushlights needed, he was given an iron holder, no more than a twisted upright of metal wire on a base, with a spring clip at the top in which the rushlight was to be held at a diagonal angle. Too upright, and it wouldn't emit enough of a glow; too horizontal and it would burn up rapidly. At the angle between the two extremes, the rushlights would burn for about half an hour and would provide adequate light for him to draw his circle and symbols on the floor of his cell with chalk.

And then there was practice of the Wracking Nerves.

"A demon of the Thirty-Third Order," the Abbess said, "is only a few short rungs down from a demon lord. This Malady—Yashash-na-Agarot—can likely endure a substantial amount of pain."

To that end, the Abbess guided him through the process of drawing upon his dawn-tide repository and forming the invisible barbs and hooks that would scour the demon's nerves—and demons did have nerves, she assured him. If anything, they were more acutely attuned to all the sensations that humans could experience. They hated more vengefully, loved more passionately, and felt pain much more excruciatingly.

The Abbess repeatedly assailed Anskar with the Wracking Nerves, though with nowhere near the force and virulence of that initial onslaught.

"Now, try it on me," she said during a session, after he had developed a tolerance to the lashings of the cant.

It felt as though he were doing something dirty as he reached for his dawn-tide repository, swept aside the bindings that contained it, and flayed the Abbess's nerves. She might have winced slightly, but didn't even whimper, let alone howl in torment.

"Don't worry," she said, "it's working, but it's nothing I've not felt before."

Days passed, long days in which he would practice in his cell, and he would study the circle of summoning, which he had sketched dozens of times on scraps of parchment the Abbess provided him with. Such study required a steady supply of rushlights, so Anskar spent his mornings in the abbey's workshop, where there were baskets filled with dried reeds and shelves crammed with jars of tallow.

When he remembered—and it was so easy to forget—he would repair to the refectory to eat stale bread, hard cheese, and limp greens with other robed and hooded people, all of them silent, locked away inside themselves, a communion of the alone.

Alone in the center of the chalk circle he had drawn on the floor of his cell, surrounded by words in Nazgrese, Anskar began the summoning.

As the Abbess had taught him, he built within his mind's eye an image of the form Malady had worn when she had accompanied Luzius Landav to Branil's Burg—a dwarfish woman in a motley jacket and pants and a tricorn hat. He tried to recall the sound of her voice, the scent of her, the "taste" of her presence. It took considerable concentration to hold the image firm, because he kept seeing the gigantic sea serpent the shapeshifter had transformed into.

His first set of seven rushlights burned down to ash, so he took a break to light seven more, careful to slant them in their holders a little further to the upright this time, which meant less light, but they would last longer.

When he seated himself cross-legged at the center of the

circle again and recommenced his visualization, the image came much easier. As he focused his sorcerous senses on it, wrapping them about the image, rendering it denser, he began to feel an unfamiliar thrill coursing through his veins. It emanated from his dark-tide repository. He felt like a fisherman with a tug on his line, but he knew he wasn't there yet.

He breathed deeply. Beneath his cowl, sweat beaded upon his forehead. Squeezing his eyes shut, he reinforced the image within his mind, fleshing it out with recollected details and embellishing it with scents and sounds.

And then he opened his eyes a crack, still holding the simulacrum firm. He could see the dwarf-demon now, both inside his head and through his eyes. He focused all of his senses on the image until he could hold it in place with his eyes wide open, not real, not a manifestation of the demon itself, but a likeness so close that it would serve as a doorway through which he could cast a line and snag himself a fish.

He began to repeat the name the Abbess had given him, at first in his head, silently, no more than a thought, but then he started to move his lips, and gradually he gave the name utterance: "Yashash-na-Agarot. Yashash-na-Agarot. Yashash-na-Agarot."

His voice rose to a sonorous chant, and he lost himself in its cadence. The syllables of the name blended one into another until he heard not the threefold name but a continuous susurrus that echoed in whispers around the walls of his cell.

And the line tightened.

The hook sank in.

He felt a quiver along the sorcerous connection. A tug. A struggle to break free.

Judging the time to be just right, Anskar cried out, "I summon and bind you, Yashash-na-Agarot, demon of the Thirty-Third

Order. I summon and bind you."

Somewhere a long way off, he heard a scream of utter rage. He flashed a look around the cell, expecting to see a shadowy form, and almost lost his concentration. Nothing there save for the dark and the damp and the mold.

He gritted his teeth and resumed chanting the demon's name. Waited till he felt a tug again, and this time the hook bit deep.

"I summon and bind you, Yashash-na-Agarot, demon of the Thirty-Third Order. I summon and bind you."

"No!" came the shrill response, again from far away. "I refuse!"

"Fuck!"—a man's voice like an echo of the wind. He spoke Niyandrian. "Where'd she go?"

"Malady?"—a woman. Also Niyandrian, but not Carred Selenas.

Anskar's skull erupted with bright light. He glimpsed the ghostly outline of a man and woman lying on opposite sides of a fire beneath the stars. He could see outcrops of rock, a moon-washed mountain peak in the distance. Gone in an instant.

As he pulled the line taut and started to reel it in, Anskar's heart began to gallop. He'd snagged her. Menselas, she was coming through!

The demon appeared in a tangle of thrashing limbs, cursing and shrieking. Not solid at first: hazy, as if she were formed from smoke. With the full force of his will, Anskar yanked on the intangible cord that had hooked the demon. A sound like the whip and snap of a sail bellied by the wind, a faint popping noise, and then she was there in front of him.

"I bind you to my will," he said with as much authority as he could muster. No effect. He licked his lips and tried again. "Yashash-na-Agarot, demon of the Thirty-Third Order, I bind you to my will."

"Whelp!" the demon spat. "You clump of stinking dog shit! Offal! Prick!"

She curled her fingers into claws and advanced on him.

In a panic, Anskar lashed her with the Wracking Nerves and she hit the floor, writhing and screaming.

"You suck on a rancid ball sack! Shit-eater!"

Foam came from her mouth. She clawed at her face, shredded her throat with cries. After a matter of seconds, Anskar let up.

The dwarf lay there for a long moment, breathing heavily. She let out a sharp hiss, then, painfully slowly, like an old woman riddled with arthritis, dragged herself to her feet.

"Luzius used to mock you behind your back, Anskar DeVantte. Said you were a failure as a knight. That the only eternal vigilance you were capable of was ogling the tits on the servant girls at Branil's Burg."

"He said that? But I thought—"

"The rules of your Order are simple," the demon said, "yet obviously not simple enough for the likes of you. I know you wet your cock between the legs of that red-skinned Niyandrian bitch. Sareya, wasn't it?"

Anskar's lips moved, but he couldn't form the words to speak. He clenched his fists at his sides, swallowed bile, felt his skin prickle with heat.

"I wanted to taste her quim," Malady said, flicking out her forked tongue. "Luzius wouldn't permit it. Not because he cared about your girl, but to demonstrate how strong his control over me was. Knowing him, he fucked her himself, anywhere he could find an opening."

"No!" Anskar lashed out once more with the Wracking Nerves. The demon slammed into the cell wall, spraying spittle as she screamed and thrashed.

"You will not bind me, you shit! I am beyond you, half-blood failure! Nobody wants you, not the Order of Eternal Vigilance, not your own kind, not your mother!"

As quickly as it had come, the rage left Anskar, replaced by a cold hardness he never knew he was capable of. He raised an eyebrow, and he laughed.

"Do you know how ridiculous you sound? How impotent you are? You're nothing more than a child throwing a tantrum. You can't harm me, Yashash-na-Agarot."

He took a step toward her, and Malady's insults petered away to nothing.

"I, on the other hand, can cause you infinite pain."

She met his gaze. Swallowed. Dipped her head. Accepted her fate.

And Anskar held nothing back. He hit her with the full force of the Wracking Nerves.

Malady screamed. Blood seeped from her eyes, purple and hissing, not the sawdust she had bled during the fight at sea. She smacked the back of her head into the wall, again and again, gnashing her teeth, wailing and moaning till she slumped to the floor.

He worried that he might have killed her.

Anskar waited and he watched, heart thudding in his ears. Eventually, she twisted her head and glared at him. Not a glare of defiance this time. Shock.

"Yashash-na-Agarot, demon of the Thirty-Third Order," Anskar said again, "I bind you to my will."

Her eyelids drooped shut, all the fight gone out of her.

"I am bound to another."

"And now you are bound to me."

"I can serve only one—"

"Right?"

She rolled onto her side, curled up like a baby. "Right," she said miserably.

"Then here's what I want you to do."

There was no ritual to speak of. No preparation of place, as Anskar had done with the circle and the sigils he'd drawn on the cell floor. Malady assured him there was no need, and he told her what she could expect if she was lying.

He felt the roil of invisible currents around the demon, an answering resonance in his dark-tide repository. Malady offered her hand, and, after a moment's hesitation, he took it.

Anskar collapsed. His stomach hit the roof of his mouth. His grip on Malady's hand tightened. The cell around them wavered, then dispersed into a scatter of lines and dots. There was a moment where everything went blank—no sights, no sounds, no thoughts.

And then Anskar's eyes opened upon dismal skies of gray and black and purple. A crimson sun hung like a bloody welt above swollen black clouds. In the distance there were twisting spires and jagged battlements.

"What is this place?" Anskar asked. "Why are we here?"

"I haven't misled you," Malady said, flinching as if she expected to be punished. "For a demon using the dark-tide to travel great distances, all paths pass through the abyssal realms. We will not be staying."

Winged shapes flew between tower tops. One veered toward them. Anskar felt a rising wave of panic, glanced at Malady for reassurance, but her eyes were wide with fear and she started to tremble.

The winged shape resolved into a horned demon with skin like molten rock. Golden eyes flashed hungrily. Anskar reached for the power of his repositories, but the dawn and the dusk were empty, and the dark … somehow he knew if he used it here, against this *thing,* he would be lost.

Instead, he went to draw his sword, but it wasn't there. The Abbess had insisted he leave *Amalantril* with her.

"He's grown strong in a very short time," Malady said, staring at the closing demon. "He must have absorbed some seriously powerful demons."

"Absorbed?"

"It's how we rise through the ranks."

"You know him?"

The demon was so close now, Anskar could smell the brimstone rolling off its molten hide. It opened its mouth and belched soot and poisonous vapor in their faces.

And then they were gone, once more back into the blackness of oblivion, the liminal space of the void.

In the absolute darkness, Malady said, "An old enemy. An old competitor. I don't say this lightly, but … Frangin-gul-terriph—there's a good name for you to remember. Summon and bind him next time you need a demon's help. Though forget you heard his name from me. Just make sure you get the bindings right, else it could end up painful for you. And extremely messy."

THIRTY-SEVEN

SWEAT DRENCHED CARRED'S SKIN as she gasped and moaned on top of Orix. He was no Kovin, and he was certainly no Marith, but on a cold night, on the cold heights, he would do.

"What's that?" she asked, glancing through the cave mouth at the star-speckled dark.

"Don't stop!"

"I thought I heard voices." She could see the glow of the campfire some hundred yards from the cave, but it was quiet now.

"Probably Taloc and Malady arguing again," Orix said.

They had done little else since they reached the foothills on the approach to Mount Phryith. Taloc resented being torn away from Vilintia, who Carred had left in command of her permanent rebels in Rynmuntithe. And he did nothing but complain about babysitting a madwoman—his opinion of Noni—and a demon.

Orix gripped her buttocks and tried to force her down.

"Ouch!" Carred winced at a shooting pain in her hip—all the excuse she needed to climb off him.

"What are you doing?" he said. Then, as she walked to the entrance of the cave, "Where are you going?"

She peered out into the night, enjoying the cool breeze on her naked flesh. She could smell woodsmoke, hear the spit and pop of the fire in the thin air. A scuff of movement, then Orix's arms were around her waist, his hardness prodding her from behind.

With a sigh, she turned and dropped to her knees in front of him.

"Oh …" Orix said. "Oh!"

But before she could start, the temperature plummeted. A fierce wind skirled around the cave, sending up swirls of dust. Carred stood, shoving Orix out of the way as she lunged for her sword.

Two figures took shape in the darkness at the back of the cave. They were holding hands. One was Malady. The other, Anskar DeVantte, who stumbled, clutching his temples, then doubled up and vomited.

"Anskar!" Orix gasped, hurrying toward him, cock only half flaccid.

Anskar wiped his mouth with his shirtsleeve, and looked up. Orix covered his crotch with his hands, too late. And then Anskar turned his cat's eyes on Carred. Shock turned to something else. He *noticed* her. Let his gaze linger too long before he dropped it, ashamed. Orix glanced from Anskar to Carred. Questioned her with a frown. He snatched up his clothes and started to dress.

"Nice tits," Malady said, eyeing Carred. "And I like the scars."

"Dangerous observation to make while I have a sword in hand."

"You can't kill me," the demon said.

"Don't be so sure." She was bluffing, but she kept her gaze cold and steady until doubt spread across Malady's face. Carred let her eyes fall on the *Melesh-Eloni* again. "Now that you've brought me Anskar, what else do I need you for, demon? And let me make this crystal clear: you are forbidden from defending yourself."

Malady let go of Anskar's hand. She looked suddenly nervous. Or perhaps Carred misread the expression. Maybe it was more … sly.

"She didn't catch me for you," Anskar said. He couldn't meet her gaze. "I made her bring me. For Orix."

"You two …" Carred said, looking from Anskar to Orix. "You're not lovers, are you?"

"No!" Orix said, fastening his pants.

"I thought it would have been obvious that Orix likes women, from what the pair of you were just doing," Anskar said.

"You sound jealous."

"Then your judgment is off. Put some clothes on before I'm sick again."

Carred swallowed, one hand covering the scar on her breast. She abandoned the effort. There were too many. If Malady hadn't giggled at her discomfort, she might have thrown her clothes on, but one thing the old man Maggow had taught her about demons was to never show them the slightest weakness. It was an act as good as any she'd employed in the past, but that didn't make it easy. She thrust out her chest and opened her arms, letting the tip of her sword rest on the ground.

"Orix wasn't sick. Neither"—and she winced internally as she said it—"was your mother."

"My …?"

"You didn't!" Orix said, tucking in his shirt. "The Necromancer

Queen!" He felt about inside his pants as if his cock might wilt and drop off.

"You sly old bitch," Malady said.

"Shut up," Carred said. "And that's a command."

"Oops," Malady said with a malevolent grin. "My bindings have passed to another." The demon gave Anskar an ostentatious bow.

"That's possible?"

He shrugged apologetically. "Apparently."

"It's getting cold," Carred said, setting down her sword so she could get dressed. Malady unbound ... She was a hair's breadth from impalement via the quim, with only Anskar's control over the demon keeping her alive.

"You came for me?" Orix said. "Not to join us?"

"Who is us?"

"We've been lied to, Anskar. All our lives at Branil's Burg we were told the Niyandrians are our enemies, that they were the aggressors in a war of expansion, a war that threatened to plunge the whole of Wiraya into darkness."

"And she told you different, did she?" Anskar said.

Orix nodded. "And I believe her. She's not the villain we've been led to believe."

"Did she convince your mind first, or your prick?"

"Did I judge you and Sareya," Orix said, "when you were in love?"

"A mistake," Anskar said. "In the past."

"Love is a mistake?" Carred buckled her belt and sheathed her sword. "Is that what the Order of Eternal Vigilance teaches?"

"Well, we're in love," Orix said, reaching for her hand.

Carred snatched it away and rolled her eyes. Only Anskar saw. Malady appeared to be sulking, and Orix looked like a child who had lost its mother and was about to cry. Like her in the forest with Nally clutched to her chest. The memory made her grimace.

"What is it?" Anskar asked.

"An old injury." Not even a lie, really.

"Your hip again?" Orix asked.

"Yes, my hip."

"Orix, put your boots on," Anskar said. "You're coming with me." Then to Malady, "I take it you can manage three?"

"If I must."

"You must."

Orix glanced at Carred. She gave him nothing. "Back where? The ship? Branil's Burg?"

"Sansor," Anskar said. "I reached the Mother House, although I'm not there … I mean, I'm here now, with you, but …"

"You didn't come from the Mother House?" Carred said. "Then where?"

"Wouldn't you like to know!"

"Anskar," she said, heart starting to race. She sensed she didn't have long, and she had to persuade him. "Why do you think we are here?"

"In a cave? Privacy while you rut?"

"In these foothills, on the approach to Mount Phryith?"

"Fresh air? Exercise? I don't know. I don't care. On the run from the Order again, at a guess."

"Wrong," Orix said. He actually sounded smug. He looked at Carred for approval. She smiled and his demeanor instantly improved. Sad. In a way, he was just as bound as Malady.

"The vambrace you wear …" Carred said. "You showed that woman in the Plains of Khisig-Ugtall."

Anskar gripped his forearm. "Her name was Blaice."

Orix chuckled and winked at him. "See, it's not just me. She sure made a lot of noise. You both did!"

"Really?" Carred said. "Sareya *and* Blaice? And with you still so fresh, so young!"

"It wasn't like that," Anskar said. "So what's your point?"

"Has your mother spoken to you about the vambrace?"

"My mother's dead."

Carred held his gaze, letting silence coax the answer out of him. He surprised her with a question of his own.

"Does she talk to you?"

"Through a moontouched young woman." The sole reason she'd brought Noni along on this madcap quest.

"Sareya is moontouched."

"I know." Aelanthe had communicated that to her before she died. "But she's not the only one. This woman I rescued from the Order's slavers."

"You know about that?"

"I didn't tell her," Orix said defensively.

"Tell her what?" Carred asked.

"There were Niyandrian slaves on the Grand Master's ship," Anskar said. He kept his expression blank, so it was hard to know whether or not he approved.

"Orix didn't tell me that, but I already knew about the Order's enslavement of my people. I discovered it for myself. Not quite as spotless as you thought, are they, these knights who raised you?"

"It's not that simple," Anskar said.

"Evil rarely is."

Malady chuckled, and Anskar shot her a glare.

"You never said anything about me laughing," the demon said.

"Well, now I am," Anskar said. "Laugh again and you can rip

your face off with your own hands. So, the Necromancer Queen speaks through a moontouched woman. What does she have to say for herself?"

"Your *mother* wants what is best for you."

"I doubt that."

In truth, Carred doubted it too. There were too many gaps in her understanding. She didn't know exactly what Queen Talia wanted, save to return from the dead.

"Your vambrace is but one piece."

"I know."

"You were supposed to find more."

"Perhaps my mother ran out of golden-eyed crows to lead me to them. I might accidentally have crushed one."

Carred frowned. "I don't understand. But there is much I don't understand about all this. I'm still working things out."

"She didn't tell you all her plans?"

"No."

"Yet you shared a bed?"

"Have you finished?"

Anskar flinched, despite the fact that Carred had forgotten herself and spoken in Niyandrian. She hadn't intended to sound so angry, but he'd hit a nerve.

"I'm here because you couldn't be," Carred said, sticking to Niyandrian and watching him closely. He seemed to be following everything she said. "When you left Niyas for Sansor, it ruined your mother's plans. She wanted you to come here … to Mount Phryith. To speak with the Necromancer Tain."

"He's still alive?"

So, he understood Niyandrian now and spoke it fluently, though with an accent. Had he been pretending ignorance before? She didn't think so. She started to narrow her eyes.

Checked herself. Now wasn't the time to pry. She might scare him off.

Carred shrugged. "She wants you to possess a full suit of Armor of Divinity."

"To what end?"

"To ascend? I don't really know."

"And be a god? No, thank you. There's only one god: the God of Five Aspects."

He was discounting Theltek of the Hundred Eyes and countless other gods worshiped the length and breadth of Wiraya, but what could you expect after a childhood being fed lies by a bunch of bloodthirsty hypocrites?

"Come with me," Carred said, then catching Orix's look, added in Nan-Rhouric, "Come with us."

Anskar switched languages too: "To meet a necromancer and find some sorcerous armor that will likely turn me into something worse than Malady here?"

The demon smirked.

"I don't think so," Anskar said. "Come on, Orix, let's get you out of here."

"No. I'm not leaving."

"Don't be a fool."

"Carred explained a lot of things to me … about what our Order has done to her people. About the powers behind every country on the mainland … greedy nobles who'll do anything to further their control and influence. And she told me about Queen Talia, Anskar, what your mother means to the future of Niyas."

"Why should you care?" Anskar said. "You're Traguh-raj."

"We've been told all this time that Carred leads a band of rebels, crazed fanatics, but it's all a big lie. We shouldn't be calling them rebels. We should call them the defenders of Niyas."

Anskar seemed to waver. His eyes darted about the cave as if he might find some counsel in the shadows. Malady was watching him closely, no doubt waiting for him to slip up. Impalement via the anus? Or did she have something else in mind?

At length Anskar met Carred's eyes. Held her gaze as he spoke. "You're being duped, Orix. This whore has seduced you and addled your brains."

"Actually, I prefer slut," Carred said in Niyandrian.

"Insult her again," Orix said, "and I'll knock your teeth so far down your throat—"

Anskar clenched his fists.

"Boys, boys," Carred said. "There's no need to fight over me. You'll just have to learn to share."

"What?" Orix said.

Anskar sneered. "See what you've gotten yourself mixed up in?"

"She was joking, you idiot," Orix said.

"'Course she was. Now, are you coming or not?"

"I already told you."

Footfalls came from outside the cave. A flickering light.

"Well, he certainly took his time," Malady said.

Taloc appeared in the entrance, torch in one hand, sword in the other. In the wavering glow of the torch, he looked impressively large.

"Where's Noni?" Carred asked in Niyandrian.

"Sleeping."

"You left her alone out there?"

"I thought—"

"Go back and stay with her. Haven't you ever heard of dead-eyes?"

With a muttered curse, Taloc turned and left.

"Anskar," Carred said, still speaking Niyandrian, "please stay. Give me a chance to explain, to convince you."

He looked her in the eye, glanced at Orix. Something was communicated between the two friends, and it didn't look good. Anskar grabbed hold of Malady's hand.

"Take me back."

"No!" Orix cried, starting toward him.

And in a swirl of dust, Anskar and the demon were gone.

THIRTY-EIGHT

THE CAVE VANISHED. ORIX and Carred Selenas vanished. It was just Anskar and Malady once more, hand in hand.

In a flash they were back beneath dark skies in hues of purple, black and gray. Gone was the crimson sun—time must have moved at a different pace here, wherever here was. Lightning forked. Stars like emeralds winked. Howls rent the darkness, along with the flap and snap of leathery wings.

And then they were in his cell at the Abbey of the Hooded One, beneath the glow of the solitary red stone in the ceiling. Anskar felt scraped out from the inside, little more than a husk. Malady released his hand and he pitched to his knees, panting.

"Release me," the demon pleaded. She started to sob. "I did as you asked. Unbind me. Let me return home."

"I don't … I don't know …"

"You must. I beg you. Justice demands it. Menselas expects it."

"And you will … you will return to …"

"To the abyssal realms, yes," Malady said, no longer sobbing.

"I …" Anskar couldn't string the words together. All he wanted was to sleep, but how could he with a demon in his cell? He just wanted to be rid of her. Licking dry lips, he gave a feeble nod. "How do I release you?"

"Here," Malady said, taking his hand and guiding it to her forehead.

Dark-tide poured from him into the demon. He saw then—not with his eyes, but with some inner sense—the inky threads woven through her mind, knotted with barbs, undulating, almost breathing. Constraining.

"Unravel it," Malady said.

"How?"

"Will it."

One by one, the threads that bound the demon slackened, then sloughed away, but even so slight an effort was enough to drop Anskar from his knees to his belly, where he lay face-down on the cold stone floor, panting for every breath.

He heard the ruffle of cloth, the scuff of boots on stone. Lifted his head just enough to see the demon's face twisted into a snarl of rage and hunger, and in that split second Anskar realized he had made a fatal mistake.

Malady sprang at him.

And screamed.

The demon fell twitching and convulsing to the floor.

At the moment she leaped at Anskar, the cell door had burst open. Waves of dark sorcery passed over his head, scouring the demon, and Malady screamed under the assault of the Wracking Nerves.

Anskar craned his neck until he could see the Abbess,

hands outstretched, the air about them rippling. Her face was contorted, her eyes blazing pits of madness. She was a hag from nightmare, a dried and wrinkled cadaver, a thing that should have long ago passed beyond life.

The demon continued to buck and spasm. Vile froth spilled from her mouth. Dark fluid oozed from her ears, and it bled from her eyes like trails of black tears.

Anskar winced at a sudden ripping, rending sound, then the crack of bone splitting. The demon's scream peaked in a terrible keening wail, then her head exploded, and the dark mass of her brains spattered the walls and floor.

Malady's body slumped down with a dull thud. It lay there, motionless, and Anskar realized the Abbess had stopped her use of the Wracking Nerves and was now simply standing and watching. Fiery seams spread like fractures throughout the demon's body, flared for an instant, and then what was left of Malady cracked and crumbled, then turned to charcoal and ashes.

"There, you are safe now," the Abbess breathed in a voice so unlike that of the old woman who had spoken with him day after day in her room. Instead, it was thickly accented, the voice of a younger woman. The voice of a Niyandrian speaking Nan-Rhouric.

Anskar felt hands on his shoulders, gently rolling him over onto his back. His head flopped against the floor, but cool fingers found his cheeks, gently caressed his face. Blearily, he gazed up into almond-shaped eyes with slitted pupils.

Cat's eyes.

And then Carred Selenas was astride him, leaning down to kiss him full on the lips. He felt the warmth of her naked flesh, and he didn't resist as she guided his hands over the ridges of her battle scars, her taut stomach, her breasts. He didn't object when her hand found his crotch and unlaced his pants. He gasped as she lowered herself onto him, breathing encouragement in his ear, whispering his name, urging him to pleasure her. She raked his flesh with hands turned to claws, drawing blood. He cried out and she clubbed him about the face with her fists.

Drained, exhausted, utterly spent, Anskar couldn't defend himself. He tried to scream, but his throat felt as if it were filled with sand. Insatiably, she rode him, punching and slapping, gouging his skin. And it never ended. Menselas, it never ended.

Anskar awoke, traumatized by the foul dream that had tormented him throughout the night—if indeed it was night. He had no way of knowing in the gloom of his cell. But then he felt the stinging of his skin—his face, his chest, his arms. And there was a lingering stench in his nostrils: ripe meat, something ulcerated and rotten.

His mind threw up images of naked flesh, of Carred Selenas above him, grunting, crying out with unabashed passion, but he knew in that moment it had been an illusion.

Then he recalled that, as that interminable torment had neared the end, some part of him had glimpsed the true likeness of the woman who had taken him against his will. It hadn't been the mature, hard body of Carred Selenas. That had been a ruse to inflame his lust. The body that had violated him had been sagging and wrinkled and bony, that of a twisted hag, one step away from a cold and putrid corpse.

With a sudden clench of his guts, he rolled over and vomited.

THIRTY-NINE

ANSKAR SAT IN THE cold gloom of his cell, expecting at any moment to be summoned by the Abbess. And he no longer looked forward to it. He felt sickened by what she had done to him the night before. Her stench clung to his nostrils. He feared he might never be rid of it.

His stomach growled with hunger, but he couldn't bring himself to leave his cell. And so he sat, and when sitting became too painful on the cold floor, he lay, and sometimes he slept. When he needed to relieve himself, he did so in a corner, and he added to the stink. At one point, he scraped the coal and ashes that were the remains of Malady into a corner.

He had the sense that hours passed into days. Water and hard bread were left outside his door, but he never heard the approach of footsteps bringing it, only found it when he thought to check. The bread tasted foul to him, rank with mold, and the water was brackish and chalky.

Time no longer held any meaning for him, but something changed within him. Subtly at first, then with growing brazenness, his nauseating recollections of the Abbess's touch, of the things she had done to him, started to fascinate him in small ways. He remembered glimpses of the form she had taken—Carred Selenas's lean and battle-scarred body. It was Carred's lips he remembered now pressed to his, her tongue, her fingers, her breasts. And though he knew it had been an illusion, he found himself craving more. He grew anxious for the Abbess to return. The longer it went on, the stronger his desire for Carred became until it overwhelmed his previous revulsion.

At some unknown hour of some unknown day—or night—he stood and straightened the black robe he had been given. He felt around his chin and cheeks, rubbing at the stubble that had grown there; ran his tongue around his filthy teeth. He grew acutely aware of the stench, the foulness he'd left heaped in a corner.

And so he left the stink of his cell and shut the door behind him, and he stalked through the corridors of the abbey until he found his way at last to the Abbess's door.

To Anskar's surprise, a cowled and robed figure waited outside. "Ah, good," the man said, apparently exempting himself from the need for silence. "The Abbess said you would come. Follow me. We are about to start."

As the hooded man led him along unfamiliar passageways, Anskar became aware of a rhythmic pounding echoing along the corridors. The closer they came to the abbey's heart, the louder the thumping became, and Anskar realized that his and the cowled priest's feet marched to the same tempo.

They came at last to a vast circular space with corridors opening onto it from every direction. Anskar counted eight entrances, each, in the dim light of the chamber, no more than a gaping maw of blackness.

The floor was dominated by a circle of brass etched with the demonic swirling Nazgrese script. The center of the circle was crammed with complex sigils and numerals drawn in chalk. Around the perimeter stood dark-robed and cowled priests. There must have been upwards of two hundred.

Upon a throne at the circle's hub—a low dais of obsidian—sat the Abbess, cowl down, wizened face fully exposed, gray hair hanging in lank and greasy strands around her shoulders.

She smiled at Anskar as his priest escort ushered him into the chamber, a dozen feebly glowing red stones glaring down from the high, domed ceiling, and a scatter of rushlights in iron holders around the floor. It was a crooked smile that made Anskar cringe. No illusion could take away the thought of what she had done to him with those lips.

"Take your place in the circle, Anskar," she said.

Following the example of his escort, Anskar squeezed in between two cowled priests, and the circle of the devotees widened to accommodate him.

"We are one now," the Abbess said, fixing him with a steady gaze. "You inside me, me inside you."

Again, he saw Carred Selenas in his mind's eye, jerking above him, writhing beneath him, kneeling before him. Anskar's stomach churned and he almost gagged.

"All here are one, through me, united in a single purpose. With the addition of your … unique gifts, Anskar, our reach grows stronger, our voice louder, our intention irresistible."

She cocked her head as she studied him. "You are no longer repulsed, I see. Usually it does not take so long. In many cases, my children come to me begging for more within hours, but you, Anskar, you held out for days.

"Be at peace now. There is no shame in giving in to illusion. What you saw is what you desire. I gave you what you most wanted, even though you may not have realized it at the time. Ask yourself which is the greater sin: me fooling your senses, or you lusting for the real thing? Because your senses delude you, Anskar, as they delude everyone else who has not come into the true light. You are enslaved by petty and bestial desires, when what you most need lies in a realm beyond sight, beyond touch, beyond speech; a realm that must be coaxed closer to ours, the veil that obscures it rent asunder.

"For what we really seek, what we all seek, if we are honest and if we truly come to know ourselves, can only be taken by force."

The Abbess shut her eyes and threw her head back—the same way she had done when she had sated her unnatural lusts on Anskar. "Sup on the dark-tide essence flowing freely between each of us present," she said, her voice thick with emotion. "Let it flood you. All of you, let it fill you to bursting. Immerse yourself in its depths and give back everything that you take. Feel the dark currents roiling between us. Speak the name of your heart's desire!"

"Nysrog," someone gasped.

"Nysrog," a woman's voice replied, breathless, almost lustful.

One after another, the priests standing around the circle took up the cry: "Nysrog, Nysrog, Nysrog!" Their chanting built to a canter, then a gallop.

Anskar felt himself caught up in the sonorous tide, felt himself swept away, wanting what they wanted, desiring what they desired as if his life, his very being depended upon it.

"Nysrog, Nysrog, Nysrog," two hundred voices chanted, and Anskar's was among them now, indistinguishable from the rest.

It was a murky kind of ecstasy, a vague and heady insanity. A part of him—a thready slip of awareness that even now stood apart and observed—warned him to pull back, not to throw himself headlong into this orgy of frenzy. But he was powerless, held enthralled, buffeted by the storm winds of their barbarous chant.

The Abbess perched on the edge of her throne, rigid and upright, eyes wild now and burning with the fire of madness. Spittle sprayed from her mouth as her lips worked in a torrid cant that skirled and snapped and barked beneath the feverous clamor of two hundred voices. She curled her hands into talons and gripped the front of her black robe. Her voice rose in shrill and bleak imprecations that clawed their way above the tumult in the room, the words unsuited to human utterance.

Anskar continued to cry out along with the two hundred: "Nysrog, Nysrog, Nysrog!"

Blue lightning flashed, then purple, then red, ghosting across the circle from some other place. Thunder rumbled, distant and echoing, followed by the beating of a drum drawing nearer.

The Abbess raised her hand, and the chanting ceased.

Like everyone else in the chamber, Anskar remained perfectly still as he stared at the fog seeping into the center of the circle. Wisps of smoke snaked together, coiling, intertwining, knotting into a writhing mass.

The Abbess stood, one hand covering her mouth.

A face began to form in the coalescing vapors. Savage eyes of violet, pupils gaping pits of blackness. Eyes of madness, eyes of despair. Around them, Anskar had the impression of a gray, scaled face. Ram's horns curled away from the head. Black lips parted to reveal row upon row of jagged crystal teeth.

Anskar gasped, then realized he had been holding his breath. His guts tightened. Ice sloshed through his veins. He trembled from head to foot, and fat drops of sweat rolled into his eyes. He wanted to run. No, he wanted to fight, to maim, to kill. He wanted to rut, to rape, and to defile. It was all of those things and none of them. He was conflicted. Tormented. Torn between extremes of savagery and terror. Waves of contradiction rolled off the still-misty face within the circle. Waves of wrongness. Insanity.

But then the demon's gaseous visage crumbled into soot that turned to smoke and dispersed on the air.

The Abbess and her followers broke into hoots and howls of ecstasy. No longer static, the cowled men and woman cavorted and leaped and embraced one another, and the Abbess sat back on her throne, eyes glittering, lips working a combination of words that tried and failed to express what she had just witnessed—or at least that was what Anskar perceived. Perhaps she was just a gibbering imbecile, her mind fractured by the sheer force of the presence that had almost come through the veil between this world and the abyssal realms.

Almost, but not quite.

"You felt it, my children?" the Abbess cried, voice grating and harsh. "You saw *him*?"

"Nysrog!" two hundred awed voices whispered in unison.

"He came!" the Abbess cried. "Closer than ever before." She turned her crazed eyes on Anskar. "Because you are with us, Anskar. Because of the boiling essence within you. Because you are one with us now, and because together we are a seething ocean of dark-tide power that even the demon lords cannot resist. Nysrog, who once walked upon the face of Wiraya, who wreaked such slaughter, all in the name of order! He heard us, the tamer of chaos! We must grow just a little stronger, my children, and then he will come again to tread beneath his mighty feet the hills and mountains, the towns and cities of Wiraya."

"Nysrog!" the cowled priests all shouted.

And Anskar shouted too. Not because he was swept up in the madness this time, but because he didn't want to arouse suspicion. He knew now he had to get out. He had to leave the abbey before it was too late for him.

Too late for the world.

And so he swallowed his revulsion and shouted when they shouted, cavorted, leaped, embraced. He forced himself to stare at the Abbess with unabashed lust, all the while picturing Sareya, Blaice, Carred Selenas, letting her think his panted breaths were for her. She smiled at him, and she laughed. Cackled like a witch who had cast her invocation and knew that she had snagged a fish.

But she was wrong.

Now she was the one laboring under an illusion.

The priests began throwing their robes off, discarding them in crumpled heaps on the floor inside the circle. There was bare flesh everywhere. Nothing but flesh, slick with sweat, greasy and hot, men and women in states of arousal. Red skin, white, black and brown, all pressing together. Anskar smelled the musk of their sex. And from somewhere, though he couldn't see where, he could smell blood. Hot hands grabbed at his robe. Lustful eyes demanded he take it off. He almost succumbed, but a fizzing sensation spread beneath his scalp. Something fought against his wards.

Partake in this, Queen Talia said, her voice distant, strained, *and you will be lost. That must not happen. It cannot. Anskar, heed ...*

And then she was gone.

He glanced frantically at the throne but saw only the Abbess's discarded robe slung over one of the arms. She was somewhere in among the mass of naked bodies, moaning, gasping, screaming with the rest of them.

Anskar shoved aside the hands groping at him and strode for the corridor he'd entered from. Once outside the chamber, he ran, leaving the sweat and the cries of the orgy behind as he threaded his way along gloomy corridors until he came at last to the heavy wooden door that led out of the abbey. It was neither barred nor locked. He recalled the looks of lust in the eyes of the naked priests back at the circular chamber, the enchantment the Abbess had cast over him during that night in his cell, and he knew then there were many ways to imprison someone, many ways to enslave.

He pushed the door open a crack and slipped outside, where it was cool and dark and wet. Despite the rain, he shrugged out of his black robe, but kept on the soiled clothes he wore underneath. With a glance over his shoulder at the building he had started to assume would end up his tomb, he fled into the night.

FORTY

THEY CAME FOR HIM in the darkness, under the uncaring gazes of the moons. They came for him as he crossed a thicket, as he fled beneath skeletal trees, as he tripped and fell and got back to his feet, struggling on, breaths ragged. He didn't recall this woodland from his trip from the Mother House to the abbey, but there was so much he had forgotten in the days—or was it weeks?—of brooding in his cell.

In a sudden panic, Anskar began to worry that he might have gone the wrong way. He uttered a prayer, but stopped before he had finished. Menselas wouldn't listen, not after the things he'd done.

Howling and gibbering pursued him, the scratch and scuff of claws. He glimpsed something over his shoulder as he ran: spindly and loping like a dead-eye, only its eyes blazed yellow.

He ran on, heedless now of the direction he took, weaving a course between the trees, feet crunching on deadfall, stumbling in depressions. Something scampered away from him into the undergrowth—a badger, maybe. An owl hooted in the distance. Bats or night birds flitted across the face of the red moon, Jagonath.

A snarl from behind made Anskar turn, panting for breath. His heart thumped in his rib cage. He squinted against the dark until he could see it: a thickening of the night beside a tree. It resolved into the vague lump of a head, peering at him from around the trunk, but then it bounded a few steps closer, coming to a crouch in a pool of reddish moonlight.

It was shorter than he was, with sticklike arms and legs. There were no ears he could see, just short, sharp horns, like a nanny goat's. The mouth was a jagged gash. There was no nose to speak of, only the dark slashes of nostrils. And there was a stench coming off the creature—rot and sulfur.

A demon.

Lesser, judging by its bestial appearance. It hissed, and its tongue lolled out, black and sinewy and reaching to the demon's waist. Suddenly the tongue lashed toward Anskar, and then he was running again, sprinting through the trees.

He glimpsed movement left and right. Behind, he heard the shrieks and howls of the demon that had come closest. There were three of them at least, herding him, hunting him as a pack, and no matter how hard he pushed himself, they kept pace with him.

He stumbled and fell again, and then he was tumbling down a bank he had not seen. Over and over he rolled, bouncing off tree trunks, crashing through ferns and grasses, until he pitched into the air and came down hard on his back. Air rushed from his lungs, and Anskar grunted. He rolled onto his front and got to his knees. Head groggy, temples throbbing, he crawled forward until he slipped and slid into a ditch that might once have been a stream.

He lay there atop damp and moldering leaves that had accumulated at the bottom. Lay there and listened. He could hear nothing save the rush of blood in his ears, his own shallow breaths, the drone of insects in the trees above the ditch.

The demons were still up there somewhere. Some unknown sense told him that, but he had lost them for now. The problem was, the moment he climbed out of the ditch, they would be onto him again, and he was exhausted.

He lay there, looking up at the star-speckled blackness, fighting back tears. He was supposed to be a knight. But was it any surprise his courage had abandoned him? Why wouldn't it, when he had abandoned so many of the traits a knight was supposed to possess, and all in the pursuit of … what? What exactly had he hoped to gain by allowing the Abbess to lead him down such unholy paths?

He had been no more than a naive child to the Abbess.

He was a fool.

Was he really so easily led astray?

Had the Grand Master known what would happen? Was that why he'd sent him to the abbey?

No, it made no sense. Yes, the Order was imperfect, but demons!

All those years protected by the walls of Branil's Burg, the terrifying stories of what might lie outside, of the things that prowled the night, and now here he was, alone in the dark, hunted.

He took a deep breath, tried to think his way out of this situation. He knew he couldn't outrun the demons, and he doubted he could throw them off his scent. So what else could he do?

With mounting panic, he set about dismantling the complex wards he had erected about his mind, and no sooner had the last ward dissolved into nothingness than Queen Talia's voice lashed out, reverberating around his skull.

Idiot, she said in Niyandrian. *Fool. Never mess with demons. They are too capricious. They probe for every last weakness, they push and cajole and manipulate, and always they serve their own insatiable lusts. Nysrog! What were you thinking?*

"It wasn't by choice," Anskar protested in a whisper. "I was sent to the abbey."

You listened to that hag's lies! Are you so easily duped? Are you even my son?

"I ..." he started, but the crack of twigs from above the ditch made him stop.

The Abbess has sent her dogs after you, Queen Talia said. *You have seen too much.*

"The Order of Eternal Vigilance doesn't know what she's up to?"

Of course not. Those servants of a five-faced god might be many things, but they are not stupid enough to wish the return of Nysrog.

"I need your help," Anskar whispered. "Please."

Do you promise never to shut me out again?

Again he heard movement from up above the ditch—the merest scuff of a foot, a sharp intake of breath.

"I promise."

First, you must shadow-step.

"Won't they just follow me?"

Not these low-caste demons. They are curs, I tell you.

Anskar's dark-tide repository was brimming from the interchange of essence during the ritual, and even now the dark-tide seeped into him from the night sky. "Where?"

As far as you can see in the dark. And then you must use your senses, find a corpse, preferably of a mainlander, for it should comprehend Nan-Rhouric.

"But—"

The dead talk to you, Anskar. Do not deny it.

"They did, before ... but—"

Now you must make them speak to others. The dead are not like demons. With the end of their life comes the end of choice, of free will. They cannot deceive. Of themselves, they can do nothing in this world save repeat well-worn patterns from the days they possessed blood and flesh and bone. But a necromancer can compel them, and they will not deviate from your orders. They are the most reliable of servants.

"But you are dead ..."

A necromancer disregards the laws of death, she replied. *Even in the realm of the dead, I still make choices.*

"But you need someone else to put them into action. That's why you need me, isn't it?"

Quickly! They are near.

Steeling himself, Anskar stood. The banks of the ditch only came up to his shoulders, so he scanned the land above on both sides, picking out the dense shadows of trees, the clustered smudges of long grasses. In the distance—he wasn't sure of the direction—he could make out a hill limned by moonlight, and at its base a moat of shadow.

A twig cracked. Something hissed and spat. And then they emerged from the darkness up top: three gangly, loping shapes.

Opening the dam that contained his dark-tide essence, Anskar let the sorcerous current flow through him as he stared at the shadows beneath the distant hill. His stomach clenched the instant he poured himself into the darkness at the foot of the ditch, then grew solid once more as he emerged in the shade of the hill, hundreds of yards away.

A moment's silence, and then the frustrated howls of the demons reached him.

Wind gusted, throwing up leaves and detritus from the forest floor. Anskar cursed. The demons were downwind of him. They would pick up his scent.

Quickly, his mother's voice said within his mind. *Send your senses below ground. The earth remembers the buried dead. Find them, Anskar. You don't have much time. The earth-tide is in your blood.*

He closed his eyes, and something awakened within him, something chill that peeled away from his marrow. Inky tendrils of vapor sprouted from somewhere within his skull and bored their way into the earth.

Give the formations their head. Let them be bloodhounds seeking out rot and bones and decay.

"How?"

Use your imagination. You've seen death before.

He pictured the skeleton in the sarcophagus he'd seen when he first left Branil's Burg. It had spoken. He saw Naul, lying in blood on the floor outside their rooms. Then the dead of Atya: Gadius, Ryala, Hendel and Gaith.

One of his tendrils pulled taut.

He followed it, allowing it to lead him to the source of death it had uncovered. He passed beyond the edge of the hill, to where a crude stone cairn stood out in the silver and red light of the moons.

Dig! Queen Talia said. *Hurry!*

With the shrieks of the demons in his ears, Anskar scraped at the mossy joins between the stones and dug his fingers in, trying to find purchase. He pulled one stone away, then another, growing ever more frantic as he worked. Fingers stinging and bleeding, he slung the rocks behind him.

And then he saw it, poking up through the lower layers of rubble: a shard of bone—a thigh bone, he thought. Before he could clear away more rocks, Queen Talia said, *That is enough. Touch it.*

Anskar hesitated. Did he really want to exchange one form of depraved sorcery for another?

Howls reverberated through the night. They were getting closer.

Do it or die, his mother said. *There is no other way.*

Anskar touched the bone shard sticking out of the debris of the cairn.

Now follow it. In your mind, follow where it leads. A bone is but an anchor for the spirit, the flesh even more so. They are separated by the veil, but where one spirit has flown, another may follow. You can follow, Anskar, so long as you retain contact with the bone.

He grasped the bone shard tightly and closed his eyes once more, emptying his mind of all thoughts. The blankness filled with all manner of images and impressions, some his own, others alien, the imprint of a life long-since gone. He flung himself into the current of those ancient impressions, allowed himself to be swept along upon the tide of memories that existed no longer as recollected images and words and actions, but as vague feelings of joy and pain, anger, love, and loss.

And then he was within a tattered landscape of gray, and he knew he had been here before. He felt a presence at his back and turned his spirit eyes to see a shadowy form, a tall and slender woman woven from the dark, a jagged crown upon her head. She raised a spindly arm to point over his shoulder with a bony finger.

He turned back to see a wavering shade, a naked man, broad-shouldered and barrel-chested, with the hard, scarred face of a warrior. There was a deep cavity on one side of the head, where the skull had been shattered. Where there should have been legs, the warrior's body ended in a wispy tail of smoke.

The shade drifted toward Anskar, the fire of rage bright in its pale eyes.

Stand your ground, Anskar, Queen Talia commanded from behind. *The spirits of the dead act as they always acted in life. It is a pattern of past behaviors, no more. You are my child, the son of a necromancer. My power is in your blood. It is your power now, the power to command the dead.*

"But what should I command it to do?" Anskar said, willing himself not to back up a step as the warrior's spirit came straight at him.

Send it for help. Now! The demons are almost upon you!

"Go!" Anskar commanded the warrior's spirit. "To the Mother House of the Order of Eternal Vigilance. Go there, to Sansor, and bring help. Tell them Anskar is in trouble. They must come at once. I am fleeing from the Abbey of the Hooded One," he added, so that they would guess the path he must take.

The rage in the warrior's eyes abated. It looked lost and sullen. But then it bowed, and Anskar was flung back into his body beside the rubble of the cairn.

And the demons were coming. He could hear their hissing breath, the pad of their feet on the earth. He could smell the rot and the sulfur.

That way, Queen Talia said. *To your right. Sansor lies to your right. Shadow-step as far as you can each time. Keep going, keep strong, and you might yet make it. If not, help may meet you on the way. It is your only chance.*

There was a bar of gray light on the horizon in the direction his mother indicated. It would soon be dawn. Just one last effort, he told himself. One final sprint and he would be safe.

Howls abounded as the demons spotted their prey, and in that moment Anskar poured himself once more into the shadows.

He couldn't tell how far he had come when he emerged beneath a tree, but it felt farther than before. He doubled up and vomited. When he'd finished and wiped the filth from his chin with his sleeve, he cast a nervous glance behind. Still they were coming.

Fixing his gaze on the east, Anskar shadow-stepped again. He stumbled this time when he emerged onto the dark-shrouded ground beneath an earthwork embankment. The summit was blistered with burial mounds. In the distance, carried by the night wind, he could hear the howls and hoots of the demons. He had created a good deal of space from them, but they were already growing louder.

He shadow-stepped again, a mere few hundred yards. He collapsed this time, face-first in the dirt beside a stream, his hand dangling in the icy water. He forced himself to his knees and dry-heaved. There was a twisting tightness inside his skull, and when he probed within, he found his dark-tide repository was not at all the infinite well he had once believed it to be. It was a sagging, flaccid wineskin from which he would be fortunate to wring out another few drops. But he had to try. He had to go on, and he didn't need Queen Talia to tell him.

Rising unsteadily, he shadow-stepped again, and this time he re-formed from the shadows with a scream. Sharp pains lanced through his head. White flashed behind his eyes, and when he glanced up, even the starlight was too bright to bear.

Gritting his teeth, he tried to shadow-step once more, but

there was nothing left in his repository for him to dredge up. Agony racked his frame, coursed through his veins—the same excruciating pain he had experienced from the Wracking Nerves. Only, there was no one afflicting him this time. No one to switch the pain off. On and on it went, wave after wave of utter torment that seemed as though it would never end. But then something cracked inside his skull and blackness collapsed on top of him.

Anskar awoke to the stench of rotten eggs.

The pain in his head had subsided to a dull throb. His limbs were limp, his bones scraped clean of all their marrow. He felt hollowed out, as if whatever essence sustained him in life had been sucked from him.

A twig snapped underfoot, followed by a sharp inrush of air. Anskar turned his head, tasting dirt in his mouth.

Do not die here, his mother hissed. *You must not die here.*

Anskar had the impression there would be consequences if he did—beyond the grave.

Get up! she commanded as a demon emerged from the bracken at the edge of the clearing.

The demon came on cautiously, as if it suspected a trap. Or perhaps it expected Anskar to shadow-step again and was trying not to startle him into doing so.

He heard the footfalls of the other two demons, one on either side.

You must get up! Queen Talia urged.

And do what? Anskar thought. Get up and fall straight back down again? He lacked the strength to walk, never mind to fight, and he had nothing with which to fight the demons in any case. He had left his armor and his sword at the abbey, and even with his full strength he doubted he would have stood a chance.

He managed to roll to his back and prop himself up on both elbows. He could see them then, all three demons, closing in slowly, almost imperceptibly. Drool glistened from fanged maws, and they were all three hard with lust.

Get up! Queen Talia screamed inside his skull.

Anskar almost felt sorry for her. It had to be a torment being an impotent spectator, watching as her schemes came to nothing. He would have laughed if he'd had the energy. He would have mocked her. This was what she deserved for concealing him from the world, for allowing him to be taken as a child to Branil's Burg and raised by her enemies, for invading his life once it had seemed to be going right for a change.

One of the demons sprang at Anskar. On instinct he raised his arm to protect his face, and the demon's razor teeth clamped down on his forearm. Instantly the creature scurried away, screeching, baffled by its inability to rip and rend flesh, to taste blood.

It had bitten the vambrace.

Again, Anskar wanted to laugh. The fear-laced laugh of a man who knew in the next instant he was going to die.

This time, one of the flanking demons came at him in a loping run that ended with a leap. He hammered out an elbow that struck the demon's chin, but the creature carried on through the blow and slammed into him. The demon straddled him where he lay, its urgent hardness pressing into his belly. It leaned in close, snapping at his face. Claws ripped through his shirt, raked his skin. Pain flared. Flesh stung. Anskar tried to shift his hips to roll from underneath, but he was too weak. The demon fastened a hand around his throat, squealing with glee.

And died.

Hot blood showered Anskar's face, rank, dark and vile.

He had heard the rush of air, the pulping thud, the crack of bones as the demon's head spun away into the thicket. Its body careened to one side, falling off him.

Help had come! Anskar rolled to his knees. From the Mother House. Lanuc and the knights of the Order.

He glimpsed the surviving demons backing away and knew he was right, that they were outnumbered and afraid. But then his eyes came into focus on the massive form looming out of the darkness, backlit by the flaming rays of dawn. A woman, huge and heavy-breasted and with a raging, terrifying face. In her hands, a monstrous sword that Anskar would have been hard-pressed to lift, let alone swing.

For it wasn't Lanuc of Gessa who had come to his aid.

It was Braga the blacksmith.

There was a crazed ferocity to Braga's eyes that made Anskar scuttle back from her. Ignoring him, she strode past, beckoning to the demons with one hand, brandishing the giant sword in the other.

"Come to Braga, spindly things," she growled. "My sword is hungry for your stinking blood."

The demons shared a look—it was only a moment's hesitation, and then their feral eyes returned to Braga striding confidently toward them. New prey, they must have thought. Fresh meat. They sprang.

Braga's sword swept down, cleaving a demon from shoulder to belly. The blade became lodged in its rib cage, and the second demon took advantage, flinging itself at Braga, claws reaching for her throat. She swatted it down with disdain, then stamped on its head. The demon rolled aside, emitting a keening wail. And then Braga ripped her sword free of the other demon's rib cage and swung. The demon's torso went in one direction, its legs the other, until both hit the ground still thrashing, then shuddering, then twitching less and less until they grew still.

Braga watched as the last of the demons slowly died, every muscle tense as if she expected another attack, or as if she wanted something else on which to assuage her rage. But then her huge shoulders slumped and she lowered her sword, dragging the tip across the ground as she turned and made her way back toward Anskar. Anger sloughed away from her as she knelt beside him, doe eyes filled with the kind of concern a mother might show for a child who had fallen and grazed its knee.

"Braga … what are you … How?" Anskar asked. His voice came out thin and weak, and he drifted farther and farther from consciousness.

"The ghost said you were in trouble." She shrugged as if it were an everyday occurrence.

"You saw him? The spirit of the warrior?"

"He said his piece then left. And so I grabbed my sword and I came looking for you."

"But the knights …" When Anskar had sent the warrior's spirit to get help from the Mother House, he had assumed knights would come in response, maybe even the Grand Master himself.

"Ghosts don't bother those cunts," Braga said.

"But they visit you? You've seen ghosts before?"

"Sometimes. Mostly they're sad bastards. Mostly they do nothing but wander and wail. But this one was different. This one had purpose. It brought a message."

"My message," Anskar said. "I sent it."

Braga frowned and looked deep into his eyes. Eventually, she snorted and turned to survey her handiwork, wrinkling her nose at the broken corpses of the three demons.

"They had their cocks out ..." she said with evident distaste.

"They were naked," Anskar said, stating the obvious.

"But they were ..." Braga looked as though she were about to be sick. "Stiff and throbbing and—"

"And now they're dead," Anskar said, not needing to hear more. "Thanks to you, Braga, they are ..."

Anskar's head flopped back against the ground, his sentence unfinished. He was tired, so tired, and his eyelids felt as though they were made of lead. He tried to keep them open, tried to remember what he'd been saying, but darkness gushed in from every side, and the last thing he recalled was Braga lifting him from the ground and cradling his limp body against her massive breasts. He swayed and rocked as she walked, carrying him as if he weighed no more than a newborn babe.

FORTY-ONE

FOR TWO DAYS ANSKAR remained in bed in the house he shared with Lanuc. Priests of the Healer came to check on him, spooning salty broth into his mouth and forcing him to take sips of cool, fresh water laced with herbs; but for the most part they simply allowed him to rest.

When red light seeped through the window shutters each morning, he felt the gentle rush of the dawn-tide filling his repository and restoring some of the substance he had lost. In the evenings, he lay atop his bed, arms spread wide to welcome the dusk. At night, the steady ooze of the dark-tide seeped through his pores, whether he wanted it to or not.

On the third day, the summons came.

"I didn't know," the Grand Master said as he and Anskar

walked alone in the cherry orchard at the fringes of the Order's compound.

Behind them, the Mother House was an indistinguishable smudge against the greenery, and the priests' houses were a scatter of specks between it and the looming spire of the basilica.

In the distance, Anskar could hear the muted hammering from Braga's smithy, and he smiled at the thought of that massive woman in the sweat-stained leather apron, swearing and cursing as she beat iron and steel into shape. He had misjudged her. She had alarmed him when first they met, but it was Braga who had rescued him, and he would be eternally in her debt. He was only disappointed she hadn't come to visit him during his convalescence, but maybe she had too much work to do. Or more likely, she felt as uncomfortable around the knights and the priests as they did around her.

"But surely someone must have said something at one time or another," Anskar said.

"By all five aspects of Menselas," the Grand Master said, "I had no idea what the Abbess was up to. I knew she was strange, that the mysteries she pursued were dark, but the summoning of demons! And to think that I was sent to that vile woman when I was but a knight-inferior like you."

"And she didn't ..." Anskar licked dry lips. "I mean ..."

"She did nothing untoward," the Grand Master said, with the merest raise of his eyebrow. "And I was never invited to the chapel at the abbey's hub. For all I know, she and her priests could have been communing with demons even then. It doesn't bear thinking about. Thank the Five your ordeal is over."

Lanuc, a large force of knights, and three priests apiece of the Healer, the Warrior, and the Elder had traveled to the Abbey of the Hooded One with orders to arrest the Abbess and her followers. The bishops of Kaile were on their way to a special convocation at the Patriarch's official residence just outside Sansor to address the issue, all of them protesting ignorance of what the Abbess had been up to.

"Either they're as blind as we were," the Grand Master had said, "or some of them are in cahoots with the Abbess. If it were up to me, I'd be bloody sure to find out. There would be screaming, there would be pain, there would be blood, but by the Five, we would find out. Not the Patriarch, though. He's too bloody weak for that, too wrapped up in meekness and compassion, for Menselas's sake!"

When Lanuc's group arrived at the abbey, they found the priests all dead, their veins turned black by some poison or cant—the priests of the Elder were still trying to determine which. They scoured the abbey, but of the Abbess there was no sign. She had fled, and fled in a hurry, so it seemed. None of the abbey's relics or valuables had gone with her, and when Lanuc had searched her chambers, he had found Anskar's mail and sword, which was now sheathed at his hip. Anskar had decided to leave the mail hauberk in his room. It was too hot for armor, and besides, there was no need, not at the heart of the Order's compound.

The Grand Master stopped and turned a slow circle, taking in the early blossoms of the cherry trees, then guiding Anskar to a stone bench that priests and knights used for their daily meditations. It was a good place to commune with the Five, the Grand Master told him when Anskar raised concerns about them coming so far from the main structures of the compound. It was also, apparently, a good place to talk in private, far from listening ears.

"Besides you and me, the Patriarch, and Lanuc and the priests who went with him to the abbey, no one else knows the full extent of what happened," the Grand Master said. "For the time being, I would like it to stay that way."

Anskar nodded.

"Even the knights who went with Lanuc don't know the things you told me, only that the Abbess had fallen foul of the Church's laws and was to be arrested. Of course, they suspect more, having seen the bodies of her followers. I want to know, though, did the Abbess at any time mention the Tainted Cabal?"

Anskar frowned, then shook his head. "I don't think so. No, I'm sure she didn't."

"I expect she would have done sooner or later," the Grand Master said. "The priests of the Elder who accompanied Lanuc to the abbey found books, symbols, certain items that confirmed what we had already started to suspect from your description of the ritual they forced you to participate in. We now believe that the abbey was a training ground for new members of the Tainted Cabal, and that under the guise of devotion to the Hooded One, the Abbess was schooling new recruits and either sending them back out into the world, or harnessing their sorcerous talents in rituals like the one you witnessed."

"I'm not sure I understand," Anskar said. "What exactly are the Tainted Cabal?"

"Evil is what they are. Fanatics devoted to the return of the demon lord Nysrog. Idiots who seem to have forgotten the terror the mad demon unleashed the last time he came to Wiraya, the slaughter, the almost total destruction of our world."

"But that's insane," Anskar said.

"Try telling them that. And besides, it wouldn't be the first time Wiraya has been bloodied and shadowed by the schemes of insane people. Take your mother, the Necromancer Queen, for instance. No, on second thoughts, forget I said that. Forgive me, Anskar, I am not known for my tact."

Anskar said nothing, but he fancied he could feel his mother's spirit smoldering with barely suppressed rage deep within the marrow of his bones.

"The Cabalists think that if they bring back Nysrog," the Grand Master said, "the demon lord will bestow his favor upon them, that he will make them demons in his image and grant them immortality. Some, it is said, are already halfway to becoming demons. They partake of human flesh and blood, and they even mate with the denizens of the abyssal realms. They are a secretive Order, insidious in all their workings. What really troubles me about the abbey fronting the Tainted Cabal's operations here in Sansor, is the sheer number of fledgling knights we've sent there to learn something of the mysteries of the Hooded One. Some chose to remain, whereas others … and this is what worries me … others returned to us, and most are now scattered across the Order's strongholds the length and breadth of the mainland, not to mention Niyas. If the priests of the Elder are right in their suspicions, then our bitterest enemies may even now be living among us, gathering our secrets, biding their time, and waiting for the command of their shadowy masters. The Five only knows how we will root them all out if that proves to be the case. But root them out we will, mark my words, though it may not always be possible to separate the wheat from the chaff."

"Then we have to assume the Tainted Cabal have infiltrated our Order," Anskar said. "Perhaps make a list of who went to the Abbess over the years. Start from there."

"Yes, a good idea indeed. But what I need to know"—the Grand Master placed a hand on Anskar's knee, gave it a reassuring squeeze—"is whether you swore any oaths or made any pacts while you were at the abbey. Oh, I know it would have been under duress, but this is important. You must answer truthfully."

Anskar glanced up at a hint of movement from farther back in the trees. He glimpsed the white cloak of an Order knight moving back behind a trunk.

The Grand Master saw him noticing and gave a nervous laugh. "You can never be too careful, eh? Even here in the compound. I always have guards watching me, but they're out of earshot, so please speak freely."

Anskar had the uncomfortable feeling the guards—however many of them there were—had been brought for his benefit, in case he didn't give the answer that was expected of him.

"There were no pacts," he said carefully.

"None that you were aware of." The Grand Master narrowed his eyes. He lightly stroked Anskar's thigh. "Did the Abbess … did she …?"

"No," Anskar said, more harshly than he had intended. "Nothing. She did nothing."

"Nothing at all?"

Anskar winced at the recollection of her touch, of the illusion of Carred Selenas astride him. Winced at the acknowledgment that none of that had been real, that the hands that had caressed him had been spindly and swollen with arthritis, the lips that kissed him dry and cracked, the breasts he had been forced to knead not firm, but flaccid, sagging sacks. And the stench—it still clung to his nostrils. Mutton. Ulcerated flesh. Piss.

"Nothing," he said miserably, hanging his head.

"What really happened, Anskar?" the Grand Master asked, pressing in close, one hand stroking Anskar's hair. "You can tell me. I would like to think that you trust me."

A strange mewing noise came from amid the cherry trees, followed by a heavy thud.

"What was that?" Anskar said, seizing the opportunity to stand and extricate himself from the Grand Master's unwanted touches.

"Probably nothing," the Grand Master said, also standing. He looked in the direction Anskar had glimpsed the knight. "Stolton, everything all right?" he called. When there was no reply, he turned to look into the trees behind. "Gavros? Chaldin?"

Silence. Just the rustling of cherry blossoms in the morning breeze, the distant clangor of Braga's forge, the buzzing of a lone bee that flitted in and out of the yellow-and-white flowers that grew among the grass.

"Deaf as posts, the lot of them," the Grand Master said, resuming his seat. "Not good enough. There will be consequences."

"Should we be worried?" Anskar remained standing.

"Not at all. It's not uncommon. They grow bored, lax in their duties. They will be punished, but not before we are finished here."

"It doesn't feel right. I sense... I don't know. Could we go look for them? What if something bad has happened?"

"It's probably nothing. You know what knights are—"

"Grand Master, you could be in danger." It was an irrational feeling, nothing more, Anskar tried to tell himself, but the disappearance of the three knights unsettled him.

"Perhaps you're right." The Grand Master stood once more. "You have your sword? Good." He drew his own blade, and Anskar followed suit.

"Stolton?" the Grand Master called again. Then louder, "Stolton? Chaldin? Gavros?"

Still no reply.

"We should head back," Anskar said.

The Grand Master sighed. "Fine, but heads will roll for this. If there's one thing I can't stand, it's … Who on earth is that?"

A lone figure emerged from behind a cherry tree some twenty yards away. It looked like a peasant or, rather, like one of the vagrants who came begging for alms at Branil's Burg. Vihtor used to permit them to enter, and the Healer's priests would grudgingly dole out scraps of food and mugs of beer. The man wore a patched and hooded cloak above mud-spattered pants and scuffed boots.

"Who are you?" the Grand Master challenged. "How did you get in here?"

"Through the trees," the stranger said, gesturing behind himself, where the orchard continued until it terminated at a low drystone wall. "Should I not have done so?"

"If it's charity you're after …"

"It isn't."

The stranger walked toward them casually, as if he had every right to be there. As if he hadn't a care in the world. Uneasy, Anskar stepped in front of the Grand Master.

"My quarrel is not with you, Anskar DeVantte. At least not until you have been given a chance to return to the fold."

"You're a Tainted Cabalist?" the Grand Master said. He spoke a cant and his golden ward sphere sprang up around him. Anskar immediately did the same, activating his own ward, and he took a firm grasp of *Amalantril*'s hilt.

The stranger halted a mere two sword-lengths from where Anskar stood protectively in front of the Grand Master. "Such a show of strength," he commented. "Yet I am unarmed." He held out his hands, palms open, to show that he carried no weapons.

"That doesn't mean you pose no threat," the Grand Master

said. “Where are my guards?”

“You only had three,” the stranger said. “I expected more.”

“Dead, then,” the Grand Master said.

The stranger gave a little bow and chuckled beneath the hood of his robe. Anskar strained to catch a glimpse of the man’s face, but there was nothing save darkness.

“The Abbess was right about you, Anskar,” the stranger said. “The mark of sorcery is strong with you. But will it prove strong enough?”

“I’ll ask you again,” the Grand Master said, stepping to Anskar’s side, where their ward spheres overlapped, forming a denser barrier of protection that covered Anskar’s right side and the Grand Master’s left. “Who are you? Did the Tainted Cabal send you?”

“I am an avenger,” the man said. “And yes, I was sent. I was sent to avenge the deaths of the two hundred priests of the Abbey of the Hooded One.”

“We are not responsible for whatever happened to those poor bastards,” the Grand Master said. “Their veins were blackened—some kind of poison or sorcery, I’m told. That is not our way.”

The man laughed. “It is certainly beyond your ability. But you must, nevertheless, be held accountable. Without you sending armed knights to the abbey, there would have been no need for the two hundred to sacrifice their lives so that the Abbess could elude you.”

“She drained them?” Anskar asked, incredulous. “She stole their essence?”

“It was hers to take,” the stranger said. “They served her willingly. They were one with her, as you are one with her.”

The Grand Master glanced at Anskar.

“I am not one with her,” Anskar said.

"She begs to differ. She carries your seed inside her. You were quite enthusiastic, she tells me."

"She what?" the Grand Master said. "Your *seed*?"

"Anskar DeVantte here, Grand Master, rutted with the old crone. Just don't tell her I called her that. She gloated about it afterwards. Said he couldn't get enough of her. She must have tired you out, Anskar. I heard you didn't stay for the orgy."

"You lie!" Anskar cried.

"I do. Most of the time. But not about this. Hyle Pausus here can see that I speak the truth by the blush of your cheeks. But still, you like a blushing boy, don't you, Grand Master? I hear things, you see. From the recruits you have so generously sent to the abbey."

"How bloody dare you!" the Grand Master shouted, and he stepped in and swung his sword.

The stranger slipped aside so quickly, so fluidly, that Anskar didn't even see him move. One minute he was there, a sword coming at his head, the next he stood behind the Grand Master, and he punched him hard, once, right through the ward sphere, in the kidney.

With a grunt the Grand Master dropped to his knees. His sword fell with a dull thud to the grass, and his golden ward winked out.

The next instant the man was back in front of the Grand Master. His hand snaked out and took the Grand Master by the throat, and with no effort at all, he hoisted him into the air.

Anskar lunged with *Amalantril,* and to his astonishment the blade struck true. His sword pierced cloth and flesh and scraped against bone. The man snarled and dropped the Grand Master, who hit the ground hard and moaned.

Anskar stood still, watching the effect of his strike, when

he should have been into the next attack. He hadn't expected the stranger to still be there. He had expected lightning-fast movement, evasion.

The stranger turned to face Anskar. He rolled his head and his neck cracked. He should have been screaming in pain from the stab. There should have been blood gushing from the hole *Amalantril* had ripped through the flesh above his liver. But there was no blood, and in place of screaming, the man just laughed.

Anskar backed away a step, and the stranger looked between him and the Grand Master, who was struggling to get to his knees.

"If you keep backing away, Anskar," the man said, "I will slay this old pervert you are sworn to serve."

Anskar stood his ground.

"Better," the man said. "But let's be realistic. What do you really think you can do to stop me from killing him anyway?"

Anskar stared, had nothing to say. He was outmatched and he knew it.

The dead guards! Queen Talia hissed within his mind. *Raise them!*

"How?" Anskar asked, not intending to speak with his lips.

"What was that?" the stranger asked.

The Grand Master made it to his feet, but the stranger back-fisted him in the stomach and down he went again.

Grant me control of your mind, Queen Talia said, *and I will do it.*

The stranger lifted the Grand Master from the ground, this time holding him by the ankle. "How would you like me to kill him?" he asked Anskar. "Quick or slow. Merciful or long and lingering. I don't mind. I am in no hurry."

You must trust me, Queen Talia said.

"I don't have a choice," Anskar muttered in Niyandrian. "Do it."

He felt the frantic rush of her activity—a writhing, nauseating sensation that reached from the inside of his skull to his belly. He winced and tried not to be sick.

"What are you doing?" the stranger asked.

The Grand Master's eyes were wide with fear as he dangled upside down in the stranger's grip.

Invisible threads of sorcery shot outward from Anskar: three questing lines. He felt their hooks bite, felt the cold rush of something not quite tangible sluicing through his guts.

"Stop right now!" the stranger commanded, and he threw out a hand, palm toward Anskar.

Immediately, Anskar's ward sphere went out. Still holding the Grand Master by the ankle, the stranger advanced on him.

Then he stopped at the sound of a groan.

The stranger angled a look to his right, where a white-cloaked knight stepped from behind a tree. The knight's head hung by the slenderest of threads from his severed neck.

Another groan, and another dead knight appeared from the opposite side, this one with a fist-sized hole through his chest.

The third knight came from behind the stranger, dragging a broken leg as he shuffled forward, the top of his head missing and exposing a mess of brains and gore.

With too little care to be called disdain, the stranger dropped the Grand Master, then pivoted and hurled dark fire from his fingers at first one dead man walking, then the second, and lastly the third. And in that moment, as all three of the slain knights who were charged with guarding their Grand Master failed a second time and burst into black flames that reduced them to ashes, Anskar reached into his dusk-tide repository, and he hurled fire of his own at the stranger, golden, not dark; bright and searing and blisteringly hot.

The stranger whirled to face him, robe going up like a pitch-soaked torch. But the man didn't screech as Anskar had hoped. Instead, he cackled as his hooded cloak burned away to nothing, along with the clothes beneath.

There was no stench of roasting flesh, no skin melting from the bone. What Anskar saw as the clothing perished, the flames abated, and the smoke gusted away, was a horned head, face twisted with malice, golden eyes ablaze with unspeakable cruelty.

The demon swelled until it was twice the height of a man, its skin a crust of magma, charred and smoking with its own inner fire. Wings of shadow sprouted from its back, bearing the demon aloft with great sweeping beats. More shadows coalesced around its molten body, hardening into a carapace of black and glistening plate armor. As it swept toward him, Anskar realized he had seen this demon before, when he'd passed through the abyssal realms with Malady.

The dwarf-demon had made him a gift of its name.

"Frangin-gul-terriph!" he shouted. "Demon of the Thirty-Eighth Order, I bind you to my will. I bind you!" he screamed as the demon showed no sign of stopping, and a blade of shadow formed in its taloned hand. "Frangin-gul-terriph!" Anskar cried again. "You are bound!"

The demon crashed to the ground, sending up clods and divots of earth amid a coiling plume of smoke. Anskar held the demon there with the force of his will, left it kneeling, glaring at him with those terrible golden eyes. But what should he do next? Already he felt the demon straining against his hurriedly formed bindings. His head began to pound. Fat drops of sweat beaded on his forehead and rolled stinging into his eyes.

And so he did the only thing he knew how to do, the only other demonic sorcery the Abbess had taught him.

He assailed it with the Wracking Nerves.

The demon screamed then. Fell thrashing to the ground, bucking and screeching and begging Anskar to stop.

But he didn't stop. He was too afraid. And so it was no measured burst of torture he delivered to the demon's ravaged nerves. It was everything he had.

With a resounding crack and a plop, the demon burst apart, its purplish innards spilling forth like molten soup that seethed and hissed where it touched the earth.

Anskar started at a hand on his shoulder—the Grand Master clutching him for support as he struggled to remain standing.

When the steam abated, the demon was nothing more than a pool of purplish ichor. The Grand Master let out a ragged sigh and slumped down on the grass. He was chuckling, and soon his chuckles became a high-pitched, girlish laugh.

Already there were knights hurrying toward them through the orchard from the direction of the Mother House, Lanuc at their fore.

"An orgy, eh?" the Grand Master said. He sounded disappointed. "There was nothing like that when I was sent to the abbey as a young man. Or if there was, I was never invited."

Anskar didn't need to point out that was because the Grand Master was lacking in the deep mark of sorcery that he had, which made him stand out from the majority of the knights. It was sorcerous aptitude the Abbess had ultimately wanted him for, his abilities with the dusk-tide and the dark. The Grand Master, on the other hand, was not at all what the Tainted Cabal were looking for.

But Anskar had the sense that, if the Abbess had extended the invitation of an orgy to him, Hyle Pausus might never have left the Abbey of the Hooded One, might never have risen through the ranks to become the head of the Order of Eternal Vigilance.

And Anskar wondered just what Menselas, the God of Five Aspects, made of that.

FORTY-TWO

"THE DEMON WAS AN assassin sent by the Tainted Cabal." The Grand Master concluded his debriefing to the hushed nods of the senior knights and the priests present.

They were seated in the long hall that served as the Order's council chamber, the Grand Master on a high-backed chair at the head of a table of blackwood, the knights on one side, the priests—representatives of four out of the five aspects—on the other. Anskar sat at the foot of the table on a stool Lanuc had brought in when they found there weren't enough chairs.

"So, it was revenge for us driving the Abbess away," Lanuc said.

"And for Anskar making his escape," the Grand Master said. "I have no doubt the Abbess informed her Tainted Cabalist masters of his worth. It's a rare sorcerous ability he possesses."

Lanuc frowned at that. "You think they'll come for him in the future?"

"Probably," the Grand Master said. "And I daresay they'll make another attempt on my life. If nothing else, the Tainted Cabal are an unforgiving bunch, and they are certainly predictable."

"Insidious," one of the other knights said.

The priests all touched their fingertips and thumbs to their chests in the sign of the Five's protection.

"I've already sent messengers to our strongholds throughout the mainland," the Grand Master said. "I want our seneschals to be especially vigilant, and I want every last Cabalist scum flushed out and made an example of. I want them impaled on tall spikes so everyone can see what happens to those who would corrupt our Order."

"But the Patriarch ..." one of the priests said—she was dressed in the drab clothes of the Mother aspect. "Shouldn't we wait until after the conclave?"

"We should not," the Grand Master said, and his knights dutifully grunted their agreement. He glared at the woman for a long while, and Anskar had to suppose the Grand Master was sizing her up, assessing the likelihood that she might be a Tainted Cabal spy.

"They are among us," the Grand Master finally said, switching his gaze to the others seated at the table with him. "We must keep our eyes open. We must listen for hints and rumors. And we must show no mercy. The Tainted Cabal is a plague. A cancer. We can afford to leave no trace of it in our midst.

"But Lanuc is correct, Anskar. The Tainted Cabal will indeed come after you again. Someone with talents like yours is too valuable for them to pass up. And what you told us about the ritual you participated in, a ritual to return Nysrog to the world, and that other matter the demon in the orchard alluded to ..."

To Anskar's great relief, the Grand Master didn't spell it out for the others present, but even so he felt heat rise to his cheeks.

"… only makes matters worse," the Grand Master concluded. "I want you out of this poisonous atmosphere. Far away, and under the watchful gaze of people I trust. Obviously, you can't go back to Niyas, not till Vihtor Ulnar rids us of Carred Selenas and her blasted rebels. But there is another option. For months I have received petitions for aid from Aelfyr, King of the Thousand Lakes in the north." Now he was speaking directly to Lanuc. "For a variety of reasons, I have not seen fit to answer those requests until now. King Aelfyr is beset with problems from the Soreshi of the Ymaltian Mountains. Those sorcery-wielding savages have been harassing his borders, stealing his flocks, and abducting his young girls and boys, though Menselas only knows why. Whatever the cause of the Soreshi aggression, something is stirring in the north, and it's about time we nipped it in the bud."

"I agree with you, Grand Master," Lanuc said. "But is this mission going to be safe for young Anskar?"

"He is a knight," the Grand Master said. "He is not meant to be safe. He is meant to serve."

"But Vihtor, Grand Master …"

"Is the Seneschal of a remote Order outpost. I am his superior. You take your orders from me, Lanuc, not him. I am not given to repeating myself, but I'm certain we've had this conversation before."

"Grand Master," Lanuc conceded.

"Good, then you will handpick a force of no more than one hundred knights, and you will take Anskar with you to the Kingdom of the Thousand Lakes. I will send messengers ahead of you to inform the King." To Anskar he said, "It will be an opportunity for you to hone your martial prowess in readiness for solemn vows next year. There," he said to Lanuc, "you can tell Vihtor that next time you write—I assume you do keep in touch? Furthermore," he told Anskar, "it will be a chance for you to balance out the darkness you've been exposed to with the light of Menselas's mercy, for the Thousand Lakes is a godly kingdom, and there you will find priests holier than anywhere else on the mainland."

The priests at the table all glowered at the slight, but not a single one of them dared to say a word about it.

Next morning, after he had greeted the dawn-tide, Anskar sat upon a knight's destrier, one of the trained and massive warhorses that could bite an enemy's face off just as easily as it could rear up and crush their skull with its hooves. It was mostly for show, he realized, gazing about at the other hundred or so mounted and armored men and women that Lanuc was preparing to lead out of Sansor's northern gate for the long journey to the Kingdom of the Thousand Lakes. Destriers were bred for short, devastating charges, and for carrying the weight of an armored rider. They were trained not to shy from battle, and to give as good as they got in the chaos and clash of steel. But they were ill-suited to riding long distances, which was why the pages behind the knights on lighter horses each held the reins of a spare riding mount. Once they were out of sight of the city, the knights would dismount and exchange their war horses for the smaller ones.

There were priests of the Healer with the company, too, men and women skilled in staunching the flow of blood, suturing wounds, and administering salves and tisanes that could stave off the rot should a wound become infected.

A crowd had assembled behind the rope barriers the City Watch had put in place. They were all dressed in the luxurious velvets, precious stones and metals of the noble elite and rich merchants. There were a few high-ranking politicians among them, identifiable by their golden chains of office. Of the poor folk, the laborers, the rogues, the serfs who were the true lifeblood of Sansor, there was no sign.

Like the destriers, it was all for show.

But as the gate inched open and Lanuc gave the command for the company to ride forth, Anskar saw that not all the onlookers were rich or well-dressed. He glimpsed Braga the blacksmith in all her oily, sweat-stained magnificence watching from an alley, while two nervous men of the Watch exchanged looks, uncertain what to do about her presence here, and clearly afraid of making an issue of it.

As Anskar rode past, he waved to Braga, but to his surprise she neither cursed nor waved back. Instead, she dabbed at an eye as a tear streaked down her face, leaving a track through the soot and the grime.

"She likes you, lad," joked a wiry older knight who rode alongside him. The man had a thick mustache and a ruddy, friendly face. "By the Mother's tits, I think she has the hots for you."

And then they were out through the gates and riding north, and the sun was climbing high in a clear blue sky, and the sweet smell of freshly scythed grass was all around them.

Anskar filled his lungs with crisp, cool air, and for the first time in ages, he felt free as the company left the city walls behind and headed for a shallow valley.

They were riding to the farthest northern reaches of the

mainland, to another realm, and with each mile they traveled, he increased the distance between himself and Niyas, between himself and Carred Selenas and the expectation that he was the *Melesh-Eloni*, the godling, the heir of the Necromancer Queen.

For a fleeting moment, he expected to hear his mother's voice in his head, chastising him for riding even farther away from his destiny. Sometimes he had the impression that she could read his thoughts, that the longer he conversed with her, the stronger the connection grew between them.

But he had re-established the wards he had set against his mother before leaving the Mother House this morning—another promise broken, but one he felt certain the Five would forgive him for. This mission with Lanuc was a manifestation of the mercy of Menselas, and Anskar wanted nothing to interfere with that, nothing to thwart what might be his last attempt to atone for past sins and to give his life entirely over to the providence of the Five. After what he'd experienced at the Abbey of the Hooded One, it seemed the only sure and certain road.

And so he laughed out loud as he cantered along at the center of this force of holy knights riding to the aid of a pious and beleaguered king, and though he drew frowns and looks of bemusement from the closest of his new companions, he didn't mind in the slightest. He felt free not only of Carred Selenas, but free also of the hold the Abbess had over him. And most of all he felt free of the specter of his mother.

And the vambrace on his forearm grew cool against his skin, and suddenly very heavy.

FORTY-THREE

FOR HOURS THEY FOLLOWED the crooked path to the summit of Mount Phryith. The higher they climbed, the thinner the air became, the thicker the mist that smothered them with its clammy touch. It was freezing, ice making the hewn rock of the path treacherous, but still Carred had to stop to wipe sweat from her eyes, and she panted for every breath. Noni clung to her hand, shivering. She couldn't see Orix and Taloc, only hear the muffled scrape and thud of their boots on stone.

"Not far now," Noni said through chattering teeth.

"Did Talia tell you that? Why doesn't she speak through you any longer?"

"She is … divided."

The ground leveled out—a ledge perhaps? Hard to tell when she couldn't see more than an inch in any direction. It was a relief Malady was no longer with them. The dwarf-demon could have gotten up to all sorts of mischief in the mist.

"Careful," Taloc muttered from behind. "Don't want to fall."

"Thanks for the advice," Carred said. "I'd never have thought of that myself."

"How much farther?" Orix grumbled in Nan-Rhouric.

"Stay here if you like." She was sick of his whining. And to be honest, she was sick to death of his neediness, his greasy skin. Theltek, she missed Marith.

It was Noni leading *her* now, one hand stretched out in front, feeling the way. When Noni stopped, Carred stopped with her.

"What is it?"

Noni guided her hand to a sheer rock face. "Look for an indentation."

Carred felt the cold surface with her fingertips till she located a groove. She traced its contours: a circle no larger than—

"The void-steel ring Queen Talia left for you," Noni said. "Insert it."

Carred drew the chain over her head and pressed the ring into the circle. A perfect fit.

"The Queen created this lock," Noni said.

"To keep something in?"

"To keep others out."

Behind her, Taloc swore and Orix gasped at the grind of stone as the rock face swung inwards. Dust swirled into the air, backlit by a violet glow coming off the walls inside—not the rough rock of a cave, but bricks and mortar, scabbed in places with flaking plaster.

"I'm not going in there," Taloc said.

"Suit yourself. Orix?"

He swallowed, puffed out his chest.

"Stay with Taloc," Carred said in Nan-Rhouric. "Hold hands if you like."

Noni hung back with them. "The Queen forbids me to enter. Tain will scent her presence within me."

"And they're not talking," Carred said. "I remember."

Retrieving her ring and hanging it around her neck once more, she crossed the threshold into a cathedral-like space.

The glow came from scaleskin fungi coating swaths of wall. Above, the ceiling was vaulted with rotting joists from which hung cobwebs like heavy drapes. Workbenches lined the walls, crammed with retorts and beakers, rusty iron stands, scraps of brittle yellow paper curled at the edges. There was a forge filled with ash, a pitted anvil, hammers, files, chisels. Offcuts of various metals were scattered about the floor, among them discarded pieces of armor—a cracked pauldron, a rust-scabbed cuirass, a battered greave that looked as though it had been beaten with a hammer in anger.

Deeper in, there was a bed frame riddled with woodworm, atop which was the disintegrating remains of a black-speckled mattress. A shelf stood at the head of the bed, crammed with ancient books that looked as if they would turn to dust at the merest touch.

In the shadows of an alcove there was a patch of denser darkness on the floor.

"Light!" Carred called back to the entrance. "Quickly!"

She heard someone enter while she stared at the dark shape, willing it to reveal itself.

"Take your time," she said, but then Taloc was beside her, fumbling with a box of fire-sticks. He struck one. Cursed as it broke. Struck another and it took. He touched the flame to a rushlight and passed it to Carred. It smelled of tallow. She stooped and cast the wavering light into the alcove. A great helm reflected the glow back at her, blue and silver, turning black.

Blue-silver again. Black, in swift alternation, as if it breathed in the light then exhaled it.

Tentatively, she touched the metal. Icy. It vibrated beneath her fingers, caused a shiver beneath her scalp—her poor, neglected repositories. She turned the helm, the better to see. No slit for eyes, no holes for breathing, its only feature a hairline crack that divided the faceplate down the middle.

"Shit!" she said, dropping her rushlight and sucking her singed fingers. Taloc handed her another, and she almost wished he hadn't.

She'd seen this helm before. Racing toward her. In her dream. When her mother left her screaming in the woods.

"Carred, are you all right?"

"Still here, then?" Orix must have come in with Taloc.

"'Course I'm still here." In his besotted little mind, he'd probably never leave her.

"Then who's with Noni?"

"I'll go," Taloc said, sounding only too happy to get outside. He passed Orix his fire-sticks and stash of rushes.

Carred set her still-burning rushlight on the ground and worked a fingernail into the seam that split the helm. She pulled. Cursed as her nail broke. Pulled again, and the faceplate came open with a squeak of its hinges.

Light blazed within.

She leaned away, shielding her eyes. Blinked then looked again as the light settled into a soft, emerald glow. Her hand slid from her eyes to her mouth as she gasped then tried not to gag.

Inside the helm, there was a head. A man's head. Perfectly preserved.

"Menselas!" Orix whispered. "That's … that's …"

"Macabre is what it is," Carred said. As faces go, it wasn't much to look at. Too long of a nose. Nostrils you could ride a horse through. Hollow cheeks, thin lips. Wisp of a beard. Waxed mustache that curled up at the ends—it had once been the fashion in Niyas, according to her great-grandmother, who lived till she was a hundred and thirty, a ripe old age even for a Niyandrian.

The eyelids fluttered.

Carred held her breath, refusing to scream.

And then they came fully open. Yellow eyes. Slitted. Niyandrian eyes. Eyes that took a second to focus, but when they did, came to rest on her.

"Tain?" she breathed.

A gurgling sound came from the head. Its lips parted, made a chewing motion. The tip of its tongue poked between them.

"I ..." the head rasped. It gave a little cough. "I am Tain. Yes, yes, I am he."

"How can you speak without lungs?"

"How can you speak without a brain?" the head countered.

"I'm not sure," Carred said. "But somehow I manage. How can you be a prick without a prick?"

"What's it saying?" Orix asked.

"Niyandrian greetings," Carred told him in Nan-Rhouric. "Don't worry, it's going well."

"What words are these?" Tain asked.

"Nan-Rhouric."

"You sully your lips with the language of barbarians?"

"Times change." Probably the mainlanders said the same thing about Niyandrian nowadays.

"You ask about my ability to speak, but not to breathe," Tain said.

"I was wondering about the lack of decay, too," Carred said.

"Kind of unusual in a severed head."

"My head has not been severed," Tain said, somewhat smugly. "It is just in a different place to the rest of me."

"You ascended?"

"There were … flaws in my design."

"Ah, yes," Carred said. "The Armor of Divinity. The reason for my visit."

She stooped to lift the helm and brought the necromancer's eyes level with hers.

"I have a proposal for you."

END OF BOOK TWO

TO MY READERS

As always, if you enjoyed the read, leaving a review supports the books and helps keep me writing! You can return to where you purchased the novel to review it or simply visit my website and follow the links: WWW.MITCHELLHOGAN.COM

There are also websites such as Goodreads where members discuss the books they've read or want to read or suggest books others might read: WWW.GOODREADS.COM/AUTHOR/SHOW/7189594.MITCHELL_HOGAN

If you never want to miss the latest book sign up here for my newsletter. I send one every few months, so I won't clutter your inbox. MITCHELLHOGAN.COM/NEW-RELEASE-ALERTS/

Having readers eager for the next installment of a series, or anticipating a new series, is the best motivation for a writer to create new stories. Thank you for your support and be sure to check out my other novels!

ABOUT THE AUTHOR

Photo copyright © 2018

When he was eleven, Mitchell Hogan received *The Hobbit* and the Lord of the Rings trilogy, and a love of fantasy novels was born. He spent the next ten years reading, rolling dice, and playing computer games, with some school and university thrown in. Along the way, he accumulated numerous bookcases' worth of fantasy and sci-fi novels and doesn't look to stop any time soon. For ten years he put off his dream of writing; then he quit his job and wrote *A Crucible of Souls*. He now writes full-time and is eternally grateful to the readers who took a chance on an unknown self-published author. He lives in Sydney, Australia, with his wife, Angela, and his daughters, Isabelle and Charlotte.